ASCENSION
THE GATES LEGACY,
BOOK 3

Books by Lorenz Font

The Gates Legacy Series

Hunted - Book 1

Tormented - Book 2

Ascension - Book 3

Reckoning - Book 4

Redemption - Book 5 – Coming soon

Indivisible Line

Feather Light

Pieces of Broken Time

The Prodian Journey Series

Rise of Alpha

Ascension

The Gates Legacy, Book 3

By
Lorenz Font

Wendy D.
Thanks for sharing my journey from day one.
With all my love.

Glossary

Incomis Sippanus—A disease that can be transmitted from vampire to vampire or vampire to human through feeding or sexual intercourse. Symptoms are similar to leprosy or AIDS, including painful lesions and clouded white irises. Consumption of human blood alleviates visible symptoms but also speeds the disease's progression. Harrow Gates is the first known carrier of the disease.

Vampire Council—Governing authority of the vampire world, consisting of ten purebred vampires called Elders.

Harem—Goran's mistresses, beautiful redheaded vampires who are trained in combat.

Dangeran—Metal with the strength and weight of titanium that has been infused with diamond bits, used in the construction of most vampire weapons. Vampires cut by Dangeran will disintegrate unless the wounded area is cut from their bodies.

Arnis—Three-foot-long wooden sticks used as a sparring weapon.

Kalimetal—Metal version of Arnis. Three-foot-long sticks infused with Dangeran. Animal pelt is woven to the handle to provide a safe grip.

Blanch Room—A large secured area inside the Vampire headquarters that houses humans before and during transition.

Mentha—A plant extract believed to have a calming, numbing effect on vampires.

Great Vampire Revolution—Uprising by a group of revolutionary vampires seeking freedom from Goran's rule in the 1960s.

Pure-Blooded Vampires—Elite class of vampires on the verge of extinction, they are able to reproduce and can read minds. Each possesses a unique gift, and they must feed from pureblooded vampires of the opposite sex to survive.

Tack Enterprises—A company owned and operated by Pritchard Tack that manufactures guns for the military and private companies. Profits are used to support a large group of fighters, researchers, and medical personnel who are working on finding a cure for the disease *Incomis Sippanus*.

Vampire Rebellion—A small resistance by vampires in upstate New York. Reason for the uprising is unknown.

Staring through the cracked ceiling at the wooden beams, Rohnert adjusted his body on the makeshift cot. He'd been hiding for what seemed like forever, lurking in the shadows, away from the vigilant eyes of the Council guards. In reality, not even three full months had passed since he left the underground facility he'd once called home.

Not a day had gone by that he hadn't thought of the place and its inhabitants, especially the bold and passionate human doctor who ran the in-house clinic. Dr. Shelly Anderson's image flashed before his eyes, and Rohnert sat up with a growl of frustration. He focused instead on the sounds of the storm outside, which had picked up momentum. The lashing winds rattled the shaky foundation of his hideaway, and the steady patter of rain continued to pelt the roof.

Rohnert picked up his favorite weapon from its resting place on the floor. The Kalimetal's familiar weight steadied him somewhat while he walked to the grimy window and stared outside. He'd been cooped up longer than he intended. Trouble was, if he set foot outside the confines of the house, he'd likely bump into a Vampire Council soldier. They had been in abundance of late.

As head of the Vampire Council, Goran had decreed that any vampire in possession of a Kalimetal was to be eradicated—no questions asked. Rohnert's big dilemma was his unwillingness to kill Council soldiers for following that order. So he remained hidden to spare the lives of the innocent.

Restless, he paced the empty room, which was an extension of a boarded-up apartment complex in a shady part of the Brooklyn. The abandoned dwelling served its purpose, providing cover until the need to venture out arose again.

He didn't know how long he could withstand the boredom that accompanied such inactivity. His sole mental exercise was trying to come to terms with the events that had taken place at the Tack Enterprises' stronghold upstate. The slaughter of his friends, human and vampire alike, might have been ordered by Goran, but Rohnert felt responsible all the same.

His mind rewound to the night Goran's Harem had attacked. The Council leader had ordered his redheaded mistresses to kill and had been willing to sacrifice them for a chance to cripple Tack Enterprises' operation. Rohnert couldn't shake the memories of his comrades' faces or of the shrieks of the female vampires as they perished one by one. Although his friends won that battle, the cost was high. Too much blood had been shed that day, and it had all been for nothing.

Rohnert ran his fingers through his hair and pulled at the roots. The damn stuff had sprouted into obstinate, snarled tangles. Before joining Pritchard Tack's band of vampires, Rohnert had been living with limited means—it had been his way of life ever since he left his position on the Vampire Council. Anything he'd acquired during his stay at Tack Enterprises was gone, too, since he had walked out of the facility with nothing but the clothes on his back apart from his weapons and Marania's black book. Without even the most basic possessions, the simple task of trimming his hair was impossible, but that was the least of his worries.

Pritchard had been a legitimate manufacturer of Grade A weapons for both the military and private sectors. Under the banner of his billion-dollar business, Tack Enterprises, he had been seeking a cure for the disease that afflicted his daughter Allison. She had been stricken by *Incomis Sippanus* when she'd been changed into a vampire, and Pritchard had vowed to help all those in need by finding the cure. His business had allowed him to create several strongholds for diseased vampires who were hunted without mercy. In the end, they had also become sanctuaries for misfits in both the human and vampire worlds, and he had given his life for them. Pritchard had left the operation in the capable hands of Harrow Gates, the vampire who had unknowingly spread *Incomis Sippanus* and had joined the fight to protect the afflicted.

Once Rohnert had joined the underground operation, he'd been a recipient of Tack Enterprises' generosity for a whole year. He'd found a place for himself there as a teacher and friend to vampire and human alike. For awhile, it had seemed possible that he had found a new home for himself.

He hadn't planned on Dr. Shelly Anderson, however. The clinic's doctor and resident ball-buster had found a way into his heart and left behind a massive void. If he'd stuck to his resolve to never tangle with a female, he could have avoided losing his newfound sanctuary. Despite knowing that Goran would go after anyone close to him, Rohnert had taken what she freely offered, her body and affection. When he came to his senses and realized the danger his actions posed to her, he'd left without saying goodbye. Not quite the exit he'd had in mind, but staying in the facility would have complicated matters further. She would never understand his rejection now that she'd felt his passion for her.

Although he had vowed to stay away from her and the underground compound, the task had proven difficult. There hadn't been a day when the human female was absent from his conscious thoughts. Every goddamn, waking hour passed at an excruciating pace because he couldn't manage to keep his mind off her.

As embarrassing as it was, he had succumbed to his weakness and dared take control of Shelly's unconscious thoughts in her deepest slumber.

Rohnert's power was not limited to the manipulation and mind reading that his fellow pureblood vampires all shared. Unknown to many, he could also mentally interact with any human or vampire when they were asleep. It was a special ability not many pureblooded vampires possessed. Each of them had specific gifts, and that was his—a power he hesitated to use due to its invasive nature. Desperate times called for desperate measures, however, so he had done the unthinkable and raided Shelly's dreams. The only excuse he could offer was his overwhelming need for her.

His last trip into her mind two nights ago had revealed that Shelly regretted the brief time they'd spent together. She couldn't have known that when he'd told her that he didn't want her, her pained expression had crushed him. Despite her attempt to mask the hurt, he'd seen what he'd done to her. There had been a sudden shift in her thought pattern that had startled him. Her thoughts had become clear and concise and were directed at him.

I might have fallen for you Rohnert, but I'll be damned if I let you walk all over me. Mark my words—you and I will never be together. Even if you beg me to love you, this woman has learned her lesson.

Rohnert had staggered against the weight of her rejection, but felt he deserved it after violating her privacy like that. He was fucked. The thought of Shelly ate at him, making his existence even more intolerable. This noble shit had to stop—she didn't need his protection. She was her own person, an independent woman who could take care of herself. He couldn't save the world, and she'd never asked him to save her. Rohnert needed to forget her before his need for her crushed him into dust.

"Damn it." If he had stuck to his plan to not get involved with Shelly, he wouldn't be in this crappy predicament. Too bad his heart had chosen to ignore his head.

"Talking to yourself again, sir?" Alonzo asked, slipping through the battered wooden door.

Rohnert pivoted and scowled at the vampire he'd allowed to squat with him for the past week. Alonzo had been one of his best students, a member of the elite guards Rohnert had helped create. Of Spanish descent, he sported a mass of thick brown curls, eyes the color of wine, and a witty personality that bordered on annoying. Zo, as he preferred to be addressed, was smart and had excelled in every weapons class Rohnert taught.

"Ditch the 'sir' if you want to keep breathing."

"Qué es el problema? Despertó en el lado incorrecto de la cama otra vez?" Alonzo said, rapid fire, in his native tongue.

Rohnert walked forward, releasing the Kalimetal from its sheath. "If you don't cut that Spanish BS, I swear in Buddha's name, I'll cut you up in little pieces."

Zo backpedaled and raised his hands in surrender. Every existing vampire knew the devastating effect of a weapon infused with the Dangeran metal, in particular when used by a master like Rohnert. His Kalimetal, which was a cross between a sword and baton, was a weapon that could tear anyone to bits. To the untrained eye, the pair of three-foot metal rods appeared benign, but their slim profile and light weight made the weapon easier to wield, providing a broader range of motion that gave the fighter an edge during an attack.

"Madre—sorry—sir, you're making me nervous."

"Translate!" Rohnert pointed his weapon at Zo's neck.

The vampire, though a head shorter than Rohnert, met his gaze with steady eyes. "You know I'd never say anything disrespectful." He pushed the tip of Rohnert's Kalimetal away with care.

"Translate!" Rohnert repeated.

"I said, 'What's the problem? Wake up on the wrong side of the bed again?' See? It's harmless." He broke into an irritating grin.

Rohnert blew an aggravated breath and lowered his weapon. "Where have you been? Don't you know that defection is a serious offense?"

"I was hanging out at the salsa club." Zo flopped onto the floor, still watching Rohnert with vigilant eyes.

His patience dipped to an all-time low. "If you want to keep on hanging out with me, lose the salsa outings and take this seriously. The minute you left the Council, your life ceased to be safe." Rohnert returned to the window and gazed out again.

"I was killing time. With you always moping around here, I needed to get some fresh air. Besides, I was armed."

Rohnert shot a quick glance over his shoulder to see Zo lift his tattered denim jacket to reveal a holster filled with every imaginable weapon, including several throwing stars, a Glock, and push daggers.

"Haven't I taught you to always stay away from those types of establishments?" When Zo nodded, Rohnert glared at him. "And yet you went?"

"I was following a couple of vampires."

"To at salsa club?" What had this world come to?

"I overheard them talking about a bunch of Kalimetal-carrying vampires, so I followed to get more information."

The mention of Kalimetal got his attention. He strode to where Alonzo was sitting and looked down. "And?"

"Some Council soldiers walked in, so I had to scram. All I know is there were six vampires." Although Zo had shed his accent, there were still moments when, if rattled, he reverted.

"Jesus," Rohnert whispered. He hadn't heard from Harrow and the rest, not that he'd given them a 411 on his location.

"Boss, what is *Buddha*?" As good as Zo was in combat, the idiotic things he spewed from his mouth were guaranteed to irritate Rohnert.

He sat on his heels and gritted his teeth, trying to keep his temper in check. "I told you I went to Asia a long time ago. To get in the monks' good graces, I had to spend hours upon hours in quiet reflection. Something I find you're not capable of." Rohnert closed his eyes and breathed deep, unsure if he should be thankful for Zo's company, or curse the day he stumbled upon him in an alley.

"You still haven't made the connection to Buddha."

Rohnert's eyes shot open. "Buddha was their savior. He grew on me."

Alonzo grinned, compounding his annoyance. "Sounds like you did a lot of traveling, boss."

"It soothes the soul." He sounded more wistful than he'd intended.

"I plan to visit my roots someday."

"You can do it now." Rohnert rose to his feet.

As exasperating as Alonzo could be, the vampire was loyal and a great soldier to have watching his back. Rohnert had instilled loyalty in every student he taught, and even combat instruction came second to that. He believed they needed their allegiance established before learning anything else. Little did he know that their sworn commitment had been directed to him, and not the Council, or its leader, Goran, for that matter.

"And leave you talking to yourself? No sir! I'm Robin to your Batman."

Rohnert couldn't help but chuckle. Wherever Zo had been hanging out, the bastard sure had learned a lot of dumb things. Pop culture had a way of streaming into one's psyche, no matter the nature of being.

"Thanks, but please keep your stupid ideas to yourself."

The winds continued to howl outside, and rain hammered against the roof. Hard. Rohnert sat down on the cot, listening to the calming sound. Funny, it seemed like his mood was the direct opposite of the weather. Go figure.

"What do we do now? It's a good day to stay caged in here. I bet we can find more people to join our little party." Alonzo stood next to him.

And add to the list of lives I'd be responsible for? He shook his head.

"I think two is already a crowd," Rohnert said. "We're staying in tonight."

Shelly entered her bedroom, feeling drained. In her years of practicing medicine, most of the patients she'd lost on the operating table had been gone even before they reached her, and there was nothing she could have done about it.

She dropped onto her sofa, not bothering to fix herself anything to eat first. Folded into a fetal position, she allowed herself to feel the weight of another life lost. Saving people had been her constant burden, and also her happiness. Having grown up in a stern household with parents who were both doctors, Shelly had felt the pressure to follow in their footsteps. She loved the profession, and the constant emergence of exciting diseases and innovative treatments had kept her on her toes. Her parents hadn't lived to see the day of her graduation, perishing in a house fire while she was away at med school. Still, Shelly could feel their presence in her life, urging her to continue their mission.

Tonight was a rough one. One of their new human fighters had accidentally fired a gun while cleaning it. She'd heard the sound and ran to the bedroom a few doors down from hers where she found the man gasping his last breaths, blood oozing from a chest wound. She called for help while performing CPR, but the man had checked out before additional assistance could arrive.

The scent of blood lingered on her clothes, but the stench of death was even more difficult to bear. In her chosen profession, she and her colleagues had to give themselves constant reminders to keep their emotions under wraps for the sake of their mental well-being. Shelly had been lucky enough to stay detached, but tonight, her inherent self-preservation took a nosedive.

She had no idea why she'd broken down and bawled like a child in front of the nurses, her determination to keep it together thrown out the window. Depleted, she had retreated to her office as soon as she had pronounced the time of death.

She was turning soft. The moment she'd allowed Rohnert into her life, everything had changed, shifting into unknown territory. Before him, she had managed to maintain her distance from emotional entanglements with men. Falling for a vampire of all things had messed her up real good. Rohnert had given her a mind-blowing orgasm, but then had immediately professed his indifference toward her. All it had been to him was sex.

That one night with Rohnert had proven to be a disaster. A big one. She had offered herself to a reluctant vampire, even though she'd known he wanted nothing to do with her. Pathetic. Had she not acted like a lovesick teenager, her pride would still be intact and her heart untouched. Maybe if she'd admitted to herself how deep her feelings for Rohnert went, she wouldn't have made herself so vulnerable. But fuck it, she'd made a mistake. She just hadn't realized how big a mistake it was until he left the facility without a word, disappearing like a ghost and abandoning everyone, not just her.

She had pulled herself together like she always did. Normally, it wasn't a problem, and yet, tonight, all she wanted was to cry her silly heart out. Shelly gave in to the misery and loneliness, letting out the tears and hoping that at the end of it all, she'd be able to forget.

The deaths she'd witnessed and the friends she'd lost at the hands of Goran's forces haunted her on nights like this. It was even worse to lose someone for nothing—a stupid accident and a waste of a life.

She succumbed to the ache she'd been trying to ignore, but after this day, she vowed, she would never shed a single tear for Rohnert ever again.

Goran paced around his chamber, seething at the most recent news from his second-in-command. Hamilton had ventured out several times in the past two months in hopes of locating Iden, a Council elder who had gone missing. So far, his efforts had been fruitless.

"Leave me." His voice boomed across the room, rattling the windows and the menagerie of fine artwork adorning the wall.

Hamilton bowed low and exited the room like his ass was on fire. Goran returned to his desk and deposited his shaking body on the chair. He wanted Iden found. There was no doubt that the vampire was in possession of something he needed.

He gave the drawer a hard pull, shaking the entire desk until the bust sitting on the edge fell on the floor with a resounding crash. No love lost there. He'd been trying to find an excuse to get rid of Grandpa's hideous sculpture once and for all. Instead of feeling a sense of loss, Goran laughed in contempt.

After he'd yanked the black book out of the drawer, he opened it to the marked page he'd read over and over. There, Marania had chronicled the popular prophecy of Gastarius—the oldest living vampire and a god-like figure to them all, both untouchable and unreachable.

Due to her position in the Council as the keeper of records, Marania had been able to secure an audience with the relic himself and found that Gastarius did possess the power to see the future, including their eventual emergence as a powerful race.

In the old manuscript, Marania had written Gastarius' prophecy:

> On the first sign of the moon's illumination, a vampire will rise into power, his heart filled with avarice. Among his peers, he will raise havoc, and death will augment the despair within. Mortals and vampires alike shall have no power to prevent the destruction he will leave in his wake. A disinclined soul shall be called, and a child borne to the rightful guide shall come to fulfill this divination.

"What the hell is the blustering idiot talking about?" He shoved the tattered tome away from him, and the black book landed on the floor with a thud. "No one speaks in riddles anymore." Goran huffed and rose from his seat.

A tumult of emotions blanketed him. With the fall of his Harem, he had no one to vent his anger on, no one to boost his flagging ego, and no one to bed and fuck. When was the last time he'd had a good lay?

His frustration mounted, increasing with every passing minute while he walked back and forth across the carpet. He made his way over to where the book lay and picked it up in haste. It had opened to the pages on which Marania had recorded the birth of vampire children belonging to Council members.

> Iden, son of Admar, and mate, Chandra welcomed their daughter, Isidora, on a bleak October morning, year 1938. Blessed with red hair and sable eyes, the babe was sequestered in the family's estate—reason not stated.

The crux of this whole damn thing was that the woman's identity was well concealed. Why? Goran had a nagging suspicion, but the answer could be supplied by none other than Iden himself. And the bastard was nowhere to be found.

He glanced at the other pages. Most entries were illegible. It appeared as if someone had made every effort to disguise the truth. Some pages were torn, others removed or tampered with. The blasted vampire, Marania, had eliminated the damning evidence because she had known of his intention. The indications of her interference were crystal clear.

His rage building, Goran armed himself with his sword and stalked out of his chamber. He walked with deliberate ease, every step filled with purpose. He entered the wing where he expected to find Hamilton. The blistering sound of wailing scaled the Council walls, anguished and terrified.

Inside the Blanch room, he found his trusted soldier sitting on the frayed Bergere chair that had been his dead son's favorite. He smirked at the thought of Demetrius. One less soul he had to worry about. He and his mother could carry on with their incestuous affair in hell.

Hamilton scampered to his feet while Goran walked toward the front of the massive room amid the weeping of petrified humans about to receive their lasting legacy. He glanced at the innumerable unknown faces before summoning Hamilton to him.

The vampire moved fast and bowed before him. "Yes, sire."

"You're coming with me tonight. There is someone I want to visit after I get something to eat." Goran was anxious to get going. His fangs throbbed with hunger. He'd held out long enough. The night was still in full bloom, and they had sufficient time before sunrise—enough to do some damage.

"How many men should I gather?" Hamilton straightened but kept his eyes averted in respect. The vampire hid none of his thoughts from him. His evil heart knew nothing except to please Goran and carry out his every wish.

"Just the two of us tonight. Prep the elite guards before you leave. I want them ready when I summon them." Goran turned and headed for the side exit.

Hamilton was quick to do his bidding, barking orders to his trusted men. Within a few seconds, shrieks filled the room and the process of creating new vampires commenced. Goran summoned the portal that would allow them to exit the Council's stronghold, and Hamilton walked alongside him through the hazy gate that appeared.

The evening breeze was welcome after the stifling confines of the

Council walls. Goran inhaled deep, feeling his immediate surroundings and gathering the thoughts of those around him. The New York City plaza was, as usual, besieged with humans. The meal he'd been putting off wasn't necessary, but he was in the mood tonight.

Glancing around, he did a quick inventory for anyone close to palatable and spotted a woman looking lost in the crowd. Concealing his sword underneath his long trench coat, he walked over to the unsuspecting human, with Hamilton close behind, and struck up a conversation.

"Miss, are you looking for someone in particular?" He offered his most alluring smile, willing his fangs to retract until they were nothing more than prominent canines.

The months following the back-to-back attacks on the Tack Enterprises strongholds had been as difficult as the day they lost their leader, Pritchard Tack. His honorary son, Harrow, sat inside the I-room alone, still devastated by their losses to Goran's forces. The battles had left them depleted and in a state of mourning. Burying the remains of their human friends had been heartbreaking. As much as he'd tried to put the past behind him, the haunting images of the people they'd lost, both vampire and human, continued to remind him that he had failed them.

Pushing back his chair, Harrow got up and headed to the well-stocked bar. The revolving door opened, and he pulled out the first bottle he touched. He poured the liquid to the brim and chugged a quick one. Then he poured another.

The door swung open, and his adopted sister Allison walked in with Tor. Harrow glanced at them through his dark sunglasses, sensing their emotional grid. As distraught as they were over the death around them, one could not deny that Tor and Allison had something to celebrate. In the midst of the casualties they had sustained, and the loss of Tor's arm in the process, they'd found each other, and their happiness radiated in spite their efforts to hide their feelings. Harrow was as elated as a brother could be.

He opened his arms, and Allison ran into his waiting embrace.

"Glad you came right away," he whispered into her hair.

Tor snorted. "Of course we did. You left us without a choice. You have this entire place on lockdown. There's nowhere for us to go." He flopped on the chair, resting his prosthetic arm on the table.

Harrow kissed Allison on the cheek before letting her go. Holding his drink, he marched to the head of the table and settled. Tor's reddish-purple eyes watched him with intensity. The vampire hadn't vacated his duties as Harrow's bodyguard, even after he'd been given the task to serve as Allison's guardian instead. As much as Harrow wanted to curse Tor for being overly watchful, he could never thank the vampire enough for sacrificing himself for Allison's sake. Losing a limb could do a number on one's ego, but Tor seemed to have adapted to his condition. He continued to perform his responsibilities without skipping a beat. He might have lost his arm in that fight, but he'd retained his grit and perseverance. Tor was a winner in Harrow's book.

While the room started filling in with what was left of their team, Harrow did a mental count of those who'd survived. The skeleton crew consisted of newly recruited vampire fighters, the diseased vampires who needed homes, and the very few humans who had been lucky enough to miss the slaughter.

Following Rohnert's departure, Allison, Jordan, and Tor had stepped up to the plate to teach the martial arts and weaponry classes that were just too much for Harrow to handle.

It had been a huge undertaking to respond to the negative comments stemming from the closure of the Tack Enterprises production line. Harrow had been in nonstop discussions with General Leo Krever, their go-to guy for damage control. Krever was in charge of maintaining contact with Tack's clients and assuring them that shipments would resume soon.

Harrow waited until the last of the remaining personnel walked in before he got up to address the group. A wave of melancholy descended upon him when he glanced at the vacant seats that had belonged to his good friends, Lambert and Cyrus. It was a silent reminder of how their operation had been crippled by losing two such integral members of their squad. He took a deep breath, suppressing the sadness in his voice.

"Listen up. I've decided to lift the lockdown. I will—"

Hoots and hollers halted his announcement as the room erupted in a jovial celebration. Despite Harrow's somber mood, he couldn't help but smile at everyone's enthusiasm. He lifted his hand to quiet them down.

"I urge everyone to be vigilant. Watch each other's backs. Our first and foremost goal is to continue finding infected vampires and offer them help. Aside from that, I'm not going to account for your time while you're out. Stay tight and don't give our location away. Whatever you do, make sure you're never followed." Harrow eyeballed every single one of this team.

"If you are in any way threatened, it's never cowardice to back down. No heroic shit here. I can't pat your back if you're dead. Rotations are still in effect. Same arrangement, two per group, and report to Tor or Firman if anything's up. Are there any questions?"

Gunner, another new recruit, raised his hand, his gray-white eyes brimming with excitement. He was a young diseased vampire, and one of Harrow's most promising students. "If we are approached by a Council guard, what do we do?"

Harrow had expected this question. "If they say they're going to take you in, you're as good as dead. They have a way of knowing which ones are infected. I will let you decide at that point which way you want to go. All I ask is that you never divulge our location."

"You've got nothing to worry about, boss," Gunner said, looking eager.

"Well, then we're good to go. I'll see everyone here same time tomorrow."

Jordan barged into the room, hauling ass. "Sorry I'm late. What did I miss?" She looked around apologetically and strode to where Tor was standing.

Harrow smiled at her before continuing. "As I was saying, we'll meet again tomorrow. Everyone must check in with Tor or Firman as soon as they arrive."

When the room emptied, he walked over to Jordan, his mate for over a year. "I'll fill you in about my little announcement," he whispered, "in the bedroom."

Cyrus woke up to a brand new day—another day in hell. He'd been imprisoned in the same room for several months at least. He'd lost count, and he was unable to recall the events following his abduction from the office building. It had been nothing but a great big blur. Considering the punishment he'd endured and how often he swam in and out of consciousness, there was no telling what day or month it was.

Performing a quick mental catalogue of his body, he wiggled his toes. All ten were still there. His upper limbs seemed fine, although his wrists were bound before him. His head, as far as he could tell, seemed intact despite the headache that stemmed from the repeated blows the night before. Even though his entire body ached and the pain of his broken leg was excruciating, he was still alive. That was always a good thing.

During his captivity, the same two humans had been guarding him. Not even once had they answered his questions. Instead, they had been interrogating him, beating him to a pulp every time he refused to give them information.

Who is the head of your operation? Why are you collaborating with the Tacks? Where is your hideout located?

Whoever they worked for, Cyrus hadn't had a glimpse of their employer. The duo operated like clockwork, showing when it was time for his rationed meal. One pint of water and three granola bars each day—just enough to keep him alive.

In the past couple of days, he'd been running a temperature. Cyrus knew it had something to do with the broken leg they had given him. Since he didn't know their names, Cyrus had dubbed them Sonny and Cher. The man he'd christened Sonny was a slight guy with a mustache and straight hair he pushed away from his face with gobs of gel. The other human, who sported a thick mass of long and curly hair, was the bigger, and dumber, of the two.

Lying on the bed, Cyrus glanced around the pale blue walls with his swollen eyes for the hundredth time. He shifted his gaze upward, toward the cathedral ceiling. It was covered by skylights, which were out of reach, but his one connection to the outside world. If his guess was correct, this was a room designed for vampires—nothing to keep the sun out, and a painful way to meet their ultimate doom.

Cyrus inched toward the edge of the bed and planted his good leg on the floor. Pushing his body to sit up was difficult, and his head began to spin. He sank back against the mattress with a groan.

"Damn it!" He closed his eyes, which were heavy like lead.

The door opened, and Sonny and Cher walked in as if they'd only been waiting for a sign that Cyrus had awoken. Though his eyes were unwilling to do his bidding, he forced his lids up and stared at the duo. Garbed in dark jeans and identical gray sweatshirts, both men stopped at the foot of the bed and watched him with critical eyes.

"Get up, asshole. It's time for your trip to the bathroom." Sonny clamped his hands on the rail and shook the bed.

"Maybe, we can just leave him to pee on himself. That might get him to talk," Cher said.

"Why don't we just let me out of this damn place?" Cyrus replied in a dead tone.

"Shut the fuck up and do as I say," Sonny shouted. He'd been the one who enjoyed treating Cyrus as if he was a mere dummy and his face was nothing but a punching bag.

"I can't fucking walk since your broke my leg, asshole," Cyrus answered, but he pushed his body up anyway. The moment he was vertical, his head started to spin again. Smothering the urge to groan, he gritted his teeth instead.

"D, drag his ass to the bathroom," Sonny ordered Cher.

"Why do I always get to do the fun part?" Cher complained.

"Because I'm your boss, and my boss is ordering me to do this. Understand?"

Grumbling, he walked toward Cyrus and pulled him upright. His leg was so not ready for this, and he hollered in pain. The darn leg was indeed broken, and the longer it was left untreated, it was going to be hell for him in the days to come.

"Stop crying, bitch, and follow me," Cher said and pulled Cyrus along behind him.

He cried out but started hobbling. He could barely move, although he tried putting his weight on the good leg. Every step was laborious agony.

Unwanted tears began to fall, despite his best efforts to rein them. Sonny smirked at the sight of his misery. When they stopped in front of the bathroom, Cyrus kept tabs on the two. He towered over them. On a good day, he could have taken them on without a problem, but that wasn't the case today. There was no way he'd get away, let alone survive.

Sonny patted his jacket, issuing a silent warning to Cyrus. Once the restraint was removed, he was shoved into the tiny bathroom. Other than the toilet and the sink, the bathroom had nothing—no frills, no windows, and no way out.

Cyrus sunk on the toilet seat in frustration. He needed to think, to find a way out of the hell hole, soon. Time was running out. He'd better get a plan in motion before the clock stopped ticking.

Rohnert was running to the house at a speed he hadn't realized he possessed, expending all his energy in hopes of reaching Lambert before things got out of hand. The desperate cry for back-up echoed in his ears while he dug harder into the ground.

He'd once considered the ability to hear others' unspoken thoughts a gift. Instead, it became a curse, forcing Rohnert to listen to the helpless pleas of his friends. He knew that they would never ask for help unless the situation was grave.

"Knox, guard the left side of the house. Peyton, take the right," Lambert ordered, running to the front of the building and locking the door behind him. *"Whatever happens, no one can enter the house."*

Jesus, there are so many of them. Where in the hell is back-up? Damn, if this is the fucking end, I should've told Peyton how I've always felt about her, Knox thought.

Peyton had been holding her ground until she was attacked from behind. Her dying thoughts were as silent as calm water.

There had been a female who jumped in front of Lambert. *"You're no match for us for our number."*

"That may be true, but I'm going to die fighting." Lambert had reloaded his Glock and another ear splitting howl had filled Rohnert's mind.

Then another gun had fired and instead of ashes crumbling to the ground, it had been Lambert's body that fell. In the few seconds it took for his light to dim, he'd thought of Gail, the little girl he'd grown to love. She was safe, he'd thought, and Lambert was ready to go.

Although Rohnert hadn't witnessed the bloodbath, he'd heard everything. It was enough. He had listened while his friends—the people who needed his help—died. He'd failed them.

Slowly, the past began to dim, and his restless mind eased back into the present, the sound of his heavy pants waking him. He sat up and let his eyes adjust to the darkness.

Then a sound of footsteps approached. *"Dios mio.* Is everything okay?"

Alonzo was right next to him, reaching out, but Rohnert raised his hands to ward him off.

"I'm good." He felt for his Kalimetal, an automatic response.

"You were talking in your sleep, sir." Zo sat on the floor next to Rohnert's cot.

"Let's go out."

Rohnert heard Alonzo's heart skip. "As much as I want to go out and kick some butt tonight, I think a thorough psyche eval is in order. This daily nightmare shit isn't healthy, not even for the great vampire."

Zo's answer infuriated Rohnert. There was no cause for concern. He had it together. "I'm fine. Let's roll." He pushed himself out of the rickety cot, the coils grunting under his weight.

Alonzo reached out and kept him from moving. "*Maestro*, no . . . you can't keep things bottled up."

He stared at Alonzo's hand on his arm until the vampire had the good sense to release him. If Zo wanted to keep his hand still attached to the rest of him, it was the smart thing to do. At the rate Rohnert's fury was building up, he needed an acceptable outlet to expel his aggression. Going out would help. He'd been cooped up long enough.

"Do I look like I need a psyche eval?"

"You're a walking zombie." Alonzo laughed and inched farther away. "If you're going to lead us, you need to have all your screws tightened."

Rohnert smirked, and his eyes blazed. "And you're the right person to talk to?"

"I'm the only person here, so that makes me qualified." Zo kept his expression even. "Unless you cherish talking to yourself? I think that's a no."

Rohnert knew he'd been spending too much time inside his head. The weight of the past and what could have been kept bearing down on him, making each waking hour an agony. He got up and pushed the horrid thoughts away.

"No talking will be done tonight," he said and threw a quick glance at Alonzo. "If you want to stay here and play doctor, you're going to be doing it alone."

Zo smirked but rose to his feet. "You know I respect you more than anyone, but if this goes on much longer, you're going to crack." He patted his jacket and felt for his weapons.

Rohnert threw a disgusted look at the persistent vampire who held his hands up and preceded him to the door. Alonzo might be annoying, but he was also right on the money, and cracking wasn't an option.

A satisfying meal never failed to put Goran in a better mood. With his hunger satiated, he could think clearer, and his disposition was much improved. Hamilton had moved the woman into the Council walls, where she'd undergo her change in the Blanche room just like the rest of the new recruits. It hadn't taken long to get what he needed, and he'd left the woman breathing enough to cross into her nether existence.

Wiping a remnant of sweet blood from his mouth, Goran walked the length of the Rockefeller Center with an amused expression. The damn human idiots glided around on their rented skates, going round and round, with no purpose and nowhere to go.

He scanned the grounds, considering what to do next while he waited for Hamilton. They had to move fast. Iden had likely built an army by now, so they would need to use the element of surprise. The capture of Iden's daughter was crucial to Goran's plans to reign over the vampire world uncontested.

Hamilton's distinct footsteps alerted him that his right-hand man was approaching. Without turning, Goran set out at a sprint, moving too quickly for the naked eye to track.

"Where to?" Hamilton asked from behind him as he tried to match his leader's bigger, quicker strides.

"We're visiting the countryside." Goran dug his heels deeper on the slick pavement, their blurred figures eliciting confused glances from people in the general vicinity.

Without an exact destination in mind, Goran began to run through the information he'd gathered, trying to trace any detail that might give away the location of Iden's hideout. The vampire Elder had disappeared like a ghost in the night, leaving no traces or clues behind. It was possible that he had found sanctuary with the motley group of deserters and diseased vampires that the Council soldiers strove to eradicate.

Hamilton had scoured the rebels' lairs, even the ones the fools believed he didn't know about, and yet all efforts to locate them had been unsuccessful. Those lucky bastards had evaded him, but it wouldn't take long before he found them—he always did. However, each trip produced few clues, and his impatience escalated every passing day.

The Vampire Council had their eyes on him, and he could feel their silent accusations of the crimes he'd committed. Goran ignored their allegations with a shrug. If they wanted to know the truth, all they had to do was ask, although they should arrange for their own funerals if they did. No one had the right to question him.

As much as he hated doing the dirty work, he realized that some things needed his personal touch, and finding Iden was a task that fit into that category. Besides, he wanted to see his bride with her mouth gaping open and horror in her eyes when he proclaimed his wish to bed her.

Damn—he meant *wed* her. The thought of hunting her down excited him. The task wouldn't be difficult if he had any leads.

Hamilton cleared his throat. "If it would not offend . . ."

Goran glanced at the vampire. By this time, they'd reached the outskirts of the city and were running at full speed. The darkness swallowed them like mere phantoms.

He knew what Hamilton was thinking and didn't give him the chance to pose his question. "Some things are better left to me to do."

Hamilton clamped his mouth in an instant and concentrated on keeping up with him. Yeah. The bastard was smart enough not to push any buttons, being familiar with Goran's explosive nature. If he wanted to keep his head attached to his shoulders, shutting his hole was a great idea.

Silence and the rushing air accompanied them for the rest of the long run to the general area Goran wanted to scour. The journey took them into the countryside. Judging from the description in Marania's book, his instinct told him he was in the correct vicinity.

Now, the question was where he should start looking.

Knocking door to door wouldn't work, since secrecy was of utmost importance. Their race had always operated underground, and he wasn't about to shake an age-old practice. Most likely, Iden anticipated that they would come at him with everything they had. This was where Goran must employ finesse and surprise.

Stopping not too far from a cluster of homes, he sniffed the air, willing his keenest sense to detect anything out of the ordinary.

Nothing.

The air held the pure scent of human, sweat, and acrid dinner leftovers. His stomach roiled, not particularly fond of the smell of human food.

He slowed into a jog, passing by a collection of houses that had seen better times. The ranch-style homes were from the forgettable fifties and were similar to each other, with low, pitched roofs, rectangular shapes, and small porches. The sole thing that set them apart was the exterior color.

"Let's walk," Goran said after they'd covered a three mile radius and come up empty. The night was young, and they had plenty of time before light pushed them into hiding again.

Hamilton stopped at the command and matched his stride to his master's. In silence, they continue to comb the neighborhood, with Goran's olfactory perception acting as their GPS.

"Sire, are we still looking for Iden?"

Goran had to smile. His second-in-command couldn't hold on to his curiosity, even if it meant saving himself from punishment.

"Yes we are. He's in possession of a precious commodity." Goran left his explanation vague. He wasn't ready to share the idea of Isidora with anyone yet.

Mystified, Hamilton's ruby reds settled on him. "But you own every rare artifact known to man." It wasn't a question, but a statement meant to appease him.

"Hamilton." He placed a calming hand on the vampire's shoulder. "You're better off not knowing yet. I have my reason for hunting Iden. The bastard vacated his post in the Council without due notification. For that, he is an enemy."

Goran had no plan of divulging more information. Ignorance was bliss, and the less Hamilton knew about his personal dealings, the better. Given the nature of the contents of the black book, any insignificant detail leaked to anyone could prove disastrous.

Out of nowhere, a familiar scent wafted in the air. Goran's hand shifted to his sword and gestured for Hamilton to halt his movement. They turned in the opposite direction in anticipation of a fight. Council soldiers and guards had been instructed to end their patrol in this specific area for fear of stumbling upon vampires who had jumped ship, so to speak. No one would be loitering in this location without his or Hamilton's knowledge.

Within a few minutes, two vampires cleared the dense vegetation, oblivious to what awaited them. One of the two, a male, was a familiar face, although Goran couldn't place him in his long list of acquaintances. The female was a nameless vampire he'd never seen before.

Hamilton hissed, cocking his shotgun.

The twosome stopped short after realizing they had company. The male, burly and wearing a muscle shirt that exposed his obvious love affair with tattoos, shielded the female with his body. His eyes flashed with hostility before recognition dawned. He dropped to his knees, leaving the female vulnerable, and she reached for the gun in her waistband.

Goran's grip relaxed, and he moved forward, signaling Hamilton to stay at ease. His second-in-command hesitated before backing down.

"What's your name?" Goran's eyes fixed on the female. As much as he tried to purge his healthy appetite for redheads, he'd be damned if he would pass on a chance to have his way with one. The woman shot him a blank, almost comical, stare when Goran powered on the charm that was unique to him.

"Harmon." The man struggled back to his feet and pulled the woman closer to him.

"Where have I seen you before?" Goran's onyx eyes flickered in the male's the direction for a brief moment.

"I . . ."

The hesitation told Goran all he needed to know. The man was a Council soldier who had left his post—one of the many who were unaccounted for. Smirking, Goran unsheathed his sword before Harmon could draw his own weapon.

Striking the vampire across the neck with one clean sweep, Goran sneered. "That's for vacating your post without warning."

The severed head fell on the ground with a dull thump and rolled to his feet while the woman's screams disturbed the quiet night. When the popping and crackling began, she began to run away.

"Clean up here. I'll be back." Goran sheathed his sword in its scabbard went in pursuit.

The female's pace was no match for his. He gained on her in no time. Before she had a chance to realize what was happening, Goran had her pinned against a tree.

"I'll be most kind to you, my dear," he whispered in her ear, when he unzipped his pants.

"No . . . no . . ." The woman clamped her legs together, denying him entry.

"This won't take long. I'll make it fun and worthwhile."

That was lie, of course. He had no intention of making the experience memorable for her. Instead of putting her in a trance, he hastened his movements, ripping her filthy jeans off her trembling body and thrusting into her. Defiance was the key ingredient to his arousal, and the pursuit made it even sweeter. It had been ages since he'd last felt the sensation of filling someone.

The female tried to put up a fight, kicking and screaming. He pounded harder, excited at her futile attempts to ward him off. He'd been so caught up in his thirst that he failed to catch the woman's thoughts right away.

Serves you right if I infected you, you sick bastard. "Get off me!"

Goran stopped mid-thrust and pulled out as if his dick were on fire. Shrinking away from her, rage replaced lust in one quick instant.

"You're sick." The statement served to cement his idiocy. Goran bristled, zipped his jeans, and once again drew his sword. He didn't need to wait for confirmation—her eyes said it all.

Without hesitation, he plunged the tip of the sword into her chest, twisting until the blade penetrated her heart. Her pathetic cries filled the feeling of gloom that cloaked him. Detesting himself for his carelessness, he spat at the woman's body, not bothering to wait for the imminent fireworks.

Zane concluded his exercise regimen for the day, donning his nylon shirt. He had been going at the punching bag with gusto for the last hour and would have kept at it for another hour if he hadn't had a pressing appointment with a very important man.

His cell phone beeped as Zane crossed the hallway to his bedroom. Picking up the device, he read the text message and smirked.

He's ready for you.

"I bet." He typed a quick text back.

I'll be there sometime tonight.

After sending his response, he strode to the bathroom for a quick shower. A few minutes later, he was dressed to impress. Garbed in his usual coat and tie, he headed for the stairs, taking the time to clear his head and rehearse all the questions he wanted to ask. The car ride took longer, since the dense crowd milling at every nook and cranny of the city slowed him down.

"Damn!" He pounded the steering wheel, wishing the ground would swallow up the humans and clear his way. If living in the city hadn't been so convenient, the traffic alone would drive him away.

Zane reached the quieter area of Little Italy a minute shy of the agreed-upon meeting time. At this point, the street was almost empty, and the crowd much scarcer. He parked his car in front of the pizzeria.

When he pressed the button to activate the car alarm, the horn sounded twice. He looked up at the faint light outside the establishment and smiled. The design of the awning reminded him of a movie he'd loved when he was growing up. Of course, most men his age worshipped *The Godfather*.

The door opened even before he'd stepped onto the curb, and a male vampire waved him in. On alert, Zane walked into the dark room and focused on the man seated at the far side of the room, away from the late night crowd.

The scent of cheese, sauces, and anchovies made Zane's stomach lurch. Though he'd been around humans most of his life, the disgusting odor of food had been a longstanding annoyance for him. Nothing could replace the tangy smell of blood.

"You're three minutes late," the familiar voice called out.

If hostility had a scent, the aroma his grandpapa emitted was the horrible stench of decayed bodies mutilated beyond recognition and surrounded by feasting flies.

"Traffic was impossible—"

"Silence! I'll do the talking. Sit and listen."

It was going to be a long night, Zane could tell. He pulled up a chair and sat across from the man who evoked both fear and loathing in him.

Shelly stepped out of the tub, feeling out of sorts. She'd thought a long, warm bath would do the trick. Instead, she was still sluggish.

It'd been a slow morning. Hell, it had been a slow week all around. The fighters were off lockdown, but there hadn't been any incidents that required her services. Most people would celebrate that there hadn't been any casualties, gunshot wounds, or even minor aches so far, but she felt like crap being idle. For lack of better things to do, her mind often wandered to the forbidden Rohnert territory. Those errant thoughts kept creeping up during her most vulnerable times.

Staring at herself in the full-length mirror, she noted her sunken cheeks, the unhappiness in her face, and the brittle smile that never reached her eyes. What the hell was wrong with her? She'd vowed to never let any man affect her, let alone a creature that in her wildest imagination she would never have believed existed.

The phone rang, and Shelly draped a towel around her body and rushed to answer it.

"You wanted to see me?" Jones asked, sounding relaxed for a change.

She gripped the phone hard. "Yeah. I was hoping we could talk." Her stomach knotted once more.

"Sure. You know where to find me." Jones paused, and she heard a sigh. "Is everything okay, Shell?"

No one called her Shell anymore, not since he . . .

"Don't call me that. Yes, everything is just peachy." She tried to hide her disdain. "I'll see you in fifteen." Shelly slammed down the phone.

Shelly was almost done dressing when a soft knock sounded on her door.

"Who is it?" she snapped.

"Shelly?" Jordan's voice came through the door.

After twisting her still-damp hair, Shelly tied it into a quick knot and headed for the door. Though she and Jordan had grown friendly after Harrow's near-death experience more than a year ago, they hadn't forged a tight friendship until Shelly had helped Gail in the aftermath of the massacre in their upstate home. With Annie's death, Jordan had taken full responsibility for Gail. Shelly had to hand it to the vampire. She was doing a wonderful job as Gail's mother.

"Coming." She opened the door. "What brings you here?"

Jordan stood outside in her usual outfit of jeans, leather jacket, and boots, minus her favored Kalimetal weapons. She regarded Shelly for a long moment before moving past her and into the little sitting area.

"Do I need a reason to visit you?" Jordan asked, settling on the leather couch.

Shelly rolled her eyes before proceeding to the kitchen. "Coffee?"

"Only if you add three teaspoons of blood." Jordan laughed.

Shelly made a face. The thought made her stomach queasy. "Eww! That is gross."

"Well, you asked." Jordan looked around before resting her amber eyes on Shelly.

Pouring coffee into a foam cup, Shelly tried to get rid of her. "I have to see Jones. Can we visit another time?"

Jordan was fast on her feet. Before Shelly could even bat an eyelash, the vampire was already standing next to her.

"I can tag along." Jordan opened the door for her.

"Can you just get lost?"

"No, ma'am. Harrow is swimming with Gail, and I have nothing to do. They shooed me away, so I'm here to annoy you." Jordan smiled. Her grin was wide enough to show the tips of her fangs.

They traveled down the long hallway until they reached the elevator. "I'm not in the mood to be bothered today," Shelly said, punching the floor number.

"I'll keep my hole zipped and be quiet as a mouse." Jordan's fingers moved across her lips in a zipping gesture.

"Fine. You can start now." Shelly took a sip from her coffee.

As promised, Jordan remained silent, and there was no conversation while they walked toward the laboratory. Jones looked up from his mountain of journals upon their arrival. His unkempt hair was a mop of brown and dark circles ringed his eyes. The scientist had been spending too much time on research.

In the year since he'd taken over his dead predecessor's position, Jones had aged. He scrambled to his feet and got up to meet them, giving Shelly a quizzical look.

"Well, she showed up, and there's no getting rid of her," she said by way of explanation for Jordan's presence.

Jones smiled apologetically. It wasn't an unusual occurrence for Jordan to show up at most of the facility's meetings. "Well, have a seat, ladies." He pointed to the chairs opposite his desk.

"If you don't mind, I'll just wander and let you guys conduct your business," Jordan made her way toward the rows of computers and printers.

Shelly watched her before sitting on one of the chairs Jones offered and getting down to business. "So have you gotten the results yet?"

Jones sat on his chair and shoved a paper across the desk. "Are you sure you want to talk about it right now?" He glanced in Jordan's direction.

Shelly nodded. "Word will get around no matter what, so we might as well start with her." Jordan threw her a menacing look. "And besides, you know about their keen hearing."

Glancing at the paper, Shelly scanned the results, heart thumping against her chest. Her suspicion was now confirmed. What in the hell had happened?

"Jones, are you sure?" she asked, knowing the answer already.

"You're a doctor, Shell . . ."

She threw him a dagger glare.

"*Shelly*, you know I wouldn't joke around with something like this."

Angry tears brimmed. "No. It can't be."

"The results don't lie." Jones dropped his voice lower. "I ran the tests several times, and I'm positive."

Shelly tore the paper into pieces. "I was on the O-ring!" She tossed the shredded pieces into the trash can.

"I wish I could give you the result you wanted."

There was a swooshing sound, and before she could react, Jordan was sitting next to her, rubbing her back. "Is everything okay?"

Shelly shrank away from her touch. "If you ask me that question one more time, I'm going to slap you back to Harrow."

If Jordan took her seriously, she gave no indication. Instead, she bit her lip and nodded in understanding.

Jones watched them with interest before he addressed Shelly. "I want to discuss my findings, when you're ready. There are other options . . ."

Shelly shot to her feet. "I'm not going to kill this baby . . . whatever it is!" She hurried to the door, aching to get away and sort out the mammoth confusion swimming in her head.

"I wasn't suggesting you get rid of the baby."

"It's okay, Jones. Let her be," she heard Jordan say before she slammed the door shut.

Isidora walked around her boudoir, snapping a hairpin into her newly chopped hair. It was a small triumph, but a triumph nonetheless. Her father, Iden, had insisted on leaving her hair long. Her red locks, her crowning glory according to her father, had reached the small of her back. Whatever his reason, Isidora refused to let him dictate what she should do. He had robbed her of many things already, and this was something she wanted too much to back down from.

She'd been sick of the long hair for as long as she could remember. The stupid mane and its weight had been a constant annoyance. Her mother, Chandra, shared her father's opinion but had been more subdued in her insistence. After years of constant battle with him, Isidora had taken matters into her own hands. Without the help of an expert, she'd grabbed a pair of dull scissors and cut off her tresses in haste.

Satisfaction came in many forms, and this was the sweetest of them all. She glanced at her reflection in the mirror and grinned. After her father got over his initial shock and her mother finished weeping, they'd stared at her like she was a creature from another planet.

The hair, now expertly trimmed by their family stylist, looked better, making her big black eyes stand out. She looked and felt prettier. Gone was the bland looking hairdo she had sported all her life. Her nose was more prominent, and her skin seemed creamier, more alive.

Isidora felt a glimmer of hope. If she had been able to penetrate her father's armor with something small, she might one day be able to convince him to let her out, even for a short time. She'd lived in their palatial house her whole life and had not once been off the grounds.

Her meals were delivered to her on a schedule, and numerous guards watched over her. Many times she'd asked the reason for her sequestration, but her father offered vague responses that were filled with holes and quite unbelievable.

"You're precious, child. You may not know it, but you are," he had said.

It irritated her to the bones that he wouldn't entrust her with the truth.

Whatever he'd meant, she wasn't buying the lies. It was a matter of time before she chipped away the remaining resolve to keep the truth from her. Whatever it was, she was a big girl and could handle it.

"Mistress," her most trusted companion said from the door. Maureen bowed and advanced into the room. "Your meal is ready."

Rolling her eyes, she patted the mattress. "How many times have I told you to stop being so formal?"

Maureen sat down next to her. She had been Isidora's confidante since they were little. They'd grown up within the confines of the grand house and its grounds. Together, they had spent many days plotting their way out, but as soon as the thought even crossed their minds, they were beset with several babysitters who watched them like hounds.

Maureen winked at her with her big blue eyes. "Your mother is somewhere nearby. I don't want her to think that I don't respect your royal highness."

Isidora nudged her friend. "Oh, shut up! Mother knows everything. There's no hiding anything from her."

"I think I have a brilliant idea." Maureen lowered her voice. "In the meantime, your food awaits."

Her interest piqued, Isidora gestured for Maureen to keep talking, but she shook her head. "Fine. When will you tell me?"

"After you eat, I'll meet you in the garden."

Maureen accompanied her to the wing that housed the feeding room and held the door open for her. The moment Isidora walked in, a piercing hiss filled the air. It was enough to stall her, and she raised her eyes to the big, menacing vampire who awaited her.

One of her recent requests was to feed straight from a vampire rather than wasting humans or drinking pure blood from a glass. Besides, human blood was not as gratifying as a vampire's, and could only last her for so long. Instead, she wanted to use one vampire alone since a vampire's veins gave more nourishment and allowed them to feed less often.

Finn rushed at her, only to be yanked back by the metal wrist restraints. He snarled in her direction, hurling the scent of his resentment at her.

"This will take just a minute," she said, keeping her voice gentle.

His eyes snapped with pure hatred. She had no idea why he'd been hostile to her, since in return, she'd made it clear that Finn would only feed from her. It was a win-win situation for all involved.

"I want you, but not like this." He growled when she inched forward.

The fight wasn't as bad as it once had been. After several near-fatal encounters, she'd noticed a gradual change, and it excited her. Upon her insistence, Finn had been stripped of his weapons and left with nothing but a deep violet robe. The color excited her, and the luxurious material made feeding more thrilling. Noble blood was satisfying, but it was the eroticism that made her want to scream.

Taking his hand in hers, she pushed Finn back against the wall. He resisted, twisting her arms behind her. Isidora purred and inclined her head to expose her neck.

"You're hungry. Take what you want." Her breathing came in erratic bursts when his fangs elongated. Finn latched on to her neck without wasting time. The first tug was the always the sweetest, causing havoc in her mind. He punctured deeper and sucked harder, pulling and tugging at her vein. Her body responded, curving into his, loving the feel of his strong muscles against her skin.

After he'd taken his fill, Finn licked the puncture site with his tongue, leaving a hot trail of desire. "You're sweet and wonderful," he murmured into her hair.

This was the play. The show they put on for everyone's sake.

"I want you now." Isidora mounted him, twisting their bodies to the floor as far as the shackles would allow.

"Take all you want, my lady."

That was all he needed to say. Isidora punched into his neck with such force that he screamed.

Rohnert and Alonzo rested at the top of one of the most prominent buildings in the busy thoroughfare. For lack of anything better to do, Rohnert had decided to watch people and immerse himself in their inner ramblings. Each one proved to be as mundane as he'd expected. He scanned the immediate area, including every alley, getting the best view from his vantage point while Alonzo chewed on his gum with furious resolve.

"What do you think we'll gain from sitting up here?"

"A little perspective."

The nonstop twinkling of lights from the nearby buildings added to the euphoria of being outside once again. Living cooped up in their hideout was a sad existence.

Rohnert needed change. There had to be something else he could do besides sitting here wasting time. He needed to get back to his roots, where he'd found peace and purpose.

The one thing I'm getting from sitting up here is nausea. Alonzo's internal blather was the loudest of them all.

"I don't mind sitting here alone if you can come up with something constructive to do." Wasn't that the truth? Rohnert didn't mind being alone.

He'd gone long enough with limited associations, and he was looking forward to an opportunity to spend time in communion with nature, in silence and meditation.

"If you're okay with me bailing, I'll meet up with you at the apartment before sunrise." Alonzo got on his feet and gave him a slight nod before flinging his body into a downward spiral.

Rohnert watched him with detached interest while he plummeted into a blur. Switching his focus back to the tangent of human emotions and thoughts, Rohnert couldn't help but think of Shelly. The woman was like a persistent itch, keeping him uncomfortable and restless. His musing took a nosedive toward the last night they had been together.

Shelly had pushed him to the edge of want. The memory of her resplendent body often haunted him, and this time was no different. A shudder rocked his core when the vision of Shelly's naked body sprawled on the bed popped into his mind.

This was the reason why getting involved with the human had proven dangerous. He couldn't think straight, and there was nothing he could do to get her off his damn mind. Rohnert might as well purge his brain of everything pertaining to the doctor. That beautiful woman had him by the balls.

A piercing shriek rang out nearby. Rohnert stood up and zeroed in on the general direction from where the sound originated. Plunging eight hundred and fifty-six feet, headfirst, off the New York Times Building got him pumped for a face-off with the aggressors. When he closed in on the ground, he twisted and spun his body until he was pointed downward. Landing near the side of the building with a soft thud, he sprinted to the exact location of the altercation.

He was about to turn into the dark alley when he realized that someone had beaten him to it. "We're not here to attack other vampires. We're done with that. If you can't rein your hostility, I suggest you get lost." The voice sounded familiar so Rohnert decided to take the back seat and scale a one-story building to watch from the rooftop.

Once he found a perfect spot, he caught a glimpse of three vampires. Although he couldn't see the face of the one who had just spoken, Rohnert was certain that it was his former comrade and student, Gentry, again. Rohnert's old friend was facing the other two vampires in the alley. It was clear that one of them was the aggressor and the other, his target.

Gentry's shoulder muscles strained against his dark tunic as his grip on his dagger tightened. Rohnert silently applauded. His serious and well-thought-out words were not a threat, but a warning. The attacker had better heed him before his head was served on a silver platter.

Instead, the self-indulgent male sneered and pointed his gun at the victim, a smaller vampire, who showed signs of being infected with Harrow's infamous disease.

"Gentry, I've served the Council well. I believe in the cause of eradicating lowlifes like him." The trigger engaged, and Rohnert jumped to his feet, not wasting any time.

Somersaulting from the roof to the ground, Rohnert unsheathed his Kalimetal and struck before anyone could react, and the gunman dropped to the ground dead, taking the diseased one with him. Gentry spun around, aiming his dagger in Rohnert's direction.

"Gentry, it is I." He lowered his weapon.

"Your grace." Gentry went down on one knee. "It's a pleasure to see you again."

"The pleasure is mine." His eyes flickered over to the pale, but relieved, victim who scrambled to his feet. "Lose the title, and no kneeling or bowing."

"What's going on here?" the diseased one asked.

Gentry got up and sheathed his dagger in his waistband, looking much too happy to see Rohnert. He turned to answer. "You're free to go," he said.

"If I were you, I would contact this number. They can help you." Rohnert recited the untraceable number to the underground facility and made him repeat the digits. Once the shaken man was sound enough to leave, he waved him off and wished him luck.

Turning his attention to Gentry, Rohnert parked his Kalimetal in his back strap and began to walk. Gentry followed him, and together they navigated the back alleys.

"I joined Iden's army as you suggested."

"And do you regret doing so?" Rohnert took quick stock of the ex-Council soldier. Warm crimson eyes met his. Gentry sported a military buzz cut that showed his preference for order. He followed orders without prejudice, but he used discretion in deciding whether the cause was worthy. A proven leader, he was a good man to have on one's team.

"Not a day," he said. "But we still need a leader. Iden is wanted by Goran, and it's quite difficult for him to operate while in hiding."

The invitation was there, but Rohnert chose to ignore it. He wasn't a born leader. There was no drive in him to lead people, and he wouldn't subject poor, unsuspecting souls to slaughter once more.

"Stay put, and you'll find a good one soon." He had no idea why he said what he did.

"Let me give you my contact number and where you can find us." Gentry recited a series of numbers and an out-of-town address Rohnert committed to memory.

"Very well. I want you to keep protecting the sick ones. The group at Tack Enterprises is researching the cure. They are good people, and they stand behind a good cause. Let Iden know that I will be in contact once the time is right, and tell him that I support his quest to find a worthy leader."

"Your message will be delivered right away," Gentry said.

"I also want you to go to this address and convince the man there to go with you. He's an asset, and he'll be able to help with tactics and training. He'll give you an earful, but once you get over your initial irritation, you'd find him tight and loyal."

Gentry agreed to do his bidding without further questions. They slapped hands before they separated and went in opposite directions. The night was young, and Rohnert had made up his mind. He knew where he needed to go —a quiet place where he could sort out his wayward thoughts and once and for all clear his mind of the guilt that continued to wreak havoc on him.

Zane was still smarting from the meeting with Grandpapa long after he left the pizzeria. Goran had been in a foul mood, a frightening contrast from the last time the old vampire had paid him a surprise visit. His phone buzzed the moment he got in his car. After engaging the locks, he scanned his phone for messages.

There were several voicemails from Hill, one of the humans tasked with guarding Cyrus. Zane listened to the messages while he navigated his car into the deserted street.

Boss, we're ready for you. He's going to be a blast.

Hill's tone reflected his excitement, and Zane shook his head while he hit the disconnect button. The human was good, but quite annoying. The same went for his sidekick. If not for their willingness to take the assignment without questions, he would've looked elsewhere. Besides, they were ruthless, and that was what he needed.

With a smirk on his face, Zane drove for a few minutes before he reached a neat row of unremarkable townhouses. Once parked, he took his backpack from the compartment and slung it over his shoulder. He wouldn't dare dirty his signature suit.

Taking the flight of stairs two at a time, he reached the rented suite in just a fraction of time it would have taken had he opted for the elevator. Sliding his key into the keyhole, he did a quick due diligence check before walking inside.

Hill and David looked up from their perch on the sofa.

"Where is he?" Zane pulled on his tie.

"In the room," Hill answered, regarding him with a critical eye.

He returned the challenging stare. "You have something to say?"

The man thought for a moment. "When are you going to pay us?"

"At the end of the day."

Zane disappeared into the spare bedroom. He changed into a black cotton shirt and jeans, folded his discarded outfit, and carefully slid it back into his backpack, and pulled out a box. He jiggled the container and grinned.

"This is going to be fun," he said to himself and walked across the hallway where his guest would be waiting for him.

The room had been prepped to his specifications, and the man of the hour jumped back upon seeing him. The blinds were drawn tight, with two spotlights primed on his target.

"Here I was hoping you were dead."

Zane shook his head, slow and deliberate. "Cyrus, Cyrus. It won't be easy to get rid of me. I have millions of questions I need you to answer before I die." He gave a laugh filled with derision. This man was the key to unraveling the mystery surrounding his father's disappearance, and the one who could lead him back to the underground hideout where Zane had once been a prisoner.

"Nothing will come out of this mouth." Cyrus's eyes burned with hatred.

Zane waggled his finger at the human and moved closer. A quick inspection showed that Hill and David had done what he'd asked of them. Good. The steel arm restraints appeared snug and dependable. He reached forward with one hand and yanked at the short chain, testing it. Cyrus recoiled and, using his restraints for leverage, went at him with a sweeping kick with his good leg. He swung back and hit Cyrus's leg, sending him crumbling to the floor with a howl.

"You'll never get the best of me."

Despite his tears, Cyrus cursed and struggled back on his feet. "I will have the last laugh. Mark my words."

Zane feigned fear and shuddered for maximum effect. Then he held the box up and made sure Cyrus was looking at it. "Can you guess what's inside?"

The human didn't answer, prompting Zane to remove the lid and take out the shiny piece of metal. It was pure entertainment to watch Cyrus's face contort into a series of expressions ranging from anger and confusion to a smidgen of fear. "That's what I want—the look of fear in your eyes."

Cyrus snarled. "I'm not afraid of you, you fuckin' bastard."

"Oh, you will be by the time I'm done," he said and tossed the box on the floor. Zane held the contraption's spoon-like segments closer to Cyrus's face. "You'll be well acquainted with fear by the time I'm through with you."

"Now we're talking. I thought you'd never lift the lockdown," Tor said as he and Harrow jumped the big puddle the recent storm had left just outside their underground facility.

"After your nonstop griping, I figured it was time to shut you up." Harrow ran faster.

"See what a little air can do for you! Check you out—I see that wild look in your eyes again."

"Just shut your hole will you? Let me enjoy a moment of silence."

Though Tor was right, Harrow wasn't about to admit to it. He'd be better off if he found a muzzle for Tor's face. Harrow laughed at the vision in his head.

"Look at you, you're even laughing. This is great! Just like old times."

Tor was swift enough to surpass him, and Harrow dug his heels deeper into the ground. True, they had been caged inside headquarters. Harrow took a deep breath, knowing that when Tor was in one of his obnoxious moods, it was difficult to get him out of it. Why fight a losing battle?

"Where to?" Tor asked after several minutes of welcome silence.

"The usual."

"Very good. I've been dying for some Silver." Tor said, referring to his favorite tequila.

Harrow shook his head. He was looking at a very long night. When they reached the city, they headed for the bar where it had all started. The night they'd met, their encounter hadn't been friendly. Tor had almost severed Harrow's head with his shitty axe. So much had happened since then. They'd been adopted into a big, dysfunctional family, and they'd made it work.

Reaching the dark club, Harrow preceded his friend. In his usual fashion, Harrow wore his Oakleys and sported a trench coat to conceal his Kalimetal. Finding a spot in the bar had never been easy, but with Tor emitting a don't-fuck-with-me vibe, seats cleared right away. The humans scurried, stumbling in their haste to get away from the two vampires.

Harrow waved at the bartender, who came for their orders. After Tor handed him two hundred-dollar bills, the man rushed to fill their orders.

Harrow couldn't help but notice that Tor continued to grin like an idiot. Even with the devastating loss of a limb, his buddy remained upbeat. Love had to be the key. With Allison around, Tor seemed different. It was difficult to explain.

It was a bummer that his other buddy, Rohnert, was nowhere to be found. Since he'd left the facility, he hadn't been heard of. Shelly had turned tight-lipped about everything in general. They suspected there had been a fallout between the two, but no one was brave enough to ask.

The bar, as usual, was filled with bottom dwellers. Hookers and drug dealers were making deals while the music blasted from the raggedy jukebox. Harrow smirked. The scent of vampires swirled around him like bad news. He stayed vigilant, but Tor seemed oblivious to everything but his drink order.

"Thirsty?"

"No sir. In fact, I'm celebrating." Tor raised a shot glass with his prosthetic limb and shot him an irritating smile, complete with fangs.

"What are we celebrating?" Harrow raised his glass in Tor's direction. Despite the dim light in the club, Harrow could see just fine. Everyone was minding their own business, and all was well.

Then someone reeking of arrogance sat next to him on a newly vacated barstool. Harrow inclined his head at a better angle to catch a glimpse of the man's face. Tor leaned forward, stared at the man sitting next to him, and laughed.

"Dude, are you the guy Rohnert didn't kill last year?" Tor said, his voice laced with sarcasm.

The newcomer rose, no doubt feeling for his weapon. "Who wants to know?" His voice was low and dangerous.

Instead of answering, Tor reached over and offered his prosthetic hand. "Tor. I was with Rohnert upstate when we bumped into each other in the clearing."

The fighter continued to scrutinize him and Harrow, his hand resting on his waistband. Though Harrow couldn't see the weapon, he was certain it was there. Brows scrunched and eyes narrowed, the man took a few moments before he laughed.

"I'll be damned. How are you?" He took Tor's outstretched hand, glancing down at Tor's artificial limb. "What the hell happened to you?"

Tor pulled his hand back and waved it in the air. "Just some cosmetic enhancement." He chuckled.

Harrow kept looking at one vampire to the other. Had he missed something? When had Tor become friendly with VC soldiers?

"Oh by the way, this is Harrow, and this is . . ." Tor paused.

"Gentry."

Tor laughed. "There you go. He's the one who dropped to his knees to pay homage to our homey, the stud muffin."

Gentry laughed at this description of Rohnert. "That's me. Speaking of which, I bumped into him about an hour ago." He sat down again.

"You saw Rohnert tonight?" Harrow couldn't quite believe it.

"He found me and an ex-friend in an alley. Your *homey* saved an infected vampire and suggested that he call you guys."

Harrow still was, and always would be, an infected one. He could run and hide, but when he surfaced, people would know he was a carrier of the deadly disease.

"We try to help as much as we can. If he calls us, he won't be turned away."

Harrow turned his attention to the bartender, watching him flip and toss bottles as he prepared customers' drink orders. Tor and Gentry continued talking shop, and Harrow's mind drifted to Rohnert. It might be a good idea to look for him. They'd been a happy unit, even though they'd had their fair share of testosterone-fueled showdowns.

"Hey, Gentry. Where can I find Rohnert?"

"I don't know. He didn't say anything." Gentry turned thoughtful. "He asked me to see someone before the end of the night. The place isn't too far from here. I was killing time. I planned to go an hour before sunrise."

"Did he say who it was?" Harrow placed a tip for the bartender on the table and, out of habit, patted his jacket for his weapons.

"No. Only that the guy is a talker but would also make a valuable member for our team." Gentry chugged his vodka and got up.

"What team?" Tor asked.

"Because you are friends of Rohnert's, I'll tell you a little. There's a group opposed to the current ruling party." Gentry followed them to the door.

Goran had made enemies everywhere, but the powerful leader remained untouchable. Lord knew how long it would take before they could surface without having to look over their shoulders all the time.

"Can we go with you to see this character?" Harrow had to ask. Any way to find Rohnert was worth checking out.

"I don't mind at all."

It didn't take long to find the rundown structure located just outside the city proper. The building screamed *bulldoze me*. They drew their weapons, prepped for a fight well before they reached the porch.

The floor grunted under their collective weight, making Tor hiss. When they reached the front door, the sound of a cocking shotgun greeted them. Eyeballing each other, Harrow took the left side of the door while Tor and Gentry moved to the right.

"Not another step, or I'll blow you to kingdom come," an accented voice shouted.

Harrow signaled to the others to keep an eye out while he attempted to talk the man out of blowing them to smithereens. They nodded, their faces alert.

"We're not here to fight—we want to talk." Harrow kept his voice low.

"We? How many is *we*?" They heard the sound of another gun being cocked.

Two guns? Or two vampires inside?

"There are three of us, and Rohnert sent us."

That was, of course, a lie. Rohnert had no idea that he and Tor would decide to tag along. However, Harrow had no idea with whom they were dealing.

"I'll open the door. If I see any weapons drawn, I will gun you down."

Harrow nodded to Tor and Gentry. The latter holstered his gun and slipped his dagger back into his waistband. Tor hesitated before clipping his axe into its case.

"We're clean," Harrow said through the door. He listened for any activity inside and was beginning to doubt the man would ever open the door.

The door rattled on its hinges, and the man revealed himself. Two guns were aimed in different directions. The three men raised their hands, showing they were unarmed.

"*Intenten algo y limpiare el suelo con sus cenizas.*" The vampire's gaze flickered at Gentry and registered recognition. "Gentry, is that you?"

Tor looked at Harrow with a question in his eyes.

"Zo, what the hell happened to you?" Gentry moved forward as soon as the guns were lowered.

"Just like you, my man. I left." The man Gentry identified as Zo smiled. He regarded Harrow and Tor for a second before giving his full attention to his long lost friend.

"I thought you were rotting in a ditch somewhere." Gentry laughed.

"La mala hierba nunca muere."

Harrow tried to come up with the translation, but his limited knowledge only produced two words—bad and dead. Not the best introduction to a new acquaintance.

"I have no problem with this happy reunion and shit, but can we speak English, please?" Tor said.

Leave it to Tor to ruin the mood. Zo hissed and turned to him, looking like he was ready to rock 'n' roll.

"Alonzo, they're Rohnert's friends." Gentry rushed between them and grabbed Alonzo while Harrow subdued his friend.

"Where the hell is your sense of humor? Flushed it down the toilet?" Tor chuckled, raising his hands and backing away.

Alonzo seemed to consider Tor's jibe before he nodded. "Yeah, I guess I did. Boss decided to bail on me." He fished inside his pocket and handed a piece of paper to Gentry.

"He left me that note and didn't say where he was going or for how long."

"And that's what brings me here," Gentry started. "He wanted me to convince you to come with me."

"Wait. You spoke with him?"

Alonzo led them into a decrepit room. The inside of the house had fared much worse than the exterior. There was no furniture, and the place was as barren as a godforsaken desert.

"Yes . . . but I didn't expect him to go anywhere. You know how Rohnert is. He enjoys his own company."

"And he talks to himself all the time." Alonzo shook his head. "Sometimes, I hear him talking about some female named Shelly."

Harrow and Tor glanced at each other.

"Do you know who she is?" Alonzo caught their very brief exchange.

"Yeah, but I'm not at liberty to talk about her. It's not my business." Harrow sighed. So his suspicions had been right. There was something going on between those two. He'd known something was off, but he had curbed his curiosity and respected Rohnert and Shelly's need for privacy.

"Well, whatever it is, Boss got it bad."

"I think you may be right," Harrow conceded.

"Gentry, how about running your offer by me again?" Alonzo smiled.

Shelly's eyes threatened to spill over as she gunned down the hallway to her room. The last thing she needed was an audience. It might take her days to regain her usual composure.

To say the news had come as a shock would be an understatement. This was a nightmare she had no hope of waking from. Shelly almost collided with Rayce, who was walking out of the I-room. She would've face-planted on the ground if the young man hadn't grabbed her by the shoulder, preventing her from falling.

"Dr. Anderson, is everything all right?"

She bit back the tears that threatened to spill. *I'm not going to show weakness. I won't embarrass myself. I can do this.* She recited the words inside her head.

Although she was certain that Rayce had an inkling of what troubled her, she nodded and continued on her way, not stopping until she reached her suite.

Once the door was shut tight, the floodgates opened. She raced to the bed and buried her face on the pillow to muffle the sound.

Anger, dread, and doubt raged inside her. The emotions were so raw. She had always been a proud woman, and nothing had ever shaken her rock-solid determination to let her head guide her decisions. Yet she had fallen in love with a vampire. She'd pursued the man, even though he wanted nothing to do with her, and now she was carrying his child. Through the fog of terror that gripped her, one thing was clear. She was going to keep it. Yeah, *It* was a good description for the baby of a human and a vampire. This *It* was her child—a living little person growing inside her. No matter what its father had done, this *It* would grow up with one of its parents. She would love *It* with everything she had in her.

But that didn't change anything. She was still fucked.

A knock came at the door. Shelly ignored the rapping and lulled herself into a stupor. She'd be okay. *It* would be okay. Repeating the words in her head, she floated into a restless sleep.

Shelly didn't dream. Her full schedule afforded her little sleep, and whatever napping time she could rake together was spent in a full-on snooze. However, she did remember dreaming when she was a child. It was far too scary for her, because in her dreams, she met creatures, scary beings hell-bent on taking her to places unknown to man.

This dream was different. She was floating on water, surrounded by a vast and picturesque landscape of blue—beautiful and mesmerizing. The water was still, with pretty eddies appearing with her every movement.

Out of nowhere came a gust of wind that swept the landscape into a frenzy of whirling water. Shelly nosedived into the water to avoid being tossed around and stayed underwater for as long as her lungs would allow before returning to the surface to catch her breath. A tug on her ankle prevented her from getting the much-needed oxygen, and water surged into her mouth when she broke out into a scream. She fought to free herself from the grip, but the tug pulled her further underwater. Small hands kept her from floating up while she struggled. Her lungs were going to explode, but she was losing ground. Before the blackness took her, a face of a young child flitted in front of her. Before she could grasp the message in its ebony eyes, oblivion seized her.

"Shelly? Open the door!"

Shelly woke up screaming to the sound of loud pounding at her door. Keen and determined, Jordan's relentless knocking persisted, and Shelly knew she wouldn't be able to hold her off for long. Shaking off the remnants of her wild dream, she swiped the tears from her face and tried to bring herself back to the present. She straightened up, determined to make things better for her and *It*.

"If you don't open this goddamn door, I will break it down." Jordan pounded on the door again.

Shelly hurried to get up, giving herself a big dizzy spell. She braced her hand against the wall and stayed still. Once her vision stopped swirling, she took a deep breath before shuffling to the door.

The mind had a canny way of wrapping itself around an improbability. Since she'd accepted that she was pregnant, her mind had adjusted to the idea that she needed to take care of herself.

"I'm going to count to three. One . . . two—"

Shelly yanked the door wide open. "What the hell do you want? Don't you know that pregnant women need their rest?"

Jordan paused mid-knock, her brow lifted. "Is everything okay? You scared me when you ran out of the lab so fast."

"I had to pee." She wanted to be left alone to try to get past the overwhelming reality that she was carrying an *It*.

If Jordan suspected the lie, she didn't say anything. Instead, she advanced into the room and sat on the sofa without invitation, making herself comfortable. Shelly took a deep breath and sat next to her.

"Okay, I won't beat around the bush. I want to know how you feel," Jordan said, tucking one of her legs underneath the other.

"Fine, but first tell me why you came here before I went to see Jones? Did you suspect something?"

Jordan hesitated.

"Give me the truth." Shelly crossed her arms over chest and waited.

"I guess it's a vampire thing. I didn't know for sure, but I sensed that you're carrying something inside you. Can't explain it."

"Is there any particular thing that gave it away?" Shelly asked, baffled.

"I can smell it."

"I smell?" she asked, amused despite herself.

"In a good way. You smell sweet, like nectar. Something I want to sink my fangs into but wouldn't. For some reason, pregnancy is revered by our kind. I don't know. It seems ingrained in us. Harrow and I talked about it. We're both mystified. Jones is looking into it, though."

"Do tell. I want to hear this."

"Well, he read Leroy's research about vampires in general. Mind you, some of his findings came from Rohnert himself."

This made Shelly pause. Jordan gave her a sweeping glance before continuing.

"Since the species is dying and reproduction has declined, half-breeds are treated like precious cargo. Also, they're not as affected by the sun as their purebred counterparts."

"Is that why the vampire they brought here for questioning survived the sun? He was a half-breed?"

Jordan nodded. "Now, with these halfsies, you have to be careful with their upbringing. If an idea is cemented in their heads at an early stage, they'll grow up believing that concept, whatever it is."

"What the hell does that mean?" Shelly touched her flat stomach, rubbing her belly like a crystal ball. She wanted her baby to be healthy and as close to normal as possible.

"The way the child is raised will determine how he or she will behave in adulthood. If they are taught that drinking blood is wrong, they are able to survive without it. There are many half-breeds living among us, ones who choose to live as humans. They ignore and resist the basic call of their vampire DNA. It can be done, but that requires the parents to make certain sacrifices."

Shelly had already made up her mind. "This one will be brought up as a human. I will give *It* everything I have—even the love *Its* father refused to give me." She let out a laugh filled with bitterness, and tears began to trickle down her face. Her raging hormones were putting in another appearance.

Jordan reached out and patted her hand. "You're not alone. We're all here for you."

"Thanks," she said past the choking knot in her throat.

"You're welcome."

Good thing Jordan wasn't a hugging type, because Shelly wasn't in the mood for touchy-feely at the moment. The prospect sounded scary, but she couldn't deny the tremendous emotion that came with being a mother. She never thought she'd be one. Actually, she never dreamed of having a child, knowing full well that she'd committed her every waking moment to her profession.

Well, check her out. She'd had a change of heart.

Bretania gazed across the table at Goran during their one-on-one meeting. She had many things in mind—this he could tell right away. "Goran, what are you intending to do with the children?" This conference didn't include the rest of the Council elders. It was between him and Bretania in her role as their weapons and combat specialist.

Goran stroked his chin. He'd been distracted the last few days after his unfortunate encounter with the infected vampire. He shoved the vile memories aside and concentrated on Bretania.

The female was charismatic and a valuable asset to the Council. She continued to serve him well, which had prompted him to entrust his six bastards to her care.

He had no use for the toddler yet, but he could work with the other five. The children were growing up fast and were well-adjusted to life as vampires. Their lust for blood was a constant source of joy for him. Too bad all their mothers had bitten the dust.

"I've no plans for them yet. But if I do, you'll be the first to know." He flashed her one of those smiles that guaranteed a sweet return.

Bretania inched closer. "Are you thinking what I'm thinking?"

"Perhaps." He watched her gaze slide down to where his shaft had gone considerably hard.

"I will take that as a yes." In an instant, Bretania was straddling him, knocking him down on the bed. Did he say she was a pussycat, too? And a darn strong one to boot.

Goran chuckled in response.

"And I thought you weren't into brunettes?" Her voice lowered into a wicked purr.

"Women aren't the only ones who are allowed to change their minds," he drawled before taking her mouth with his. This game was what he missed now that his harem no longer existed. Bretania's appetite seemed that of a lioness who hadn't fed for weeks.

Goran's pants grew tight. He'd love to take advantage of her offer, but if that bitch in the forest had indeed been infected, there would be a chance that she'd passed on an unwelcome gift to him.

His shaft turned to jelly at the thought, softening like a marshmallow, and his companion noticed the change.

"Is there something wrong with me?" Bretania's eyes were filled with uncertainty.

Goran shook his head.

There might be something wrong with me.

"I'm tired. Please leave."

Without another word, Bretania picked up the hem of her dull yellow gown and departed, but her face was filled with concern and regret.

Cyrus' eyes blazed like fireballs, and his hatred for Zane spiked like a furious geyser. The cocksucker had the balls to smile at him. God, if he was given a chance to kill the bastard with his bare hands, vampire or not, he'd take him on in a heartbeat.

"Be careful, Cyrus. Anger is a malady of the soul."

"Bastard! Let me out of these chains, and I'll give you a good fight." He hissed under his breath. His leg was killing him. The pain had become more unbearable with each passing day, and every movement was excruciating. If he were lucky enough to get out of this hellhole, he'd walk with a fucking limp for the rest of his life.

"I'm just showing you the same gracious reception you guys gave me back when I was your guest." Zane laughed and inched forward.

"You deserved it. You and the legions of fuckers you brought to our facility."

Zane's smirk disappeared, and he blurred away from Cyrus, making it impossible to track his movements. All Cyrus could see was a figure moving around, followed by a piercing howl, and then the lights came on. Adjusting his eyes to the rude glare from the ceiling, Cyrus saw the gadget Zane was holding for the first time. The obscure piece of shiny metal looked harmless, but Cyrus wouldn't bet on it.

He recoiled, sending the chains rattling with a loud clang against the wooden floor. Zane's scarlet eyes flashed with fury.

"What do you know about Demetrius?" Zane whispered in a low, restrained voice.

The name sounded familiar, but it took Cyrus a few seconds to jog his memory. Demetrius was the vampire who had led the attack on their underground hideout. He had also been instrumental in the deaths of three of their loved ones.

"I'm sure his father doesn't miss the bastard."

"But his son does." Zane didn't wait for him to answer. "So I'm going to ask you one more time—where is my father?"

Cyrus thought about how to answer. Tell the truth or lie? The dude was nothing but a bad memory after all.

"He's dead," he said in a flat tone, sounding neither apologetic nor jubilant.

The last thing he'd expected was Zane's reaction to this news. Cyrus had seen some pretty weird things throughout his life as a bounty hunter. None of it had made the hair at the back of his neck stand up the way it was doing at that every moment.

Zane slumped down on the floor like a withered leaf, dropping the instrument as he went. His tangible grief tore at the thick walls that surrounded Cyrus's hardened heart. This was not good. He sized up the vampire before him. An angry vampire could be very lethal, half-breed or not. Jerking the chains, Cyrus tested their strength once more. Solid. He was going nowhere.

After Zane had contained his anguish, he picked up the apparatus and pushed his body from the floor. There was a resolute expression on his tear-stained face. Cyrus's heart began pounding hard against his chest—something that never happened to him. This had to be the end.

God, just make it fast. I want a clean and quick exit.

Zane oozed hatred. His face contorted into a sneer and his lips curled back, exposing teeth meant to inflict pain. The incident in the I-room during which Zane had torn Rohnert's flesh sprang to mind. The Halfling was more fearsome than the other vampires he'd encountered in the past. Even so, Cyrus stood his ground. He wasn't about to project fear.

"Now, tell me where I can find whoever killed my father." Zane's voice dipped lower.

Cyrus shook his head with vehemence.

Zane stalked forward, letting the gadget dangle from his fingers. "You will take me to your hideout."

"No. You can kill me, but I won't say anything."

"We'll see how well you do against this."

Taking him by surprise, Zane swiped Cyrus's leg out from underneath him so fast he fell, kept upright only by his chains. Before he could react, Zane's fist rammed into his skull.

As much as Rohnert hated to leave, even vampires could crack, and he was nearing his saturation point.

It had been easy to avoid detection at the airport, slipping in and out of entry ways and security checks. Finally, he'd made it inside the baggage area of a plane headed for his intended destination. It hadn't taken him long to select an idyllic location, a perfect place where he could regroup. Upon arrival in the Philippines, Rohnert avoided the busy streets, opting to trek along lengthy stretches of rice fields. He retraced the once-familiar lands where he'd spent the years after he'd left the Council. Snores came from the cluster of shanties indigenous to the region.

At the end of the longest field, he reached a big gate made of sturdy bamboo. Although it was imposing on the outside, he was certain that the interior had remained the same. He didn't bother knocking. Instead, he scaled the barricade without giving it a second thought.

He landed on the other side and moved with the ease of familiarity, proceeding to the front of the temple where his old friend would be waiting for him. The heavy carved Nara door creaked when he let himself in the darkened room.

"I didn't expect to see you back here so soon," a rich baritone voice said.

Rohnert smiled. "I didn't expect to get myself into trouble so soon."

"Well, you've come to the right place."

Rohnert hadn't even gotten a chance to set his Kalimetal down when a kick landed on his chin. He staggered back, not having expected a direct hit from the old man.

"Some things just don't change." He rubbed his jaw.

"I hate change. I'm too old for it." Isagani came into a patch of light streaming in from outside the temple. He flashed his fangs and then enveloped Rohnert in a warm and welcoming embrace.

After the rather awkward hug, Rohnert stepped back and regarded his old friend. Isagani had become his master and had imparted the knowledge of Kali-Eskrima to him during the darkest moments of his existence. He'd come full circle, running back to the place he had always regarded as his home away from home.

"She's what?" Harrow's eyes rose, looking from the rim of his sunglasses.

"You heard me." Jordan flopped on the edge of the bed and glared at him. "Shelly's pregnant." She made a big round arch with her hand on her belly for emphasis.

Harrow sat next to her and removed his glasses. "But who's the father?" He had an inkling but needed confirmation.

"She didn't say, and I didn't ask."

He hated it when Jordan tried to keep him in the dark. "C'mon, I'm sure you have a guess." He snaked his arm around her waist and drew her close, sniffing her hair. He loved her scent. The woman didn't go for perfumes. Nothing fancy, just straight up wash and wear.

Jordan laughed and tried to inch away, but his arm tightened around her.

"Do you have a guess?" she asked him.

Harrow pretended to think and rubbed his chin with his free hand. "Um, not really. You know I have better things to do than speculate on other people's affairs." That was an outright lie, of course. Though Rohnert never discussed his personal affairs with anyone, Harrow had caught him glancing at Shelly more than once when the doctor wasn't looking, and vice versa.

"You men are worse gossips than women." Jordan rolled her eyes. Although she was acting huffy, she snuggled closer, wrapping both arms around his waist.

"Maybe we are, but why don't you just tell me anyway?" He nuzzled her hair.

Jordan inclined her head to give him better access, so Harrow ran his mouth across the expanse of her neck, pausing at the pulsing jugular. He wished to the higher powers that he could feed from her.

"Take me." Her voice was a mere whisper.

Dear Lord, what the hell was he supposed to do? He'd take her in a heartbeat if Jones could be positive it was safe for them.

Harrow raised his head away from the damning temptation. "It's not safe." His words were strangled, defeated. He tried to move away, but her hand locked on his.

"But you can still make love to me. It's been working for us." She flashed a smile that could melt even the steeliest of hearts.

His lips lifted into a wicked smile, revealing his fangs. There was no reason to deprive himself, and he wasn't about to make her wait.

He pushed her down on the mattress, going to his knees to begin undressing her. Peeling away each layer of clothing from her body felt like Christmas morning all over again.

Harrow unclasped her bra and skimmed his fingers along her mounds, starting at the base and moving up to the tips of her nipples. They perked up, as eager as he was. He grinned and dove down to taste one, licking the tip and swirling his tongue around it until she moaned and gave an involuntary shiver. Her back arched while he circled his tongue around her breasts. Jordan grabbed his hair and pulled his face up to hers. She was as beautiful as the first time he'd laid eyes on her. When she seized his mouth, her hunger manifested in the wild strokes of her tongue.

Yeah. The lioness is in the house.

Once they surfaced for air, he had to ask. "Where's Gail?"

Part of fatherhood was knowing whether they were free for the rest of the night.

"She's asleep."

They both jumped out of bed, each intent on making use of this precious opportunity. Jordan squirmed out of her jeans, and Harrow shrugged off his clothes as fast as possible. Not bothering to turn off the lights, they shoved the heavy bedcover down to the floor and dove onto the mattress, Jordan on top and him on bottom.

She wanted control, and Harrow didn't mind giving her free rein. The end result was all that mattered—both of them breathless and satisfied. He grinned when Jordan lifted her body, positioning her center against his shaft.

"I don't think I can wait a minute longer," she murmured before she lowered her body onto his.

He held her while they moved in a rhythmic pattern, slow and deliberate. Jordan changed from the slow seductress to a high-speed nymph once he was inside her. Harrow stifled a scream when her walls began to create a delicious friction against his engorged penis.

The little noises she created drove him wild. He pumped into her body with wild thrusts until he couldn't breathe. They slid against each other, their sweat mingling at every point of contact.

Jordan dug her nails into his flesh when she exploded with an enviable orgasm. Her cry of satisfaction filled the room.

Harrow gave her a few seconds to recover before he twisted their bodies on the mattress. Her glorious red hair sprawled along the pillow, some strands sticking to her sweaty face. He took her with the ferocity of a wild animal until he shattered in ecstasy.

Jordan gasped when he pulled out of her. "Jesus Gates, you're amazing."

"I aim to please." He smiled and collapsed next to her.

They stared at the tiny crystal chandelier on the ceiling, holding hands while they tried to catch their breath. Silence sounded weird after the show Jordan had put on.

"Who in the hell is the father?"

Jordan chortled. "And here I thought you'd forgotten."

"Pillow talk, woman. It's a must in every bedroom." He snorted.

Her voice turned somber. "I know it's Rohnert."

"I'll be damned." And the vampire was nowhere to be found.

It had been a hell of a month since Shelly had found out about her pregnancy. She'd adjusted to the demands of the life growing inside her, and she was thankful that the facility and its remaining inhabitants had been cooperative, demanding less of her time. There had been no gunshot victims, no emergency amputations, and Gail hadn't even turned up with a sore throat or an ear infection. By the looks of things, she'd be giving birth in the early summer—that was, if half-breeds behaved the same way as human fetuses did.

She tried hard not to think of *Its* father. Nothing would bring him back, and even if he were around, she still wouldn't acknowledge his presence or accept his help. For her, he was nothing but a sperm donor. No love lost there.

Of course, that was a lie. She knew it, but she wouldn't be caught admitting the truth. Their relationship had ended when he walked out on her that night, and his words still stung.

This is not what I want. You and I won't happen again.

Rohnert had spoken those words with conviction, and with the passage of time, she had learned to accept it. She was alone. She watched her own back, scratched her own itches, and she would never beg another man, human or otherwise, the way she'd done for him.

With the extra time on her hands, she was able to plunge into new avenues of research regarding her unborn child. Since Jones had some time in-between his own projects, they often spent time engaged in long conversations—and sometimes arguments—about her pregnancy, the expected symptoms, and the birth.

Today was like any other. She and Jones were poring over ledgers and journals Leroy had left behind. In his quest to understand the creatures of the dark, he'd stumbled upon some facts concerning these so-called "Dhampir," or half-breeds.

"Have you read this?" Jones asked, sliding over a thick folder filled with Leroy's scribbles.

Shelly shook her head and leafed through the papers. "Similar to vampires, no weaknesses?"

"That's what most of the available information is saying." Jones rubbed his temple. "Remember that one guy they brought here who bit 'you know who'?"

Kudos to Jones for not mentioning *his* name. Shelly gritted her teeth nonetheless. It was difficult to think of *It* without slipping into thoughts about *Its* seed contributor.

"Yeah," Shelly answered, distracted.

"He was strong, fast, and unaffected by the sun. Your baby is going to be the same, I can feel it." Jones rubbed his hands together, looking like a clown instead of a respectable scientist.

"*It* is going to be fine, and I'm going to raise *It* as a human. None of that blood-drinking crap."

"I don't understand why you call your child *It*." Jones shook his head and watched her with those knowing deep-set eyes.

Shelly met the challenge of his gaze. "*It* is neither human nor vampire. *It's* a combination of two like and unlike beings. Therefore, *It's* an *It*." *For now.* "Why don't you stop asking me irrelevant questions and give me more facts?"

"Fine." Jones flipped a page in the large binder. "Here's one. Some children of mixed heritage are stillborn."

Jones stopped once he realized that Shelly had grown still. She'd always seen the long, winding road ahead of her and *It*, but she'd never considered that her child might not even live to see life outside her womb.

Her lips quivered with undisguised fear, something she hadn't experienced in a long, long time.

The scientist got to his feet and rushed to her. Laying a comforting hand on her shoulder, he sat next to her. "I'm so sorry. I didn't mean to frighten you. Those are a few reported cases. Most of the known half-breeds are thriving."

That might be true, but Jones's addendum couldn't erase the uncertainty that was now weighing on her mind.

The door swung open, halting their conversation. Harrow walked in with his usual swagger and a look Shelly knew so well. He was a man contented with his life, with his mate, and everything in general. She felt a sudden pang of envy. Could she ever put her life back together the way it had been pre-Rohnert?

"I'm going to visit with General Krever. I'm taking the girls with me. Leo wants Gail to play with his grandkids, so Jordan will stay with her for the weekend. I'll be back tomorrow night."

The scent of her fear didn't escape his notice, and he knelt on the floor next to her. "Shelly, what's wrong? Is it the baby?"

"No." She shook her head. Yes, I want someone to promise me that It will be okay.

Harrow gathered Shelly in his arms and tried to comfort her. "I'm here for you. Everyone in this facility will help you get through this. I promised you that there won't ever be a time when you'll be alone."

Jones agreed in a hushed voice, but Shelly knew that even though the offer was good, she would still be facing mountains of questions and rocky paths alone. The long uphill climb had started, and all she could do was say what she always did in dire situations.

"Bring it." She gave a shaky laugh.

In true Shelly fashion, she pushed Harrow away and squared her shoulders, meeting his surprised gaze with remarkable calm. "Gates, go on and get that family of yours out of here. And kiss Gail for me." She stormed out of the lab with her head held high, leaving Harrow and Jones watching her with surprised expressions in their faces.

It was a perk of being pregnant—the liberty to have mood swings and not have to explain any of it. Shelly huffed while she made her way back to the sanctuary of her office, where she could immerse herself in baby-related books.

Shelley awoke with a start, her body drenched in sweat. The juncture between her legs was wet, too. When was the last time that had happened? Had she ever had wet dreams before?

"Damn you!" Seething in the darkness, she slid her body out of the tangled blanket. She scooted closer to the nightstand and flicked on the lamp, hating the rude glare that bathed the room.

This has to stop.

She leaned against the headboard. She'd be fine. She had been on her own for a while now, and being pregnant and alone wasn't any different from being *not* pregnant and alone. Her feet slipped down to the cold hardwood floor, and she stood up, hating the tightness in between her legs.

Shelly walked to the bathroom and straight into the shower. If cold water didn't work, she had no idea what would. She had been trying to focus on her research instead of thinking of *Its* father. Just when she'd thought she had forgotten him, he crept into her dreams and sent a fire raging through her body.

The icy water cascaded down her body, giving her the shivers and washing away her ill-timed arousal.

She had better things to focus on. The chilly blast continued to pound against her numbing skull. Good. That was what she needed.

After rinsing off, she dried herself and donned a shirt and pair of yoga pants—the only clothes she had that weren't yet tight around the waistline. She gave the elastic a tug to try to loosen it a bit more. She reined her damp hair into a ponytail and rushed out of her room.

The facility was quiet. Their vampire friends would still be out on patrol, and the ones on rotation would be likely to converge in the training room. She walked the deserted hallway until she reached the exercise room. Quiet—the place was damn silent, which suited her just fine.

She got on the treadmill and began a slow walk. Once her heart rate started to speed up, she increased the speed to a run. With the noise of her pounding footfalls overpowering the silence, she let her mind wander.

The baby was growing on schedule. Although she couldn't be happier with *Its* development, she still had a nagging, empty feeling.

"Anderson! Stop thinking," she scolded herself.

Then the sound of laughter echoed in the stillness of the room.

"Yeah, Anderson! Stop with the mind fuck." Harrow stood in the doorway.

"Eavesdropping now, Gates?" She threw him a disgusted look, but kept up her pace on the machine.

Harrow cleared the threshold and sat on the nearest chair. He lifted his sunglasses to watch her. "What are you doing running like you're on a mission? Aren't pregnant women supposed to take it easy?"

Shelly rolled her eyes. "Easy and I don't get along. And besides, pregnant women aren't that fragile."

Harrow snorted and regarded her for a few moments before he spoke again. "It's clear to me that you operate with a different mindset, but as your employer, I have to remind you that I don't want you overworked. I can opt to bring in other medical personnel, you know."

That sounded like a threat. Shelly slammed on the button to stop the treadmill and stepped off, glaring at him. "Gates, let's make things clear. Mind your own business and we'll get along just fine.

Harrow rubbed his chin and chuckled. "Someone woke up on the wrong side of the bed."

She huffed, hating the damn vampire for being able to read her like an open book. "I always wake up on the wrong side of the bed."

His laughter ebbed in an instant. "It's tough, huh?"

Shelly wasn't about to crumple under his compassionate words. It was much easier to keep up the façade and maintain her distance. She wanted to avoid any emotional breakdown, not that she was going to subject herself to such humiliation. "Nah, it's all under control, morning sickness and all."

As if on cue, nausea hit her at full blast. She shut her eyes and braced her hand against the treadmill handle, steadying herself.

Harrow jumped off the chair and ran to her side, where he hovered without touching her. "Are you okay?"

She raised her hand to stop him, and Harrow stepped back, looking at her with his kind eyes.

"I'm fine. Get out of here and check in with Jordan."

"If you need anything, a day off or whatever, just let Cheryl know. I'm all for a healthy baby." He winked at her and turned toward the door.

The last thing she needed was a bunch of people worrying about her. "Every day here is a day off." That much was true. After the number of available fighters had been cut in half during the last conflict, their facility had been like a ghost town.

"Jordan and Gail are leaving for the week, spend time with them," she said before the door closed behind Harrow and another wave of nausea hit her. She hated the goddamn feeling of being helpless. Clutching her mouth, she waited for the dry heaving to stop.

Six more months. She could do this.

Goran felt like he was walking on pins and needles, and the upcoming meeting added to the anxiety building up inside him. He paced the length of the Assembly room, having arrived early to clear his mind. He needed to talk to what was left of the Council elders—the ones he thought would stick with him for the long haul.

The soles of his shoes left indelible marks on the plush carpet that bore their race's crest. The mighty oak bush reminded him of their most cherished motto—*we shall prevail*. He swore that he would, no matter the cost.

Fear took hold of him without warning. Was it possible that his momentary lapse in judgment with that blasted woman in the woods would bring an eternity of pain and distress? He damned himself for not taking precautions before he'd used her.

Outside the Council doors, the muffled sound of approaching footsteps made him conceal his worried expression. In haste, he smoothed his black velvet robe and squared his shoulders. This was an important day.

Today, he'd be gauging the mindset of the remaining Council elders before proceeding with his plan. Though the disappearance of several members had been rumored, Goran had been quick to brand them cowards and issue an official decree to terminate on sight. The deaths of their record keeper Marania and the wise, rational Alphonsus had sent tongues wagging, but Goran had played his part to perfection, providing a sympathetic ear to the mourners and vowing to bring the killer to justice.

When the door opened and the members trickled in, their behavior lacked the usual bravado commensurate with their position and power. Goran watched each one with intent eyes while they took their respective seats.

Goran knew he could trust a few of the remaining Council Elders. Bretania was on his side, as well as Wendell and Serena. August was old, but he was good at his job, so there was no need to rock the boat. Who knew how long the old one would last? Randolph was not in attendance, and Constance was dead.

Each of the Council members appeared tense, and Goran took advantage of their vulnerable state. Soaking in their general emotions with one greedy sweep, he seized their innermost ramblings right away. Their thoughts revolved around fear for their safety and that of their families, as well as the questionable disappearances of the Council members.

Goran swept his gaze across the room. Before he could speak, the heavy doors opened and Randolph came rushing in.

"I apologize for my tardiness, but there were matters that couldn't wait," Randolph said, making his way to his assigned seat. Whispers spun around the room while the other members awaited Goran's reply.

"No need to apologize, my friend." Goran's voice was smooth, yet laced with venom. He knew that Randolph was a snake lurking in the background, waiting for the right time to strike.

Randolph dipped his head with false graciousness, hiding his thoughts. He was too smart for his own good, but even the toughest bastard would let his guard down. One little moment was all it would take for Goran to gather and build up evidence against the vampire.

When the murmurs had settled down, Goran stood up and walked the length of the expensive carpet, gathering his thoughts.

"I've heard from my most trusted men that Constance is dead." Gasps spread like wildfire, to be followed by stunned silence. It was time to play the part of the distressed leader. "I am saddened by the loss of several of our great elders, and I vow in the name of my father, and those who came before him, that I will not stop until justice is brought upon the wrongdoers."

Sympathetic agreement came from all present except Randolph, who directed narrowed eyes at Goran. Still the vampire refused to lower his guard.

August cleared his throat, looking distraught. "You must do everything within your power to avenge the death of our good friends." Though his tone was meek, his urging was firm and resolute.

"I'm concerned about our safety and that of our kin." Wendell's eyebrows creased in a worried frown.

Goran dipped his head in Augusts' direction. "My old friend, your wish is my command," he answered with all sincerity. "Wendell, I will assign a guard to you and your family. Leave your fears behind. I won't allow any mishap to befall you or your loved ones."

He gave each of them a thorough looking over, giving them a false sense of security. Everyone seemed to buy his promise but Randolph, who continued to regard him with careful scrutiny. Goran shrugged and continued with his agenda.

"With the loss of our dearest Marania, I will stand as the official record keeper for the time being. Is there anyone opposed to this idea?"

The room fell into an uncomfortable hush. Goran flashed a smile and continued digging through their unguarded minds for any helpful revelations.

Randolph bristled but said nothing. The vampire was beginning to irk him. To Goran's surprise, he rose and bowed his head low. "I am certain that you will protect our Council's private documents to the best of your ability," Randolph said and planted his hand over his heart.

The others followed suit, which pleased Goran. Now that he had the suckers in the palm of his hand, he could begin to explore his clandestine strategy to keep his reign free from challengers.

Discussions about other matters followed. Goran began plotting while August ran the show, although he was delighted by each report concerning their profitable investments. Once he got out of there, he had a very important phone call to make, and he expected the bastard to be ready to execute his orders.

It had been a week since Rohnert arrived in the Philippines. Isagani had made several passing comments about his state of mind during their sparring practices, accusing him of being distracted. Rohnert was in no position to argue, knowing his friend had hit the bull's-eye with his observation.

A mean round house landed on his chin, making him stagger backward. This was one of those days.

"See what I'm saying? You're in one of your moods again." Isagani chuckled. He flicked his fingers, beckoning Rohnert.

Rohnert shook his head while rubbing his chin. If this continued, his pride would be a thing of the past, like everything he had left behind in New York.

He raised his hand for a little time and then brought his palms together, drawing on his inner Zen just like his mentor had taught him.

Breathing deep, he closed his eyes and summoned calm. He focused and rid his mind of clutter—no matter how much each thought affected him, he pushed it back.

"I'm ready," he said, snapping his eyes open.

Isagani's sparkling brown eyes smiled in understanding. No matter how old the vampire was, he hadn't lost his touch. Rickety as he claimed his knees were, his kicks still packed a mean punch. His once-ebony hair was dusted with flecks of gray and was held back with a piece of thin leather. Short in stature, barely reaching Rohnert's shoulder, he was considered one of the most prominent vampires on this side of the globe. He was the most sought after as well. Many asked him to impart his knowledge and craft, but he had been picky about with whom he shared his martial-arts wisdom, thus creating a long list of enemies in the process.

However, Isagani also had legions of loyal followers lurking in the shadows, ready to sacrifice their lives in exchange for his. Why the old vampire had decided to take Rohnert under his wing was still a mystery to him, but he didn't question his luck.

Isagani brandished his Arnis and waved it in a slow moving pattern. Mesmerized by the motion, Rohnert drew his weapon and aimed at his teacher. They circled around the bamboo floor, and each step of their bare feet created a crunching sound that filled the temple. The candles flickered then stilled as if holding their breath in anticipation. Rohnert calculated his every movement, careful not to break eye contact. The old guy had impressed on him during his training that he needed to pay close attention to his opponent's eyes.

"Everything you know is from me." Isagani was employing a tactic to make Rohnert doubt his own abilities.

Rohnert snorted. "As great as the teacher might be, the student is younger, more lithe, and ready to kick some big-talking vampire butt," he said, drawing the first strike.

The clashing of sticks followed. With fierce concentration, Rohnert moved, striking with left to right sweeps. The old vampire blocked each hit with precision.

"Big words from a very lonely man." Isagani appeared unimpressed.

"Put your money where your mouth is," Rohnert said, landing a surprise hit across Isagani's shoulder, leaving the old vampire stunned.

Isagani smirked. "Do you know why Magellan lost the battle and eventually died?"

"I'm sure you will tell me." His teacher would share the wisdom with him whether he asked or not. Not bothering to stop, he advanced, weaving both sticks at a fast, unrelenting pace and parrying every blow from his opponent.

"Because he was too distracted and thought with his head in his ass." Isagani made an unexpected spin and smacked the stick against his back, but Rohnert pivoted in time to block the next hit and dish out one of his own. Isagani snickered as he tumbled away. "Magellan thought the locals were an easy conquest, but he was mistaken. Glory isn't something you grab with both hands. You need to take time to understand first and approach with caution. He did not take into account the reefs surrounding the island, and his cannons and muskets were out of firing range. To make matters worse, their heavy armor became a liability."

Rohnert grunted while he followed his mentor with his eyes, readying himself for another clash. Isagani danced around him with agile footsteps.

"I'm not going to fall for your attempt to distract me."

"Oh, really? You're thinking of that woman, the pretty blonde doctor, and the friends you left behind. You're questioning your loyalty toward your race, and you're angered by the direction in which your life is headed." The old man crisscrossed his sticks with a swishing sound. "You distracted yourself from the most important thing."

"And that is?" Rohnert flashed forward before dropping down to slide, swiping at his master's legs. Isagani fell on his back, and Rohnert took advantage of the small window to whip the stick away from his grasp. He seized his mentor by his neck, close enough to see his veins straining under his skin.

"You haven't stopped to embrace the big picture. Go ahead and open the black book. Stop guessing your destiny."

Even flat on his back with Rohnert's Arnis pointed at his neck, his teacher managed to grab his wrist and nab the stick from him. Rohnert responded by striking with his free hand, which Isagani blocked before jumping to his feet.

They laughed and bowed to each other.

"And that is a draw," Isagani acknowledged and kicked the stick on the floor with his foot. The Arnis went flying in the air, and he caught it with one hand. With a flourish, he handed the weapon to Rohnert.

"One of these days, I'm going to beat you. I'm done with draws."

Rohnert patted his friend on the shoulder.

"One of these days, you will come back here without so much baggage," Isagani said in his usual know-it-all manner. They slapped their hands together in a firm handshake and settled on the floor in front of the altar, which was filled with fragrant flowers and candles. Isagani lowered his face to the floor, arms outstretched, and began to chant.

"How did you know I carried a black book?" Rohnert spread his legs and planted his palms on the wooden floor.

Raising his head, Isagani turned to him. He smiled, showing uneven teeth, and pointed at his temple. "I know everything." He winked. "You have carried that thing like a burden, when it shouldn't be."

"What do you suggest I—" Rohnert felt a tug in his belly, a pull so hard it radiated throughout his body, leaving him stunned and unable to breathe.

"Your tender act has produced an heir." Isagani glanced at him, not a trace of worry on his face.

Through his discomfort, Rohnert stared at his mentor with questioning eyes. "Heir?"

Isagani nodded in a slow, thoughtful manner. "You heard me. Now, the question is, what are you going to do about it?"

"Who?"

Stupid question. There was just one person it could be.

"Yes, and you know what's best."

"Is that a sign?"

"You're a first time father. Pure blood feels every creation, although most sense it later in the pregnancy," Isagani said in a matter-of-fact way.

With his mind tossed in a grinder and set on maximum speed, Rohnert jumped to his feet, grabbed his Kalimetal, and ran to the nearest exit.

"You're welcome!" His teacher called after him with a chuckle before the door closed.

Another die had been cast, and Rohnert needed to be an active participant in whatever destiny had in store for him. He must hurry before events passed him by.

⚜

Harrow was in the middle of a business conference call with General Krever, Allison, and Tor when Rayce's voice crackled over the intercom.

"General, I'm going to put you on hold for a moment," Harrow said and took Rayce's call. "Yes?"

"Boss, come over quick. I just finished decoding one of Dante's files."

The eagerness in Rayce's tone wasn't lost on him. "We'll be there." He depressed the button and returned to Leo's call. "Listen, I have to go. Let's get together in a week or so and finalize our plans."

Leo chuckled. "You sound like Pritchard. Give me a call, and we can set the plan in motion."

"Kiss the girls for me?" Harrow's chest tightened. Jordan and Gail had been away for a few days, and it felt like months.

"I sure will. And give my goddaughter a big hug. Keep that mate of hers busy, too. He looks like he is ready to crack," Leo said before hanging up.

Tor's laughter echoed in the I-room. "The general knows me so well."

Allison uncrossed her legs and leaned over. "That's because you look like a sullen child." She planted a tender kiss on Tor's lips.

"Kids, let's go." Harrow stood up and secured the sunglasses over his face.

Tor and Allison followed him. Whatever information Rayce had deciphered must be significant for him to interrupt an important business meeting. Harrow's mind began to work furiously. After Dante's sudden demise, Rayce had been hard at work decoding the intricate secured files he'd left behind. Most of the confidential information unraveled in the past had to do with the business, but this felt different.

Rayce wore a wide grin when they entered the control room. Harrow pushed his sunglasses up on his head. Focusing on a screen, he saw what looked like a chute. "What do you have for us, my man?"

"Okay, look at the screen. They're located inside the boiler room." Rayce punched at the keyboard, and the monitor showed three identical troughs.

"What are they?" Harrow bumped heads with Allison while they tried to scrutinize the image at the same time.

Tor snorted. "So we have a laundry chute. Yippee!"

"Sir, it's not a laundry chute." Rayce chortled. "It's sort of an escape drain."

"A what?" Allison asked.

"According to Dante's records, the chutes are emergency exits. Each one ends in a different place. He'd been working on the maps on the night of his death." Rayce tapped another set of keys to reveal the entry's date stamp. "It's obvious that he and Pritchard had been working on this in secret."

"Why?" Allison asked, sounding distressed.

"I don't know, Ms. Tack." Rayce scratched his head apologetically.

"You know how your father's mind worked. He was thinking ahead in case we needed to evacuate. He wanted a way out." Harrow turned his attention back to the monitor.

Tor prodded Allison. "Let's check it out."

"Hold it, tiger. We can't test it yet. It's the middle of the day, in case you didn't notice. If you like yourself as is, better wait until sundown just in case the chute spits you out in the middle of an open field."

Tor considered Harrow's words and let go of Allison. "We can still check the location of the chutes and maybe go for it later." He wasn't going to quit once an idea had been planted in his head.

"Fine. You can be our test dummy." Harrow grinned.

"Let's do it." Tor took Allison's hand and led her to the door.

"Jesus, you're relentless." Harrow was right on their heels.

In true Tor fashion, he began running as soon as they hit the hallway. Two floors down, they took the stairs to the basement, where the big boiler room was situated. Harrow turned the lights on, and the three of them separated to look for the chutes. Within a few seconds, Allison squealed.

"I found them."

Harrow and Tor shot to her spot and found the three identical chutes. The unremarkable doors had little numbers on their lids painted in white and were big enough to hold an average size human.

"Hmm . . . interesting." Harrow opened the chute, and darkness stared back at them. "Let's try it tonight."

"Sounds like a plan. I'll take one with Ally. Hopefully, it doesn't end up in a sewer or something," Tor said, chortling.

"Then you'd better wear something comfortable." Allison smiled.

"Okay, I'm taking the one on the right. Tor, you and Ally can take the middle one, and I'll have one of the guys take the left."

Zane dropped the phone into his pocket, cursing under his breath. He hated the idea of working for anyone, but his grandpapa in particular. The sucker had blindsided him with an offer he couldn't refuse. The part he hated was the damn underlying threat. He had to be smart. If his father's testimony had been true, Demetrius' sire packed a shitload of wrath and trouble. It would be in Zane's best interests to stay under the radar and do Goran's bidding.

Thinking about their long phone conversation, he had to admit that the offer of assistance had been heaven-sent. Zane had enough manpower to accomplish his plan, but the additional force would guarantee success. The goal was to bring the motherfuckers down once and for all. He'd wanted a lot of things in his life, but nothing as much as avenging Demetrius' death. He wanted it so bad he could taste it.

A knock on the door brought him out of his mind's rage. "Come in."

"We're ready," Hill said from the doorway.

"I'll be out in a minute. Is he breathing?"

His minion hesitated. "Barely."

"Get him ready and bring him here," Zane said.

Hill nodded and left. The bastard was showing weakness. Zane hated any sign of a flaw—in particular, any hint of sympathy. He heard another knock on the door.

He gritted his teeth, uncertain if he was doing the right thing. If he wanted this operation to succeed, then he had to carry this out. "Bring him in."

Dragging footsteps echoed from the hallway. Hill and David had carried Cyrus into the living room by the time he came out. A quick check told him the human was knocking on death's door.

"Put him on the sofa." Zane rolled up his sleeves.

The men propped up Cyrus on the sofa. Without support, he leaned sideways, his slow breathing labored and faint.

"Leave us." Zane waved them out.

Hill wavered. "Do you need help?"

"Leave!" Zane's voice thundered. The two disappeared so fast it was almost comical. God, he was tired. Revenge was a tough emotion to overcome, and it raged inside him like wildfire. He took a deep breath and walked over to the sofa. The stench of blood overcame him.

Without as much fanfare, he dropped to his knees next to Cyrus. His mouth was agape, and his lids were shut after the repeated beatings he'd received. Coarse facial hair had grown on his chin, and his engorged lips were slashed in several places.

Zane was beyond compassion. "An eye for an eye, right?"

Summoning his energy, he eyed the target and shoved all his inhibitions away. This would be his first, and it wasn't your normal garden-variety greet and suck. With one quick motion, he latched his teeth onto Cyrus's neck, tugging at his jugular. He drew enough blood to feed and to restart the bastard to a new life. Maybe there would be a thank-you note or a hug for him afterward.

When more blood gushed down his throat, he felt revived and ready to go. Stopping after taking what he needed as his father had taught him, Zane knew he needed to give the progression time to take place. At least the bastard would love him for it. Zane wiped his mouth clean of blood while his body surged with raw energy. Watching Cyrus for a moment, he searched for the telltale signs of the eventual change. Cyrus' breathing ceased. He picked up his gun on the table and tucked it in his waistband.

Flicking on his phone, he speed-dialed a number and spoke in clear, distinct voice. "We're ready to go." Then he slung the human over his shoulder as if he weighed nothing.

Harrow had barely opened his eyes when his phone chimed, alerting him with the caller's distinct ringtone.

"Hi, gorgeous." He smiled and breathed deep, imagining holding Jordan in his arms and inhaling her sweet scent.

"You sound happy." Jordan laughed on the other line.

"Because I'm talking to you."

"Well, I'm missing you. I thought I'd give you a call before you go on patrol." He could imagine the pout from those luscious lips.

"I'm glad you did. I miss you and our little girl. How is she?"

"She's knocked out. She and Lindsay played all day. I'm on doll overload here."

Harrow smiled at the mental picture. Jordan, by her own admission, had been a tomboy growing up. She hadn't played with dolls, and her parents had taken her to commune with nature every possible chance they got. Harrow hadn't seen Leo's grandchild, but going by the general's description, she was as much of a handful as Gail.

"So are you bored to death yet?"

Jordan sighed. "Only because you're not with us, but I'm happy for her. It makes a big difference when she's around kids her age. Just being around a bunch of vampires and old farts can do a number on a child, you know."

"I want what's best for Gail. Do you think we should get her a tutor here in the facility?"

"Harrow, we want her to go to a regular school in the outside world. We want her around other kids."

"You're talking about her going out during the daytime when we can't watch her. I don't think that's a good idea, love." Harrow knew an argument was coming and braced himself.

"As much as I want her with me twenty-four-seven, we have to think about what's fair for her. She's missing out on a normal life. I want what's best for Gail."

"What's best for her?" Should he even ask?

"Leo and I had a long conversation today, and he offered to have Gail stay with him. We can visit every night before we go on patrol, and we'd take her home on weekends. It would be is a small price to pay for her to have a chance at normalcy."

Harrow closed his eyes and let the idea sink in. "Is that what you think would be the right thing to do?"

"I do," Jordan's answer came faster than he'd expected.

"Then we'll give her the best life we can manage under the circumstances."

"Oh, Harrow! Thank you. When we get back, let's talk to her about it."

"Why don't I let you do the dirty work?" He laughed when Jordan clucked her tongue. "I'm going to be the good guy she comes crying to when she complains about you trying to send her away."

"You're not playing fair. Let's talk to her like normal parents would."

"Who said we're normal?"

"I'm not playing here."

"Fine. We'll talk to the princess together."

The facility alarm went off just as they were saying goodbye. "Jordan, I'm going to have to call you back later. I have to check on this first."

"Is everything all right?"

"I don't know. I gotta go."

He couldn't even wait for her response. This was the warning for a perimeter breach, something they would test from time to time. Rayce hadn't mentioned a test run today. Jumping out of bed, Harrow grabbed his Kalimetal, not even bothering to find a shirt or shoes. He ran into Tor and Allison in the hallway.

"What the fuck is going on?" Tor asked.

"I have no idea." Just like him, Tor was running without a shirt and shoes. Allison was in her robe and also barefoot. At the very least, they'd all had the sense to grab their weapons.

They made to the control room at a sprint, and Jones and Shelly made their way in amid the blaring sound of the alarm. Firman followed, looking like he'd just made it to bed.

Harrow did a mental headcount. "Where are the rest?"

"They're coming," Firman answered

"What's going on?" Shelly looked bedraggled.

"Where's Rayce?" Harrow said when they found the room empty.

Tor ran to the control board and tinkered with several keys. Soon after, the piercing sound ended. Harrow watched the monitors, wondering where Rayce was, when something caught his eye.

"Run a rewind on the camera." He moved closer to the monitor. A side exit door was open. "What the hell?"

"Here." Tor pressed a button, and the playback started.

On the video, two cops appeared by the front gate, carrying Cyrus between them. One spoke into the camera, but the sound was faint.

"Volume!" Harrow was getting impatient.

"We found him in an alley, and he gave this address. Why don't you come out or let us in?" the uniformed officer said.

"Let him speak," Rayce's voice answered.

"He passed out after he gave us the address," the other cop said. "Here, maybe this would help." The same officer lifted Cyrus's head for the camera.

The camera zoomed on his face, all bloodied and bruised.

There was no conversation that followed until they saw Rayce streak out one of the side exits. Everything happened so fast. The next thing they saw was one officer pointing a gun at Rayce and firing a shot.

"Fuck!" Tor screamed just as the sound of gunfire exploded.

Harrow had no chance to think. His first instinct was to keep the women safe. "Tor, take Allison and head for the chutes. Jones, follow them and take Shelly with you. Whatever happens, don't come back here until I find you."

Tor was about to protest, but more gunfire erupted. By the sound, they were in for a long fight.

"Go! Just fucking go!" Turning to Firman, he ordered. "Cover me!"

While Tor led the others out of the room through a side exit, Harrow grabbed the emergency gun that was located underneath the desk and started firing on the mother boards, the recorders, and the monitors, destroying every item that might give their secrets away. Reloading, he continued to fire until the whole room was covered in smoke. Gunfire continued to sound outside, and he knew that their numbers wouldn't hold out for long. He had to make a decision whether to perish with the others or pick a fight he could win.

"Firman!" Harrow said, not raising his voice above the noise. "Let's hide in here and see if we can set a trap. Don't do anything stupid—just follow my lead." The vampire nodded, though Harrow sensed that he was jonesing for a good fight.

He pointed to the ceiling. It would be a good hideout. "Quick!"

Harrow was replacing the last of the ceiling panels when the door swung open.

"Check all the rooms. Turn over everything, anything! Kill anyone you find breathing," a familiar voice ordered.

Receding footfalls sounded while Harrow racked his brain. Where had he heard that voice before? He scanned through his memories like the phone book, trying to come up with the name. Footsteps advanced into the room, then the sound of furniture being toppled followed.

Soon after, the gunfire ebbed, leaving nothing but an eerie silence. Harrow could sense some of their human friends had checked out. The scent of their blood wafted through the air around him. He gestured for Firman to stay quiet. Whoever was down below was in a bad mood with the amount of cursing he was doing. The man stopped raining expletives when the some of his people came back.

"Zane, this is a ghost town. No one is here, and the rest are all dead."

Harrow's mind registered and recognized the name. It was the vampire they'd caught, but who had gotten away. Aching for payback, he clamped his mouth shut and kept himself from blasting out of his hiding place to kill the bastard. He needed to pick his battles wisely, and this was not the time.

"Tell Goran's men to leave. We're good here."

"And you?" one man asked.

"I'm going to stay for a few minutes. I will meet you back at the house."

The room fell silent once more.

Zane's time was up. Harrow signaled to Firman to stay put. This bastard was his to kill. Once and for all, he would end Zane's existence.

Harrow took a deep breath, kicked the panel, and let his body fall downward.

"Your time is up, Zane."

"Jones, we're going back," Shelly said the moment they'd cleared the long-ass chute that had taken them two blocks north of the facility. The underground secret outlet had saved their lives. Whoever designed the emergency exit had spent a lot of time planning the door that led to the street. Judging by the comfortable ride, the architect had to have been Pritchard.

She glanced around to see if anyone was watching them when they made their way out the ordinary-looking door. No one was paying attention, so it was easy to blend into the foot traffic right away.

Jones' face was the picture of incredulity. "Didn't you hear what Harrow said?"

Shelly dusted her pants and felt her stomach. *It* was protesting but alive. "I heard what he said. You saw the video. Are you going to leave Cyrus and Rayce out there?"

"I was ordered to take care of you," Jones protested.

"Then you will drag your butt with me, and we'll help those two." She turned in the direction of the facility, ignoring the possibility of danger.

"And when we get there, where are we taking them?" He looked like he wanted to bolt. "They need medical attention."

"And that's exactly what I'm doing to do. I have a place that I still maintain here in the city. I have enough supplies for emergency procedures —"

"You're going to play doctor?"

Shelly raised her eyebrows. "I *am* a doctor. The more we argue about this, the less time we have to save their lives. If you want out, go ahead."

"I don't have a place to stay. I gave up everything when I started working for Pritchard."

Shelly saw the vulnerability in Jones' eyes and knew she'd baited her trap well. "As I said, I have a place. You're welcome to stay until we can regroup."

They walked in silence. The air was crisp, and the exercise was good for her. It had been a long time since she'd gone out of the facility, even though she was free to come and go.

When she'd agreed to work for Pritchard, she had given up her career at the hospital. She had wanted a different setting, a change of pace, but to still be able to do what she loved best.

They reached the deserted patch of the road that led to the facility within minutes.

She stopped. "Do you have any weapons?"

"I have the gun Harrow gave me." Jones reached inside his trouser pocket and produced the handgun.

"Do you know how to use it?" She had taken a few lessons herself, but she didn't believe in bearing arms.

"Cyrus gave me a few lessons."

"Will you use it if necessary?"

"No doubt."

"That's all I need to hear." She led him into the thick bushes to hide. "This is what I'm going to do—I will walk over to Cyrus and Rayce and pretend I stumbled upon them. If anyone approaches us, shoot."

"You want me to shoot without asking?" Jones sounded unsure.

"I want you to shoot." It went against her principles as a doctor, but she had people to help and a baby to nurture into this ugly world.

"Okay." He sounded more certain this time.

Shelly took a deep breath and stepped out of the vegetation. Using the moonlight to guide her, she found the men's bodies sprawled on the ground about five feet away from each other. She checked on Rayce first since blood was still oozing from his wound.

How long had it been since he was shot? If her guess was correct, over twenty minutes had passed. This could be bad. When she took his wrist, she could hardly find a pulse. She had to work fast. Running toward Cyrus, she sensed something different about him the moment she touched him. The distinctive thud-thud of his heart was something she'd seen before.

Shelly pulled out her rarely used cell phone and dialed. She looked around, waiting for someone or something to jump her, but nothing happened. The area was quiet.

When her call was answered, she said, "I need a taxi right away." She gave the directions in haste. Tossing her phone back into her pocket, she took off her white coat. "Jones, come here!"

He was at her side in an instant. "What's going on?"

"Give me your jacket. We can't have anyone seeing this blood all over Rayce."

He shed his jacket while Shelly's mind focused on what needed to be done once they reached her place.

"What are we looking at?"

Shelly shook her head. "Rayce may not make it."

"And Cyrus?"

She gritted her teeth, hating the answer. "He's not going to be happy when he wakes up."

"What do you mean?"

Shelly lowered her voice. "He's going over to the dark side."

A sixteen-hour flight could drive any person nuts, and Rohnert's patience had already been stretched to the limit when their flight was delayed for an additional six hours. It was impossible for him to get back any sooner. Even if he went on foot, moving nonstop, he'd still make better time on this flight to JFK.

Grinding his teeth hard, he lurked in the shadows while airline crews tinkered in the cockpit. He snuck into the baggage compartment when no one was looking and made himself comfortable.

Shelly had been in his mind all along, refusing to give him even a second's reprieve. Ever since Isagani had told him she was pregnant with his child, Rohnert had been struggling to understand how it could be real. The whole situation was impossible.

How had it happened? God, even his questions didn't make sense. She had assured him she was safe. He'd taken her at her word, and that moment of weakness had brought forth a child.

He'd heard stories about his kind having children, but he'd never paid close attention to the details. The one detail he did remember was that once a purebred male decided to father offspring, not even the sturdiest steel could stand between him and his young. An overwhelming urge to protect the mother and child swelled within him.

Isagani's words came back to him. You have carried that thing like a burden, when it shouldn't be.

Had the old vampire recognized Rohnert's destiny all along? His mentor had been around longer than anyone he knew, and whatever gibberish he spoke always came to pass. Rohnert was inclined to heed his advice, even when it didn't make sense to him.

Pulling the book from his waistband, he smoothed the wrinkled edges. It was time to uncover the secrets of the Council. If Marania had deemed him worthy, then he must be. Turning to the first page, he glanced at the neat script.

Rohnert:

This manuscript was given to me for safe keeping until the moment I was instructed to hand it to you. Time is our enemy—as well as the evil hearts that grow in our midst. You are the purest of us all, as was foretold by Gastarius. The fate of our race lies in your hands. Despite the iniquity that flourishes within our Council walls, the truth will soon be exposed. Only you hold the key to the survival of our race. The burden you bear is also your glory.

Your friend,
Marania

Confused, he stared at her words over and over before closing the book. How could Marania have been so certain that he even deserved to lead their people? She could be presumptuous at times, but he'd never thought she would be careless.

As far as he was concerned, he was just a vampire who'd had enough of their tyrannical ruler. His one wish was to live a quiet life.

Over the sound of the plane's engine, Rohnert heard the announcement that they had been cleared for take-off. He opened the black book again and searched for something that made sense. Thick and filled with the collective wisdom of their race, the information it contained was not any one person's opinion but unassailable truth.

Slowly, he went through the list of births and deaths before reaching the record of disappearances. Unable to believe the record at first glance, he turned to another page, hopeful to find an entry that would make sense.

On the first sign of the moon's illumination, a vampire will rise into power, his heart filled with avarice. Among his peers, he will raise havoc, and death will augment the despair within. Mortals and vampires alike shall have no power to prevent the destruction he will leave in his wake. A disinclined soul shall be called, and a child borne to the rightful guide shall come to fulfill this divination.

Bullshit. Goran was in power, and his children would follow after him. Though Rohnert doubted that his Halflings would ever make it to power, he was convinced of Goran's ability to produce an heir to continue his legacy.

Shaking his head, he closed the book once more and tucked it inside his waistband for safe keeping. The moment he figured who the new record keeper was, he'd surrender the book like it was hot potato. This sort of information was better in the hands of a person who knew how to interpret it.

Marania had been a good friend, but he figured that at some point, her judgment could have been compromised. Goran had a way of manipulating people to do his bidding, and there was no reason why she should have been any different.

Once the aircraft was airborne, Rohnert rested his head on top of a suitcase and let slumber take him. His nerves were frayed by the time they landed in New York City, and he ached to stretch his legs. Slipping out of his hiding place and leaving the airport undetected was an art he'd perfected long ago. He tore through the city streets at a high rate of speed, toward the underground facility.

It didn't take him long to arrive in the vicinity of the compound. He scanned his surroundings, utilizing his sense of smell. Right away, he could tell something was off. Drawing out his Kalimetal, he proceeded with caution. By the mouth of the entrance, the aroma of blood hit him. A few feet ahead, he saw a pool of red on the muddy ground. Crouching, he touched the blood and brought it up his nose. Hard to tell which human it had come from.

With his heart drumming, he ignored protocol, proceeding before he'd secured the area. Instead, he raced down the lip of the tunnel, banging on every entrance until he found an open side door.

Carnage greeted him. Dead humans, blood pooled around them, were surrounded by mounds of ashes littering the floor. A crippling fear ravaged him.

"Shelly!" he screamed, rushing through the hallways, kicking at every door in his way until he reached her suite. Her bedroom door was open, but no one was there. Rohnert looked at the unmade bed and flew out of the room to get to the clinic.

Horror gripped him when he found the lifeless bodies of two nurses.

"Damn it!" He was racing out of the room when he heard the sound of sobbing. Running back into the clinic, he called out. "Who's in here?"

The linen closet opened, and Cheryl spilled out of the little space.

"It's me." Her voice was almost inaudible.

"Cheryl." Rohnert rushed in time to catch her fall. "Where is Shelly?"

She shuddered with unspoken fear, and he braced her body against his.

"Where is Shelly?" he repeated.

"She . . . they all ran when the alarm sounded off, and we stayed behind —"

"Where did she go?" Rohnert roared, panic filling his veins. He never panicked.

"To the control room to see if it was an . . . unannounced drill." Cheryl continued to sob.

Not wanting to leave her to her own devices, he led Cheryl out of the room. He pulled her into a run, keeping his weapon poised for action. They burst into the control room but found it empty. "Where the hell is everyone?"

At the sound of approaching footsteps, he pushed Cheryl behind him and pivoted. With a snarl, he let his aggression rise like an angry flame.

"Don't attack. It's me."

"Firman! Where the hell is Shelly?" His body vibrated with fury.

Isidora looked up from her book at the sound of squealing brakes and the subsequent opening and closing of car doors. "What's going on out there?"

Maureen rose from her lounger and ran across the indoor pool room toward the brick wall that surrounded the area. Standing on the planter, she strained to look over the wall.

"I don't know, but there are several cars. I see Gentry with a man in a fine robe, and there's another one I haven't seen before. They all carry weapons." Maureen was more familiar with the personnel since she had the opportunity to observe activities in and around the mansion. There were places that Isidora wasn't supposed to see, let alone enter.

Her friend's little discovery piqued her interest, so Isidora gathered up her book, tucked it under her arm, and ran toward the garden at the side of the house where her father held his meetings.

Growing up, she'd been very curious and asked many questions. Some of those questions were never answered, no matter how often she asked her parents and tutors.

One of those unanswered questions was the reason for her seclusion. Without Maureen's companionship, she would have gone mad. Then there was Finn—why couldn't they exist as normal beings? What was the reason for them to be locked inside a room and separated right after feeding?

She wanted answers.

There was rustling of clothes behind her. She pivoted to see Maureen gesturing for quiet.

"If you want to listen, I have the perfect spot."

"Show me." Isidora let her friend lead the way.

Maureen's long black hair swayed with her movements as they rushed through the door that led them to the interior of the house. Most of the servants had retreated for a short break and would be back after a few hours for their meal before sunrise. Isidora's excitement mounted at the prospect of playing sleuth. It had been a boring existence for her, and this was one of the first times she'd openly defied her father's wishes.

They reached the second floor of the mansion, and after running through the quiet hallway, Maureen led her to a guest bathroom directly above the meeting room.

"How are we going to hear them from here?" Isidora wasn't certain why she was whispering.

Maureen once again gestured for silence, and she followed her friend to one of the walls. From her hair, Maureen produced a hair pin and inserted it into a little hole. Isidora watched in utter surprise when the wall swung inward to reveal a small passageway.

"From here on, we're going to be quiet. Not a peep, because we're going to be right on top of the meeting room," Maureen whispered. "Just follow what I do."

Isidora nodded, and they tiptoed across the small room to a spiral staircase. When they climbed up to the landing, they crouched on the floor. A small square air vent offered a glimpse of the proceedings below.

Several people she recognized were present, her father, mother, and Gentry among them. There was also an important-looking gentleman wearing a robe similar to her father's, although the lapel bore a different crest. The gentleman must be of the same social standing as her father.

The other man was more roughish. He wore dark jeans and a black shirt, and his movements were calculated. He listened more than he spoke. When he did, it was with a slight accent.

Isidora strained to hear the conversation.

"Randolph, have you broken your ties with Goran?" Iden asked, addressing Mr. Important.

The man her father called Randolph nodded. "I'm as good as dead in his eyes, but he won't be able to get to me."

For someone marked for death, Randolph didn't seem at all fazed. It sounded like there was more to the situation, and she was dying to know what it was about.

"What makes you so sure?" her father inquired.

Randolph shrugged. "Even the mighty Goran has moments of weakness. I got what I needed to know." He looked at the others. "And I'm certain that he is looking for your daughter. He needs an heir."

She gasped, and Maureen was quick to cover her mouth.

Daughter? They must mean her—she was an only child. Who was this Goran? All she could do was hold her breath and wait to hear more.

"He won't find her. I've kept her here because I always knew what Goran wanted." Iden sounded livid. "My daughter won't be used to help him remain in power."

"Goran has mobilized the elite guards, and they're going to find her. If I were you, I'd take her as far away from here as possible." Randolph's tone was certain, and it was hard to dismiss his advice.

Iden spent some time in thought before turning to the other newcomer. "Is this true?"

The man agreed. "I left the elite company. Goran is going to run us into the ground. Without Rohnert, I have no idea what's going to happen to the rest."

Iden shook his head. "We need Rohnert. He's our only hope."

For the first time, she saw fear manifesting in her father's eyes.

"What do you suggest we do, Iden?" Randolph asked.

"I'm willing to fight. I have enough people to pose a challenge."

"We're outnumbered," Gentry said.

"That may be so, but I refuse to hide. I would have stayed in the Council, but I felt that Goran was just buying time before he axed me next. I'll be of more help alive than dead." Randolph smirked.

"What are your thoughts on this, soldier?" Iden turned to the other newcomer.

"The name's Alonzo, but call me Zo. My allegiance is to Rohnert, but I will stick around if you have room for me in your army."

"Do you think more will come?" Randolph asked, sizing him up.

"I believe so. From what I heard, there is an organized group that is strong enough to be worthwhile allies." Alonzo glanced around before raising his eyes in the direction of the small vent.

Isidora held her breath, and Maureen did the same. The vampire narrowed his eyes and stared. They were inches away from the vent, careful not to create the slightest noise. It took a moment before Alonzo turned his attention back to the men in front of him.

"We're honored to have you with us." Randolph patted Alonzo's shoulder.

"We're facing dark days ahead." He crossed the room, stopping by the window to stare into the darkness surrounding the mansion. "Your daughter might be the key to stopping Goran."

Isidora covered her ears, refusing to hear anymore. She must do something about this.

Maureen looked at her and shook her head, but she didn't speak until they'd crawled out of hearing range. "I don't like it when you have that look."

"What do you mean?"

"The look that tells me that you're up to no good."

Isidora got to her feet, smoothed her skirt, and breathed deep. She was definitely up to something.

Shelly never felt fear in her life, but while she and Jones raced to unload Cyrus and Rayce from the taxi cab, she realized that she was about to lose another person she cared about.

Reality bites, doesn't it?

"Take Cyrus to the bathroom and close the door," she instructed while situating Rayce on the floor. Blood continued to escape from the wound, and his heartbeat was faint.

She began pumping on his chest to revive him, stopping to blow air into his mouth.

"C'mon, Rayce, I'm not giving up on you. Stay with me."

"He's not going to make it," Jones said from behind her, sounding resigned.

"Stop it, Jones." She refused to admit the possibility. Even if she was in way over her head, she wasn't going to give up yet. "In my bedroom, open the closet, get the box of supplies, and be ready to help."

Shelly continued CPR, the dim pulse at his wrist giving her enough encouragement to keep going. When Jones came back, she worked fast, cutting off Rayce's shirt. She found the entry wound on his lower abdomen.

"I need you to continue monitoring him while I remove the bullet." She snapped on latex gloves. Her stomach was roiling, but she wasn't going to worry about herself.

The removal of the bullet was easier than she thought. That was the beauty of Dangeran. The suckers were not made to kill humans. The only issue was the affected area. Whoever had shot Rayce had no idea that he was human or they would have gone for the chest area. Not having a damaged vital organ was always a plus.

Rayce coded once more while she was stitching the wound closed, but Jones was able to resuscitate him. After he was stabilized, Shelly slumped on the floor to catch her breath then placed a phone call to a colleague she hadn't spoken to in a long time.

"Rick, I need a favor."

There was a sharp intake of breath. "After the way you left, you call me and expect me to help you?"

So the anger hadn't ebbed. She was expecting this. Bracing herself, she cupped the phone and spoke in her no nonsense tone. "It wasn't going to work out, and you know it."

"You didn't even give me a chance."

His accusation hit a nerve. Rick Whitaker had every reason to sound the way he did. He'd wanted to show her how two career-driven people could manage a relationship, except she didn't stick around. The budding feelings she felt for him had frightened her, so when Pritchard offered her a job, she'd accepted and run.

"I didn't feel the same way, Rick. You're better off without me." But here she was, calling her old boss to ask him for help.

A long pause followed. After a moment he spoke. "I haven't gotten over you . . . and I don't know if I ever will."

"You're wasting your time. If you can't help me, just say so." She was ready to hang up when she heard him sigh.

"What can I do for you, Shelly?"

"I need my old job back."

"Answer me!" Rohnert's voice thundered inside the room.

Being a father was a foreign emotion, but he was prepared to move mountains and kill anyone who stood between him and the mother of his unborn child.

Firman inched away. "Harrow ordered Tor, Allison, Jones, and Dr. Anderson to leave and not to come back until he called for them."

The answer should have put his mind at ease. Instead Rohnert felt more agitated knowing she was out there on her own. His body shook with frustration, and a growl escaped through his gritted teeth, startling Cheryl.

Firman spoke as if he'd read Rohnert's mind. "Shelly and Jones are together, so she is not alone."

"Where the hell is Harrow?" he asked, trying to distract himself.

"He's in the I-room with a prisoner. I think—"

He was out the door before Firman finished, shouting over his shoulder, "Keep an eye on Cheryl."

Rohnert flew along the corridor, half-crazed and primed for a fight. His body was itching for a confrontation, anything to get his mind off Shelly and their young.

He reached the open door, and Harrow's head whipped toward the sound of his approaching footsteps. "You came back."

"I want Shelly." And he wasn't kidding.

"I sent them away when this bastard raided the building."

There was no way he would have recognized Zane if not for the throbbing from his shoulder scar. It brought back the memory of the vampire who had bitten off a huge chunk of his flesh not too long ago. Rohnert ground his teeth while he surveyed Harrow's handiwork. Zane's head hung back, limp. He'd been tied to a chair and beaten to a pulp, and every orifice oozed with blood. The bastard's face was beyond recognition.

"What the hell happened here?" Rohnert stalked to where Zane was sitting, clutching his Kalimetal and ready to strike.

"He wouldn't speak. One thing I know for sure—he's with Goran."

Rohnert roared at the idea of Goran getting within striking distance of Shelly and his friends. The foundation shook beneath his rage, and every piece of glass around them shattered.

"That bastard would stop at nothing to—"

"You killed my father." Zane opened his swollen eyes to stare at the ceiling, his voice weak.

"And I will kill everyone in your family. Just give me the chance." Harrow shot back.

Rohnert moved closer and touched the tip of his weapon to Zane's exposed neck. "Why are you doing this?" He knew about the estrangement between Demetrius and Goran. But where in the puzzle did Zane fit?

"Goran made me do it."

"What's in it for you, Zane?" Rohnert pressed the tip of the Kalimetal into his skin.

"He . . . would tell me where Melissa, my grandmother, is."

"The motherfucker is manipulating you, just like he'd done with everyone else." Rohnert shook his head, unable to feel compassion.

Zane gave him a blank stare.

"He had Melissa lead his harem to their deaths. They're all gone."

Despite Zane's weakened state, he still managed to pull his head up. For a brief moment, Rohnert felt a sliver of pity, but he dispelled the unwanted emotion and focused on his hatred. He was better off feeling damned unforgiving.

"She's dead?"

Harrow answered this time. "She ain't coming back. Your granddaddy used you, just like he uses everyone else.

Beneath Zane's haggard breathing, his breath caught in a sob. Rohnert lowered his weapon, feeling the other vampire's frustration and the sting of betrayal.

He turned to Harrow, who was burning the floor with his pacing. "What are you planning to do with him?"

"Kill him." Harrow didn't even flinch.

Rohnert understood his friend's reasoning. Zane had caused enough damage to them. Harrow's thoughts revealed that he had killed Cyrus, too. What the hell?

"Cyrus is dead?" This was fucking crazy. It was difficult to grasp the succession of shockers he'd been given.

Harrow nodded.

"He is not," Zane whispered.

They surrounded him in a heartbeat, Harrow grabbing a handful of the vampire's hair to hold his head up.

He hissed under his breath. "What do mean?"

"I . . . turned him . . . before he died."

Harrow screamed and landed a mean backslap across Zane's face before Rohnert had the chance to stop him. The impact toppled Zane to the floor.

Rohnert understood Harrow's pain and concern. Cyrus had been like a brother to him. They had forged a strong friendship during Harrow's early days in the facility.

"We have to look for him." Rohnert racked his brain. Where would a newly transformed vampire hide himself? Bloodlust was another cause for concern. Unguided, a new vampire could go on a rampage, unable to quench the thirst for blood.

"Where in the hell do we start?"

"Where did Tor find you?"

Harrow's eyes blazed. "I will scour every bar in town."

"What about him?" Rohnert secured his weapon on his back and knelt down, inspecting each laceration and bruise running along Zane's exposed skin. They weren't life-threatening, he supposed. Harrow had experimented on their prisoner. Shards of Dangeran were lodged in his skin. The fragments wouldn't kill him, at least not yet, but they would slowly burn his skin, damaging his flesh until he begged for death. It was enough to keep him immobile, unable to summon his energy, and he would be permanently incapacitated from prolonged exposure to the metal.

"I will keep him alive until I find Cyrus." Harrow spat on the floor, which was littered with paper, chunks of broken furniture, and splintered glass. "I don't care. We can leave him here."

"What about the facility?"

"This place is compromised, along with our safety if we stay."

Harrow was a leader they respected and followed, but his judgment in his present state of mind was questionable. Rohnert knew he had to step up. "I have a place. It's not by any means comfortable, but I think it will do until we can regroup."

"Fine. Let me call the rest." Harrow pulled out his cell phone and punched a button. "Fuck!"

"What's wrong?"

"The lines are all fucking dead. I shut them down. We have no record of everyone's phone number once the main computer is disabled."

This was not something Rohnert wanted to hear. He felt the tiny glimmer of hope of locating Shelly disappeared. He bellowed a cry of desperation and thrashed any available furniture he could get his hands on.

He didn't stop until Firman and Harrow pinned him down to the ground.

"Then how the hell am I going to find Shelly?" he cried. God, did he cry.

Cyrus flopped against the hard tile when he surfaced from the weirdest dream ever. He looked around and found himself lying on a bathroom floor.

Then bit by bit, the memories hit him. He could still feel the gut-wrenching pain, how the widening of the gadget tore his skin, little by little.

Except there was no pain at the moment.

He sat up with caution, expecting to be hit by the aches he'd been battling for months. No searing pain came, not even from his leg. In fact, he felt better, although a strange sensation in the pit of his stomach made him retch and lunge forward.

Cyrus stood up after the wave passed and braced his hand on the immaculate sink. Wherever he was, it wasn't the damned prison he'd grown accustomed to. Gone were the skylight and the white walls.

He looked up on the mirror and inspected himself. He looked the same, except for the facial hair he now sported. The bruises were gone, and the swelling all over his face had subsided. He checked his clothes. They were the same ones he'd worn ever since his capture, dried blood and all. Then a new barrage of memories from his gruesome torture hit hard.

Embarrassment swamped him at the thought of what had been done to him. God, he felt like a pussy. Maybe he should've died then.

Not wanting to rely on his eyes alone to check for damage done to him, he ran his hands along the rest of his body. An odd mix of strength and energy flowed through his veins.

He felt strong—different, like he'd been given a new lease on life.

He focused on the wall opposite, wondering about the changes in him. Tiny fissures in the paint showed up like they were under a microscope. He blinked once, twice. Each time he opened his eyes, his sight grew clearer.

His ears tingled. Every single decibel demanded awareness, clamoring for attention and confusing him.

What the hell is wrong with me?

Cyrus jerked his head, astounded at the vast space in his mind. He had been a good student before, but juggling multiple ideas had been impossible until today. What had happened to him?

Then out of nowhere, a fevered burning engulfed his body, and he began to move toward the door. Scared, he choked back something thick at the back of his throat. He faltered at the raging fire in his gut. It was a sensation he had a sudden urge to extinguish, to satisfy in some way. Staggering back, he sat on the toilet, hoping whatever it was would subside soon.

A faint, almost imperceptible moan came from outside, and an overwhelming scent caught his attention. He resisted the compulsion to cry out. Fear was something Cyrus had always rejected. He'd learned early on that it crippled people, stunning them into inaction. This was different. There was yearning in him that he couldn't understand. As the hunger grew stronger within him, shouting its need to him, he felt more and more helpless.

Unable to restrain himself, he got up and walked out of the bathroom and into a quiet and unfamiliar hallway. He wandered toward the living room until a scent overpowered him. The appealing aroma made his mouth water. He barreled his way into one of the rooms, focused on satiating his deep hunger.

Cyrus recognized Jones amid the fire and haze that clouded his mind. In one clumsy movement, Jones aimed a gun at him.

"Step back, Cyrus. I won't hesitate to shoot you if you take one more step forward." Jones was a good man and had become a friend over the short period they'd know each other.

He knew that Jones was bluffing—but *how*?

Cyrus took another step forward, and the gun didn't go off. He smiled and saw the horror in Jones' eyes.

"I will shoot!"

His hands came up in an attempt to appease the scientist until the person lying on the bed caught his attention, and his stomach churned yet again. A deep-seated desire clawed at him—the need to feed. The thirst clouded his mind. He was about to take another step, when the sound of a shotgun cocking behind made him turn.

"If Jones won't do it, I will. Don't push me, my friend."

"Shelly?" His throat burned, scorching him.

"This is not a restaurant where you're free to dine at your leisure." She aimed right at his head. "I don't like guns, but you once told me that I'm a natural. Don't make me use a Dangeran bullet on you."

Dangeran? I'm not a. . .

"What the fuck?" Stunned to inaction, he stared at Shelly while the facts began to click into place. He fell to his knees.

"That's right. You're a part of the merry band of bloodsuckers now." Shelly was being her usual self, and he doubted she was bluffing. "If I were you, I'd go sit out in the hall and take this with you."

Two bags of blood were tossed onto the floor in front of him.

Oh God, he was going to lose it.

Zane squirmed against the bindings that kept him tied to the chair. The duct tape was secure, and there was nothing he could do unless he managed to Houdini his way out of it, which was close to impossible. Extreme fatigue overcame him, but it couldn't rival the pain of the gaping hole in his chest. Everyone in his life was dead.

Everyone he'd ever cared about.

Growing up, he had never understood why he'd been so detached. Compassion hadn't been a part of his make-up, and Demetrius had drilled into him that mercy was for the weak—real men confronted their fears, ignored their doubts, and never pardoned.

Everything he had believed fell at his feet like dead flies, and his resolute hunger for revenge died along with it. Goran had manipulated him, his father, and Melissa. Good god, she was dead, too. He'd known his grandfather had been stringing him along, but his inner macho wanted to prove that he could do the job and maybe earn a seat next to the bastard.

Now, he was in this terrible predicament. There was no doubt he'd waste away soon. The mother fuckin' Dangeran would damage his skin since the wound it created would grow bigger until the pieces were removed. The way things stood, the chances of getting any help soon were slim to none. His skin had started to tingle, and the discomfort soon would progress to intolerable pain.

What a way to die. A slow motherfuckin' way to die.

With his depleted energy, even turning his head toward the door became a task. His neck muscles had tightened, becoming rigid. In the quietness of the surroundings, he heard the raised voices of two agitated vampires, one of which was the guy he had bitten in the past. Funny how his past found a way to catch up with him and bite him in the ass. Rohnert, the full-blooded vampire, didn't seem to hold a grudge until he'd found out that a certain doctor was missing.

The things that remained sharp were his hearing and his goddamn mind. In a matter of days, delirium would set in. It would be a welcome respite from this ongoing hell.

"If you want him alive, go babysit him. I'm getting out of here," Rohnert said. There went the hope of any warm and fuzzy feelings from that vampire. A long silence followed after Rohnert had left. Zane wondered whether they would leave him there. If that were the case, he figured in two weeks, tops, he'd be on his way to hell. He doubted Hill would come back for him—the bastard had been paid for his services and wouldn't show up until he was summoned.

Whoopee—he was on his own.

Goran wouldn't even bother sending his men, knowing that the raid had eliminated most of the facility's inhabitants. Any remaining forces would have scattered and wouldn't be likely to return to a compromised stronghold. Zane was fucked.

Slight, hesitant footsteps approached, faint and scared. All he could see was a pair of white shoes and the bottom hem of someone's white pants. The newcomer stopped a few feet away from him. Unable to move his head, he tried to speak, but his throat clogged, and the words got stuck.

Then the sweetest voice he'd ever heard spoke. "Harrow asked me to watch you until he gets back."

"I . . ."

His mouth refused to form the words. The Dangeran bits Harrow had used on him were taking effect.

Zane tried again. "What's your . . ." Two words. He was making progress.

"I'm not supposed to talk to you. I'm just here to make sure you don't get away." The female said, her voice betraying some unwillingness.

"O—kay . . ."

The woman walked over to the far side of the room. Guessing from the ensuing sounds, she was tidying up the strewn furniture. He listened to her pick up a broken chair and set it aside, and the scratching sound must mean she was hauling another piece toward the wall. Zane fought to stay awake, blinking his eyes so he wouldn't fade into sleep.

"You shouldn't have killed our friends."

Zane stayed silent. He couldn't answer. There were no answers to give.

There was a rustling sound, then a chair was propped closer to him, and she sat down. She didn't cross her legs. By the positioning of her feet, he pictured her sitting with her spine rigid, and he could practically smell the rage inside her, though her soft voice could've fooled him.

"We're a quiet group of people here. We fight for a cause. None of my friends kill for sport. We help unfortunate victims turn their lives around by giving them hope. Why did you have to come here and destroy everything we've worked so hard for?"

Again, he had no answer to offer. Even if his voice box hadn't been affected, he suspected he'd have nothing to say. Closing his eyes, he felt his muscles shiver in response to the sorrow in her voice.

What was with the sudden attack of guilt? It must be the damned Dangeran imbedded in his skin. The stupid shards were toying with his mind. They might as well kill him now instead of this slow torture.

"I'm sure you had a reason to barge in here with your big army." The once-sweet voice rose, and he detected hysterics bubbling to the surface. "Answer me. Why did you come here and destroy the place we call home?"

Home? She's not a vampire. Why would she call this facility home?

"What's . . . yo . . . name?" His voice sounded gravelly.

Her shoes scraped the floor. Before he knew what she was doing, her face came in his line of sight. Staring back at him were the greenest eyes he'd ever seen, big and glistening with unshed tears. "I don't know why you want a name. You showed no mercy. You killed without remorse."

"Cheryl! Didn't I tell you not to get near the bastard?" Harrow's voice shook the room.

Once he'd walked out of the facility, Rohnert had no idea where to start. He'd comb the city if he had to. Running as fast as he could, he created a blur around him, becoming invisible to human eyes. At this point, no one had better cross his path, because he was seeing red. He'd kill anyone who dared slow him down.

If Harrow hadn't destroyed the computers, the phone lines would still be operational, and he'd have no trouble contacting Shelly. He couldn't blame Harrow for doing what was necessary to protect their safety and keep their operation a secret, but thanks to the vampire's quick thinking, Rohnert would have to scramble to locate Shelly.

How had things escalated so fast? And how had Goran and Zane discovered their underground facility? Piecing the puzzle together was the least of his worries, but without a safe hideout, the operation was compromised, which made his friends more vulnerable than ever.

Before he could begin looking for Shelly, he had to prepare the abandoned apartment for the survivors. With its flimsy walls, broken windows, and good-for-nothing doors, the place was no fortress. Any persistent burglars or determined vampires could penetrate the building without much difficulty.

First things first, he had to gather the weapons from his previous hideout and move them to the more secure apartment. With human tenants residing in the property he used to use, any danger would likely involve them, and that was not acceptable. The humans had no business being bothered with the otherworldly presence around them. They had enough chaos, killings, diseases, and inequality that had to deal with.

Rohnert arrived at his old stomping grounds in Harlem, an area he knew was not frequented by the VC guards. This had been his hideout following his departure from the Council. Nothing had changed in the year since he'd been gone. The apartment building was still in bad need of repair, and the bricks that made up the building were crumbling.

A few street kids glanced at him when he strode past, and he tried his best to blend in. Instead of using the front door, he walked to the side of the building. He glanced around, and when he was certain that nobody was looking, scaled the two-story wall until he got to the exterior fire escape. With ease, he lifted his window's wood frame until it rattled open. It was hardly a deterrent against burglars. He could only hope his collection was still where he had left it.

Fitting inside the opening was tricky, but Rohnert was able to squeeze himself through the gap after some careful maneuvering. He decided against turning on the lights since he wanted to avoid attention.

The place seemed intact. It had survived the clutches of transients looking for a place to crash for the night, although dust had collected on all the furniture and cobwebs dangled and littered the walls. The floor squeaked underneath him as he made a beeline for his bedroom. When he pushed the door open, it protested, reminding him of the many days he'd spent cooped up in there, bored out of his mind.

Rohnert kneeled by the side of the bed and pushed it against the bare wall. He tapped the floorboard until it clattered and the rusty nail holding it in place rattled loose. Then he began the painstaking task of removing each strip of flooring until the hole was big enough. He reached down and brought each weapon out into the open. One by one, he inventoried every shotgun, dagger, axe, and Kalimetal he had collected over the years. The suckers might be ancient, but they could kill just as well as their modern counterparts.

Rohnert was replacing the floorboards when a glimmer of metal caught his eye. Reaching down to retrieve the object, he remembered the reason he had chosen to set the piece of jewelry aside. The octagonal metal necklace had been a reminder of the past he'd rather forget. Once he'd turned his back on the Vampire Council, he gave up his right to partake in the legacy. He blew away the dust that had accumulated on the flat surface until the oak bush that symbolized the existence of their race stood out. It was an icon that represented their strength, endurance, and worth. He might be unworthy to adorn himself with such high distinction, but it would be the perfect gift for his child—an introduction to his father's roots and the pride of belonging to a peace-loving bloodline.

Pocketing the distinguished heirloom, Rohnert finished replacing the rest of the wooden boards and returned the bed to its original position. He walked to his closet and pulled out a duffle bag, sticking the weapons inside it. Determined to get his comrades situated, he marched out of the apartment and set out, running at a fast speed.

In a matter of minutes, he made it to the place he had called home after his abrupt departure from the facility. Sniffing around, he caught the familiar scent of Harrow and Tor. So they had been looking for him.

He just might avail himself of their assistance sometime soon. After depositing the duffle bag under his cot, he took out the black book and glanced around the room, looking for a perfect spot to hide it. With the absence of furniture and given its sensitive contents, it wouldn't be smart to leave it available to prying eyes. It wouldn't be of any worth to humans, but in the wrong vampire hands, the revelations it contained could prove devastating.

Deciding against leaving such precious treasure behind, he tucked it back in his waistband and headed out the door. He was ready to look for Shelly. Rohnert hoped to convince her that welcoming him back would be the best decision to make for herself and their child.

Somehow, he doubted she'd make it easy on him. He had treated her like shit on their last night together.

God, he was tired. And also the biggest ass there was.

Goran was plucked out of his nightmare-plagued sleep by a pounding on the door. When his eyes caught the luminous digits on the clock, he gritted his teeth. It was too early to be bothered with inane Council matters. But then again, there weren't many Elders left. He had killed them all. The thought brought a smile to his lips.

He willed the lights on and sat up. "Come in."

Hamilton strode in, acting like his usual smug self. He stopped at the foot of the bed and bent low. "I apologize for waking you, but I have some good news."

"And it couldn't wait?"

His loyal soldier shook his head, eyes sparkling with unbridled excitement.

"Spit it out, then."

The beauty of reading other people's minds was that Goran knew what would be said before the first word was uttered. He bared his fangs and smiled.

"I think I've zeroed in on Iden's location."

"You think?" He slipped out of the luxurious sheets and walked toward

Hamilton. "You know better than to give me half-assed news. You're either sure or you're not."

Hamilton blinked, on the defensive in an instant. However, he kept his voice low and respectful. "Sire, I am certain it's the right place."

Much better. "Tell me about the location."

The other vampire relaxed. "We tracked him to the city of Utica. His mansion is located close to the Mohawk River. It's well concealed. The walls are high, and the fortress is guarded by a private security team."

"Utica?" Talk about remote—it was a place he wouldn't have even considered checking. Score one for the soon-to-be-dead vampire.

"Yes. If you give me permission, I would like to test our muscles and see if we're good enough for an actual battle."

Hamilton's eagerness made Goran laugh. "Let's utilize the hybrids for now. I'm sure you're eager to see what our new army can do, but I want to make sure we're not walking into an ambush."

He watched Hamilton's face fall. "My lord."

"You will stay back and let the mongrels swarm the place. Get a trusted man to direct them while you watch from the sidelines. Kill everyone in sight, but bring me the woman."

Hamilton bowed his head. "How will I know which one she is?"

Even Goran had no idea what Isidora looked like beyond the color of her hair. At the thought of acquiring a new red-headed lover, his cock jerked. Some things never got old. He turned around and walked to his desk and sat, not wanting his minion to see how aroused simple thoughts could make him.

"If she has red hair, take her. Simple as that."

"Your bidding shall be done," Hamilton said before proceeding to the door.

Goran called after him. "Leave at the next sundown."

He inclined his head and took his leave. Goran rubbed his chin, thinking of his unfortunate brush with that infected vampire. He shuddered at the possibilities. The only thing he could think to do about it was to summon the great shaman. She would be able to heal him if the bitch had indeed transmitted the dreadful disease to him.

Thought transference had long been a dying art. They had abandoned the practice when the numbers of hybrids and Halflings had grown. The rapid increase of tainted versions of themselves brought the risk that vampire abilities would be compromised and the race exposed. Even so, he was going to use it.

Goran hurried to his walk-in closet and pulled out a battered chest made of oak. It had been ages since he'd called upon the medium, and he felt a growing apprehension as he dragged the heavy box to the center of the room. Collected dust fluttered around him when he lifted the lid. He took out a set of dark purple votive candles and beads of gingko nuts. Considered to have healing abilities, the gingko tree was believed to have survived one hundred fifty million years.

He pushed the trunk aside and lit the candles. Sitting on his haunches, he rolled his head back and closed his eyes. Willing his mind to relax, Goran took a deep breath while clutching the beads, running his thumb and forefinger along each. He chanted the sacred words to beckon the shaman. He waited a moment and then repeated the process. Minutes ticked by before a gush of wind came from nowhere, brushing past his cheek, signaling the acceptance of his summons.

After several more minutes of silent communication, he blew out the candles and settled back on his heels. It would be a matter of time before his requested company showed up. He donned an embellished black velvet robe and sat on his desk to wait.

Within an hour, there was a knock on the door. Instead of calling out, Goran walked to the door to welcome his guest. She was late but he was willing to let it go.

"Lukan, it has been a while." He regarded the woman with deep appreciation. Her long, light brown hair was like honey, cascading down to her petite shoulders, thick and luscious. Big eyes the color of darkness scrutinized him, no doubt sensing his turmoil.

The priestess took a step forward and dangled her hand close to his face. With practiced gallantry, he reached out and planted a kiss on the top of her palm.

"It's rare for you to call on me these days," she said, smiling.

He led her inside, savoring her sweet thoughts. "I have been busy." Goran stopped by the sitting area and gestured for her to sit, releasing her hand.

"And here I was thinking you didn't need me anymore."

Her honesty was like a breath of fresh air, and Goran chuckled. "I will always need your expertise, my dear Lukan. You're a rare jewel." He sat in the chair opposite hers.

"Flattery won't get you very far." She beamed and then sniffed the air. "What is it that ails you?"

Goran didn't have to say much. Lukan would know. Never once had she shielded her mind's ramblings from him. "The reason I summoned you," he replied in a whisper.

He watched the woman grow silent, her brows pulling together in a frown. She hummed a calming tune before she spoke. "You think you caught it?"

"I wouldn't know." Wasn't that the question of the century? The mighty, proud Goran succumbing to the disease he'd made his life's mission to eradicate.

Without saying a word, Lukan got to her feet and made a sweeping gesture with her hands, as if conjuring unseen spirits. She swayed until her ankle length robe swirled around her like a breath of wind. Intoning words way too fast for Goran to comprehend, she continued chanting while her hands beckoned, drawing forward some unseen force.

Goran remained still until the wait became unbearable. He stood up, walked over to the bookshelf, and pulled down his favorite book. He flipped the pages while half-listening to Lukan, arriving at the worn-out page he'd read over a dozen times.

> All warfare is based on deception. Hence, when we are able to attack, we must seem unable; when using our forces, we must appear inactive; when we are near, we must make the enemy believe we are far away; when far away, we must make him believe we are near.

Pondering the written words, he took comfort in knowing that with the elite guards stabilized and reformed, his army was strong. Therefore, his continued rule was guaranteed.

"Goran, come forth."

He placed the book back on its perch and strode over to where Lukan stood in the middle of the room. The scent of faint smoke whirled around him when he stepped into the glowing circle she had conjured.

This was something he hadn't seen before. For the first time, he couldn't reach Lukan's mind when he tried. Drawing a blank, he stared at her serene face and waited for her guidance.

"Your worries can be laid to rest," she said, laying one hand over his forehead and chanted out a tune in their ancient language. "The burden is now lifted. Give mercy to the wicked no more, for they have seen the light. Endow our gracious leader with long life, remarkable health, and stalwart resolve, that he may counter the intentions of malevolent spirits."

Goran stood there, face ashen, almost on the verge of laughing. As much as he wanted to believe the priestess, the whole performance left him skeptical. But then, he had no reason to distrust her. Over the years, she had aided and saved countless lives, and he wasn't about to jinx himself by disbelieving.

She moved closer, her warm breath caressing his check while she blew incantations over his ears, his eyes, his nose, and then his mouth, where she stopped and hovered. Opening her eyes, she glanced at his lips with nothing short of desire.

Though she was not his type, he wouldn't mind trying the great shaman. Who knew, he might even get lucky. An up-close and personal brush with a powerful figure was a good thing. Pillow talk wasn't bad, either. All he had to do was make her feel desirable, and he was the king of BS—he could make it happen.

He lowered his defensive mental armor and focused on her sweet lips. Without hesitation, he snaked his hand around the small of her back and pulled her forward. Surprise was etched on her face, but she offered no resistance. Her hands went to the nape of his neck, bringing him forward until their mouths were almost touching.

"This is not going to work, Goran. I don't mix work with pleasure." She smiled a slow, lazy grin, and it was enough to get him hard.

"Lukan dear, where is that free spirit of yours?" He wanted to capture her mouth and taste the luscious red lips.

"You needed my help, and I've cleansed you. You have nothing to worry about." She planted her palms on his chest and pushed back.

Under normal circumstances, such rebuff wouldn't have been acceptable. But since Lukan had been gracious enough to heal him, he decided not to press the matter this time. He saw that behind her apologetic smile, she trying to mask her desire. The thought of affecting the great healer in a sexual way excited him. Yet he beat down the urge and let her go.

Lukan did an elaborate curtsy before a wisp of smoke took her away, leaving Goran to his own devices once again. With his worries now buried, he'd be able to pursue the elusive Iden and the woman who had been kept from him.

If Hamilton's information was good, then he was within striking distance. Iden had better come up with a better hiding spot to escape Goran's wrath and keep his daughter safe, because he was coming. He was ready to take his bride—the one female who would seal his permanent position on the seat as the leader of the Council.

He bit his lower lip in wicked anticipation, imagining the faceless woman with red hair. His shaft began to twitch. Such perversion fueled his desire, which was the one thing that kept him going.

Rohnert paused outside the lip of the underground tunnel and glanced around. In the absence of the slight sound of the moving camera, the place seemed eerie, haunted even. He sniffed the stale air, taking stock of anything out of the ordinary to make sure he was alone.

When his surroundings checked out, he proceeded to walk the length of the secret passageway. He took another sharp breath. The place was no longer a secret after the breach that caused the dismantling of their organization, and the disappearance of Shelly.

His chest tightened at the thought of the woman who had captured his heart, his mind . . . damn, his everything. There was no time when he wasn't thinking about her and their child. If he didn't locate her soon, he'd go nuts.

When he reached the entrance, he pushed the heavy metal door open. The place was like a ghost town—strange, dark, and abandoned. Gone were the echoes of laughter shooting across the halls while the inhabitants slung friendly banter back and forth. Gone were Harrow's constant announcements over the speaker system, reminding everyone to be safe before they embarked on their missions. He even missed Rayce's tasteless repertoire of elevator music, playing nonstop and torturing the rest of them.

Rohnert made his way into the control room and started clearing the debris from what was left of the ransacked office. Shards of glass littered the floor, and every single one of the expensive toys their facility had invested in was beyond salvageable. It was obvious that Harrow had made a good call when he destroyed any evidence. However, this meant loss of all pertinent information regarding every single member of their tight-knit group. There went any hope of locating Shelly the easy way. All that was left to do was to hang around in establishments she might visit and hope that his paternal GPS would give him hints.

What if she'd fled the city to a place he couldn't reach? He swore under his breath. It took a monumental effort on his part not to lash out at every failed attempt to locate her. Without any knowledge of her background, he was drawing a blank.

Pulling out drawer after drawer, he checked for anything that would spark an idea of how to find her without resorting to stalking hospitals in the city. Nothing but unimportant supplies stared back at him from every drawer he'd opened so far. He moved to another desk.

"Doesn't anyone keep an old-fashioned fuckin' address book these days?"

He fumed and slammed the drawer shut with frustration, rattling what used to be a very expensive computer system. The U-shaped desk shook with the force, trembling with the weight its spindly legs were carrying. It creaked once more before it went crashing to the floor with a loud bang. A domino effect swept across the room, bringing all that had been left standing to the ground.

After the cloud of dust dissipated, Rohnert glanced around at the shambles he'd created and shook his head. The clean-up crew, should Harrow ever decide to restore the place, wouldn't be happy. Then something caught his eye. A square case had been duct-taped to the underside of Rayce's desk. Walking over the rubble and kicking debris out of his path, Rohnert ripped it from the wood. It was the size of a CD, and he wondered what the hell was in it. He tore through the metal casing like paper to reveal . . . well, a CD.

Rohnert sprang fast, scouring the area for a place to view the contents of the damn disk. The first few offices and bedrooms on the top level had been turned upside down. Desperation led him a couple of floors down, and his feet of their volition took him to Shelly's room. Her suite was as neat as pin. Nothing seemed out of place. Shelly's bedroom looked like it had been spared from the ransacking Zane and his men had given to the rest of the facility. Her bed hadn't been slept in, the throw pillows still stacked like quiet sentinels.

Rohnert shook off the vicious wave of longing that gripped him, strode to the entertainment center, and popped the disk inside the player. Not knowing what to expect, he flicked on the television on and stood and waited.

Instead of the voice recording he'd hoped to hear, odd numbers flashed across the screen. Codes, he figured they were. With his temper rising to a dangerous level, he wasn't in the right frame of mind to decipher it. He pressed fast-forward, and the screen blurred before him until he got to a picture of a nondescript house with an unremarkable door. Rohnert closed his eyes and racked his memory, trying to recall if he'd seen the place before.

He had to rewind the recording several times before his brain produced an answer. Anxious to get going, he popped the disk from the player and glanced around. He knew he was coming back here, even if it was just to inhale Shelly's scent. Rohnert ran through the hallway to the nearest exit. He would find the house and discover its relevance. It was the single clue he had to work with until he was sane enough to figure the rest of the code.

"I'm leaving for work now. Are you sure you can handle Cyrus?" Shelly asked from the doorway of her office, now Jones and Rayce's bedroom for the time being.

Rayce looked up from the book he was reading and nodded. Shelly glanced at the handgun sitting on top of the desk, a silent reminder of the threat that hung over their lives.

It had been several weeks since their underground facility had been attacked. It was a miracle that Rayce had survived his wounds, but his recovery had been slow. She and Jones had taken turns nursing him and Cyrus back to health. During Cyrus's crossover to a full-fledged vampire, they made sure that he had an ample supply of bagged blood.

Sad to say, they hadn't heard from anyone in the facility. Although her landline had been reinstated, Shelly had no way of contacting any of their friends with the main line destroyed. Rayce had promised to do whatever he could the moment he was vertical.

Shelly stopped by the living room and spotted Cyrus standing by the window, his shoulders hunched and his muscles coiled like ropes.

"Are you going to be okay?"

He turned around and his blood-red eyes gave the answer she already knew. "I'm fine. Do you want me to walk you to the hospital?"

She hesitated for a moment. Cyrus was an ordinary vampire, so there was no immediate threat to his life, unlike their diseased friends. It would be good for him to get a chance to catch some fresh air and clear his head, and Jones was too skittish to be any help.

Lord knew how crowded her two-bedroom apartment had been for the four of them. Good thing Cyrus seemed solid and safe around humans. After his initial frightful thirst for human blood had diminished, he had been satisfied with the donated blood she had managed to access through Jones' contact.

"Sounds like a good idea." She preceded him to the door while buttoning her jacket. Thanks to the loose-fitting scrubs, her growing belly wouldn't be noticeable for some time yet. Since it was her first day at work tonight, she wanted her colleagues' attention focused on her return and not her pregnancy.

Yeah, baby's daddy is a vampire, and he wanted nothing to do with me. It wasn't the type of casual conversation she wanted to have.

They walked onto the almost deserted street in silence. A furtive glance told her that Cyrus was deep in thought. She couldn't blame the guy. It wasn't every day you found yourself having difficulty appreciating regular meals and developing a deep craving for human blood.

Shelly tried to keep up with Cyrus's long strides until they turned the corner. She considered herself fit, but this brisk pace was making her sweat. If she was going to be on her feet all night long, they had better slow down.

"Are we trying to win a race here or something?"

Cyrus gave her a sideway glance and stopped. "What?"

She continued walking and looked over her shoulder. "I think you've forgotten that I can't walk as fast as you vamps can."

"You don't walk, my dear Dr. Anderson. You waddle." Cyrus was suddenly by her side, wearing a stupid grin.

Shelly snorted at his reference to her growing belly. "It seems like you're back to your old self. That's good," she muttered.

"There's no point in feeling like shit when I've got a little Superman in me." Cyrus placed an arm around her shoulder.

The wind picked up, and Shelly found herself shuddering. After a long time being cooped up in the underground facility, she'd forgotten what it was like to be outside. She pulled her jacket closer and leaned into Cyrus.

"If this is the schedule you're going to keep, I'm going to walk you to and from work every day. I'm going to do a little investigating while you work. Besides, it'll give Jones a little breather. Mr. Einstein is a bit jumpy around me." Cyrus chuckled.

Shelly couldn't help but smile. True, Jones had been skittish around Cyrus. Under the circumstances, she would have acted the same except she knew Cyrus well. He would kill himself first before he harmed his friends. She might be putting too much faith in him, but what else could she do?

"Just make sure you keep yourself out of trouble and your nose clean. Here, take this." She stopped and reached into her backpack, which was filled with almond cookies and chocolate bars, to produce a Glock.

Cyrus stopped and red eyes focused on her. "Whoa. I can't believe you brought this with you." He took the weapon from her and checked the chamber while keeping tabs on their environment.

"I thought you might want to have something with you. I'm afraid we don't have the fancy bullets you prefer." She rolled her eyes and resumed walking. "My shift is done at seven in the morning. Since you're now a child of the darkness, don't worry about me. I'll be fine. Besides, it's just a ten-block walk."

"Of course I'll worry about you." His brow lifted.

"I'm a big girl. It's Jones I'm worried about. He's been jumpy, and I'd hate for him to find a reason to flee." Shelly turned on her heel and crossed the street to the hospital. Cyrus watched her until she made it past the automatic glass doors, and then he walked away. She shed her jacket and slung it over her shoulder and made her way to the employee lounge.

Who would've thought she'd be back working in the ER again?

After seeing the good doctor off, Cyrus sniffed the air. He was still getting used to his new and improved self. Closing his eyes, he thought about his next step. It had been less than a month since he had been turned by that motherfucker Zane. There were still a lot of aspects he had to learn before the hunting began, but the day of reckoning would come soon.

If he followed Tack security protocol, he would find the rest of his men, regroup, and get situated. Cyrus thought of the place where most of his kind would congregate, normal or diseased. He smirked at the idea—which of them was normal, anyway? Aside from bars frequented by their fighters and the Council soldiers, there was one other place where the Tack Enterprises crew stalked their enemies.

He looked around and took stock of his environment before heading in the direction of a good starting point. Now that he was able to go out by himself, there was no stopping him from doing what he loved best.

Crossing the street amid the blaring horn of a speeding taxi, Cyrus cleared out of the way just by kicking his heels a bit harder before breaking into an easy jog. He could get used to this new and improved body. He grinned while snaking his way through the throng of people loitering on the street. Upon reaching the famed Rockefeller Center, he tried to blend in, keeping his head low and avoiding eye contact. His vision was great, but he doubted the humans would react to his bloodshot eyes well.

Cyrus strolled by the edge of the skating rink, familiarizing himself with the scent of the humans. He watched for any abrupt movements from nonhumans, but no one had caught his eye. During his foray into the jungle of people milling around, his intense concentration backfired. Before he knew it, he heard the soft click of a trigger engaging.

He whipped around, palming the Glock that Shelly had given him, but the human was fast.

"Bang bang, you're dead, sir." Angus, a young human he'd recruited before his abduction, chuckled. He lowered the weapon he'd concealed with his heavy jacket and bowed.

Cyrus had yet to learn to control his new vampire temperament. He fisted Angus's collar and drew him close. Baring his gleaming fangs, he hissed. "Don't fuck with me."

The shock on Angus's face was comical, and Cyrus released his hold. It took a few moments for the human to regain the composure to speak. Beads of sweat began trickling down the side of his face. "You're a . . . um . . . not human anymore?"

"You mean, am I a vampire now? Yes."

"What the hell happened to you, sir? We have been looking for you."

Cyrus grabbed the newbie's arm and steered him away from the dense congregation of revelers in the plaza. Only when they reached 50th Street did he let go. "Where are the others?" He looked around to ensure no one was paying attention to them.

Angus took a step back. "I—I was out on patrol with John the night the facility was attacked, sir. When we came back—"

"Listen to me. Don't ever bow to me in public, sensei or not. You're making me a target when you do that." Cyrus gritted his teeth. The young man was a newbie, and the fact that he was out meant that Harrow's fighter rotation had gotten screwed up.

"Yes, sir."

"And cut the sir crap, too. Where in the hell is John?' Angus looked uncomfortable and took another step back, which made Cyrus chuckle despite the aggression building up inside. "Answer my question."

Angus swallowed hard before he answered. "John suggested we part ways since he's infected. He thought I'd be better off without him in case the Council guards find us again."

"And what are you doing here?"

"The same thing you're doing here. I'm looking for any members of the team who survived the breach."

"Where are you holing up?"

"Here and there."

Knowing the young man's history, Cyrus felt a pang of pity for him. Angus' vagueness was a by-product of multiple foster homes, and he had seen his fair share of life on the streets. A smart fellow, Angus had problems with authority at first, but once Cyrus had a long chat with him, his attitude had done a one-eighty.

As much as Cyrus wanted to invite him to Shelly's apartment, he was concerned about their living arrangements. She had been kind enough to take them in. How much more space could she provide? The place was already too crowded.

"From now on, you're my patrol partner."

Relief flooded Angus' face. "Thank you."

"Do you have ammo?"

"I have some left." Angus fished inside his tattered bomber jacket and produced a round of Dangeran bullets.

Cyrus took them and smiled. "I'm going to need these."

"There's more." Angus handed him two throwing stars and a push dagger. "I think I can manage with just my Wesson since you're around."

"Atta boy. Now, we're going to start looking for our guys. Stay low. Don't instigate any fights. You hear me?"

Angus nodded with the eagerness of a child. Cyrus began walking. "Let's head to Fury," he said. Fury had been a dive bar he'd frequented with Lambert before his abduction.

"Fuck!"

"What's the matter, si—"

He shot Angus a baleful glance. He needed learn to control his volatile temper in the presence of humans. "Did they give Lambert a proper burial?"

"Yes. He was a good friend to us all," Angus paused, "and Harrow hasn't lost hope of finding you."

Cyrus nodded. Harrow was indeed a piece of work—loyal to a fault, but he was a man he'd come to respect as their leader and love as a brother and friend. Cyrus took a deep breath, fighting the mixture of ire and uncertainty that had started to plague him.

They reached the entrance of the bar. "Remember, we try to blend in. We don't attract attention." This order was directed more to himself than his student. If anything, it was he who should be concerned about fitting in. He was wearing an ensemble Shelly had put together—beige trousers, plaid sweater, and moccasins. Not the killer duds he was used to wearing.

Angus seemed to be thinking along the same lines. He looked at Cyrus' outfit and snickered. "Okay . . ."

The duo walked inside the dark and crowded smoke-filled room. Angus flagged a newly vacated table and called for the waitress. The woman slunk in their direction. Her hips swung to the rhythm of the music playing overhead.

They placed their orders, and Cyrus began to scan the immediate area. After he'd satisfied himself that it was clear, he began to relax. One glance at Angus showed that he was enjoying the techno beat pumping from the speakers. Cyrus had begun to loosen up when he experienced a prickly sensation at the back of his neck, and he knew someone was watching him.

He forced himself not to jump up and do a man-to-man search. *Maintain control*, he told himself. He glanced across the room to the crowded section of the bar and started to look for anyone showing interest in him.

"Is everything okay?" Angus leaned forward, resting his elbows on the little round table that separated them.

"Just doing the usual." He trained his eyes on his young student.

The younger man shrugged and worked on chugging his beer.

Even in the darkness, Cyrus was able to monitor each movement in the room like it was goddamn daylight. Every soul seemed to be minding their own business. In the case of some of the leather-clad men, it was obvious their interests lay inside the skirts of the few women in their midst. No one was paying attention to Angus and Cyrus.

Chalking up the uneasy feeling to his hyperactive imagination, Cyrus downed the rest of his scotch and rose. Angus pinned him with a questioning look.

"There are other nights. Let's roll and check out the facility."

Just before they reached the side exit, there was that prickle on the back of his neck again—the nagging feeling that someone was watching him.

Shelly had gone through the first four hours of her shift. So far, very minor cases had been brought in. Two automobile accident victims had required minor stitches, a lady with an intense pain in her stomach had been referred for an emergency appendectomy, and a little girl had swallowed her mother's pearl earring. Piece of cake, considering she was used to treating knife and gunshot victims and performing amputations.

She headed to the employee lounge for a ten-minute break to elevate her swelling feet. The room was quiet and empty, which suited her just fine. Shelly grabbed a bottle of water from her locker and was about sit down when Dr. Rick Whitaker walked in. Still looking every bit as handsome as day they'd first met, Rick was almost the same except for the flecks of gray hair at his temples.

"I heard the brilliant Shelly Anderson was back from an über-long absence," he said, standing in front of her.

When Shelly looked up, her gaze landed on a familiar pair of green eyes. It was a face she hadn't forgotten, and he'd once been a very close friend before emotions and attraction had gotten in the way

"Dr. Whitaker," she said, rising to her feet.

"You haven't changed, Shelly." His voice dipped into that lazy drawl of his.

She'd missed her friend, even if she couldn't teach herself to return his affection. "Actually, I have. If you'll excuse me, I have to get back to work and save the world."

So much for resting her feet. It wasn't so much his affection that made her want to flee, but the realization that she was just too screwed up to take advantage of the opportunity. Here was a man who could offer her a normal life, but she had to stir things up and fall in love with a vampire who didn't want to be around her. Now she was knocked up and hiding the fact from her boss. Gee, what a way to start a professional relationship.

Before she could get past him, Rick took her arm and pulled her against him. "What does it take for you to at least try to see if we can make it work?"

Rick was one of the gentlest souls she'd ever come across. It had been unfair to string him along back then, and it'd be a shame to do it now just because her life was falling apart.

"Rick, c'mon. I don't need this right now. Can't we just go back to being friends? I'd hate to feel that you just hired me back because you wanted something more—"

"Whoa, hold it there. As the chief of staff here, no one can challenge my decision on who I hire. I'm certain no one would question your capabilities as a doctor."

"Then let's keep this professional. I don't know if I can handle anything more than friendship at the moment." She placed her hand on top on his and squeezed. "I have to get back to work."

"I'm always around if you need me." His tone dropped deeper, and she could almost hear his breathing next to her ear.

"Thank you," she said and hurried to the door without sparing him another glance.

She stormed down the lit corridor and past the cafeteria until she reached the door that would lead her back to her post. It had been a bad idea to return here, but she needed to keep busy until *It* arrived. God knew the last thing she needed was to get tangled up with someone of the opposite sex. Men were nothing but trouble, and even though Rick was a fine man, she wouldn't trust anyone for a long time. At least with Rohnert, she'd offered herself to him freely. He had tasted but decided she wasn't good enough for him. Hurtful as it was, she'd gotten past it. There would be no more sleepless nights, and not another tear would be shed for him.

Keep telling yourself that, her inner voice said.

The rest of her shift was spent in a blur of frenetic activity. A victim of domestic violence was brought in with multiple stab wounds. Shelly passed the remaining hours of her shift intent on doing what she did best, and it provided the distraction she needed.

Rohnert stood in front of a well-maintained brick building in the better part of the Soho district. He stayed in the shadows until a group of tourists passed. The façade of the building was similar to the one he'd seen on the disc. So were the rest of the townhomes he had visited. It didn't matter. If he had to comb the entire city, he would.

He emerged from the dark and was about to cross the street when the main door opened and Shelly walked out with a man. Rohnert had never experienced rage in its purest form until he recognized her companion. He reached for his Kalimetal with every intention of slicing and dicing the bastard he had once called friend. It took every ounce of restraint to keep from rushing them. Rather than acting while in the grip of his fury, he followed them close enough to catch some of their hushed conversation.

But why did Cyrus put his arm around her? What the hell had Rohnert missed during his absence? This wasn't what he'd expected to see, and it took tremendous discipline to refrain from attacking the bastard. It wasn't easy to fall back when all he wanted was to claim her as his.

Sure he'd fathered her child, but he had also walked away from her. By human standards, what he'd done was considered abandonment. This knowledge made him maintain his distance until the two reached the hospital. Another piece of the puzzle fell in his lap. Shelly had been working while pregnant.

The idea pained him. Females of his kind never had to work, and pregnant women were required to stay off their feet when carrying their young.

Rohnert remained on the opposite side of the street, hiding in the shadows while making sure they didn't see him. He caught a glimpse of Cyrus glancing left to right, the same way he'd done in the past, keeping tabs on his surroundings. Still plagued with the nagging feeling he couldn't place, Rohnert decided to follow Cyrus after Shelly disappeared behind the double glass doors.

He'd be back for her. For now, he and an old friend needed to have a talk.

Recon and patrolling had been an enjoyable activity for Rohnert during his stint at Tack Enterprises. The last thing he'd expected was to be trailing one of their own. The vibes he'd been getting from Cyrus were those of fury and revenge. There were so many questions running through his mind, and all his ire was directed at Zane—understandable since the half-shit turned him into a bloodsucker.

Although he needed answers, prudence made Rohnert follow Cyrus with caution, giving him enough space to avoid confrontation. His gut told him that Cyrus remained tight, but after being abducted, it was hard to tell how fucked up he'd gotten. Rohnert continued to trail the vampire to Rockefeller Center, where Cyrus met up with one of the new recruits, and then to the bar.

One thing that had escaped him was that Cyrus' thoughts weren't as decipherable as they should have been. Normally, he could read anyone like an open book. The sporadic and incoherent images coming from the new vampire were impossible to grasp right off the bat.

Once they exited the bar, Rohnert took to the rooftops to keep himself hidden. The late evening air was cool, the fog rolling in provided additional cover. When the two headed back to the facility, he decided it was time to make his move.

When they reached the rim of the tunnel, he called out from behind them, "Evening Cyrus . . . Angus." He tipped his head but kept a hand inside his jacket for good measure.

The two whipped around, and Cyrus' relief upon seeing him gave

Rohnert the much-needed assurance that nothing had changed. He wasn't a threat. Angus stood unmoving and speechless.

"You came back." Cyrus grinned.

"Yes, brother." Rohnert flashed closer and offered his palm, which Cyrus slapped in welcome. "I see that things have taken a rough turn for you."

The new vampire patted him on the back and resumed walking. "You can say that again." He showed off his brand-spanking new fangs. "You've been following us."

Rohnert wasn't surprised by Cyrus' vigilance and chuckled. "Just doing my job." He turned to Angus and nodded. "You tight, kid?"

Angus bobbed his head several times. "Are you back for good?"

"We'll see . . ."

"Can I have a word with you?" He asked once they reached the facility. He glanced at

Cyrus, who was looking quite disgruntled at the tumbled mess around them.

He led Rohnert to the I-room, leaving Angus at the hallway. Remnants of broken furniture littered the floor. "What do you want to know?"

"You're okay, my man?" he asked.

The vampire chuckled. "Just dandy. Next question."

He had a general idea of how Cyrus felt, but he needed to hear his conviction to gauge his mental well-being. "What do you plan to do with your creator?"

Cyrus's face clouded, and it took a long moment before he responded. "Nothing for now. We have better things to do, like finding the others and securing a new hideout." He made his way to the front of the room. Pushing a button for the secret stash, the wall revolved to reveal the bar that held Pritchard's cherished alcohol collection. It wasn't a surprise that it was left untouched.

With their proximity, Rohnert was able to get a read of the complete scenario without the need for words—all his friend's pain and the vicious torture that had led to this ultimate fate.

"Fuck!" He sucked in a deep, agonized breath at the graphic punishment his friend had received. Rohnert took out his frustration on the debris, kicking it away from him.

"Scotch?"

Rohnert nodded. With this new knowledge, he understood Cyrus's need for revenge, and he couldn't blame the man.

Cyrus came back with a glass. Their eyes met and without a word, they raised their glasses. They both downed their drinks in one gulp.

"I've seen Zane," Rohnert said.

Cyrus was breathing down his neck in a blink of an eye. "Where is the fucker?" The vampire radiated hostility.

"He was here a week ago, in this very room."

"That has to be the offensive scent I caught when we walked in." Cyrus began to pace, his drink forgotten. "Where could he be?"

"I haven't spoken with Harrow since the day the facility was attacked. I don't know where he took the bastard. I'm guessing he'll be back here soon since we haven't established a new mode of communication."

Rohnert watched Cyrus's jaw clench, and he waited for the inevitable explosion. None came. Instead, Cyrus returned to the bar to refill his glass. "We need a new place to shack."

"We do, but without money, we can't do much at the moment."

"Is cash our main concern right now?"

"As far as I know. I have some toys we can use while we're rebuilding."

"Don't worry about the cash. Pritchard didn't believe in putting all his money in one place. He told me where he kept his liquid assets. As far as weapons, all we need is to have the production line create more toys for us."

How could he have forgotten that Cyrus knew as much as Harrow and Allison about the Tack operation? "Now we're talking. I have a shack not too far from here. Let's split up tonight and see if we can find more of our friends, and we'll meet up before sunrise."

Cyrus nodded and took a long pull at his drink. "Wait, I can't."

Rohnert bared his fangs, feeling a sudden burst of aggression. "What do you mean, you can't. Don't tell—"

The new vampire raised his hand. "Oh no, don't even go there. There's nothing going on between me and your woman."

My woman? "I don't think she'll take me back after the way I left."

"Shelly took me in, and I can't just leave her without telling her where I'm going. I have to see her first."

Rohnert relaxed a fraction. "Okay."

"You've been wondering about her, haven't you?" Cyrus glanced over his shoulder.

"Yes."

"The woman is still a pain in the ass. Nothing's changed. She can boss anyone around like a drill sergeant, but I think she's coping well under the circumstances. She's braver than any woman I know."

This was not a surprise. The woman could annihilate a platoon with her sassy mouth. But Rohnert's main concern was her overall well-being, and he had no idea how to voice it. This was new territory for him.

"Tell me something I don't know," he muttered after a few moments.

Cyrus chuckled before handing him a glass filled to the brim. He paced the room and took another big gulp.

"Well, she's, you know . . . expecting a child." Cyrus' declaration didn't come as a shock, but it felt odd to hear it from someone else.

"My child," he said.

"You knew?"

"I can feel him. Did she tell you anything else?"

Cyrus sighed. "She's not saying anything. She's not very happy, and the baby's going to be making a splash in five months."

Rohnert stopped dead in his tracks. "That fast?"

"You tell me. I'm a new vampire. I have no idea how this shit works."

"I'm afraid I haven't been around pregnant women before. What did Jones say?"

Cyrus roared at the question. "Jones is a bomb waiting to explode. He's scared shitless to have me around. I think all his research did not prepare him to see an actual transition happening right before his eyes."

Rohnert could imagine the good scientist having a nervous breakdown. Regardless, Jones was as hard-working as they came, even if he couldn't stomach surprises.

"Is Shelly okay?"

"What do you think? The woman is a workaholic. Nothing can stop her. Not hail, not an earthquake, and certainly not a roomful of adopted friends." Cyrus chuckled.

Somehow, the thought of Shelly being exposed to men in such close quarters didn't sit well with Rohnert. There would be changes. His female would get the best of everything, even if he had to move mountains.

The weeks following the breach of their underground facility had been hellish for Harrow. Being cooped up in Leo's house was not his idea of productivity, and he couldn't accomplish much if he had no communication with the others.

His team had scattered, and Cheryl and Zane had been added to his long list of worries. Cheryl had taken responsibility for watching the incapacitated vampire until Harrow could figure out a way to get everyone who was left in one place.

If it wouldn't have been too much of an imposition on Leo, he wouldn't have let Cheryl out of his sight. Upon Tor's advice and Cheryl's insistence, Harrow had relented and checked her in at a local motel, with an adjoining room for Zane. He wasn't planning on letting the bastard go until Cyrus was found. It was up to his mentor to decide the fate of the vampire. He and Tor had been scouring the city for a suitable bunker that would house whomever they had left. They had come across a warehouse that belonged to the military, which only high-ranking officials knew about. The property was close to Battery Park and had been recently placed on the market.

Once he'd checked the place out, all he had to do was utilize one of their overseas accounts and make the purchase. With Leo handling the negotiations on his behalf, they had purchased the building, and the wheels had been set in motion to get it renovated for their use. Harrow had been dividing his attention between the construction of the new facility and their business operations.

The warehouse would retain its outward appearance, but it would be fortified inside. Now, if he could find Rayce, then he could rest easy. Though they could afford the best tech guy out there, he wouldn't trust anyone else to install the security except Rayce. This could be a bit problematic, considering they hadn't had contact with him.

"You tight, my man?" Tor slapped him on the shoulder, bringing him back to the present.

Harrow grunted and landed a punch on Tor's arm. "Tight as a coil. You ready to paint the town red?" He slipped on his sunglasses.

If it wasn't for Gail's safety and the sense of normalcy they wanted for her, Harrow would have preferred to bunk somewhere in the city. Even Jordan was getting edgy from the enclosed quarters. It would be another week before their new warehouse hideout would be ready. It wouldn't be as fancy as their upstate house had been, but it would nonetheless be a place they could call home.

The two of them stood outside General Krever's mansion, ready to hit the road. Thanks to Tor's quick thinking, Harrow had used Gail as a good excuse for Jordan and Allison to stay. This would buy them another week, but after that, the women would be back to patrol duties, whether he liked it or not.

"I'm ready to tango," Tor said and kicked his heels against the ground. "Where to?"

He matched Tor's speed. "How about our usual place?"

Tor's response was a hearty chuckle.

"Did I say something funny?" Harrow asked, feeling his temper shooting up.

"Dude, I like you . . . a lot. But not that way. I'm in love with your sister." Tor waggled his eyebrows at him, which deepened his irritation.

Harrow smacked him on the shoulder with his palm. "Bastard. I want to start there and work our way through all the clubs, bars, and shitty holes one more time. Maybe we missed something."

He increased his pace, not wanting to listen to Tor's shitty comebacks, but the other vampire caught up with him right away. "Much better, because you're not my type."

Their banter continued until they reached the little bar. The place hadn't changed at all. It was still crowded, with odors ranging from sweat, smoke, bad alcohol to the scent of lust, drugs, and prostitutes.

"Some things never change," Harrow muttered, proceeding straight to the bar.

"Hey, stranger. You're looking good." The same waitress greeted him. Her lips were huge with collagen, her skirt short, and her boobs were the size of melons.

Harrow nodded in acknowledgment. "Give us a bottle of Patron Silver." Tor rescued him from further conversation with the interested server.

"How about a bottle of your finest scotch for me?" a familiar voice said from behind.

Harrow turned around and broke into a big grin. "You're freakin' late."

Cyrus raised an eyebrow and opened his arms. "Oh, yeah? What are you going to do about it, kick my butt?"

He walked into his friend's waiting embrace and held on. A few moments into the reunion, Cyrus shoved him aside. "I have a reputation to uphold. I happen to dig chicks."

At his words, Tor broke into fits of laughter, joined by Rohnert and Angus. Harrow socked Cyrus on the shoulder.

"Glad to see you, Cyrus."

He flashed his fangs. "We're still in business, right?"

Harrow understood the underlying sentiment and nodded. "Fuck yeah," he said, and then summoned the bartender for additional glasses.

Maureen stared at Isidora and shook her head. "That is the stupidest plan I've ever heard." She eyed her with disdain.

Isidora shrugged. "If what Randolph was saying is true, I'm not going to wait for that Goran character to come here and make me his bride. There's no way I'm going to let it happen."

Her friend continued to shake her head at her half-assed plan. "You heard your father. He isn't going to allow that to happen. And you've seen that newcomer, right?"

True, the vampire appeared capable of taking anyone in his path, but why would she place her trust in someone she didn't even know?

"He looks like he can do some ass-kicking. I say you should stay put and just wait it out." Maureen settled on the chaise next to her.

"Wait like a sitting duck? No way. I'm done sitting around. It's time I took my destiny into my own hands. Besides, even if Goran doesn't get to me, who knows what Papa has planned."

"You sound like you have your mind all made up." When she nodded, Maureen's eyes widened. "Where do I fit in this cockamamie plan of yours?"

Isidora faltered. She wanted to get out of the mansion and as far away from the absurdity of her situation as possible, but she hadn't given much thought to how to go about it. "I don't know yet. I need your help to me get out of this place, and maybe get word to Finn to meet me somewhere," she whispered.

Even to her own ears, her request sounded like it had disaster written all over it. But the idea of getting away from the stifling confines of her father's house was far too appealing to ignore. Isidora smiled in spite herself.

Maureen jumped up and began pacing. "This whole situation is making me nervous."

Isidora stood up and moved to the window. She gazed out into the darkness and sighed. "Admit it. You know this is not going to end well."

Maureen stopped next to her. "I can sense that there is more to what we heard. I just can't imagine what your father would do if you left."

"I have been hidden here all my life, tucked inside these four walls without knowing what's going on. This is my life. I think it's fair to have a say in it. Besides, I don't think I can stand being taken away from Finn and betrothed to another."

Maureen released a long breath and turned to her. "If I help you, I'm going with you."

"Whatever you think will work."

"When do you want to do this?" Maureen's voice dipped low.

She could tell that the wheels in Maureen's head had already gone into motion. "Tomorrow night?" she asked, not daring to raise her hope.

"Stay out of sight and do what is asked of you. I will try to locate Finn, and we'll take it from there."

"I'll do whatever you say," she said.

Maureen took her hand and squeezed it. "Good. I don't fancy seeing my head on a silver platter if this plan goes wrong."

"What will you tell Finn?"

"Everything." She left the room looking like a woman on a mission.

Long after her friend had left, Isidora remained glued to her spot by the window, thinking about her decision. There was no doubt that her parents would be hurt by her actions, but it was time for her to think for herself. Whatever plans they had for her, it didn't include Finn, and that thought alone resolved her.

Although her communication with him was limited to their feeding rendezvous, their unspoken feelings for each other had been communicated effectively. It was safe to assume that he'd understand and support her wishes.

If they could pull this off, she'd be stepping out of the walls of the mansion that had been her palatial jail as long as she could remember. Her endeavor wasn't going to be easy. She knew nothing of life outside the fortress she called home.

Isidora tore her gaze from the window upon hearing approaching footsteps. A soft rap on the door followed.

She dashed to the door. "Who is it?"

"It's Gentry. Your father wishes to see you."

She opened the door a fraction, not sure if it was a good idea to be subjected to her father's scrutiny at the moment. His mind-reading ability was no secret, although she had managed to shield most of her thoughts from him with success.

What if?

"Did he say what he wanted?" she asked, looking through the small gap at the tall guard who was standing outside.

Gentry regarded her with mild interest. "He didn't say. Should I tell him that you're indisposed at the moment?"

Why would he lie for me? "Thank you, Gentry," she said and closed the door.

It wasn't until the footsteps grew faint that she was able to release a sigh. All she needed was another twenty-four hours to complete her escape. Soon she'd taste the freedom that had been denied her all her life. If she could keep her nose clean and her thoughts clear until the next day, everything would be fine.

Zane surfaced from a troubled sleep. Or had he passed out? He couldn't remember. The last thing he recalled was Harrow reprimanding Cheryl for engaging him in the one-sided conversation that had ultimately led to them to this place—wherever they were.

"I—"

Cheryl didn't even let him finish. "Don't say anything. I did this for myself, not for you."

Zane tried to raise his head to get a glimpse of the woman who'd challenged the great Harrow. She was his keeper, but until when?

Until you die, you moron. He closed his eyes and breathed deep.

The muscles in his neck refused to do his bidding. His vision reached her mid-thigh, still garbed in the white slacks she'd worn since he first saw her. He swallowed against the dryness in his throat and marshaled his wits enough to speak.

"Che-ryl. I need . . . drink."

It took a lot from him to say it, and he felt more tired than ever afterward. The Dangeran fragments were sucking the life out of him—the slow, painful exit that he no doubt deserved.

The mattress dipped under her weight when she sat next to him. With his hands tied behind his back and his face down on the mattress, he couldn't do much but wait for her next move.

"I want you to die. You have it coming after you killed my friends. You know that? You deserve to die."

The catch in her voice alerted him to the upcoming waterworks. In the past, he'd hated tears as a sign of weakness, but at this most vulnerable time in his life, he wanted to cry with her. He wanted to weep for the people he'd loved and lost, and for this woman who was hurting because of his actions.

"Soon . . ." His throat tightened, and he coughed. Every slight movement caused him so much pain, imbedding the granules of Dangeran even deeper into his skin. He tried to bite his lips to keep from crying out. It wasn't enough that his body was taking a beating—his ego had to take a huge hit, too.

Cheryl didn't say anything.

After a few minutes, he felt the mattress rise when she got up. He listened for her movement. His eyes were swollen shut, and the mere effort of keeping them open expended too much energy.

"Get up," Cheryl ordered when she came back.

Zane raised his head only to slump back down. "I . . . can't." His voice even sounded pathetic to his own ears.

God, just let me die!

Without a word, she brought her arms around his armpits and hauled him up. The Dangeran particles burrowed deeper into his skin, and he shouted.

"I'm so sorry. I'm so sorry," Cheryl said with so much remorse in her voice that he ached to reassure her, but he couldn't get his mouth to work.

She didn't deserve to feel like she had done wrong. Feeling terrible for causing her undue guilt, Zane attempted to sit up on his own, just to end up where he'd started, flat on his face.

"I'm going to help you into a sitting position so you can drink." Cheryl's voice quavered.

Zane nodded in response. When she hoisted him up, he struggled to keep from howling in pain. Leaning in an awkward position against the headboard with bound hands behind him, he tried to watch her while she took the glass from the nightstand and placed it next to his lips.

He drank the water in greedy gulps, not stopping until it was gone. The drink eased the burning in his throat, and for the first time, he was able to swallow without the sandpaper texture in his mouth.

"Thank . . . you."

"Just because I gave you a drink doesn't mean we're fine and dandy. I still wish you were dead."

Zane nodded, ever so slowly. He understood. If he had the strength to lift his limbs, he'd shoot himself for her and end both their misery.

"Kill . . . me."

"I will not stain my hands with your blood. I won't give you the satisfaction of missing what Harrow has in store for you."

He was such a pussy. Or was his heart thawing? It had to be the effect of

Dangeran on him. It was clouding his mind, making him feel like he'd made a monumental mistake.

Yeah, sure. You'd be killing anyone in your path if you weren't tied up and grappling with extreme fatigue.

Was that right? Did his cruelty recognize no bounds? Would he kill these people after learning that their woes were the product of Goran's wicked machinations and his own stupidity?

"I'm . . . sorry," he said.

Cheryl's bitter laughter filled the room. "You know nothing about remorse. You're a monster. Killing you wouldn't give me any satisfaction." She continued to laugh until her voice grew hoarse and she was reduced to tears.

In spite of the arduous effort it took him to keep his eyes open, he watched Cheryl with a helplessness he hadn't felt before. Her moss-colored eyes were clouded and miserable. He longed to reach out and console her, but what good would it do? He had done the deed, and he was going to repay the debt with his life.

Cheryl's body sagged on the bed, and her cries became muffled.

Between the pounding ache in his head and the weight crushing his soul, he wished he were dead, too. Could he finally be developing a conscience?

"Why don't we continue this reunion where we can have some privacy?" Harrow said and downed his drink.

"I'm all for talking, my man." Cyrus chugged the remainder of his scotch and slammed the glass back on the counter, startling the rest of the company.

Tor chuckled and slapped him hard across the back. "I think you need a little lesson on being inconspicuous, unless you're dying for attention."

Cyrus snickered and shook his head apologetically. "I sometimes forget I'm not what I used to be."

"And what is that?"

"Human?" Cyrus stood up and straightened his shirt.

"As far as I can tell, you still are. You're just sporting a new set of fangs," Tor said.

Angus was already waiting for them outside next to Rohnert, who had grown quiet during the course of the night.

"So where to?" Harrow asked. "Any place we can talk and set this rebuilding shit back in motion?"

"You guys know where my place is, right?" Rohnert glanced left to right.

"Yeah. We met your buddy, Zo, there the night you went on your vacation." Tor chuckled.

Rohnert wasn't in the mood for teasing. All he wanted was to see Shelly.

"You guys can use that place until we find something suitable. I'll meet you there in a bit." He was ready to go.

"You're going to see Shelly?" Cyrus asked.

"Damn right, I am. I have to talk to her." This wasn't right. All his life, he'd never been compelled to explain himself to anyone—especially about females.

"I don't think it's a good idea, Rohn."

This added to Rohnert's aggravation. Since when had Cyrus become Shelly's appointed bodyguard? As far he was concerned, it was his responsibility to watch over the doctor.

Sure, but you left. That makes you a deserter, and you don't deserve her.

"I don't think I can bear another day." Rohnert took a deep breath. "I'll see you guys at the shack in a few hours." He left without saying another word.

He walked in brisk strides, blending with the foot traffic. It was about damn time he followed his heart. The nagging suspicion surfaced again. What if Shelly turned him away?

Rohnert reached the hospital and waited outside. Damn, it would've been nice to know her schedule unless he intended to wait out here until sunrise. Without giving it much thought, he crossed the street and walked around the building to the rear of the structure. The unloading area was deserted, and it was a perfect place to start the search. He glanced up and did a mental assessment before beginning the long climb up. With his Kalimetal dangling from his back, he scaled the walls, passing by unlit offices, empty operating rooms, and quiet wards.

All the while, Rohnert took in the voices drifting around him, picking out each one until Shelly's thoughts came across, loud and clear. Diagramming the layout of the hospital, he pinpointed her exact location. He turned around and made his descent. She was in the second floor employee lounge. And she had company.

His aggression flared up in an instant. From the small gap of the bathroom window, he saw her hunched over the sink. A man was rubbing her back.

No sir. No one touches his woman.

"Are you okay? What's going on? Are you catching the flu?" the man asked.

Shelly shook her head and retched. Damn. You'd better be a good baby right now, It.

Asshole better stop touching her if he wants his hands still . . . It? Did she just call the baby 'It'? Rohnert pounded the concrete outside in a sudden fit of rage.

Shelly whipped her head in the direction of the window, and he hurried to move away.

"Did you hear that?" she asked.

"It must be those stupid birds," the man, who was wearing scrubs similar to hers, answered.

Rohnert kept still and held his breath until the focus switched away from the sound he'd made. His body quivered from the new emotions that filled him. Sure, he was jealous. He should be holding her at this very moment, not some human interloper.

He had a good excuse if he elected to eradicate the bastard who had his hands on his woman. Yeah, and Shelly better quit calling their child *It*.

"If you need to take a day off, I can rearrange the schedule. You've just been back for a few days, and you're working yourself into the ground already."

"Don't start with me, Whitaker."

"I'm your boss . . . and a friend. You will listen to what I say."

Had Rohnert detected hesitation in the man's voice? Was there anything going on between these two he needed to know about? The answer came right away from the man himself. Shelly's boss, Dr. Rick Whitaker, chief of staff, was an admirer and still hoping.

Rohnert inched back to the window to see Shelly turning around to face

Rick. Her eyes, though glassy, showed defiance. "You may be my boss, but I know my body better. I'm fine. It might have been the sandwich from the vending machine."

The doctor seemed to value his head atop his shoulders and took a step back, his hands raised in surrender. "I'm just worried about you. Let me know if you change your mind."

"Fine." Shelly went to the paper towel dispenser and pulled out a couple sheets to wipe her hands, then her mouth.

Rick walked to the door, his hands inside his pockets, and then turned around. "Would you like to have a coffee after your shift?" he asked, looking hopeful.

Shelly's answer came fast. "Sorry. When seven rolls in, all I want to do is to crawl into bed. Rain check?"

Rick nodded.

Good boy. Go on your way and stay away. Rohnert took a deep breath and closed his eyes. Seven in the morning. Would there be a chance to talk to Shelly?

It was close to eight when she signed off on her last patient of the day. Shelly's back had been voicing its protest by the time she waddled out of the hospital. Hugging her jacket around her body, she walked the ten blocks back to her apartment.

Too bad. As much as she wanted to get home faster, her tired legs were uncooperative. The other pedestrians walked past her, cutting her off to get ahead. Shelly sighed and kept moving. She was hungry, but sleep sounded much more appealing than food. Besides, *It* hadn't been a happy camper last night. She wondered why. For the most part, her pregnancy had been tame compared to the stories she'd heard.

The scent of cocoa caught her nose the moment she hopped off the elevator. With the added sweet scent of freshly baked bread, her mouth started to water. She closed her eyes and savored the flavor in her head, wishing she had the strength to make herself a cup, but she was beat. The one thing that stood between her and her bed was the damn long hallway to her apartment door.

It came as a surprise to find the source of her bliss got stronger as she neared her apartment.

"Guys, I'm home," she called out and closed the door behind her. Her eyes darted to the table, and she gasped. On it was a carafe of something that looked hot and delicious, as well as a tray filled with pastries. She shed her jacket, dropped her backpack on the couch, and moved closer to the feast.

"Good morning, Dr. Anderson." Jones waved from the dining area.

From the big grin on his face, Shelly could tell he was in a very good mood. When she moved closer, she noticed omelets, sausages, and bacon. It reminded her of days at the facility when Darryl, Pritchard's personal chef, would prepare mouth-watering feasts for them. Even the presentation, from the little flower in a crystal vase, down to the doilies, was done with class and was reminiscent of Darryl's flair.

"What's going on here? Did you cook?" She took a chocolate croissant.

"Today's a good day." Jones joined her at the table.

She paused mid-chew and sniffed, hard. "Where's Rayce? Did we have a guest while I was away?" Maybe it was her pregnancy that made her sensitive to every single odor, but it was Jones' stupid smile that made her ask.

"Rayce is resting. He already ate. And yes, we had some guests tonight." He seemed happy, elated almost. Gone was the long face he'd been sporting since their unscheduled departure from the facility.

She raised an eyebrow. "Oh yeah? Who?"

Shelly had insisted that they not associate with anyone or let people into her apartment. She happened to like her privacy. Besides, those bastards from the Council might be combing the city to find them.

Okay, that was reaching. No one knew they worked for Pritchard. Their association had been a closely guarded secret. Her paranoia was just a byproduct of her need for control.

"Harrow called before he came here with Cyrus, Angus, and Tor. Can you believe it? They found us. And Harrow promised we'll be outta here and in a safe place within a week." Jones pushed his glasses up his nose and grinned.

"Wow. Really?" She continued chewing, unable to shake her feeling of melancholy. It was good news indeed, but she didn't feel the same excitement. Could it be that her freedom was about to come to an end?

"Yeah. Harrow wants us to sit tight while they're getting the last details ironed out. He asked me to tell you that he's grateful for all you've done for Rayce, Cyrus, and me."

Shelly smiled. Harrow was sweet like that. *Someone* could take lessons from him. At the errant thought, she smirked and took a long sip of cocoa.

Jones continued, seeming oblivious of her silence. "He'll send Firman and Angus here tomorrow night to pick up Rayce so he can check the wiring at the new place. Harrow said he will make sure that Rayce doesn't exert himself."

The vampire knew her well, and that made her smile again. So much for her stint at the hospital. It seemed like she was going to leave even before she'd received her first paycheck, but that wasn't the problem. This felt like the calm before a storm, even though she was safe in the company of her friends.

Shelly felt a sharp tug in her stomach. Her hand automatically moved to her belly and rested there. "I'm going to bed. Can you handle the cleanup here?"

"I can hoover down all these pastries if you don't stop me," Jones said, smiling.

Once Shelly had gotten in bed, her mind wouldn't stop churning. If she was being truthful, she was beginning to enjoy the freedom of breathing the air again, of being a part of the outside world. She'd liked the idea that she'd have the chance to give *It* a normal life.

Perhaps she needed to rethink her position. This might be a good time to reflect on whether she needed a change of pace. A new beginning.

In an attempt to shake the gloom that blanketed him, Rohnert sprinted back to his hideout. He was relieved to find his friends waiting for him but also somewhat annoyed that he wasn't going to get any time alone to sort out his thoughts.

Tor looked up the moment he walked in. "My man, why the long face?"

He shook his head to discourage any further probing, but Tor didn't heed his unspoken caution.

"Did you find Shelly?" He got up and had walked over to Rohnert, placing an arm around his shoulder.

The trouble with this vampire was that he didn't understand letting someone lick their wounds in peace. Rohnert broke away and sat on the cot. Everyone else was seated on the floor in a semi-circle. Harrow seemed withdrawn, a sign that the man had things on his mind, while Cyrus was hunched over a bunch of what appeared to be blueprints.

"I did." He wasn't eager to disclose what he'd seen and how he hadn't gotten a chance to talk to the doctor.

"Was she happy to see you? Tor continued to torment him.

"Tor, I think Rohnert is not interested in sharing the details with us. Lay off, will ya?" Harrow said. "Rohn, here's the draft of our new place. It's not too far from here. We're going to take Rayce to see it tonight."

Cyrus slid the bulky proposal over to him.

Rohnert did a quick inspection of the drawings and sighed. "So this is an abandoned warehouse?"

Harrow nodded. "We retained the dilapidated outside appearance, but the building has been gutted from the inside, making way for the creation of an underground dwelling."

"Sounds expensive to me."

"That's true, but this project is going to be similar to the place we have upstate. Subterranean complex with bulletproof windows, steel shutters, and a state-of-the-art alarm system. Name it, we have it."

Changing the subject, Rohnert asked the question that had nagged him since he found out about the breach at their facility. "How many of us are left?"

Harrow sighed. "Well, all of us here, the girls, then Firman, Cheryl, and a few more we haven't located since they were out on patrol the night of the attack."

Rohnert counted in his head. Less than fifteen souls. "How are you planning to proceed?"

"The workload will resume now that Cyrus is back, but with the changes . . ." Harrow coughed and glanced in Cyrus's direction. "I think we may need to bring in someone who does not have an aversion to sunlight."

So much bullshit around him. All these things were happening because of one man. If it hadn't been for Goran's decree to kill every diseased vampire and annihilate Kalimetal-carrying fighters, they wouldn't be in hiding. "Are we still looking for the infected ones?" Rohnert asked.

"That remains our primary goal, just the way Pritchard envisioned. If we can find extra manpower, though, we'd be better off. Right now, we're the only ones left to fight and patrol. We have the women to think about, and a child—well, it'll soon be . . ."

Damn it. Was this the world he planned to bring his child into? What a crock. Gail, Rohnert's child, they deserved something better, a safer place where violence and death wouldn't be a constant threat to their survival.

"I know a few people we can add to our little group. Has anyone been in contact with Zo or Gentry?"

Pirating employees was not something he made a habit of doing, but these were desperate times, and he was going to call in favors wherever he could.

"Gentry gave me his number, and Zo is with him," Tor said, already checking his cell phone. He dialed the number and handed the phone to Rohnert.

Nodding, he took the device and waited. After a few rings, the voicemail kicked in. "Gentry, this Rohnert. Call me when you get this message." He hung up.

"What about Cheryl?" Tor asked.

Harrow took a moment to answer, and Rohnert knew why. Was it a good idea to relay the truth to Cyrus about Zane's capture?

Rohnert glanced at him and gave a nod of encouragement.

"Cyrus, I think you have to know this. When the facility was attacked, I managed to capture Zane and—"

Cyrus was up on his feet in a flash. He pulled the Glock from his jacket. "Where is the motherfucker?"

Tor wrapped his arms around Cyrus, restraining the vampire in case he decided to run. Harrow jumped to his feet, removed his precious sunglasses, and tried to placate the new vampire.

"Cy, my man, calm down." Harrow placed his palm on Cyrus's shoulder and gave a gentle squeeze. "I did a little experiment on him, and the bastard is very much incapacitated."

"What experiment?" Cyrus's eyes brimmed with hatred.

"I embedded Dangeran bits into his skin. Just like I imagined it would be, the effect is debilitating. They put the bastard out of action."

Not mollified, Cyrus moved forward and pushed against Harrow, even though Tor tried to pull him back. "That's not good enough." Fury radiated from him.

"I kept him around until I found you." Harrow took a step back and assumed a defensive stance.

"Take me to him." Cyrus spat.

"Hold on, tiger. In case you hadn't noticed, the sun is up. Unless you fancy getting your ass grilled like a goddamned steak, I suggest you stay put until nighttime hits," Tor said, grunting with the effort of holding him back.

"C, listen . . . you'll get your chance later. Just hang tight for now." Harrow wiped his brows and shook his head.

Cyrus remained skeptical, but this body began to relax. "We will go the moment sundown hits." He shook off Tor as if he weighed nothing.

The raid was about to commence, and Hamilton was beside himself at the prospect of a massacre. Goran had groomed him to feel no remorse, to go for the kill and follow given orders without question. This was going to be a piece of cake.

After accomplishing a diligent study of the compound, he had determined that considerable losses were possible, but victory would be theirs. Upon Goran's strict order to use the newly created vampires, this endeavor was also certain to be messy.

They had settled about half a mile away from the mansion at a point overlooking the river. At half past eight, Hamilton gave the order, and the vampires rushed the compound, surrounding the entrance in the blink of an eye.

While he watched from afar, Hamilton wished he could be part of the fun. Every soldier lived for this day, and he had been ordered to miss the party. However, those orders had been given by a man who wasn't even around to know if he followed them.

With his mind made up, he dug his heels into the ground and decided to crash the party.

Isidora was awoken by a voice in her ear, followed by a whole lot of shaking. She peeled her eyes open and yawned.

"What? I don't want to wake up yet," she said and closed her eyes.

"Issy, get up." Maureen continued shaking her, half-dragging her out of bed.

"What's going on? What time is it?"

A loud boom sounded somewhere in the compound, making them both jump.

"Just do what I say. You need to trust me and stop asking so many questions. Wear this." Maureen shoved a pair of dark jeans, a black sweater, boots, and a wig at her.

"A wig?"

"Yes. Do it now!" Maureen ran to the window and gasped. "Hurry!"

Isidora did was she was told, slipping into the pants and sweater. Cries and the sound of guns firing nearby rang in her ears.

"Maureen, what's going on?" she asked while trying to fit the awkward black wig on her head.

Instead of answering, Maureen dropped to the floor next to her bed and pulled out a box. In a blur of movement, she yanked another wig from the container. It was a red one, the color of Isidora's hair. She began putting it on. Then Maureen removed her clothes and slipped into Isidora's discarded nightgown.

"Are you . . ."

Her friend gave her one fleeting glance and pulled her inside the walk-in closet. "You're going to go now, and you won't look back. Run as fast as you can once you clear the tunnel. I was able to send word to Finn to meet you. Follow me."

Maureen moved to the far side of the wall and removed one of the mirrors.

"What are you doing?" Isidora asked. Was there something they weren't telling her?

"Be quiet. The mansion is under attack. You have to get out of here." The other woman pulled on a latch to reveal a little door and tugged on her arm. "Go now, before it's too late."

"No! How about you? Papa and Mama? Everyone?" She began to take a step back, her eyes stinging with tears.

"You're more important. This is a part of the plan. Go." Maureen pushed her to the small opening. "Don't stop, keep going. Remember, take a right and after about fifty feet, there'll be some boulders, Finn will be there."

Sobbing and growing more scared with each passing second, Isidora wrapped her arms around Maureen. "Will I see you again?"

"Remember our good times together." Maureen choked back a sob and broke away from her embrace.

She nodded, hurried to the chute, and jumped into the unknown. Before she could look back, Maureen closed the secret exit, leaving the tube dark and muffling the noise from the mansion.

Isidora began crawling. Her forward movement was slow as she pulled her body with her elbows. Inch by inch, she progressed along the secret passage. The only sounds were her beating heart and her uncontrolled sobs. By the time she reached the other end of the sluice, she was out of breath and feeling claustrophobic. She found a round wheel and rotated it until a hatch opened.

She spilled out of the opening and ended on the muddy ground. Despite feeling shaky, she was able to close the door after several tries. Isidora turned around and tried to orient herself in the darkness. She counted in her head and took a quick right, then broke out in a dead run. Minutes later, she spotted the boulder that Maureen had mentioned and found two men in dark robes standing close to it. With their backs turned to her, they didn't sense her arrival, which gave her a chance to hide behind a tree.

"Are you sure we can kill this one?" one of the men asked.

"Yeah. Hamilton ordered us to kill any strays. We're going to start with him." The other one sounded impatient, pointing his weapon to another person.

Isidora peeked from her hiding place just in time to see a third vampire she hadn't noticed before. Even in the darkness, she recognized the male's identity—Finn.

Her mind began to race. What could she do? Unarmed but determined, she emerged from her hiding spot.

"Hey, boys. I'm lost here. Can you show me the way to the road?" she said in a syrupy voice. In spite of her trembling knees, she tried to sway her hips in what she thought would catch the men's attention.

All heads whipped up to look at her. Caught in surprise, the two vampires bared their fangs and sneered.

"Look, we have dinner, too." One of the men grinned.

In one quick movement, Finn kicked at the vampire closest to him. The sudden attack bought him time to grab the sword and strike the other on the head. Isidora rushed to help, but Finn had it covered by the time she got close.

He jumped up to avoid a dagger flying his way and swung at the other vampire's torso, catching him with a clean sweep across the shoulder. In a matter of seconds, the crackling and popping signaled the disintegration process. Isidora dared not move until the fireworks ended, then she rushed into Finn's open arms.

Her heart pounded hard against her chest, making her dizzy.

"I got here just in time." She sobbed against his chest.

"Oh, baby. I'm glad you're safe." Finn kissed the top of her head, holding her tight.

In the haze of her confusion and tears, her knees gave out, but Finn kept her upright. His familiar scent filled her with comfort, and they stood in the middle of the forest, holding each other.

"Should we go back?" she asked after she'd regained the semblance of control.

"Word got to me that we should stay far away from there."

"Where should we go?"

"I was given a name of a person who could help us," Finn said. Then with a swift movement, he swept her off her feet and carried her deep into the forest.

Rohnert felt like a taut coil ready to spring. Enduring a ten-hour period cooped up with five other males had been a challenge. Although the banter had been light, it was difficult to keep his head straight. Shelly was all he could think of.

He was anxious and ready to go by the time darkness arrived. He was practically dragging Firman and Angus out of the building so he could get to Shelly. He could've gone by himself, but having the other men with him could provide a buffer in case the doctor threw a fit.

His plan was to arrive as a member of Rayce's escort. He wanted to case her apartment, check its safety and defenses should any unwanted visitor show up on her doorstep. The thought of danger to her made him grit his teeth. If he had a choice, he'd have Shelly safe in the company of his friends, therefore guaranteeing the wellbeing of their unborn child as well.

He could sense his child. The connection between them grew stronger with each passing day. Aside from this association, he had his mind dead set on making Shelly understand how wrong he'd been to leave in the first place.

Breathing deep, he set the pace. Firman kept up with him with very little effort. Since humans weren't able to keep up with their running speed,

Angus drove one of the bulletproof cars that hadn't been trashed in the latest attack. As usual, the busy streets made it difficult to navigate through the maze of bodies, and Rohnert's patience was wearing thin by the time they reached Shelly's apartment.

Firman took the lead the moment they stepped out the elevator, since they'd agreed Rohnert should fade into the background at first. After several knocks, Jones answered the door, his face breaking out into a wide grin.

"Welcome, my friends," he said and opened the door wider to let them in.

"Is Rayce ready?" Firman asked, looking around.

"I heard the doorbell. Who is . . .?" Shelly walked into the living room, her hair wrapped in a towel like a turban, smelling like sweet shampoo. She stopped in her tracks upon spotting Rohnert standing behind Firman. It was difficult to read her, since she schooled her expression to hide her emotions.

"What are you doing here?"

"I wanted to say hello to you and our child," Rohnert said. Although he had practiced what to say, the vision of Shelly made him forget his rehearsed introduction.

She turned around to rush back to her bedroom. Rohnert caught up with her and held her by the elbow, but she shook off his grasp and slipped inside. He shoved his foot in the door to keep it from closing.

"Not so fast, Dr. Anderson. We need to talk." Another blunder. He should've used her first name.

"We have nothing to talk about, Rohnert." Shelly advanced into the room, allowing him to follow her inside. He closed the door behind him.

The intonation in her voice made it quite clear that she was angry, but its effect made Rohnert more aware of her presence and his need to hold her.

"I made a big mistake for leaving the way I did, and I want—"

Shelly turned around, her eyes flashing with rage. Rohnert had been prepared for this. To be quite frank, he would rather deal with her fury than her silence.

"You don't deserve my time or to have *It* . . . my baby grow up knowing you."

"Shelly, don't you dare call our child *It*. That baby is not a thing, and he or she was created by two people who wanted each other."

Shelly snorted and shook her head. "It was only me who wanted you. As I recall, you made it clear you wanted nothing to do with me." She threw her hands up in the air in a display of frustration. "You didn't spare my feelings back then—don't you dare start now."

Rohnert moved closer, wanting to establish a connection, but Shelly's rigid body made him think twice. "If you can take a moment to listen to my explanation, you'll understand the motives behind my actions."

She spun around and walked up to him, close enough to let him smell her sweet breath and the fresh scent of her soap. He could feel her body humming with fury. It took a tremendous amount of restraint to keep from reaching out to touch her.

"You want me to take the time to listen to your lies? Oh, cut the crap, Rohnert. Our child doesn't have to know that *Its* father is full of shit."

Abandoning caution, Rohnert snaked his hand around the small of her back and pulled her closer. Before he could listen to the voice of reason, he seized her mouth and claimed her in a long and punishing kiss.

Shelly resisted at first, pounding her fist on his shoulder and trying to create some space between them. Instead of letting her go, he deepened his kiss, making sure she felt his body's response to her proximity. Shelly's resistance weakened after a few moments, and her hands relaxed at her sides. Although she didn't kiss him back, she swayed under the power of his closeness.

Rohnert let his tongue roam inside her mouth, seeking a reaction, any sort of response, but Shelly remained impassive. At long last, he gave up, but he didn't let go, not wanting to lose their connection.

"If you're done proving how much you want me, you can close the door on your way out," she said.

Rohnert's mind-reading gift came in handy here. When Shelly let her defenses down, he caught a sliver of her real feelings, but they weren't what he'd expected at all. This enraged him, and for the first time, he lost his cool.

"You're not going out tonight."

"You're not my father. And quit reading my mind."

He wondered who had given her the 411 on his ability, but it was beside the point. The woman wasn't going anywhere.

"It's not safe for you to be out there."

"Oh c'mon. Don't try that bullcrap on me." Shelly planted her palms on his chest and pushed.

He kept his hold on her, refusing to let go. "Listen to me. You're carrying my child, and it's in his best interest that you not get yourself killed by being stubborn."

Shelly turned her face away. "You're not going to tell me what I can or can't do. Stay away from me, and let me live my life the way I see fit." With another hard push, she broke free from him.

"You're not listening to reason."

"I'm done listening. Now, if you'll excuse me, I have somewhere to be." She walked to the door, opened it, and waited.

Rohnert walked out the door, conceding this time but by no means accepting defeat. Shelly slammed the door after him.

He returned to the living room to find Firman, Angus, Jones, and Rayce deep in conversation. They all looked up at him, and it was obvious that they were aware of his dilemma. No one said anything, but from their furtive glances, he sensed their pity.

"You got what I need?" he asked Rayce.

Rayce stood up with difficulty, clutching on to his stomach and flinching "Yes, here it is." He produced a set of keys and handed it to him.

Rohnert gave him a pat on the back. "Thanks. I'm glad you survived your wounds."

"I'm glad Shelly didn't give up on me. Don't let her—"

Rohnert raised his hand to stop him. He knew what the human was about to say, and by the grace of the gods, he wasn't going to let Shelly give up on him.

Firman broke the awkward silence that descended upon them. "Shall we?"

"Before I forget, I kept busy while I was recuperating and got a few cell phones activated with Jones and Cy's help." Rayce produced identical cell phones and handed them out. "Each one of us is assigned a symbol for speed dial. Memorize them and delete the note."

"Sounds good." Firman saluted. "Now, do you want to me to carry you to the car?"

Rayce chuckled. "If you don't mind slow, I'll rather keep my ego intact."

"After you." Firman shot Angus a knowing look, and the human preceded them to the door. "Are you joining us?" He turned to Rohnert.

"Tell Harrow I'll catch up later. Call if anything comes up."

They all left the apartment, leaving Jones behind. The scientist was thinking what a pathetic being Rohnert was. He clenched his jaw, agreeing with the human.

With his idea of a happy reunion thwarted for the time being, he was left to lurk in the shadows, unwilling to let Shelly go out by herself. He would have to guard her from afar.

After a few minutes, she emerged from the building. Shelly glanced around, but if she sensed his presence, she gave no indication. She took the same route that took her to work, but she stopped in front of a café a few blocks before reaching the hospital.

She made a beeline for the entrance, which left Rohnert to figure out how to maintain his surveillance. In this type of establishment, people were expected to remove their coats while dining. If he did this, the enumerable weapons he was packing would be revealed. Keeping tabs on her up close was out of the question.

Rohnert parked himself across the café and resorted to listening from his vantage point. It was difficult to hear to everyone's ramblings while separating out Shelly's and the doctor's thoughts. It didn't make it easier to learn that this human had been in love with Shelly for a long time, and the one thing that kept him at arm's length was her refusal to return his affection.

Bonus points for Shelly.

"Hey, I'm glad you called me," Rick said.

"I wanted to tell you something."

Judging from the echo of their voices, they had settled into a cozy spot.

Rohnert hated the elation in the male's voice over being sought out. "Would you like to eat first?"

"I'm fine. I can't keep anything down."

"Is it the flu?" Concern laced Rick's tone.

"It's not the flu. Actually, there is something I wanted to ask you."

"I'm all ears."

"I'm pregnant."

Rick's tone soured. "Who's the father?"

"It's not important. I'm raising this child alone."

"The hell you are," Rohnert muttered.

It took Rick a considerable time before he could gather his thoughts together. When he spoke, he sounded defeated. "What can I do for you?"

"This is a delicate matter, and I can't see another doctor without being asked too many questions. I need your help to deliver this baby."

"What?"

"I . . ."

How can I tell him that the father is not your garden variety human? Damn it!

Shelly's unspoken concern was understandable, but she wouldn't have to worry about this if she would allow him to help. Rohnert sighed. All he had to do was summon the great Lukan. The shaman had been the redeemer for every pregnant woman of their race, although Shelly was human, and that made their situation a bit tricky.

"What, Shelly?" Rick asked, pulling Rohnert from his ruminations.

"This is not your regular pregnancy. There might be some complications. I don't know how to explain. I want this baby safely delivered, and you're the only one I can trust."

The way Shelly rushed through her explanation made Rohnert pause. He hadn't given the pregnancy much thought. A human mother giving birth to a vampire child wasn't something he'd come across before. Was it even possible?

"I'm not an obstetrician, Shelly. It would be unethical."

"I wouldn't ask you if I had any other option." Shelly sounded almost desperate.

Isn't this my lucky day? The great Rohnert at the end of my blade.

Rohnert swung just in time to avoid being hacked by a deadly blow to the head. He jumped away while unsheathing his Kalimetal, sizing up his attacker. Two vampires fell upon him. One he recognized, and the other was one of those mongrels Goran had created.

"Rubius," he said to the one he knew. "I never thought the day would come when you would turn against me."

"The prize is too high for me to ignore," Rubius answered.

The other vampire fired his gun, narrowly missing Rohnert's shoulder. Rohnert's reaction was swift. He lunged, throwing a star at the newbie before striking him in the sternum. The impact threw the younger vampire several feet away.

Rubius reacted faster and swung at him. Rohnert deflected the hit with his Kalimetal, and they parried. This type of situation was bad, considering they'd attracted a few onlookers. With the disintegration process happening under their noses, inevitable questions would be asked by the witnesses.

"Didn't I teach you to keep conflicts away from human eyes?"

"Special circumstances." Rubius took another swing at his torso, which Rohnert blocked.

Damage control came with a price. Rohnert wasn't going to gamble with the chance of attracting more bystanders. Moving at a distorted speed, he crisscrossed his Kalimetal, aiming to confuse his former student. He landed a swift blow to the head and finished him off by slicing through his right shoulder down to his hip.

With the fireworks crackling, Rohnert turned and performed an efficient sweep of every witness. He chanted ancient words while erasing the memories of what they'd just seen. With a snap of his fingers, the unsuspecting humans were brought back to the present, and any recollection of what they'd witnessed cleared away.

As if nothing had happened, Rohnert wiped the filth from his blade and sheathed his weapon before resuming his reconnaissance mission.

All in a night's work.

Zane awoke to the sound of his moaning. Day four of the excruciating punishment he so deserved. He forced his weak eyes to open and took time to focus. When he did, he found Cheryl sleeping next to him. Exhaustion marred her features, and her mouth was drawn into a straight line. Even in her sleep, the horror she'd experienced was reflected by her tight fetal position. Her arms hugged her body, as if she were holding herself together.

The woman deserved better. He didn't know her by any means, but she had managed to touch his black soul with her accusations. Her words had burned him, and for the first me, he felt like a waste—a poor excuse for a living, breathing creature.

Another searing pain caused by the Dangeran blasted through his spine, making him groan. Zane shivered with cold, even though the windows were shut. He moved his body a fraction, inching closer to Cheryl for warmth, and he discovered in the process that his hands were no longer bound. She had removed the bindings. Who else would've done it?

Instead of running away the moment he learned he was free, he mustered enough strength to wrap his arms around her, watching Cheryl shudder in her sleep. His body temperature must be dipping lower. Soon, shock would make its way into his system.

Moving at a slow pace, he used his short fingernails to pick out some of the Dangeran bits lodged in his skin. Wherever he could reach, he took them out, feeling instant gratification as each piece was removed. After a long time had passed and he'd extracted as much as he could, he was able to settle into a more comfortable position.

With his body heat regulating, he felt some of his strength return. It wasn't enough for him to function at his normal capacity, but it would be enough to flee. The thought of leaving Cheryl made him flinch, but he'd die if ever Harrow or the others came back for him. What good would his being dead do him or her?

Cheryl shuddered once again. Zane got out of bed and staggered to the mirrored closet. He glanced at his reflection and realized for the first time that the Dangeran had created lesions all over his body. Even with the removal of the hard metal from his skin, the damage would remain. It was a small price to pay for the havoc he'd created. Sliding the closet door open, he grabbed a blanket and brought it back to the bed. With caution, he spread it over Cheryl.

Zane wobbled to the nearby desk and found paper and a pen. Hopefully, the sleeping angel would find it in her heart to forgive him. He wrote his apology, placed it in her pocket, and departed.

Shirtless, barefoot, and barely able to walk without stumbling, he made it to the back exit without encountering anyone. His mind worked to concoct a plan, but first he needed to find safety. He decided against returning to his penthouse, since it was a place his grandpapa knew. The single place he would be safe was the townhouse where he'd held Cyrus captive. How ironic. The place he had used to torture the human was now where his tortured soul would seek solace. It was amazing how fate had a way of turning the tables. He was now the hunted.

Walking the streets in his condition was not the smartest thing to do, but under the circumstances, he was better off in the company of humans. The creatures he'd considered inferior were now his saving grace.

He turned just in time to see a car approaching, and vehicle stopped on the side of the road next to him.

"What's wrong?" the driver asked after rolling down his window.

"I was robbed at gunpoint. I need a ride back to my apartment."

"Get in." The locks disengaged. "Where do you need to be dropped off?"

Zane slid into the warmth of the passenger seat and closed his eyes. He recited the address. Next thing he knew, he was in front of his townhouse.

"You should call the cops," the man suggested. "If you need anything, here's my card. Give me a call." He handed Zane a business card.

Stunned at the man's kindness, he opened the passenger door and got out with care. The remaining Dangeran still imbedded in his skin made it difficult to move, but at least he was somewhat mobile.

"Thank you very much for your help." He glanced at the card. "If there's anything I can do to return the favor, you know where to find me."

The man tipped his head and sped away. He lumbered his way toward the front door, and the doorman rushed to his aid.

"Mr. Drew, what happened to you?"

"I lost my keys, Abe. Can you let me in, please?"

What a shocker. He'd been saying thank you and please as if the words were familiar to him, but he hadn't uttered them before. This whole experience was goddamn turnabout. Abe supported Zane's weight by sliding his arm under his shoulder. "No problem, sir."

They made it to his townhouse, and before Abe left, he asked, "Is there anything else you need? Do you want to order take-out?"

"I'm fine. Thank you very much."

Alone, Zane stumbled to the sofa. Before he passed out, his mind reflected on two names—Cheryl and Goran. The latter left a bitter taste in his mouth and a hatred so deep, it turned his heart to ice.

Goran decided to take an evening stroll, away from the maddening silence of headquarters. Hamilton was leading the army, and Goran was left bored and antsy. Stepping out of the walled box sounded appealing. This was also the perfect opportunity to pay his dear grandchild a visit. Zane had ignored his calls for several days.

He sped through the fringes of darkness, away from the awareness of humans, until he reached the expensive penthouse on Fifth Avenue. As usual, he opted to scale the high-rise instead of taking the stairs.

When he reached the correct floor, the sliding door from the balcony wouldn't budge. What a shame. He took another route—this time, through the open bedroom window. Upon inspection, he found the place hadn't been slept in for days. Zane's scent was stale. Goran took his time to check the dwelling for any hint to the boy's whereabouts. He moved from the bedroom and out to the living room, but the place was clean. There were no clues to lead him anywhere or tell him what Zane had been up to as of late.

He caught a glimpse of a laptop on the kitchen table. Technology was a tricky bastard. Aside from the usual operations with which he was familiar, the rest gave him headaches. Even if he wanted to snoop for contents, his limited knowledge wouldn't get him far and just might get him into trouble.

Zane was the spitting image of his father, right down to the red hair. Even their expression and responses were alike. Demetrius had been belligerent, often questioning his father's motives. Though he would follow orders, his driving force was self-gain. What a family they made.

Returning to the balcony empty-handed, Goran leapt off the ledge and plummeted to the busy street. The wind brushing across his face was a welcome change. With his long hair fanning back like a cape, he tucked his legs, spinning with the speed of his momentum until he reached the busy street, which was still littered with hapless humans. He broke into a jog, phantom-like in his dark coat, but stopped when something caught his eye. A television in a shop window was flashing breaking news, and he moved closer to watch the report.

Well, well. It seemed that his favorite vampire had been busy—and careless. The homemade clip showed Rohnert battling with one of the elite guards. It could have passed for a normal street scuffle if the other man hadn't disintegrated in the end. All caught on camera. Since Rohnert was gifted with the ability to erase memories, the person behind the camera must've escaped his notice. How convenient for Goran.

He moved to another television flashing the same bit, and Goran studied the background for clues. The setting was telling. That hospital was not too far from where he was, so all he needed was to do a little snooping on his own.

Goran had sent Hamilton to secure his future bride, but he also needed to eradicate the one person who posed a challenge to his reign. Feeling like he'd just won the lottery, Goran decided to swing by the hospital to check. What could be there that Rohnert wanted? It was unlike him to be sloppy.

He was calculating, smart, and prudent. It didn't add up at all. However, his mistake gave Goran information he could use against him.

Exhilaration brought a spring to his steps while he made his way across the city to the medical center. Careful not to be detected, Goran shut his thoughts and cased the environs from the shadows. He rounded the building to look for anything that would give Rohnert's goal away.

Opting against spying any further, he knew what he'd be doing in his spare time. Rohnert would be back, and Goran would be, too. It would be his personal task and would produce successful results. The possibility of finding out more about the dealings of the elusive vampire made up for the wasted trip.

Hamilton reached the compound just as the butchery began. He was focused on one goal alone. With stealthy movements, he bypassed the clashes around him, noting several familiar faces, Gentry and Alonzo among them. This would make Goran happy and would win him the highest favor. His group of bandit vampires was reckless but hungry, and they kept everyone busy, leaving Hamilton to search for his master's coveted prize.

He entered the mansion, blowing past the ashes of fallen vampires, and went from room to room, killing anyone who didn't fit the description. It was easy until he reached the last room on the second floor.

With care, he opened the door and aimed his gun. He advanced into the dark room to find a lone soul at the balcony, a silent witness to the bloodshed around them. He wasn't into redheads like his master, but the sight of the red tresses falling behind the woman's back sent a prickle through his body.

"Don't move. Drop that dagger if you want to live to see another day."

The woman turned around while her grip on the dagger loosened, and it hit the floor with a thud. "What do you want?" she asked.

Beautiful was the first thought that came to mind. "You will come with me without a fight, and all of this will end now," he said, moving toward her.

Her mouth quivered, and tears made their way down her porcelain cheeks. His master knew how to pick them. In one swift movement,

Hamilton used the butt of his gun rendering the woman unconscious.

It wasn't his most glorious moment, treating a woman with such savagery, but it was the most effective way to get her out of the compound. Resistance wasn't an option, and this was one way he could transport her without causing unwanted commotion.

Cyrus and Harrow reached the motel where Cheryl had checked-in with Zane. If it hadn't been for Harrow, Cyrus would've torn down the door off its hinges. Armed with better toys this time, he was primed to fight, and his thirst for vengeance had clouded his better judgment.

Several knocks produced no result. His nerves were shot, and his patience was nearing its last thread. "What if something happened?"

"How about chilling, my man?" Harrow slipped the card key through the slot.

"Why didn't you use it in the first place?"

"Because I believe in privacy."

Cyrus hissed. What a perfect time for the vampire to acquire scruples. With a soft click, the latch released, and Harrow pushed the door open. Cyrus rushed past his friend.

They found the room dark. Cheryl was lying on the middle of the bed, alone.

"What the fuck?" Cyrus's voice boomed.

Startled, she bolted upright. She glanced around, and surprise crossed her face.

Harrow rushed to her side, placing a gentle hand on her shoulder. "Cheryl, where is Zane?"

The human shrank back, and terror spread across her face. "I . . . don't know. I must've fallen asleep."

Cyrus let out a roar that shook the room and rattled the windows. "What do you mean you don't know?" His new fangs sharpened and throbbed, something he couldn't control.

Fine, he was acting like a lunatic, forgetting his manners in front of a lady. The thirst in the back of his throat was overriding his better sense. Regardless, revenge had been within his grasp, and now what?

"I fell asleep. I don't know what happened." From the look on her face, it was hard to doubt her conviction. Cyrus was almost certain she wasn't lying.

"Did you talk to him at all?" Harrow asked, inching away from the frightened woman.

Cheryl nodded before she ended up sobbing. She took one look at Cyrus and covered her face. Was it from fear? He'd never know, and frankly he didn't care. Harrow took one look at him and shook his head.

Cyrus walked away, fighting to control the wrath that consumed him. He glanced through the balcony door and tamped down on his emotions. This vampire thing would take some getting used to. He considered himself a reasonable guy, but this was beyond his ability to suppress. The need for revenge was too strong—he could almost taste it.

"I did most of the talking. He spoke a little, but it was just to apologize."

"The motherfucker doesn't understand the first thing about remorse. He is beyond redemption."

"I tied him up really well. How did he get away?" Harrow asked.

Cheryl shook her head. "I don't know." Her voice barely audible.

Something was off, but Cyrus couldn't put his finger on it. "Has he got you fooled?"

A pained expression crossed her face. "I'm so sorry."

Cyrus took a deep breath and bit his tongue before he slung an angry retort at the frightened woman. This, after all, was beyond her responsibility. If they weren't shorthanded, someone would've been assigned to Zane. He summoned his energy in order to project calm despite the deluge of violence within him that was aching for release.

"Cheryl, I'm sorry. I didn't mean to take this out on you."

Harrow whispered calming words meant to put the nurse's mind at rest. "You did what I asked of you. Don't worry about it. We'll catch him one of these days."

Frustration made Cyrus pace the room. "What now?" he asked.

"We're going to take Cheryl over to Shelly while we wait for the completion of our new hideout." Harrow paused. "Are you still interested in working for us, Cheryl? I will understand if this is too much for you. You're free to go."

She nodded and raised her head. "I want to continue to work for you, if you still want to have me around." Uncertainty laced her tone.

Yeah. They were all staying because they had jobs to do. Doubt crept into Cyrus's psyche. He made a vow to Pritchard to see this whole project come into fruition, but the call for vengeance was much too strong. As a man of his words, he would honor his oath and let go of his agenda.

For now.

Shelly tossed and turned that night, but sleep wouldn't come. After several minutes, she kicked the cover and got up. In the darkened apartment, she made her way toward the kitchen and filled a glass with water.

Sitting in the dark, she couldn't help but replay the whole conversation with Rohnert. The vampire had the gall to ask her to listen to him. What had he been thinking? Did she have *stupid* written across her forehead?

She sighed and took a big gulp of water. Hunger gnawed at her, but she was afraid to eat anything solid. Throwing up wasn't appealing at all. However, the little one needed something more nourishing than the bananas she'd been eating. Besides, she had been salivating over the strawberry milkshake from the café at the corner. She glanced at the luminous time on the microwave.

It wasn't too late, and the café was open twenty-four-seven. She could make a quick trip. She hurried back into her bedroom, slipped into comfortable sweat pants and a matching top, and grabbed her wallet.

Since Jones had fallen back into a normal sleep pattern, the house was quiet. Rayce was still out with the rest of Harrow's crew. Shelly snorted, hating the way Rohnert's image crossed her mind.

When she opened the door, she almost stepped on the item sitting in the hall. It was the very thing she'd wanted—a strawberry milkshake. Glancing left to right, she listened for any noise, but there was just silence. It took a tremendous amount of restraint to keep herself from hurling the offering across the hallway, but it saved her the trouble of making the trip. And why waste a good milkshake?

She picked up the drink. Closing the door behind her, she muttered, "Don't even think for one minute that this means anything."

Returning to her bedroom, she laid the tall cup on her nightstand and stripped out of her clothes, leaving on her rather large underwear. Her belly had grown bigger in the course of few days, and *It* seemed content. She recalled an intense response from her unborn child in its father's presence. Had they been bonding? Was that how it worked?

The thought should've warmed her heart, but her displeasure with the sperm donor strengthened her resistance.

In the comfort of her bed, she downed the remaining milkshake. Satisfied, she carried out her bedtime ritual and decided she was ready for bed.

Once sleep had claimed her, one dream after another plagued her. Shelly woke several times during the course of the night. At six o'clock, she gave up, donned her robe, crossed the hallway, and knocked on Jones' door.

"Jones, I need to talk to you," she said.

He met her in the living room, his hair disheveled and his eyeglasses missing. "Shelly, what's on your mind?" He settled on the far end of the couch.

This meeting was not the first. During their first week cooped together in her tiny apartment, she had called on him to calm her fears with words of wisdom derived from his countless hours of research on vampires. She tucked her legs underneath her and got comfortable. Although the temperature in the apartment was set at sixty-eight, she felt a chill creeping up her body. She hugged her robe closer.

"You spent hours talking to . . ." She couldn't even bring herself to say his name. Shelly took a deep breath and tried again. "You had several talks with him in the past. Did he ever mention anything about being able to communicate other than speaking?"

Her inquiry was vague, but she had no idea how to form the question. The idea was as ludicrous as her whole situation.

Jones hunched forward and rested his elbows on his knees. "You mean talking to humans in their sleep?"

Bingo! "Yes," she said.

"I'm not at liberty to disclose the details of our conversation—"

"Don't hand me that bullshit. Just give it to me straight." So much for niceties. She was not going to be thwarted by a confidentiality clause—not when she was being manipulated during her sleeping hours.

"Will you let me finish?" Jones huffed.

Shelly nodded, biting her tongue.

"In light of your present situation and your involvement with Rohnert, I'll tell you what I know. One of Rohnert's talents is being able to communicate with people in their sleep. Because of the invasive nature of the ability, he has been reluctant to use it. He said that the few times he did, it landed him in trouble. Why do you ask?"

She sneered at the revelation. So the great Rohnert wasn't impervious to temptation. "I think he used his power on me."

"Why would you say so? Do you remember any of it?" Jones scratched his head, but the gleam in his eyes reflected his growing excitement.

"I don't remember any detail in particular, but the sustained dreams, their vividness, and their nature raised my suspicions." Not to mention the wet dreams she'd had in the past, which she had no intention of discussing with the scientist, even if it could prove useful as part of his research. It was her dirty secret to keep.

"I'm not going to jump in and say what's immoral or what's not. I suggest you square it with Rohnert. His motives might be self-serving right now, but I believe the man relies on his conscience. I found this out about him. He never acts on impulse alone, no matter how dire the situation might be. If Harrow is the Last Boy Scout, Rohnert is the Sir Galahad of vampires."

Shelly rolled her eyes. Rohnert seemed to have snagged a new fan to add to his list of followers.

"I don't know about that, but I'll give him the benefit of the doubt. If you ever come in contact with him, just relate my exact sentiments to our *friend.* He needs to butt out of my head and out of my life. He impregnated me, but that doesn't give him the right to invade my subconscious."

"Ouch." Jones flinched, and then nodded. "You know I still need Rohnert to complete my research. Whether you like it or not, we need all the information he can give us. He's not your regular vampire, and who knows what this pregnancy will entail. I think it's wise to keep him around, even if it's at arm's length."

"What I think is that you should keep your research going and let me decide what's right for my sanity," she retorted. Okay, that was uncalled for. Jones didn't deserve her hostility. "I'm sorry. That was out of line."

Jones didn't appear offended at all. He gave her a sheepish grin. "No worries. It's that hormonal imbalance speaking on your behalf."

"Go to hell, doctor!"

"Right after you, Dr. Anderson." Jones laughed.

Rohnert had barely left the milkshake on her doorstep when Shelly opened the door to her apartment. He hid in the stairwell by the emergency exit and waited. With her thoughts guiding him, he was able to stay one step ahead of her.

Sure, he was using his ability for his own gain, but at this point, what else could he do? She refused to listen to him and abhorred being in the same room with him.

Listening to her inner ramblings gave him a glimpse of what she thought about, including him. He also found her more endearing and less threatening, the more he got to know her. Too bad it wasn't on a personal level. It would have been nice if they were talking face-to-face and deciding what the future held for them.

This planning shit wasn't his style. He hadn't been able to find the right woman, and Marania had called him picky. Rohnert wasn't wired the same way as the others. He'd never been interested in a lay in the hay, until Shelly had come along. Now, he was screwed.

He waited close enough to hear her mind. When sleep beckoned her, he took the opportunity to beseech her subconscious for answers. As much as he wanted to keep his visits chaste, the doctor, with her beguiling lips, smart mouth, and enchanting face, always managed to snatch away his resolve. It didn't help that she had curves that his hands begged to trace.

Rohnert swore that he had no business being with a woman who wouldn't be an acceptable mate by vampire standards. However, a clandestine affair wasn't his style. Hopping on the solo saddle suited him just fine, until she'd gotten pregnant with his son. Everything had changed from that moment on.

True, it sounded selfish for him to come back for that reason alone. He couldn't blame Shelly for thinking that his sole focus was their unborn child. In reality, he doubted he could've stayed away from her much longer. The thought made him shudder. This was all he'd ever wanted, but he faced the impossible task of convincing the woman to take him back. The need to take care of her and protect her had been so strong that most days he didn't know what to do with himself.

While the Council's edict didn't forbid taking a human woman as a vessel, they weren't seen as equals. As a pureblooded male vampire, he was obligated to breed babies and propagate their race.

Tonight, he took comfort in holding Shelly and in learning her real feelings for him, even if it was just in her sleep. Damn him for being weak. If she hadn't inadvertently expressed her true sentiments in her dream, she would've been considered untouchable in his book. As it was, he was a bastard for not keeping his hands off the woman he loved. He couldn't deny the impulse to hold her or even stroke her hair in her sleep.

He left Shelly's apartment just as she stirred and bolted upright. His situation must change soon. Their facility would be ready in a few days— just a few goddamn days before he could snag her from her new routine and put her under his protection. This stalker shit was beginning to get old. He had started the countdown until Shelly could be back safe in his arms, along with their child.

In the waning hours of the early morning, darkness was giving way to the light, Rohnert decided to visit an important person he hadn't seen in years. As much as he wanted to continue to stay uninvolved, the changes in the Council's direction were too drastic to be ignored.

He took out his cell phone and punched in Harrow's designated code. The vampire answered on the first ring. In the background, Rohnert could hear Jordan and Gail's voices, and his chest tightened. He could have the same thing, if only.

"Hey, I have some people I want to see. I won't make it back until nightfall. Holler if you need anything."

"Sure, my man. Anything else?" Harrow's voice sounded contented, no doubt because of the people that surrounded him.

Don't go there. Don't you dare go there, Rohnert told himself.

"I know we're a little low on manpower, but can you assign Angus to Shelly's apartment as a favor to me?" That was a tall order, but his paranoia wouldn't let him rest until he found someone to watch over her in his absence.

Harrow chuckled but didn't press for further explanation. "You know Shelly's too smart. She'll notice if we assign someone to her."

The guy had a point. Rohnert racked his brain for an excuse. "Why don't you tell her that Angus can't get along with one of the vampires, and you'd hate to have his blood on your hands?" That sounded convincing enough.

"Rohnert, I never thought I'd see this day."

"Zip it, Gates."

Instead of proceeding to their temporary meeting place as usual, Rohnert's unplanned detour led him to Randolph's doorstep. The warm reception of the Council elder told him that he'd made the right decision in seeking his counsel.

Upon hanging up the phone with Rohnert, Harrow couldn't help but grin. Jordan caught it right away.

"What are you smiling about?" Soft hands snuck around him from behind.

"Our stud muffin has got it bad," he said, turning around and taking her in his arms. He pushed her back against wall and pressed his body close.

She smiled and planted a sweet kiss on his lips. "I knew it was only a matter of time before he caught the bug."

"He's paranoid and jumpy, worse than Tor and me combined." Harrow wormed his hand inside her shirt, running it along her curvy body and loving the softness of her skin under his touch.

"That's what you think. As I recall, you were pretty pathetic back at Pritchard's house when you confessed your feelings for me."

"Hush, woman." He silenced her with a punishing kiss, which Jordan returned with equal fervor. Minutes flitted by while their impassioned desire took them closer to the edge.

Jordan broke away, glancing at Gail, who again had fallen asleep on their bed. "Not tonight, honey."

Harrow groaned and took a deep breath. "I can't wait to have our own bedroom again."

"Oh, be quiet. You should be grateful we have a roof over our heads. Leo has been very gracious." She nudged him off her.

"I'm thankful for many things, but not when I have to take a cold shower again." Harrow laughed in spite of himself. It wasn't just him who had been belly aching. Tor shared his sentiments, although the vampire's problem had more to do with his inability to keep the noise down.

"I'm going on patrol tonight and finalizing the arrangements on our new headquarters. Then I'll visit Shelly to see how things are going with her."

"Taking Angus with you, too?" Jordan smiled. There was no doubt that she'd overheard Rohnert's request.

"That, too," Harrow said and then sighed.

"What about me? You have to put me back in rotation."

Jordan had mastered the art of seducing and then diving in for the kill. True, with the recent attack on their underground facility, Harrow's paranoia had reached new heights. He had grounded Jordan and Allison against their will. It wasn't fair, but with Tor backing him up, he was able to hold off the women. He'd known it wouldn't be for long.

"You can go out with Firman tonight. Allison can go with Cyrus." They were the ideal babysitters for the women.

Jordan shook her head but accepted the assignment without question. "When are we moving into the new place?"

"If all goes as planned and Rayce gives me the go-ahead, we're scheduled to move over there tomorrow night."

"That's great." Jordan walked over to the bed and rearranged the sleeping angel in the middle. "Shall we?"

Harrow smiled. This was the life he'd always dreamed of, and Pritchard had made it happen. Although there were still many kinks to iron out, such as the cure, the ongoing battle with the Vampire Council, and the business, life was good. He wasn't going to complain.

Harrow slid under the goose down and cradled Gail in his arms, while Jordan settled on the other side of the bed. He was on the verge of sleep when a rude knocking pulled him back to reality.

"Harrow, get the door before it wakes up Gail."

With an irritated grunt, he padded over to answer the door. He yanked it a bit too hard and found Tor standing outside, wearing the same expression of irritation on his face.

"Gentry called. He wants to talk to you."

It took him a few seconds to register the name. "Fine, give him my number."

Within seconds, his phone was ringing. Sleep became a distant memory. "Harrow here."

"It's Gentry. Iden's compound came under heavy attack last night. Iden has been killed, as well as his wife. His daughter is nowhere to be found, but according to reports, she was able to escape. We suspect it's Goran."

"Have you contacted Rohnert?" Great. Another dilemma to pile on his ever-growing list.

"Rohnert?"

"He's back."

"We had no idea. Would it be possible to contact him?" Gentry, he'd learned, was a faithful soldier, and his loyalty belonged to one man alone.

"Of course. Hold on, let me get the number for you." Harrow recited the digits.

Gentry turned quiet for a few seconds before he spoke again. "I need a very big favor."

"You got it. What exactly do you need?" Although their ranks had dwindled to a terrible low, he wasn't about to turn down a comrade's plea for help.

"We need a place to stay. I doubt that it'll be safe for the survivors to stay here." Gentry's voice held a hint of misery.

Then the warehouse would have to be ready, no matter what. "You are most welcome to join us. How many are left?"

"There are twenty strong and several injured. We might need some medical help, too. We had to do some emergency amputations."

Harrow knew what he meant. "Can you get them to us tonight? We have a doctor and a nurse. I'm sure they can work on the injured."

"I believe we can. Where do we take them?"

Harrow gave Gentry the address of the abandoned apartment. "Take everyone to that address by nightfall. And then by tomorrow, we'll have a permanent place for you to stay."

"I'm sure they'll be able to work on a limited capacity."

"You have nothing to worry about. Call Rohnert and have a talk with him. I'll be waiting for you tonight."

"Thank you."

Gentry's relief was obvious. Although it wasn't in Harrow's nature to turn away someone in need, the living situation would be a bit tricky. The new quarters were designed for forty, tops. With this recent development, they would have no other choice but to double up.

He could make it work.

"Don't worry, it will all turn out just fine," Jordan whispered into the dark.

"I'm crossing my fingers."

Randolph, one of the respected members of the Council and one of the few vampires that Rohnert trusted, welcomed him into his secret hideaway with open arms. This location, known to just a small number of allies, was a designated meeting place.

"Brother, I thought you'd never come back." Randolph pulled him into an embrace. "I am glad to see you."

"As I am to see you, my brother."

"Come and sit with me."

The vampire led Rohnert into the dining hall. Although the dwelling was smaller than his official residence, this place offered the same luxury. Randolph was slightly shorter than Rohnert, with flecks of graying hair at his temples. He had a commanding presence and possessed the wisdom of the old ways. A stickler for following the strict rules of the Council, he was also known for his intelligence and fairness. No wonder he had fallen out of Goran's good graces.

The ornate wooden table was dressed with the finest china and a feast for two. A butler walked in holding a silver pitcher once they were seated.

"You must be thirsty," Randolph said and gestured for the man to begin pouring.

"You haven't changed one bit." Rohnert watched as blood filled his goblet.

His friend chuckled. "I happen to like drinking from fine crystal."

It was a known fact that after Randolph's mate had perished in childbirth, he'd vowed never to take another mate. It had been a century since his partner's demise, and celibacy suited him just fine.

If vampires were vulnerable during the birthing process, then no one, especially not a mere human, could be protected from the same fate as Randolph's mate. The thought made Rohnert shudder.

He pushed the errant worry away and focused on the man before him. "You're looking well, my friend."

"I feel great, considering the circumstances." Randolph took a long sip from his glass and rolled the liquid in his mouth.

"I heard that we've had some restructuring in the Council." Rohnert pushed the goblet away, declining the real deal even if he had zero options when it came to feeding. His scruples were going to be a long-term problem, but he pushed the concern aside.

The vampire grunted and shook his head. "More like house cleaning. Goran is up to something. I've been keeping tabs on him, but since he added me to the shoot-to-kill list, I haven't gotten any new intelligence."

Rohnert assessed his friend's mindset and figured he was telling the truth. When their minds were unshielded from each other, it was as honest as honest came.

"I'm in possession of the black book."

"We suspected Marania would entrust it to you. What are your plans?"

Rohnert shook his head. He hadn't given anything much thought lately —he'd been so consumed by Shelly and their child. "I don't have the slightest clue. When I left the Council, I stopped hoping for change, but the killings . . . they're worrisome."

"Your mate is with a young." The vampire smiled and patted him on the arm. "Congratulations."

Rohnert inhaled deep, wishing the circumstances were different. "I impregnated a human and left before I knew. Now, she wants nothing to do with me. I can't say I blame her. I treated her unfairly."

Randolph stood up and paced, his dark velvet robe swaying with his every movement. "It could be a problem once word leaks out. With your current status, you and your family are sitting ducks. Have you thought about telling her the truth?"

"No. There is no convincing Shelly at this moment."

His phone rang, an unknown number flashing on the display. Rohnert answered but didn't speak.

"Your grace, this is Gentry. Harrow gave me your number."

"Gentry, it's been a long time."

"Indeed. I bear some bad news."

"Tell me." He gestured for Randolph to come closer.

"Iden's mansion came under heavy attack last night. We sustained massive losses, including Iden, Chandra, and most of their personal guards."

"What about his daughter?" If it weren't for the black book, Rohnert wouldn't have known what the motive could be for such an attack.

Randolph, hearing this news, gave an anguished cry.

"We have no idea what has become of her. Although we had a plan in place, we don't know if it was successful."

"What plan?"

It wasn't Gentry who answered. "We had one of Isidora's trusted friends standing close by should anything like this ever happen. She was to take her to the secret tunnel and then pose as her," Randolph said, sounding broken.

"There are signs that the tunnel had been used, and our investigation led us to traces of ashes. There's no way of telling. We did what we could, but there were too many of them," Gentry said.

Goran might have the woman in his possession, which meant trouble. Time had become their enemy, and swift action must be taken. Where would they start?

"How many are left?"

Gentry grunted. "A few at best. I contacted Harrow for help. We had to perform some haphazard amputations, but the wounded need further medical attention. He told me to meet him at your apartment tonight."

Shelly! It had to be. Who else would Harrow bring in?

Rohnert cursed under his breath, and his chest tightened. "Is Zo still with you?"

"Yes, sir, and some guards that defected."

"Good. I'll meet you there as soon as sundown hits."

"Yes, sir."

"Gentry?"

"Sir?"

"Lose the sir shit. Good job staying alive. Hang tight, my man."

After disconnecting the call, Rohnert couldn't sit still. He paced the length of the room along the carpet that bore Randolph's family seal. The nightmare just wouldn't stop. What had become of their great race?

"My friend, have a drink and spend the time with me until sundown," Randolph said, holding a glass filled to the brim.

"I swear I will kill Goran if I get a chance."

Randolph smiled and projected his thoughts as clear as possible. *That's right, my friend. Rise to the occasion.* Then he raised his glass to Rohnert.

Shelly was getting ready for her shift in the hospital when Jones knocked on her bedroom door.

"It's open." She grabbed her backpack and turned down the volume of her favorite rock band.

"Harrow wants to speak with you." Jones handed her a cell phone.

Apart from the short talk she had with Harrow a couple of days ago, she hadn't heard from him, but he'd promised to keep her posted on the move-in details.

"Harrow?"

"Shelly, how are you doing? How's the pregnancy coming along?"

"I'm fine. What can I do for you?"

"I have some vamps who need medical attention. They're coming tonight. Can you see them?"

Although she was still on Tack Enterprises' payroll, she had to be on duty tonight at her other job. What would Rick say about her calling off at the last minute? It was a bit hairy, but she couldn't imagine saying no to those in need of help.

"What do I need to bring?"

"I have some supplies en route from headquarters as we speak."

"Let me call work right now and tell them I'm going to be late."

"I'll send your pick-up in a few minutes." Harrow sounded relieved.

"Okay."

She ended the call and handed the phone back to Jones. "You're coming with me."

Shelly took out her own cell phone and dialed. When Rick answered, she feigned a weak voice. "Hey Rick, I'll be late tonight. My stomach is a bit queasy." He was instantly worried, which made her feel rotten for lying.

"Is there something I can do?"

"I'll be okay. Can you find someone to cover for me until I get there?"

"No problem. I'll have Hastings stay over until you get here. If you don't think you'll make it, just give me a call."

Once they hung up, Shelly headed to the living room, where Jones was waiting for her. "Some doctor I am."

He shook his head. "Don't be too hard on yourself. I'm sure they'll find someone to cover."

A black sedan was waiting out front by the time they reached the front door. Angus got out and held the passenger door open for her.

"Evening doctor." He offered a gracious smile.

"Hello, Angus."

Shelly had no idea where they were headed, but she soon realized that they had entered an unsavory part of Brooklyn. The buildings and houses were run down or condemned. She focused on the thrill of doing what she loved best, although the anticipation was doing a number on her stomach. It wasn't good that she hadn't had much to eat except some toast.

She took a deep breath and tried to settle her stomach. The car went a few more miles and stopped in front of a decrepit building. Overgrown weeds bordered the property, and its plywood-covered broken windows completed the structure's ramshackle image.

"Here we are." Angus parked the car and ushered them toward the building. Jones acted undeterred by their surroundings, and since Angus looked relaxed, Shelly felt silly for being concerned. Harrow would make sure they were safe and uncompromised. There was nothing for her to worry about except getting the job done.

The floorboards grunted under their collective weight, and she grabbed Jones's arm when the front door opened with a loud creak. She felt her heart jump to her throat once she recognized the tall and imposing figure waiting inside.

Shelly's response was instantaneous. She pivoted and was poised to flee, except Rohnert was too fast. His hand closed in on her arm, stopping her forward progress.

"Angus, Jones, we'll meet you inside." His message was clear. He wanted no one to witness their exchange. How very convenient.

"Let me go," she said, shaking his hold on her.

"Shelly, I've been waiting for you." Rohnert's low voice enveloped her like a warm cocoon.

"You can wait all you want."

"Please stay." It sounded like a caress.

Shelly leveled her gaze at the vampire. "Don't use your charm on me. You might get away with it in my sleep, but I won't let you manipulate me now."

Rohnert was focused on her. Those black eyes watched her as though she were only thing that mattered. She wanted to believe it. When her knees grew weak and her pulse started racing, she knew it was a matter of time before she balked under the intense effect of his stare.

"I'm done being exploited. Let me do my job and just stay away from me." She saw him flinch, but she hardened her heart. There was no way she'd let him chip away her walls.

"I can't stay away from you, but I will let you do your job without interruption."

With those words, Rohnert guided her into the decaying structure. It was filled with fighters, most of whom were vampires. If her count was accurate, there were only three other humans, not counting . . .

"Cheryl?" she exclaimed in surprise.

"Dr. Anderson. I'm so happy to see you." Cheryl wrapped her in an excited embrace.

Tears stung her eyes. "I'm glad you survived. Are there any others?"

Cheryl shook her head and choked back a sob. "But I brought Led Zeppelin," she said, attempting a smile.

Just like old times. Shelly took a deep breath and put her game face on. She looked around the sea of weary faces. "Who's first? And where in this god forsaken place am I going to be able to do some damage?"

At the corner of her eye, she saw Rohnert's lips turn up into a smile.

Rohnert managed to keep his distance from Shelly for the time being, giving her enough space to work on the injured soldiers. Some faces were familiar, and some had been recruited after he'd vacated his position on the Council. While he paced the crowded hallway, he tuned out all but one person's thoughts. All he could hear were Shelly's ideas, louder than her preferred rock music, while she planned the best prosthetics she could create for the fighters with missing limbs.

"Sir, there are enough scuff marks on the floor already without you adding to it." Alonzo stepped into his line of vision, looking bedraggled but alive.

Rohnert smirked. "Good to see you, too." Although the elite soldier was a pain in the butt, it was a pleasure to see him unscathed after the attack.

Zo walked closer to Rohnert, out of earshot of the vampires hanging around in the hallway. "Are you back for good?"

He blew a quick exhale and nodded. "There are things that need to be done and matters to address."

The gleam in the soldier's eyes was one of triumph. "So we're back in circulation."

Rohnert gave the same answer he would give anyone. "As soon as we're situated, I think we need to regroup and figure out what's best for everyone involved."

This seemed to appease the other vampire. "You know I have your back."

He patted him on the shoulder. "I never doubted that."

Although Rohnert was glad to see people in high spirits, his own mood was bottoming. If it hadn't been for Shelly's presence, he would have preferred to be alone to sort out his thoughts. The six-floor apartment building wasn't big enough for them all, but he managed to find a quiet space in the rear of the building, and he parked his ass by the stairs. It was dark, and the westerly winds had calmed down, to be replaced by a softer breeze. Rohnert looked up at the dark sky sprinkled with stars and sighed.

With his mind still focused on Shelly's activity, he pulled the black book from his waistband. The tome had been his constant companion, but he had no desire to discover something new. The thought of reading its contents felt like an invasion of someone's privacy. Whatever it contained, Marania had sacrificed her life to protect it, and so should he. Then why did he keep attempting to leaf through the pages? It had to be the curiosity Isagani had stirred within him.

He stared at the cover before opening the book in the middle, to the part that often called him to take a peek. Even in the darkness, the words were luminous, and the pages seemed to take a life of their own. The familiar sentence stared back at him.

A child borne to the rightful guide shall come to fulfil this divination.

Every time he read that phrase, one conclusion came to mind. Goran. Would this be the reason for his inexorable thirst to find the right mate? Was Goran the rightful vampire to guide them through the dark hours? That idea would take a lot of getting used to, given his knowledge of the vampire's tempestuous nature.

"Mind if I hang out here with you?" Jordan asked from behind him.

The woman was like a breath of fresh air, and he welcomed the intrusion. He closed the book and replaced it in its regular hiding place. "Mind if I don't feel like talking?"

Jordan sat next to him and spread her legs in front of her. "It doesn't matter. You'll answer anyway."

He didn't have to see her face to know she was smiling. Her tone said it all. They both stared straight ahead into the darkness in silence. Shelly's music was on full blast, and Rohnert could tell that she was in her element. Then Jordan injected her own thought.

Aren't you glad to be back?

He ignored her silent question and closed his eyes.

Is she happy to see you?

Rohnert hissed and inclined his head in her direction. "Silence, I heard, is golden."

Jordan laughed and faced him. "You have to keep trying. It wasn't easy for her when you left."

Sometimes, he wished he no longer cared. It would be best if he were alone. Peril followed in his wake, and everyone he'd ever loved had been taken from him. He would do Shelly a great service if he left her alone.

"I haven't discussed my early life with anyone, but growing up was no party for me. Everyone one I ever cared about almost always turned up dead."

Jordan's face reflected understanding, and she took his hand. "I'm here to listen."

Her offer tempted him to open the floodgates, and before he remembered he should hold back, he was spilling his guts like there was no tomorrow.

Rohnert's childhood had been a complete haze. He grew up in extravagance, with servants waiting on him hand and foot. His parents had loved him dearly, and he'd returned their affection with equal zeal. Although his young life had seemed promising, Rohnert couldn't shake the feeling that something was wrong.

His father, Arron, had an exquisite pedigree, and his house was the next in line for the coveted seat as the head of their race. From a young age, Rohnert had been groomed to take his father's place after the reign of the current party expired. Leading hadn't been his calling. He preferred to fight and nurture young fighters, and he dedicated his time to this chosen endeavor.

Arron and his wife, Hedy, had doted on him like any parents to their only child, but Rohnert had always felt like he was an outsider, as though he didn't belong. No amount of assurance from his parents put his niggling suspicions to rest.

On Rohnert's hundredth birthday, Arron spoke of a secret that he would divulge to his son in due time. However, the next winter his parents, along with several members of the Council, perished in a gruesome murder during a retreat to a secluded location. Nothing made sense, and no one could offer an explanation for their deaths at the hands of the unknown assassin. Arron's secret was taken to his grave, along with Rohnert's hopes.

A familiar ache made it difficult to breathe, and he snapped out of his trance when he heard a sharp cry not too far from him. He released Jordan's hand and was up on his feet in an instant.

"Dr. Anderson, for crying out loud, I could've gotten it myself." Cheryl helped her up onto her feet.

"Oh for heaven's sake, I'm fine. I just pulled a muscle or something." That was, of course, a lie. Her back still burned even once she'd straightened up, abandoning the scissors she had dropped on the floor.

The vampire, Mort, looked at her with sympathy despite his own personal torment. She had just finished cleansing and dressing his wound when her balance went all crazy on her.

It had just been six hours and five patients—piece of cake.

Mort tugged at her arm. "Is everything okay, Doctor—"

The flimsy door was torn off its hinges like a piece of cardboard. "What the hell is going on here?" Rohnert's voice rattled everything around them, sending the bottles of precious anesthetics to the floor with a loud crash.

"Don't you ever knock?" Shelly wobbled to the nearest chair and flopped onto it clumsily.

"I heard you cry. What's wrong?" Rohnert rushed to her side, ignoring her question, and placed his hand on her belly.

It could have been the warmth of his touch or some quack medicinal magic, but her back felt instant relief. Shelly had wanted to deny him the privilege of connecting with their unborn child. Instead, she smothered a moan at the glorious reprieve he brought to her. She was much too proud to acknowledge how his presence soothed her.

"Nothing's wrong. I probably pulled a muscle when I bent down to pick up the scissors." She tried to move away from him, to disconnect herself from his touch.

Cheryl took one look at Rohnert, and without a word took her leave. Mort scrambled to his feet and followed suit.

Rohnert kept his hand on her back. "You're lying." He peered at her.

Shelly bit her tongue to keep herself from lobbing another furious retort. She looked away, focusing on the exit. He had no right to look so attractive and virile, and her heart shouldn't be hammering against her chest the way it was. Under his close scrutiny, she felt vulnerable, naked almost, and she hated the sexual stirring in her gut.

"You look tired."

"I'm fine. It's my normal. I have to go to work now."

"You're done working for the night." Rohnert's eyes bore into hers. The command in voice would have sent others seeking for cover.

She was no pushover. "You're not telling me what to do."

Shelly stood up and bolted past him.

Rohnert was quick to restrain her, and he spun her around to face him.

"I'm not doing this to annoy you. You have to look after yourself and our child. Your schedule doesn't allow you enough rest."

Sure. He was going all gallant on her, showing concern. It was a bit too cozy and little too late.

"No, it isn't," he said, answering her unspoken words. "I left because I wanted to protect—"

"Oh spare me the details. You left because you're afraid to show you care. Now that I'm pregnant, you come waltzing back into my life to take control. If you're concerned for the child's well-being, don't be. I'm going to let *It* know who the sperm donor is."

She watched his face harden. "Do not call our child *It*. We're going to give him a name, and I'm not just a donor. I intend to be a part of his life every step of the way."

So he had been eavesdropping. Just for kicks, she pushed on. "And how do you propose that we go about doing that?" Shelly held Rohnert's gaze with enough challenge to discourage any man.

His features softened, and his eyes crinkled. "I want a ceremony to bind us. I don't want my son to be born a bastard."

As in getting married? Her chest felt weird all of a sudden, inflating at the prospect, but she tamped down her excitement. *Where in hell does this man get these silly notions?*

"And if I won't do it?"

Rohnert smiled, exposing the tips of his fangs. "You won't deny your child the life he deserves."

Too cocky for his own good. Shelly snorted and shook her head. "This child deserves to live in peace away from the violence and without the fear of getting killed." It was obvious that she'd struck a nerve when his nostrils flared. Shelly stifled a smile.

"I will protect my child with my life." He pulled her closer until their faces were almost touching and held her chin with his thumb and forefinger. "You won't get rid of me, even if you try."

Without giving her a chance to answer, he cupped her face with his big hands and captured her mouth in a hungry kiss, demanding her to respond.

Shelly planted her palms against his chest and pushed. Rohnert didn't budge. He growled against her lips and deepened the kiss, rendering her breathless and weak in the knees. Her hands relaxed then fisted in his jacket, finally feeling the burn of his mouth.

Oh, God. How could she think straight? She prided herself on being tough, and she usually stuck to her resolve. Yet Rohnert short circuited her brain, making it difficult to think of anything but getting him between her legs.

His hands wound down to the small of her back and pressed her body until there was not a hairline of space between them. She felt lightheaded. This had to stop. She wasn't going to . . .

Shelly moaned, unable to stop herself from touching his face. If she were truthful with herself, she wanted this and needed him like air.

She also needed a doctor. It was obvious she was sick in the head. She had vowed not to allow him walk all over her, and look at what was she doing —letting him trample her will and moaning like a sex-starved kitten while he did it.

Rohnert released her mouth and whispered. "Stop fighting your attraction to me."

Shelly met his feral gaze and released a sigh. "This is for our child." It sounded believable to her ears, just enough to salvage her pride. All it had taken was one kiss, and she was ready to make a go of it.

Goran ground his teeth until his jaw cracked. Menace rolled off him like a cloud of dark smoke, choking everyone in his midst.

Hamilton staggered backward, cupping his mouth and relaxing his hold on the female vampire's neck.

Goran hissed. "I specifically asked you to stay back."

"I wanted to get the job done right." Hamilton looked scared, unable to retreat farther once he hit the wall.

"You're a brownnoser. You want to be in my good graces, don't you?" He stalked forward. Each step was precise, calculating. Goran towered over the cowering vampire.

"Yes, sire." Hamilton's head was bowed low, and his gaze was trained on the floor. "I thought it would please you if I brought the woman."

Goran bellowed a cry so fierce that everything around them rattled and trembled. Clenching his fist around Hamilton's collar, he picked up the soldier like a ragdoll. "Do you have any idea who you brought here?"

Gasping for air, Hamilton lifted his eyes and stared at the female vampire. "I . . . den's daughter. You . . . said she has . . . red hair."

Goran dropped the vampire on the floor, where he lay sputtering and catching his breath. "You brought me an imposter." It took three long strides to cover the length of his chamber to reach the woman.

The young female backpedaled at his predatory approach, her eyes sparking with terror. "Get away from me!"

Her attempt to run away prompted Goran to grab a handful of hair, yanking her back. Her body spun, and she fell on the ground. Goran's hand came up clutching the red wig.

His mouth turned into a cruel line, and his eyes narrowed into fine slits. "Look who's here with us—a fraud."

Hamilton's eyes grew as big as saucers, and he stuttered. "I . . . had no way of knowing, sire." Panic suffused his face, and fear shook his voice. "I apologize for my mistake."

A wicked smile was Goran's response. He hurled the hairpiece across the floor and took a deep breath, tracking the woman's movement even while his eyes were trained on his soldier. This was going to be a tough decision, considering his depleted army, but things had to be done his way.

Not one to waste a perfectly good opportunity, he sneered at the plan forming in his head. "You and I will talk after I have a word with her. Wait for me in the Blanch room."

Hamilton nodded, seeming relieved to escape. He crawled to the door, dragging his body in haste while the tip of this sword scraped the floor behind him. The grinding noise should've irritated the crap out of Goran, but it sensitized his wicked soul. He turned to the woman, whose hair was long and black.

"What's your name?" He used the gentlest tone in his arsenal, keeping eye contact with her. Jesus, she was just a girl.

"Maureen," she whispered, then covered her face with tiny hands.

"Maureen . . ." He let the name roll off his tongue. "What are you doing pretending to be my future bride?"

Her fingers spread apart, and she peeked through them. "Bride? Who are you?" Her voice trembled.

His lips grazed her neck, and the scent of fear she emitted fueled his lust. "You've been too sheltered. Iden should've let you out once in a while to smell the flowers." He cradled the frightened female and took her to his bed.

Willing the lights to dim, he shrugged off his robe and began chanting. Maureen looked up at him, her fear diminishing more with each mesmerizing sound he produced. Her body turned languid, prepping for him.

She was beautiful and young. It would be a big waste once he was done with her. Her undulating body was heating up, and the thrill of the lay kept him interested for the time being. Goran raked his eyes along the delicate figure underneath her pink shirt and jeans.

"I think you'd be prettier without your clothes on," he said, and released her from the confines of her stifling garments.

Maureen watched him underneath a veil of thick lashes, her whole body humming while she rearranged her body to his liking, spreading her legs wider for easy entry. There was no resistance on her part, and he was willing to bet that his incantations had worked and she was well on her way to oblivion.

Just like any other woman he'd possessed in the past, he gathered all the information from her memories while she was in her most vulnerable state. In bed, at the edge of orgasm, her thoughts would spill like a waterfall.

The dutiful friend took the place of his future bride. This Isidora could be dead or running free somewhere out there. The idea of how he'd been thwarted made him thrust a bit harder, and the easy glide was forgotten.

He pounded into her with furious vehemence, as if every lunge would produce more information. She moaned, and he pounded some more.

Soon enough, she was crying in his arms. Ecstasy? For sure. It was his turn, and without fanfare, he latched his fangs onto her jugular while drilling his erection harder into her body. Her squeal could have been one of pain, but he didn't care. Goran tugged hard, and she arched her body, tilting her head to give him more room. He drew back and took another vein until he was near satisfied. Using his fingernails, he pressed into her skull until she screamed.

Her cry reverberated inside the chamber walls while she kicked and flailed. Blood oozed from the pressure points, and he kept puncturing different areas while he pounded his body into hers. She kept fighting, but with every movement, more blood squirted from her head.

As his groans of release intensified, her cries diminished, signaling her imminent demise. The beating of her puny heart faltered and finally stopped.

"So you wanted to be a redhead? It seems like you got what you wished for." He pulled out of the body of yet another hapless being who'd dared take him for a fool.

Today was the big move, the day everyone had been waiting for, and Harrow was torn. They were fortunate to have a bunch of workers who were willing to move mountains and had worked night and day to finish the project, but this meant he'd be missing their little girl. It was decided that it was in Gail's best interest if she stayed with the general during the week so she could attend a regular school.

"Momma, why is Daddy saying I'm going to stay here at Grampies' house?" Gail asked while watching television in their bedroom. Harrow looked up from the laptop and blanched. Grampies was Gail's name for Leo.

Jordan whipped her head up fast, startling the little girl in the process. "When did he say that?"

Harrow flinched. He had forgotten that he and Jordan agreed they'd talk to the little girl together. He glanced across the room to catch her lips lifting into a snarl.

Gail looked at him, and then back at Jordan, who concealed her fangs just in time. The temperature dipped, and Harrow readied himself for a good tongue-lashing. That would be in thirty minutes, the moment Gail fell asleep.

"Daddy told me yesterday."

Gail's innocent answer had to be clawing at Jordan's heart right that minute, and he felt like an idiot for breaking the news to their little girl alone. In his defense, Gail had wanted to know if they could adjust her bedtime to accommodate the Brady Bunch reruns, which were her favorite these days. She'd begged for a thirty minute extension, which he thought was best decided by Jordan.

If she could only read his mind, it would save him the trouble. He offered an apologetic smile, but aside from the dagger glares she shot in his direction, Jordan ignored him.

"Did he also tell you why?"

Gail sat up and rolled her eyes, thinking of the answer. Harrow turned his attention back to the computer, but kept his ears open for their adopted daughter's answer.

"He said Heather's school is great, and he wants me to go there. It would be easier if Grampies can take us to school together."

Silence followed. If it weren't for the irritating jingle blasting from the television and Gail's voice singing along, Harrow would think Jordan had left the room.

"Daddy is right. You won't have to wake up so early since the school is a few blocks away from here."

"That's what I thought." Gail stroke her chin, something Leo did often. "That's why I asked if I could have an extension on my bedtime."

Harrow turned around and stared at Gail. Last time he checked, she was six years old. Had she matured into a teenager overnight? He shook his head and caught Jordan smiling, no doubt thinking along the same lines.

"And what was Daddy's answer?" Jordan asked.

Gail narrowed her eyes, as if catching on to the silent agreement between her parents. "He said it's your decision. C'mon, Momma. I think Greg is groovy."

Jordan laughed. Her laughter was filled with such pure glee that Harrow found himself joining. The shared joke was lost on Gail, who pouted and crossed her arms over her chest.

While Jordan was handling the tough decision, Harrow's phone rang.

"Rayce, are you a bearer of good news?"

"Yes, boss. We're all good to go."

He breathed a sigh of relief. They'd been cooped up in Leo's house for weeks, and he was afraid they were wearing out their welcome. "Tell everyone to pack up and meet us there at sundown. Keep it under the radar."

By the time he'd hung up, Jordan was chastising the inconsolable girl. One would think she had been denied the right to breathe. Harrow chuckled and shook his head.

Jordan looked up and gave him a wink. It was a sign that he was forgiven. Harrow stood up and walked over to the bed.

"Gail," he whispered, sitting right next to his daughter.

She refused to look up, but the pout was too prominent too ignore, as well as the tears brimming in her eyes. Oh, the problems of a child.

"Let's make a deal. I want to see your grades for the whole year first. If they're good, then we can negotiate later on." Really, he was striking a deal with a six year old. Time indeed had changed him.

Gail didn't respond right away, but she blinked a couple of times while she contemplated his offer. In his peripheral vision, he caught Jordan biting her lips to keep herself from laughing.

After a few tense moments, Gail met his gaze. "Fine, Daddy. We'll negotiate again."

Where in the hell did kids get their ideas nowadays? If he had a choice, he would outlaw television. Harrow kept himself from laughing. "Fine. Show me the grades, and we'll see."

With that crisis averted, Harrow went back to the laptop to finish his research while Jordan read Gail a bedtime story. In fifteen minutes flat, Gail was asleep, tucked in Jordan's arms. This was his cue to take the little angel to the bedroom she shared with Heather, Leo's granddaughter.

At the far end of the mansion's hallway, he ran into Leo, who asked him to join him in the study. With a nod, Harrow agreed. He tucked Gail in bed and kissed her on the cheek before slipping out of the bedroom.

He found Leo seated behind his desk, a bottle of brandy sitting on the desk with two glasses. "So how's it going with the warehouse?" Leo poured them both a generous portion.

Harrow took the leather chair across the table and downed the glass. He pushed his sunglasses up his head and sighed. "Rayce said we're good to go. I'm planning to get everyone situated tonight."

The general pulled a long one from his glass and smiled, leaning against his chair. "That's good to hear. I'm a little concerned with the recent sighting of Rohnert on television, killing that Council guard."

Harrow shook his head. The vampire had been careless, and these types of situations required damage control. "Is it that bad?"

Leo weighed his answer before speaking. "Well, there are a lot of strange things happening around us, so playing it down wasn't too difficult. To neutralize the video, I contacted a travel photographer, and he circulated footage taken during his journeys that shows how something like that could be staged."

"How much did that cost you?"

"He owed me a favor. We're now even." He proceeded to refill their empty glasses. "I have one thing to ask of you."

The slight shift in the general's emotional grid warned Harrow to brace himself. "Of course, anything."

"There are questions from NCS about this particular sighting. Although we downplayed it as prank, I'm afraid there are believers who say this is the real deal. You have to round up your boys and lay low for a while. There's nothing much I can do once they decide to look further into the validity of the recording."

Harrow digested Leo's warning. As if he didn't have enough crap to worry about, he had to play Merlin and make the vampires disappear. Sure, sir, got this all figured out. No worries. Thank you very much.

He downed the brandy and let the effect of the alcohol work down his system. "Yep. I got this." Harrow stood up and reached out his hand. "Thanks for the warning, Leo."

The general rose to his feet and clasped his hand. "Don't mention it."

Harrow turned to walk away, but before he cleared the door, Leo spoke again. "And watch our good friend Cyrus. I think the man is a tad bit too intense. I'm worried about him."

"No worries. I got his back," Harrow said.

Phase one of his groveling had worked. Whether he needed to use manipulation or pity, Rohnert was going to get back in Shelly's good graces. He'd do whatever it took to be around Shelly once again and get the chance to hold her.

The kiss made him painfully aware of his attraction. The bond they shared through their child was strengthened by the realization that she'd had him by the balls the moment he laid eyes on her.

His goal was to wean her from her current job at the hospital and get her back at the facility full-time, but Shelly's bullheadedness might get in the way. For someone who was used to taking charge and giving the orders, it wouldn't be easy to let someone else call the shots. Feminism was something his race hadn't had to deal with before. Since he'd fallen in love with a human, Rohnert had to adjust.

Even baby steps would lead to an open door. At least, that was his hope. After the kiss they'd shared, it had been close to impossible to take his hands off her again. He glanced at Shelly's sleeping figure and sighed. It would be morning soon, and he'd kept vigil all through the night. For a change, she had listened to his plea to stay off her feet and rest, instead of marching straight to the hospital as she'd initially intended. He suspected the good doctor recognized her own body's limits.

Rohnert planted a soft kiss on her lips before he left. Daytime was his foe, but for her it was a blessing. Any creature of the dark would have to wait for nightfall before they could get to her, and he'd be waiting for them if the time ever came.

Stepping out into the waning darkness, his skin prickled at the imminent daybreak. He hastened his stride, breaking into a run. The orange tentacles of the early morning sun were threatening by the time he reached the new hideout.

Surrounded by untidy vegetation, the warehouse sat near the tip of Manhattan, facing the harbor. Some might consider it an eyesore, but the building stood as a reminder of a bygone era of bootlegging and gang violence.

His keen senses made him aware of the countless number of unseen cameras that were trained on him, and he knew that Rayce was more than ready to blast any intruder without a second thought.

An outer door opened as he passed it, and he backtracked to let himself in. The maze took him into another portal leading to a foyer. Looking around, Rohnert had no idea what direction to take until another door opened. He walked through it, knowing that their beloved tech guy was guiding him to the inner sanctum.

At the end of a short hallway, another door opened and Harrow stepped out to welcome him. "What do you think?"

"I think I'm lost." This facility, though small, was a fortress. There were multiple doors, a labyrinthine design meant to confuse, and the mirrors all around were a great addition. Aesthetically speaking, it was right up minimalist alley, but this new set-up would buy them time should they come under attack again.

Harrow flashed a thumbs-up and ushered him inside what was clearly the new I-room. It was a smaller version with no windows, but its bare walls were covered with monitors. The cameras zoomed in from every direction like watchful eyes. A big, rectangular table sat in the middle of the room with chairs surrounding it, and the mammoth television on one wall was the main attraction.

Remembering the former facility's meeting area, Rohnert had to know. "Don't tell me, there's a bar here somewhere?" He checked out the seams of every wall and laughed.

Cyrus got up from his seat and headed to the front next to the television. He took a remote control and pressed a button. A small version of Pritchard's libation station rolled around.

"What's your poison?" Cyrus asked, flashing his fangs.

"Single malt." Rohnert took the last vacant chair at the end of the table.

He took stock of all the vampires and humans around him. Zo was standing against the wall polishing his blade. He gave a reverent bow when their eyes met. Gentry sat next to Tor, having a conversation. Firman, Angus, Jordan, Allison, and several vampires Rohnert had trained while connected with the Council gave him respectful nods. A few new faces, some wearing dark lenses, checked him out, awe written all over their faces. Aside from Angus and Barth, there were no human fighters on the payroll. It was a good thing—less connection to the outside world.

Rohnert grunted his approval and returned his eyes to Harrow, who stood up with his sunglasses perched on his face and gestured for silence.

"I'm sure most of you have questions. First, this is our new HQ. You'll find the accommodations more comfortable than what we've had the last few days—"

Someone from the back of the room coughed, and the room erupted in laughter. It was a much-needed release.

Harrow cleared his throat and continued. "You will each share a room with another person, and Rayce will explain the safety features of each room. All I ask is that you respect the property as your own and keep your noses clean. We've been under tremendous pressure, as most of you know, and I want this transition to be as painless as possible."

"Sounds like I'm rooming with my girl." Tor winked at Allison, who sat across from him. Allison, in her usual feisty self, smiled and puckered her lips.

An errant thought crossed Rohnert's mind. Would Shelly mind shacking up with him? *Christ, don't even go there.*

"Okay, kids. We have Tor and Allison sharing a room." Harrow rolled his eyes. "Let's address our goals. First of all, we will continue to come to the aid of those in need of protection. The spread of the disease has slowed down, thanks to the animal blood diet, but it is far from eradicated. The Council hasn't eased up on hunting the diseased. In fact, from what I hear, no questions are asked anymore. It's just straight up shoot and kill."

"Fun!" Jeremy, a new recruit, said.

"That's it." Harrow laughed and paced to the front. "Next, let me introduce the new members of our team. Let's welcome Alonzo—"

"Call me Zo if you want me to reply," the vampire interjected.

Rohnert blew a loud breath, avoiding Alonzo's narrowed eyes. He tuned out the rest of the introductions, his mind focused on the task at hand. With most of the fighters in their team well-trained and informed, his priority should be getting some of the Elders to safety. Of course, before that, he'd have to convince Shelly that it was time to move into the new facility. An idea popped in his head that just might work.

"I'm not going to lie. I'm holding that bastard Goran accountable for all the killings in our midst. I realize it's ambitious, but I'm not giving up on the idea that we'll find a way to retaliate, if necessary." Harrow looked straight at Rohnert.

This time, Jordan pounded her fist on the table, looking more ferocious than ever. "Damn right we're not going to give up on that idea," she said with a hiss.

Atta girl! It seemed like some people couldn't sweep their thirst for vengeance under the rug. Rohnert watched his friend, and her spirit renewed his own. He was not likely to forget the more important things that needed to be done. Goran remained a formidable foe, a phantom striking from the shadows, and always a step ahead.

Gentry raised his hand to speak. "The Council's stock of recycled humans is expendable and easy to replace. With the reintroduction of the Elite Guards, we're looking at tougher opponents."

Zo snorted. "We can still take them with careful planning."

"Wait, no one said anything about going head-to-head with anyone, especially an army like that. We're going to sit tight and do damage in our own way. That being said, our production line will continue taking orders on a smaller scale for now. Cyrus will continue to oversee that side of the business, but since he can no longer conduct business during daylight, I'm going to assign the last few humans we have to the task of acting as Tack Enterprises' liaisons."

Listening to Harrow talk, Rohnert could empathize with the weight the vampire was carrying on his shoulders. "Tor, Firman"—Harrow looked to Rohnert with a silent request in his eyes, and he agreed with a nod—"and Rohnert are in charge of training and patrol assignments. We're all here as one unit. We have each other's backs. If you have any questions, don't hesitate to ask. Familiarize yourselves with the safety precautions. Other than that, we're going to take the night off to get settled."

Once the room had emptied of all but the core members of their group, Tor rose and marched over to Allison, pulling her to her feet. The big vampire, as fierce as he was, was a total lamb in the presence of his mate. Jordan stayed in her seat, while Cyrus parked his rear next to the bar, pouring one drink after another.

"Now, we can talk about the more private details of our lives, as they affect the group as a whole." Harrow sat down at the head of the table and removed his sunglasses. Leave it to Harrow to inject a major topic and make it sound casual. "Let's start with you, Rohn."

Rohnert knew where this was going. He straightened in his chair. Since it'd be easier to think if his body was in constant motion, he stood up. "Tell me what you want me to address first," he said.

"You and the doc. Do you think she'll want to come back with us?"

Yep. There it is. "I'm working on it," he replied.

"The baby . . . how long before she gives birth?" Harrow sounded like a goddamn machine gun, firing personal questions he tried to push away at the back of his mind.

Rohnert stopped pacing and walked up to Harrow. He braced his palms on the table, his face mere inches from the vampire's grill. "I'm not sure, but I'm going to sit with Jones soon and get it all figured out." He gritted his teeth and moved away, hating to sound so defensive and useless.

"Hey, take it easy," Cyrus piped up. His voice was commanding, but his demeanor remained relaxed—just an average newbie struggling to sift through his ever-changing emotions.

Rohnert raised his hands in deference to his buddy. "I will let you guys know what Shelly decides. It's difficult to protect her when she's out and about in broad daylight."

Harrow's slight movement caught his attention, and he inclined his head to see him better. Rohnert knew what his friend was about to offer.

"I'm going to assign Angus to watch her during the morning hours. She can't say no to me. I will put a pressure on her to return since she's still under contract. That should get her back here faster."

Harrow's way of thinking was right up Rohnert's alley. With Shelly, it was better to give her the terms point-blank. "That's a great option."

"Perhaps you and I can pay her a visit." Jordan smiled.

"I'd like that. Maybe your friend will listen to you."

"It just might work. I have to watch out for her."

"So that's settled." Harrow swiveled his chair to face Cyrus. "Are you tight?"

Cyrus chugged the contents of the glass and nodded. "Tight as a drum." He flaunted his fangs. "In case you're wondering, I still want to skin that motherfucker alive."

Tor burst into laughter, and Allison popped him on the shoulder to shut him up. "Dude, I was hoping you'd forgotten about your *daddy*," he teased.

Cyrus flashed his middle finger and gave him a fiendish grin. "My memory is better than ever."

Shelly awoke feeling refreshed, despite the ache between her legs. She stretched and adjusted her eyes to the soft morning sunshine that filtered in through the blinds. Deep down, she felt Rohnert's presence and knew with a degree of certainty he had been around. The vampire was complicated, methodical, and paranoid—a terrible combination. She knew he'd be obsessing over his unborn child. The thought made her pause. He'd pledged to protect their child with his life, and that thought alone should make her happy. So why did she felt left out? Shaking her insecurities aside, Shelly gave one final stretch and then got out of bed. She walked straight to the bathroom for a quick shower.

It had been some time since she'd had a good night's sleep. As much as she hated to give Rohnert the credit, his insistence that she march straight home, instead of working the remaining hours at the hospital, had proven beneficial. Her body had been adjusting to pregnancy, and although her research had given her some information about what to expect, it still wasn't enough. Jones had been helpful, but most of his data dealt with conditions after delivery. Shelly had yet to meet a pregnant woman carrying a Halfling, let alone the child of a purebred vampire. Most of women on record had perished in the battle upstate.

She was on her own with this one. Unless Rohnert . . . did she expect his help with this?

Her phone rang, and the caller ID flashed Harrow's name.

"Hey, Gates. What's up?" She looked at herself in the mirror. "Aren't you supposed to be sleeping?"

Harrow chuckled. "Hello, Dr. Anderson. I'm working late today."

"What can I do for you?"

"Our new headquarters is up and running. I would like a meeting with you tonight, if at all possible."

"Sounds good. What time should I come? And where is the new headquarters?"

"I'm going to have a car waiting for you at nine. Also, I wanted to tell you that while you're not with us, I've assigned Angus to be your babysitter in the daytime."

"I don't need a sitter." The nerve. How could Harrow do this to her?

"Of course you do. I intend to take care of my people."

Her eyes narrowed in suspicion. "Did Rohnert put you up to this?"

"Your boy had nothing to do with my decision, although you know him well enough to guess that he agreed with my idea right away."

"He's not my boy." She seethed at the inability of these people to understand what privacy meant. "Fine, warn Angus that I'm grumpy and not a great company. It's best he keep his distance for his own sake."

"Why don't you tell him yourself?" Harrow chuckled. "He's on your doorstep right now, waiting for you to let him in."

"You people are insufferable." She hung up.

Shelly threw on a pair of her loosest jeans and a beige sweater and hurried to the door. Angus stood outside, grinning at her. His longish brown hair was pulled into a ponytail, and he was dressed in beige slacks and black shirt. He looked more like a starving artist than a lethal soldier.

"Good morning, Dr. Anderson." He flashed a boyish smile.

Shelly was instantly annoyed. *It's going to be a long day.* She opened the door wider to let him in. "I don't talk a lot, unless I'm working. If you must be my babysitter, I would like you to call me by my first name." She closed the door.

"I was given a fair warning, Doctor . . . Shelly," he said.

"Coffee? Bagel?" She proceeded to the kitchen. "Sit and make yourself comfortable."

"Yes, thanks." The young man sat on the sofa and looked around. He must have been somewhere in his mid-twenties. Why a young man would choose to get into this line of work was a question she kept asking herself.

She pressed the start button on the coffee maker and popped a bagel in the toaster, wondering where her sudden appetite was coming from. Clearing the dishes, she checked her phone for messages. There was one from Rick.

Shelly, I thought about the thing you asked me. I want to talk to you about it. Call me.

She pressed his number on her speed dial, and he answered on the third ring. "Whitaker here," he said.

"Rick, you left a message for me to call you."

"Yes. I'd rather talk in person. Would you like to have dinner tonight?"

The invitation sounded harmless—just two people talking over a hot meal. She could call Harrow to move their meeting. "Sure. Where should I meet you?"

"I'll pick you up at seven-thirty. Wear something nice."

Nice didn't mesh well with her these days, but what the heck. "Fine. But make it an early dinner, I have to go somewhere at nine."

"That's okay. See you at seven, then."

A beep sounded—the coffee was ready. She gathered two cups and got the bagel out of the toaster. "Cream and sugar?"

Angus nodded and walked to the kitchen. "You got a date tonight?" The question didn't bother her as much as the tone.

"It's my boss." She didn't want to get baited in explaining further.

"Finn, we've been walking for three nights straight. Do you have any idea where we're going?" Isidora asked.

It wasn't an exaggeration. She wondered if they were lost or just winging it. They had gone through the denser part of the forest, hiding from any unfamiliar sounds and avoiding crossing anyone's path. For years, she'd imagined the outside world away from the stifling confines of the mansion. Now that she had the opportunity to experience it, she couldn't shake the terror that built within her.

Maybe she had made a big mistake by leaving. But what could she go back to? With the compound under siege, she was lucky to have gotten out alive.

Isidora had heard about the city from stories, magazines, and television. She'd thought she knew what to expect, but as they neared their destination, panic got the best of her. From afar, the twinkling lights had been like gems sprinkled in the night sky. The closer they got, the unaccountable scents created images in her head of death, misery, and danger. Stimulating as it was, a bad feeling began to nag at her.

Isidora faltered and held Finn's arm. "I don't know if we should keep going."

He glanced at her, and his expression softened. "Let's give it a shot. If we can't find the place, then we'll figure something out."

She nodded, unable to come up with a better alternative. Each sight and sound reinforced how naïve and closeted she had been. The fringes of the city scared her.

"It's okay. I'm here with you," Finn whispered. He took her hand, and they walked past the border, trying to stay unnoticed.

It was quite dark, and the roads were emptying of cars. The fear remained. Isidora took comfort in Finn's touch while they waded through the maze of Brooklyn's streets. Finn took out a paper from his pocket to orient himself.

"I think we're pretty close." He tugged at her arm.

The street was poorly lit, with lampposts standing about fifty feet from each other. In the dark, she noticed several people converging. They moved away from one man who approached them and hastened their steps. Turning onto another street, they came upon the right address.

"Here we are."

Isidora looked up at the decrepit building and shuddered. "This is the meeting place?" she asked. From its exterior appearance of the structure, the place didn't look safe enough. A small child could break-in.

"This is the address Maureen gave me." Finn checked the paper again. In the dimness of the night, she could see his jaw tightening. "Wait here and let me check."

"No." The place gave her the creeps. She'd rather walk into the unknown with him.

Finn studied her for a moment and nodded. They climbed a couple of steps and knocked on the door. When not a sound came, Finn decided it was time to prowl the property. "This might get ugly."

Her hands tightened on his. They walked around the building and spotted a broken window that big enough for them to fit through. Finn took the lead and hefted his body into the opening, and then reached out for her.

"Don't make any noise."

Isidora didn't need the reminder. She held her breath while they combed through each room. There were traces of scents from vampires and another aroma she had been getting accustomed to smelling over the last few days.

"This place is empty," Finn said after they'd covered the two levels and all six apartment doors.

"They conspire with humans?"

"This is the outside world. Anything goes. From what I've heard, most vampires exist among humans." Finn placed his throwing star back in its holster.

"What are we going to do now? How would we find them? Do we even have a name?"

"Slow down, Isidora. We're going to be fine. We'll start with the establishments they frequent. Maureen told me to look for someone named Rohnert."

Isidora had heard the name but couldn't remember when or where. This was becoming a nightmare. "I'm scared."

Finn offered a smile. "Don't be afraid. We'll be fine. I'll find a way to get you to safety." His words did very little to alleviate her concerns.

They left the abandoned building in favor of searching elsewhere. They walked the length of the street until they reached a place that gave Isidora sensory overload. Lights, noise, and the overwhelming scent of human blood assaulted her from every direction. Her heart started racing, and the now-familiar tang was beginning to cause havoc in her gut. She felt like she was going to snap, and she tugged at Finn's arm when she spotted a dark alley. It offered a reprieve from the bustling activity around her.

"Let's hide here."

He shrugged, no doubt sensing her emotions. "Are you okay?" he asked once they found themselves alone on the deserted pathway.

She leaned against the wall and buried her head against his chest. "There are so many of them. I can't control my thirst."

"Don't worry about them. Come feed from me." He began rubbing her back while inclining his head to offer his neck.

One look at his thick vein made her fangs throb with anticipation. "Right here?"

"No one's looking."

Hunger took over her better sense, and she dove in. Ecstasy clouded her mind at the first pull, and her body arched with need.

"We're just in time for dinner, boys." An unfamiliar voice came out of nowhere.

She felt Finn stiffen and pulled away. Blood dripped from the puncture wound, and she stared at him in daze.

"We don't want any trouble." Finn exposed a weapon-filled holster she hadn't seen before.

"And I want what you're having," the man said, walking out of the shadows.

"What are you going to do about it?" Finn pulled her behind him and crouched.

"I'm going to call my friends and help myself to your lady friend after we kill you." The gleam from the man's eyes was filled with wicked intentions, and Isidora felt instant revulsion. Several men came out of the shadows, sporting fangs and weapons of different shapes and sizes.

It didn't take a smart person to know when they were outnumbered. "Please let us go. We were just passing through." The plea was out of her mouth before she had a chance to think.

Instead of listening to her request, the four men surrounded them. "Whatever happens tonight, you're going to look for a man named Rohnert. Remember the name." Finn's words were clear.

"She's not going anywhere except with me," the head of the group said, brandishing multiple daggers. The rest followed his lead and unsheathed their weapons.

Finn's movement was like a bolt of lightning. He pushed her to the ground, and then he unleashed multiple throwing stars, striking two vampires at once. No matter how fast he moved, the remaining vampires were just as quick.

An order rang out from close by. "Stop this."

It was too late. Two daggers flashed toward Finn, hitting him in the chest and leg.

"No!" Isidora's screamed.

The newcomer was just as quick to hand the attackers their exit tickets, striking one with an ax and the other with a dagger. Isidora crawled to Finn. Pulling out the dagger lodged in his leg, she cut through the healthy skin, aborting the process of disintegration.

He caught her hand. "No . . . there's nothing we can do with this." Finn pointed to the gaping hole in his chest and coughed, his eyes filled with terror. "I've always . . . loved . . . you."

Right before her eyes, his body began to disintegrate. Ashes blew from the cavities and then he fizzled into a heap of dust. She cried at the horror of it. Her vision blurred, and anguish smothered her, a blackened haze descending to remove her from this insanity.

"How was your first day on the assignment?" Rohnert asked the moment he spotted Angus in the training room.

"It was interesting."

"How so?" He feigned nonchalance, continuing to do his stretches on the mat.

"Well, Dr. Anderson warned me right off the bat to stay away. Said she's grouchy." Angus chuckled and took his place on the treadmill.

Rohnert could just imagine it. Shelly could make any confident man swallow his balls with her sardonic remarks. "And did you?"

"I may have overstepped and butted in at one point." The sound of the treadmill and Angus's feet pounding the rubber surface almost drowned out his answer, but Rohnert heard him loud and clear.

"You're good. Don't let her scare you. She's a great woman."

"No doubt about it." Angus saluted.

Rohnert collected his Kalimetal from the floor and exited the training room. He went for a quick shower and dressed in presentable leathers before gathering concealable weapons for his patrol.

Since he was planning on relieving Alonzo, he took the stairs to the top level of the structure that held their cars. He wasn't about to let Shelly take a cab and risk questions or exposure. Tonight, he would be escorting Shelly back there for her meeting with Harrow, and then Jordan would approach the doctor with a follow-up offer.

Hopefully Shelly wouldn't pose any resistance. Zeroing in on Shelly's location from Angus' thoughts, he set his mental GPS and put the car in drive. Once outside HQ, Rohnert took a bit of time to get his bearings. He reached the swank restaurant in thirty minutes and found Zo pacing across the street, looking like an average idle citizen with nothing better to do.

"Boss, what brings you here?" Alonzo asked once he spotted him.

Rohnert scowled. "I'm going to dinner."

To his annoyance, the vampire chortled. "Dying to try their veal?"

"I heard the ribs are great. Go on, I'll take it from here."

Alonzo bowed and turned to leave. His silent parting thought was, *Maldicion, esta vampiro esta obsesionado.*

"I heard that. In English."

"I said, damn, this vampire is obsessed."

Before Rohnert could digest the meaning behind the observation, Alonzo took his leave.

Kidding or not, Alonzo had hit the bulls eye. Rohnert had indeed taken his interest in Shelly to a new level. He was about to risk exposure by dining in a restaurant to stalk the object of his affection. Regardless, he wasn't about to stand in the shadows and watch from the sidelines.

He tossed the key of the Lincoln Continental to the valet and walked inside. The expensive establishment was intimidating, but Rohnert had other things on his mind. He focused on Shelly's thoughts alone. Furtive glances were thrown his way while the host ushered him to a cozy little table at the end of the room across from Shelly. Rohnert had to smile at the cautious stares, knowing that he looked like trouble waiting to happen.

"Is this to your liking, sir?" the host asked.

"This is fine."

It helped that the room was dimly lit, making it easy for him to stay undetected. From his vantage point, he could see past the table between them and could hear Shelly's conversation just fine. After the server took his drink order, he was left to peruse the menu and eavesdrop.

"So this man who got you pregnant, does he want anything to do with the baby?" he heard Rick ask.

His muscles stiffened in anticipation of Shelly's answer. Rohnert looked up from the menu in time to see Shelly blow out a hard, long breath. "Actually, he wants to be a big part of the baby's life."

"Why are you not with him?"

"It's a long story, and to be quite frank, unbelievable."

"I'm listening," Rick said and leaned forward to take Shelly's hands in his.

Rohnert hissed under his breath and saw red, crumpling the menu with his fists. Shelly drew back, but her expression remained impassive.

"Sir, do you need another menu?" the server asked, placing a glass of scotch on the table and distracting Rohnert from his eavesdropping.

"I'll have the prime rib—rare," he said in a dismissive tone.

The waiter scampered away, and Rohnert tuned back in to hear Shelly's reply. "I'm telling you this because despite everything, you're a good friend. I trust that you'll keep my secret."

"You can trust me."

She didn't speak right away, vacillating over whether to mention the V word. In the end, her deep desire for the safe delivery of her child made her tackle the task of telling Rick the truth.

"I fell for a vampire, and I got pregnant."

"Is this a prank?" Disbelief was written all over Rick's face.

Rohnert couldn't blame the guy for reacting that way. To him, it would seem like an absurd idea.

"Rick, do I look like I'm kidding?" Shelly asked, her voice sounding earnest.

Her boss shook his head, but skepticism lingered on his face. "So are we talking about an incubus?" The question was dripping with sarcasm.

Rohnert took deep breaths and worked on calming down. He was no incubus. In the first place, he hadn't taken Shelly in her sleep. Also, she had been in complete control when it happened. The doctor had better watch his mouth if he intended to keep breathing, even if he didn't understand the true significance of his words.

"You're not making this easy for me," Shelly complained.

"Because you're not making sense."

"I'm being serious."

"And I'm trying my best here," Rick said. "You are asking me to believe there are actual vampires. I mean, we're in the twenty-first century. Superstition and myths belong in fiction, not the real world."

"Can you just listen?" Shelly sounded impatient. When the doctor nodded, she continued. "I met this purebred vampire where I used to work. Well, I still work for them. Anyway, I got involved with him, and it went downhill from there."

"The unyielding doctor finally fell for someone?" Rick sounded broken.

Shelly sighed. "Hard."

Rohnert's chest puffed with pride, but shame replaced his elation. She deserved someone better than him, and he was a prick for even coming here and listening to a private conversation.

But you're here to protect her, the voice inside his head reasoned.

"And this vampire is willing to take on a family?" Rick scratched his head.

"He wants to take care of us," she answered.

"Then what do you need me for?"

"I have no idea how this pregnancy will go. We've done research, but I haven't come across a human who survived the pregnancy."

Rick stared at her, aghast. "Then why are you going through with it?"

"Because I love it . . . him." Shelly's voice quavered.

"And you're ready die for that love?"

"If you're going to question my principles, then it was a mistake to ask you." Shelly pushed the chair to get up, and Rohnert was doing the same when Rick grabbed her hand to stop her.

"Shelly, look. I'm sorry. I just can't wrap my mind around the concept."

Rohnert sat back down. For the first time, he had a clear picture of her dilemma. Shelly sat back down, her face ashen. "I can't either, but it's true."

"So you need help with the delivery? How about check-ups? Do you know what you're having?" *Vampire? Human?*

Rohnert seethed. "A child, damn it," he muttered.

"I'm in my fourth month, and from the very little information we've gathered, females don't appear to go full term. The most would be six to seven months."

"I'm not an obstetrician."

"But you're a surgeon, and I have another doctor and nurse on staff."

Rick scowled. "What kind of people do you work for?"

"Good people who help others."

Her boss appeared dubious. "Why can't this doctor on staff help you?"

Shelly sighed. "Because he is a scientist. His focus is research."

"Great!" Rick shook his head. "I'm supposed to perform an unprecedented delivery of a vampire's baby, and my assistant will be a scientist? Jesus, Shelly. That is screwed up."

"Yeah, well, what's your answer? Are you going to help or not?"

From afar, Rohnert could tell by the bend of Rick's body that he was going to relent. "Fine, I will help you. Just be prepared for me to call in a professional if there are any complications, or if it's beyond my expertise, I will take you to a hospital. Do you understand?"

Shelly considered Rick's proposition and nodded. "Thank you."

Rohnert's prime rib arrived, but he just stared at it. For the remainder of the meal, Shelly and Rick engaged in conversation about the hospital, their patients, and the staff—things he didn't need to worry about. He concentrated on chewing the meat, which tasted like cardboard. After a few bites, he gave up and called for the check.

He walked out of the restaurant, feeling like shit. The valet returned with the car, and he waited inside it for Shelly. She and Rick emerged fifteen minutes later, and Rohnert got out of the car.

"Shelly, I'm here to pick you up." He affected his calmest voice.

Her surprise at seeing him was borderline comical, and Rick was on guard with Rohnert's full focus on him.

Shelly regained her composure quick enough to perform introductions. "Rick, I want you to meet Rohnert. Rohnert, this is Dr. Rick Whitaker, my boss."

Rohnert extended his hand, and the doctor clasped it.

"I'm pleased to meet you." Rick's eyes narrowed.

Sure you are. "The pleasure is mine." Rohnert turned to Shelly. "Shall we?"

"Thanks for dinner and for being so understanding," she said to him before Rohnert led her to the car, leaving Rick staring after them. "Have you been waiting long?"

"Not too long." He opened the passenger door and helped her settle in before coming around to the driver's side.

Once the car was in motion, they remained silent. Shelly's thoughts wandered between the shock of seeing him and her conversation with Rick, leaving Rohnert to wonder about what the future had in store for them.

Goran stepped into the shower, still reeling from the exhilaration of the kill. Under the hot spray, he cleansed the blood from his body and cleared his mind. One complication after another had derailed his plans, and he was ready with a backup strategy. He prided himself on careful planning, groundwork, and thorough execution. The disappearance of his future bride-to-be had altered his course and pushed him to initiate the next phase of his plan. With his gut satiated and his balls tingling with aftershocks of the lust the girl had stirred in him, he donned his harem pants and velvet robe. Once his sword was strapped across his shoulders, he walked to his desk.

He picked up the telephone and dialed. "Devereux, it's time."

"Yes, sire," the elite guard answered.

It was done.

He had a meeting, and he hated to be late. As much as he hated handing down a harsh sentence, he was a stickler for respect. Once that respect was compromised, there was no solid foundation on which to continue to build. Goran stepped out of his chamber into the quiet hallway. Aside from the distant sounds of children giggling and playing, there was no sign of other occupants nearby.

Hamilton knew how he hated people loitering about, and Goran's children were safe and tucked away. Since Bretania had assumed the role of babysitter after their mothers perished, he was free from domestic responsibilities.

He reached the Blanch room and wasn't surprised to see it primed for use, just as he'd wanted. With its walls scraped of blood from the most recent batch of new recruits, the place smelled downright sterile.

He found Hamilton seated on the Bergere chair waiting for him. His second-in-command rose to his feet upon his arrival and bowed low.

"Are you ready to talk?" he asked.

Despite the calm façade Hamilton tried to project, Goran sensed the terror he harbored deep inside. "Yes, your highness."

He eyed the weapon strapped across the soldier's body and decided to make it a fair fight. "I have an idea. Let our swords talk instead. Just an exercise. I haven't gotten the chance to practice for quite some time." Goran unstrapped his sword and placed it on the chair.

The hesitation was obvious, but his subject inclined his head, making Goran smile.

Shedding his robe, he picked up his sword and walked to the middle of the room. The tile flooring absorbed the sound of his footsteps, and the surface felt good against his bare feet. Hamilton followed, and they maintained a few feet of distance between them.

He raised his scimitar in preparation, and Hamilton pulled his broadsword from its scabbard, prepping for the game.

"Ready?"

"Yes." The vampire's eyes were focused on him.

Tuning out the slightest noise around him, including the rambling thoughts coming from his opponent, Goran smiled and lifted his sword above his head, assuming a defensive position.

Hamilton waited, positioning his weapon perpendicular to his body. Bretania had taught him well, but Goran had a few tricks up his sleeve. Pulling a fast maneuver, Hamilton took several steps forward and thrust his weapon. Instead of blocking with his much lighter sword, Goran sidestepped and pushed his leg out, swiping at his opponent. Hamilton stumbled but quickly regained his footing.

"Concentrate." He pointed the tip of his sword at the man's neck.

Hamilton blocked the taunt, positioning his blade vertically, then without hesitation slid his blade in a horizontal sweep, aiming for Goran's legs. He almost caught them, but Goran jumped away.

Goran smiled, feeling the chill in his veins, and tightened his fingers on the hilt. With rapid movements, he lunged, and Hamilton blocked, the clash of their swords creating the grating sound.

He parried and swung a blow to the shoulder. Hamilton evaded by stepping back and blocking. "You're good." Another strike blocked.

Hamilton sneered. It was obvious that Goran's misses had given the vampire enough confidence to attack. He stretched his arm forward with a quick thrust. Goran dodged, letting the flat of his sword absorb the blow.

He slid to his left to avoid the continued attacks, assuming the defensive position, and dished out a counter attack by slashing Hamilton's pant leg.

"Mistake number one. You're overconfident." Goran rolled onto his back, away from Hamilton, who stumbled forward.

Adrenaline, rage, and humiliation sealed Hamilton's fate. He ignored the taunt and rushed Goran when he jumped to his feet, his sword vertical to protect his head from the blow.

He avoided the strike by mere inches, pivoted around, and countered with another thrust to Hamilton's torso. "Mistake number two. Know when you're defeated."

With the last hit, Hamilton dropped to his knees, releasing his weapon to clutch his stomach. He looked up at Goran, his eyes beseeching leniency.

"Mistake number three. You didn't follow my orders. And now you're good as dead," Goran said through gritted teeth. He lifted his sword and swung from the left, slashing through the man's neck.

Tears trickled from his soon-to-be-ex-second in command's eyes before his head separated from his body and dropped to the floor. The severed part rolled a few feet away.

"Mistake number four. You fucked with me." Goran inspected his scimitar, tracing his finger along a notable nick on the edge. He took a quick glance at his once-favored soldier and walked away. The fizzle, pop, and frizz began as he closed the door behind him.

Voices floated around Isidora just as she slipped back to reality.

"You shouldn't have attacked the way you did—you scared the poor child," a low, soothing voice said.

Someone hissed. "If we'd come any later, the poor child wouldn't still be around."

She heard boots scraping the ground, and her eyes fluttered open. Two rather rough-looking characters were staring down at her. "Don't . . . kill me," she whispered.

"We're not going to kill you," the one with the calm voice said, sitting on his heels in front of her.

Isidora looked up to see the other character wiping his weapon on his jeans. He glanced at her and flashed his fangs, then smiled. "You're safe with us."

The belated aftereffect of shock rocked her body, and she cried. "They killed Finn."

"There now, don't cry. Let's get you out of here." A pair of strong hands hefted her up from the ground. "What is your name?"

She shrank back, wrapping her arms around herself. What was she going to do now? "It's Isidora," she answered after a moment.

The larger of the two vampires rubbed his chin, studying her. "Why is that name familiar?"

"Everything to you is familiar since you're always sticking your nose in everywhere," Mr. Soothing Voice said before turning back to her. "I'm Cyrus, and this is Tor."

Isidora looked around, and found what was left of Finn's ashes on the ground. A gasp escaped her, and she dropped on her knees to gather what she could of the remnants of the man she loved. She stashed the dust in her pocket, sobbing. Before she realized what was happening, the two vampires were on their knees beside her, helping with the collection effort.

"I think it's time for us to go," Cyrus said once the clean-up was done.

Her body shuddered, and her eyes blurred with tears at the thought of being alone. "Where are you taking me?"

"To a place where you'll be safe." Tor removed his jacket and placed it on her shoulders.

She started when she saw his artificial arm and hand. "You survived . . ."

Tor glanced at his prosthesis and grinned. "Like the boss I am. C'mon. This is not the place for a female like you."

"Don't you think we should at least give Isidora an idea of what's in store for her?" Cyrus asked. Unlike Tor, she could sense a fire blazing inside Cyrus beneath his calm exterior.

Tor considered for a moment. "Fine. We're a group of *good* vampires and humans, and we help whomever we can." He smiled, seeming proud of his short explanation.

She digested the information. What choice did she have anyway? The one person she'd trusted was dead. Without help, she would be as good as dead, too. Taking a leap of faith, she took a step forward.

"I'm ready to hang-out with the good vampires." She attempted a brave smile.

Tor led her out of the alley while Cyrus walked ahead of them. From the bulges under Cyrus' jacket, she could guess how many weapons the vampire was packing, and the thought gave her a little sense of security.

When she began to feel dizzy, Tor sensed her distress. "Are you okay?"

"I'm scared." Desperation made it easy to admit her fear.

"Don't be. We'll be outta here in no time." With a wave of his artificial hand, he summoned a yellow vehicle, which stopped in front of them. Tor waited until she got in then took the seat next to her while Cyrus rode in the front passenger seat.

The driver glanced over his shoulder and stammered. "Where to?"

Isidora didn't hear what Cyrus said, but it was clear the driver was filled with fear. The ride gave her a chance to compose herself and prepare to face the unknown. From this point forward, she was on her own. She hoped to find the man Finn had been seeking to help her. The driver did not even wait for Cyrus to close the door, slamming on the gas the second they were all out of the vehicle. Dust trailed after him, making Tor chuckle.

"Why did you have to scare the poor cabbie?" He nudged Cyrus.

"He looked at your face and decided he was going into the priesthood. There are too many sinners in his midst." Cyrus took a small cloth from his jacket pocket and waved it in front of Isidora's face. "I'm going to blindfold you for now. It's for the safety of everyone involved."

Apprehension gripped her heart once more.

"Don't worry. We're model citizens. We don't kill anyone unless they threaten us."

She nodded feebly. As soon as her eyes were covered, Cyrus guided her along an uneven path. One door opened and closed, and then another. Several feet later, the blindfold was removed.

The glare of the fluorescent light made her shield her eyes, but not before she caught a glimpse of a man wearing sunglasses.

"Who do we have here?" he asked.

Tor led the man away from her and explained the events of that evening. Confused and scared, she glanced around through her tears, taking stock of the room. It was some time before their discussion ended.

The door swung open, and a fierce but very glamorous woman walked in, her blonde hair tied in a coil above her head. Looking very regal in a leather outfit, she gave Isidora a sweeping once-over and then glared at Tor.

"Is it your life's mission to bring home every female vampire you can find out there?" she asked, her tone filled with scorn.

Tor blurred to the woman and wrapped his arms around her waist. "C'mon, Ally baby. I can't help it. Her mate was just killed. There was no way I was going to leave her out there by herself." His voice was placating, a far cry from the menace she'd witnessed earlier. The blonde smiled a little and rode up on her tiptoes to kiss Tor.

"C'mon, sister, don't tell me you're jealous. You got the man by the balls," the vampire wearing sunglasses said, walking in Isidora's direction.

"Hush, Harrow." The woman gave her another glance, but this time, sympathy replaced her earlier ire.

The man called Harrow smiled then sobered. "Is there anyone you know who lives in the city? Where are you from?"

Despite the multitude of emotions hitting her, Isidora felt at ease with

Harrow, as if he was the answer to her prayers. His comforting presence gave her a chance to breathe easy.

"Finn and I were looking for a man here in the city. My courtier said this man would be able to help us."

"What's the name?" Harrow tilted his head.

"I believe he said the man's name was Rohnert," she said.

Everyone in the room turned to her, their faces reflecting collective curiosity and apprehension.

"Did you say Rohnert?"

She nodded and wondered if the character she sought was an enemy of the group in her midst. If so, did it mean she was damned?

Rohnert had just cleared the gated fortress when his phone vibrated. He held the phone to his ear while navigating the car into the parking space. Shelly gave him a sideways glance.

"Harrow, what's up?"

"Where are you?"

"Parking the car. Shelly's with me." He returned her gaze, trying to get a sense of her overall emotions.

"Good. Meet me in the I-room right away. I have a woman here looking for you."

"A woman?"

"Yeah."

"I'm going to get Shelly settled in first, then I'll call you." Rohnert hung up and turned off the ignition. "Shall we?" He rushed out of the car just in time to open the door for Shelly.

"What woman?" she asked.

He shrugged. Without an idea what the hell was going on, he couldn't give her a better answer. Rohnert sensed an immediate shift in Shelly's emotional grid, and he felt like a bastard for causing her undue stress. To put her at ease, he placed his hand at the small of her back to guide her down the four levels of stairs and into the corridor that would lead them to the I-room.

"Hey." He spun her around.

"Hey what?" She scowled.

"You look beautiful tonight."

Her eyebrows lifted.

"Every night." He grazed his lips across her forehead. Then he pushed the door open.

Everyone inside the room turned in their direction. The silence turned thick, making Rohnert uncomfortable. It took a few more moments before Allison squealed and Jordan raced toward them.

"Easy." He extended his arm to stop the barreling vampire before she ran Shelly over.

Jordan skidded to a halt just short of knocking Shelly off her feet and wrapped her in a hug. The doctor looked a bit uncomfortable with this display of affection, but she seemed relieved to see her friends again.

"I'm so glad to see you," Jordan said, inspecting Shelly like she would a piece of meat at the market. "You've gotten bigger."

"Thank you. I love your fangs. They look sharp," Shelly retorted. That was the Shelly Rohnert knew and loved.

Laughter erupted from the guys in the room. Cyrus dipped his head at Rohnert while Harrow clapped him in the back. Tor, on the other hand, just grinned from ear to ear.

Harrow got down to business right away. "Why don't you kids give us a few minutes to talk?"

"I will see you after. There is so much to talk about," Jordan said to Shelly before heading to the door.

"And we need to plan your baby shower." Allison winked before hooking her hand in Tor's arm and following the rest to the door.

Rohnert hesitated, but Harrow gestured for him to stay. "If it's okay with Shelly, I want you to hang around here."

She shrugged and took the chair to Harrow's left. Rohnert removed his weapon and laid it on the table before flopping into the seat next to her, lifting his leg to rest on the chair's arm.

Harrow waited until they were settled before he laid out the agenda. "I'm glad you're doing well with the preg—"

"Gates, cut the crap. Let's hear what you have to say." Shelly leaned forward and rested her arms on the table.

"Bam," Rohnert muttered, unable to stop himself. It seemed like Shelly was back to her usual no-nonsense self.

Harrow chuckled, not taking any offense. "Well, how about telling me when you're going to be back to the grind?"

Rohnert crossed his arms and waited for Shelly's answer.

"I took a job at the hospital to occupy my time until we regroup."

"I'm aware, but I want you back now."

To her credit, Shelly took the subtle command with grace. Instead of huffing like she normally would, her mind began to race. To Rohnert's surprise, Rick's name didn't come up in her thoughts. Her concerns were directed at the post she would vacate and the possibility of leaving the hospital high and dry.

"I need to give two weeks' notice," she answered after a long and thoughtful deliberation.

Harrow considered her request, glancing at Rohnert. Shelly narrowed her eyes but waited.

"As you might have guessed, everyone has already moved in. Since you'll be alone, I'll assign Rohnert to be with you until you're back here."

"Do I have any say in this?"

Rohnert found himself uttering the answer in a hurry. "No."

Her eyes grew large. "And why not?" She directed her question at him, leaning close enough for him to smell the passion on her breath.

He straightened in his chair and squared his shoulders. This could be a very long night. He would have to remember to wring Harrow's neck for putting him on the spot. Regardless, Shelly's safety remained his utmost concern. A pregnant woman carrying a child sired by a pureblooded vampire could be easily tracked, making her an easy target for those who were familiar with the scent.

Not everyone was aware of this, so he wasn't going to broadcast it and risk two lives in the process. "First, you're carrying precious cargo, our child." The moment he uttered the words, he felt his whole body warm with reverence.

"Are you telling me I won't have any privacy until I deliver this baby?"

He ignored her question and reached out to take her hands in his. When she didn't pull back, he continued. "Second, I won't forgive myself if something happens to you while you're outside on your own."

"Oh." A hint of vulnerability was evident in her eyes, and he pulled her to him, wrapping his arms around her shoulder. He knew how much his words affected her when she leaned against his chest. It felt good to thaw the anger she'd harbored against him.

Harrow cleared his throat. "Do we need to hear the third reason?"

"Shut it, Gates," he said, then kissed Shelly's hair. He had been waiting for a chance to hold her without restraint and without reservation. Shelly snaked her arms around him, and the knowledge that she relied on him for strength felt good.

Rohnert wasn't about to let this woman slip from his grasp ever again. His macho attitude was a thing of the past, and he'd do anything to make her happy, even if he looked like the kind of sap his friends Harrow and Tor had become.

"Well, I hate to say this, but we do have a bedroom reserved for you guys." Harrow chuckled. Rather than throwing Harrow a glare meant to shut the vampire up, Rohnert sighed in contentment. Harrow leaned against his seat and rested his hand behind his head. "I love happy endings."

When Shelly stifled a laugh, Rohnert knew that everything would be all right. Everything in his world had aligned, and his course was clearer than ever.

Before Shelly could process the last ten minutes, Harrow called the boys back in, and Jordan and Allison were ushering her toward the elevator.

"So two more weeks, huh?" Jordan glanced at her and smiled

knowingly.

"I'm so glad you're back. It was so crazy after the raid, and I've been worried about you." Allison gave her a hug, her eyes glistening with tears. "Tor wouldn't let me out of his sight and forbade me to go out until we were all settled here."

This was the sort of girly thing she wasn't in the mood for. Even Jordan of all people had a dreamy, faraway look in her eyes.

"Let's get one thing straight, ladies. I'm not the huggy, touchy type. Yes, I'm back, but I will assume my old position. No special favors and definitely no baby showers." Shelly got in the elevator as soon as the steel gates opened.

Allison pouted but didn't argue. Jordan, on the other hand, snickered. "You're a party pooper."

"That's Dr. Party Pooper to you."

Jordan shook her head while Allison's laughter filled the small space. Shelly watched the pulley, which was visible from the tiny enclosure, start rolling. They traveled several floors down. Once the elevator opened, they walked into a dark hallway lined with red carpet.

"Harrow went all out with this one. He wants the best accommodation for everyone. If I didn't know any better, I'd think he wanted to relive Daddy's love for the finer things." Allison's wistful tone reminded Shelly of her former boss, the man who had started Tack Enterprises operation. Allison's father had hoped to find a cure for the vampire disease that afflicted his daughter.

A familiar ache settled in her chest at the memory of their fallen leader, making it difficult to breathe. Shelly reached out and squeezed Allison's hand. "He is wining and dining where he is right now."

Allison smiled, seeming comforted by her words. Jordan led them to the last door on the right. If her count was correct, there were ten rooms on this floor alone. They walked into a suite that held a seating area, an entertainment unit with modern toys, and a humongous bed that sat in the middle of the spacious room. To her left were double doors that concealed a huge walk-in closet. That would have been useful if she had a wide array of clothes aside from her scrubs, exercise clothes, and jeans. Maybe Rohnert was a clotheshorse. The thought made her smile.

"Um, mind sharing?" Allison teased.

Shelly shook her head. "Private."

"Harrow thought you'd like this, too," Jordan said and opened a door to reveal a smaller adjoining room. "He figured you might want the baby to have his own room but still have him close to you."

Dumbfounded, Shelly found she couldn't utter a word. She gaped at the extravagant nursery room before her, with all the furniture and gadgets a baby would need. The walls were covered with lavender paper featuring a tiny handprint design. A white crib in the middle of the room caught her eye. She wandered closer and ran her fingers along the fine wood.

Feeling tearful all of a sudden, she sniffed and checked herself.

"Hormones." Jordan's comment made sense.

Allison stopped next to her. "This is so exciting. We'll have two children in the house."

Shelly turned to Allison and smiled. "You two will be the best aunts a child could ever have."

That much was true. There was no one else to call family since her parents had passed away. These women were the closest people she could call her own. It would be all right. She had a building full of people who cared about her.

"Do you have any other requests?" Jordan asked.

She shook her head. "I have everything I want and need right here."

When they stepped out into the hallway, they ran across a vampire Shelly hadn't seen before. His enormous eyes looked at her with familiarity, so Shelly couldn't help but ask, "Do I know you?"

The male had thick brown curls and wine colored eyes. He smiled and shook his head. "But I know you," he answered. "I'm Alonzo. Zo to my friends."

"Shelly." She offered her hand. "How do you know me?"

She caught the gleam in the vampire's eyes. "Well, my boss, your man, can't stop talking about you, even in his sleep. So that makes me very familiar with you. All I needed was a face to go with the name." He smiled.

"And you, my friend, will be late for your date with Cyrus." Rohnert was suddenly next to her, working his arms around her waist, claiming her.

Zo saluted. "That is my cue to get lost. It was nice meeting you, Shelly." He jogged to the end of the hallway before disappearing from sight.

Shelly turned around and planted her palms on Rohnert's chest, loving the feel of the strong muscles underneath the black cotton shirt. "Your baby has his own room," she whispered.

Where was this tenderness coming from? She thought she had steeled her emotions and guarded her heart. Did this mean the past was forgotten? Dead and buried?

"I'm glad. I want our child near us," he murmured into her hair. Then he turned to Jordan and Allison. "If you ladies would excuse us, I think my woman has a lot of questions."

The vampires glanced at each other and nodded before walking away. Shelly didn't hear their laughter until they'd reached the elevator.

Indeed, she and Rohnert had a lot to discuss. She placed her hand in his and allowed him to lead her inside the bedroom.

Rohnert was already undressing Shelly with his eyes the moment the bolt on the door engaged. Man, it had been a while. This time, he would initiate every damn thing. He had a lot to make up for—the lost time, the way he'd left, and overall, his idiocy.

He'd led her to believe that he couldn't love her. Who had he been kidding? She was the very air he breathed, the single reason why living was bearable. Now that she was carrying his child, he'd treat her like the queen that she was. It didn't take half a brain to know he'd screwed up, and he wouldn't take her forgiveness for granted.

Ever.

"So we need to talk," he said, running his hand along her collarbone.

Shelly closed her eyes, and her expression told him the talking could wait. She had better things in mind. She wanted to make love to him.

He stiffened, and so did his cock.

"What are we going to talk about?" Her voice took a nosedive, becoming husky, and she wormed her soft hands around his waist, her lips parted like an invitation to a playground.

Okay, initiation on his part didn't happen. The woman was fast. The scent of her lust wafted in the air, and his nostrils flared.

"I want to show you how much to mean to me." He threaded his fingers through her silky hair.

"How much?" Her hand wound to the hardened bulge in his pants.

Rohnert jerked on contact, welcoming the intrusion. "So much that I'm aching,"

Her eyes spoke volumes, and her lips curved into a playful smile. "You like it?"

He shifted, allowing more room for her to navigate. The pleasure of her fingers grazing his skin made him tremble, his knees weakening under her touch.

"You have no idea."

So much for making the first move. Shelly was in the driver's seat, and he was just going along for the ride—which was wrong. It was his turn to give her pleasure, but her hand cupping his erection made it very difficult to think.

Rohnert moved his body to give her space to work. He was such a selfish bastard, but one look at her gave him absolution. She was enjoying this as much as he was.

"You can tell me what you think." She worked on his button fly and released him from the confines of his jeans.

"I think you're a tease."

Shelly shifted, and he could feel her rubbing her legs together. The idea of weaving his hand between her thighs and spreading them apart made him groan. The entry would be sweet and worth every ounce of his patience.

"What are you going to do about it?"

The vampire in him was supposed to think with a clear head and self-control, but the woman was reducing him to a pile of want, and he was unable to make heads or tails of the sensations she evoked in him.

He grunted, sucked in a deep breath, and held her hand. "You're making it impossible for me to think."

Without another word, he lifted her and marched to the king-size bed with its gazillion pillows. With a sweep of one hand, he sent the cushions flying in all directions and laid her in the middle.

"Are you taking charge?" she asked demurely.

"Yes, ma'am."

He dropped onto his elbows, securing her legs between his, and lowered his mouth to hers. She wanted him, that much he could tell, and he wasn't going to keep her waiting. She'd waited long enough, and he'd been dying to taste her again.

Patience wasn't a virtue he needed at the moment, so he let his instincts take over. Rohnert lapped her lips with his tongue, seeking entry to the warmth she offered. He kissed her until she gasped for air. Wild eyes stared into his, and he buried his mouth in her softness once again, making sure she understood his hunger for her.

He pulled away after a minute. "I want you to know that I fell for you that night we spent together." Yeah, perfect timing.

Shelly stared at him and stammered. "But you . . . you said you wouldn't let yourself fall for me."

"And you believed a fool?"

"There was nothing for me to hold on to," she admitted ruefully.

"I thought it was best to keep you believing I wasn't interested. For your own good." Rohnert moved his hand to the buttons of her blouse. "I felt like a cold-hearted bastard for hurting you."

"I can warm you up."

"I'd like that." He grinned when her buttons offered no resistance. Her creamy swells peeked out from the dark brassiere she wore. For the love of God, he wouldn't be able to keep his hands off her any longer.

"I believe I've already started." She broke into a teasing smile.

The invitation fueled the fire inside him, and he dove to the space between her breasts, inhaling. Dark hunger jacked in his gut, making it impossible to stay calm. He twisted the front closure of her bra and freed her. He tongued one pink nipple while his fingers pleasured the other.

Shelly pressed her body against his, and the hunger multiplied. He realized that this sensation wasn't just about taking her body. Her blood appealed to him more than he cared to admit.

"Shelly . . ." He tried to create a little gap between their bodies.

"I can't have you drinking from me, but I'm sure I can make other arrangements. Don't think, Rohnert. We've lost too much time already." She pulled on his neck until his face was close to hers.

"I don't want to hurt you."

"You will never hurt me by loving me." Shelly's mouth prevented any further conversation.

He responded like a man possessed, hungry to take everything she had to give. The rest of her clothes came undone with one swift movement. Overheated and dying to possess her, he raked his eyes over the expanse of her chest and the creamy bump of her growing belly.

He shivered. "Shelly, I can't do it." He pulled away.

Hurt and rejection flashed across her face. "What have I done?"

"I don't want to hurt the baby. Maybe it's better to wait."

It took a few seconds for Shelly to catch his drift. Then she laughed. "I'm the doctor here. I think I know what will hurt the baby. And if you don't do this, *you'll* get hurt."

Her threat brought him back to the land of the living. "Tell me if I'm getting too rough."

Shelly answered with another laugh. "I've yet to see that." She tugged him closer.

Rohnert answered with yanking her hair. "You're a little lioness, aren't you?" He flashed his fangs, and he swore he felt her getting wetter.

So his little vixen wanted a wild ride.

He allowed her to undress him, her eyes widening at the reintroduction of what he had to offer. With deliberate teasing, he lowered his length to the juncture of her legs and she responded with a groan.

This welcome was enough to get him excited. Rohnert slid into her, grunting at the friction. He grabbed her hips and thrust inside, slowly at first, then increasing the pressure. She moaned with pleasure while her body adjusted to him, and the satisfaction cranked his desire higher. Her slick heat engulfed him, and heaven was within his grasp.

Rohnert drilled into her, possessing her body as well as her mind, taking stock of her ecstatic thoughts. He smiled in contentment. Within minutes, her voice echoed through the room while she erupted in her first orgasm.

He lifted her legs onto his shoulders and kept pounding into her for his own release. There was no greater pleasure than hearing her groans of satisfaction,

"Oh, Rohnert, I'm coming again."

For the next half hour, he gave her the wildest night of her life. He took her to the heights of ecstasy, and her answer came in explicit moans and gasps of delight. Her cries spilled from her lips and filled the room with the sound of her pleas for more.

Collapsing next to her, Rohnert rested his face on the pillow while his arm splayed across her body, staking ownership.

He gave Shelly a sideway glance and caught her sighing in contentment. His world was spinning on its axis again, and the rest of his worries fell away.

Sleep came too easy this time. Rohnert had lost track of time in her arms. Half the day was gone before he was roused from deep sleep by the incessant ringing of the phone.

"Hey, Romeo, Harrow wants to see you in the I-room stat." Tor's annoying voice broke through the comfortable cocoon of sleep.

"What's going on?"

"The woman, remember?"

"Give me five," he said and hung up.

Rohnert checked Shelly's sleeping figure and resented the fact that he had to leave her side, but duty called. He hated his inability to turn his back on his responsibilities even for a few indulgent hours.

Rohnert lifted Shelly's arm off his chest and slid away from the bed as quietly as he could.

"Leaving already?" Shelly peeked out of one eye.

"Keep sleeping. I'll be back after the meeting." He kissed her on the cheek.

Seeing her smile, he knew she understood. Bless her heart.

"I'll be waiting," she mumbled, already succumbing to the call of sleep.

He picked up his discarded clothes from the floor and got dressed in a hurry. After holstering his weapons, he tested the locks before slipping out of their bedroom.

Tor, Harrow, and Cyrus were already in the I-room when he arrived. "Where are the others?" He settled next to Harrow.

"On their way." Tor leaned back and put his legs on the table, crossing them at the ankles. "I take it you're back in business, my man."

Rohnert sized Tor up. "Mind your own goddamn business." It was difficult to hide his emotions from the very people who had seen him at his worst. He turned to Harrow, hoping his friend wasn't going to jump onto the bandwagon and start teasing him. "Where's the woman? And what's all the secrecy about?"

Harrow leaned on the table and removed his sunglasses, leveling white irises at him. "You're aware that Iden and his wife perished in the ambush right?"

Rohnert nodded, not quite sure he understood Harrow's sudden interest.

"And you're aware that Goran is on a manhunt to find the missing daughter, right?"

He nodded once more. "She's here with us?"

The door opened, and Gentry, Zoe, Firman, Angus, and the rest came rushing in. They bowed their head in his direction before saluting Harrow.

"Cyrus, why don't you get Isidora?" Harrow said.

He left without a word. The room buzzed with questions while Rohnert digested the new information. This was going to get down and dirty pretty soon. Goran wouldn't hesitate to turn the city upside down to find the woman.

"Have you told anyone about this?" he asked, gesturing for Gentry to come forward. "Is there anyone else who would know that she made it out alive?"

"No, sire." Gentry sat next to him. From the expression on the soldier's face, Rohnert could tell that this new development both pleased and scared the shit out of him. "There were traces that she'd made it out of the secret passage alive, but when we got to the clearing, we found ashes. We assumed they got to her first."

Cyrus came back a few minutes later with a young woman. She had striking short red hair and skin as pale as paper. Her eyes gave away her fear, and her body swayed even with Cyrus supporting her arm.

Harrow jumped to his feet and offered his chair. "Don't worry about anything. Rohnert is here," he said in a soothing voice.

The young vampire raised her eyes, scanned her surroundings, and finally settled her gaze on him. An overwhelming instinct to protect flashed through him.

"I'm Rohnert, an ex-Council member just like your father. You're safe here. You know Gentry, right?"

She barely moved her head in response.

"He's a loyal soldier of the Council and has served me and your father as well. You can rest assured no harm will come to you while you're under our protection."

"Where are my parents?" she asked Gentry.

There was no need for verbal answer. Gentry's obvious misery gave away her parent's fate.

Isidora buried her face in her hands and wept—a low wail that crept underneath Rohnert's skin and made its way to his heart. He knew the feeling so well. He had lost his parents as well. It was a difficult pill to swallow, especially for a young soul.

Cyrus walked behind her and rubbed her back to soothe her while everyone around the room looked at each other with unspoken questions.

Harrow started pacing the room.

Rohnert knew what he was thinking, and it was absurd. "I don't think it's smart to involve the rest in the Council's problems."

Alonzo cleared his throat. "With all due respect, the Council's problems are everyone's concern. We're all connected here in one way or another. Goran is running the race into the ground, and we'd be fools to let him get away with it."

Rohnert raised an eyebrow. He recognized Alonzo's zeal, and the guy was as tight as they came. "What do you suggest we do?"

Alonzo met his gaze head-on. "I say we don't allow him to rule any longer."

"And after that?"

"You can lead us. Everyone thinks you should challenge Goran," Alonzo said without hesitation.

Rohnert smirked. "Impossible. I've removed myself from the Council."

Gentry sighed. "But you can't turn your back on your people."

True. He'd done that in the past. Look how the race had suffered. Perhaps he could help without getting too involved.

"I have no intention of ruling. I'm a fighter, and I best serve my purpose out there. Maybe I can talk to some of the Council members, and see what can be done."

It would be difficult. Goran had invested time and patience into establishing loyalty among his peers. It wouldn't be easy to find Elders who were willing to risk their lives by thwarting Goran's plans.

"If you're the Rohnert my courtier and friend spoke so highly of, then there's no doubt you can pose a challenge to that evil man." Isidora's statement showed more inner strength than she'd dared to project before.

It was the one task he wasn't ready to take on. Not then, and not now. It would take a great deal of lobbying to find the right vampire to confront the head of the Council. Rohnert wasn't the one. He would bet his life on it.

"Cheryl, meet me at the clinic in fifteen minutes," Shelly barked into the phone.

"Sure, Doctor." Cheryl was ready to get down to business, and Shelly was glad at least one of her nurses had escaped the attack on their main headquarters.

"Um, where is the clinic anyway?" How funny—she'd come to the facility to talk to Harrow, but she'd gotten more than she planned on. *Get it together, girl. One night isn't going to change your life, so get with the program.*

"From your suite, take the elevator two floors down and turn to your left. It's marked." She could hear the amusement in Cheryl's voice.

"Thanks."

She slid out of bed and planted her feet on the plush carpet. Her legs were still weak from lovemaking. It would be interesting to see how walking would feel. She'd wanted rough sex, and Rohnert had obliged. Damn him for reading her mind.

Taking a step to the bathroom, she savored the tingling sensations from the night before. She grabbed a handful of her hair and sniffed it. Traces of Rohnert's scent lingered there, making her think that showering might not be a good idea after all. Muttering, she shook off her desire. Being deprived of sex for so long had done damage to her brain.

"Get in the shower and stop thinking with your pussy," she said to her reflection in the mirror.

"What's wrong with thinking with your pussy? I happen to like it," Rohnert said, taking her by the waist and spinning her to face him.

She hadn't heard him come in. That was going to take a lot of getting used to. "Only one good thing comes out of it." And she pointed to her belly.

"I don't have any problem making more, if you want them." He kissed the nape of her neck, grazing his sharp teeth along her skin.

Here we go. We're never ever going to get things done if this keeps up.

"I don't have a problem with not getting anything done today, either," Rohnert answered her unspoken sentiment. "It's the middle of the day, and I have nothing better to do."

"Don't you have any training to conduct? Good deeds to perform?"

Rohnert shook his head and continued with his assault on her skin. Shelly could feel her pulse quickening.

"You'll have to keep yourself busy. I have something to do." Using a trick Rohnert had mentioned the night before, she quickly pictured a beautiful seascape to cover her tracks. She could tell by the way he clenched his jaw and narrowed his eyes that he was trying to read her mind, but she wasn't going to let him in on her small project. "You'll have to wait and see."

His expression grew more frustrated, but he didn't argue. "I'll wait for you. Come back as soon as you can. I'm not done helping myself to you," he said and walked out of the bathroom.

Left alone, Shelly took a quick shower and helped herself to the new scrubs hanging in her closet. Brownie points to whoever had gone out their way to shop for her. She'd had no idea they made maternity scrubs, but she was glad to have them.

Rohnert had made himself comfortable in the seating area. His eyes were fixed on her, following her until she went out the door.

Remembering Cheryl's directions, Shelly was able to find her way to the clinic. A smaller version of the clinic at headquarters, it boasted the same state-of-the-art instruments and gadgets for surgeries and examinations.

Cheryl walked out of a small adjoining room with a handful of towels and supplies. "Good morning, Dr. Anderson."

Shelly cracked her knuckles. "Ready?"

"As always." Cheryl attempted a smile that failed to reach her eyes.

This made Shelly pause. Her nurse seemed off. She didn't have time to pursue it now, but she would find out what was wrong soon enough.

"I need a syringe, a bag, and a sterile tube." She took a visual inventory of the well-stocked cabinet.

Trained not to question a direct order, Cheryl went to gather everything. Shelly sat on the stool and prepped her arm.

"You'll have to do this for me."

Cheryl nodded, and snapped on the gloves. "How much am I taking?"

"Enough for one feeding." She stared straight ahead. If her assistant had any qualms, she gave no indication, and Shelly wasn't about to divulge her business. This wasn't a popular practice in their facility, since most of their vampires were satisfied with blood acquired anonymously. This was an isolated case aside. If Rohnert wanted to taste her, Shelly would let him.

The erotic vision of him taking her vein was too silly to even consider, but the idea got her hot and bothered nonetheless. She couldn't help fantasizing about offering herself to the man she loved. It was a bond she hoped they could share, although in her present condition, she wasn't up to being sucked by a vampire. In fact, she wasn't equipped to offer her vein because she was human. For that reason alone, she wouldn't stand a chance at survival unless she fancied being turned into a vampire.

"Dr. Anderson?"

Shelly snapped back to reality. "Yes?"

"Are you ready?"

"Do it." She breathed deep.

The process didn't take long. Once the bag was half-full, she decided it was in her best interest to stop.

"I think we've got enough."

Cheryl pulled out the needle and tossed it in the biohazard bin. When Shelly stood up, the room began spinning.

The nurse was quick to steady her. "Are you all right? You look faint."

"I'm fine. Just a dizzy spell." Shelly waved her hand in dismissal.

"Do you want me to call Rohnert?"

"No. I'm fine." She grabbed the warm bag and walked to the door, albeit unsteadily. "Thank you." And she pulled the door shut.

Goran smirked at the ashes that used to be Hamilton and proceeded to the room next to the assembly hall. Since this was an unofficial gathering, he'd opted for the smaller venue. The hall buzzed with lively conversation before he slipped in.

He soaked in the collective mood before making his presence known. "Is this everyone?" he asked, walking to the center of the room. The floor there bore his family's seal—the dark ruby with vines spiraling downward was a symbol of longevity and worth, and a tribute to a long line of great leaders.

"Sire." Devereux and the rest of the elite soldiers all bent low at the waist, bowing their heads in reverence. Devereux was one of their best warriors—he had smarts, expertise, and the right amount of ruthlessness. The elite vampire straightened and waited for orders, his crimson eyes watching Goran while his body twitched with anticipation.

Goran inclined his head in response. "I'm delighted with the swiftness with which you gathered everyone here, Devereux." He moved to sit on the lone chair at the front of the room.

"Your command is mine to uphold, sire," Devereux responded.

"How many strong men do we have?" Goran took stock of the sea of faces. This elite unit had been started by Rohnert but had been dissolved when the traitor left. Although the vampires were still on active duty, their roles were limited to official Council business. Relegated to routine patrols, they had been bored out of their minds and eager for change.

"Two hundred, your grace."

It was going to be interesting to see the outcome after he unleashed this powerful army. With all of them trained to use every weapon imaginable, they were going to be a force to be reckoned with and the most brutal unit to ever walk the darkness.

"I want you put together ten in each group, and I will specify each group's assignment. No one is to question my orders. I want results, and I expect every of you to follow your instructions to the letter." Goran sized each of the men, soaking in their enthusiasm. Turning back to Devereux, he said, "You're going to lead the fiercest of your men on a special assignment."

"Anything you ask, sire." Devereux bowed, the light glinting off the Council's golden oak bush on his breast.

For the next half hour, Goran went into detail about the alarming spread of *Incomis Sippanus*. The soldiers had been sheltered from current events, and their response to his news assured him they would be glad to carry out the tasks assigned to them.

It suited him just fine.

"Also, we have several members of the Council who have renounced their position without notice, and that, my men, is inexcusable. I want them captured and brought to me. If anyone dares question the authority under which you're acting, I give you permission to eradicate them without delay. Our one concern is to keep order in the Council and establish which members are loyal to the race."

Each fighter nodded, and the electric atmosphere made Goran's body tingle with excitement.

"Does anyone have a question or matter they wish to address?"

A hand came up, and Goran zoomed in, welcoming the question even before it was asked.

"Yes, Rocco," he said and gestured for the soldier to come closer.

"If I may ask, what are we expected to do if we come across Rohnert?"

Goran pretended to consider the question while gathering the overall feelings of the man who stood before him. Rocco's loyalty was divided— not the thing Goran wanted to see at the moment.

"This is what you should do." Goran stood up and unsheathed his sword. "Do not think twice about cutting him down."

He took one swing, severing Rocco's head from his body to the shock of everyone in the room.

"Rohnert is a traitor, and anyone who would think twice about sparing his life will end up just like your comrade here."

The room fell silent, and he straightened to replace his weapon. "Do I make myself clear?" he asked.

Murmurs of agreement came at once. The hallmark of a great leader was the ability to instill fear in the hearts of those he ruled and demand loyalty. There would be grave repercussions for those who strayed from the chosen path.

Satisfaction coursed through Goran's veins while he gauged the soldiers' reactions. He had gotten his message across, loud and clear.

Shelly made it back to their suite, but she was still feeling dizzy. Before she could pull the keycard from her pocket, the door opened, and Rohnert took her in his arms. She was supposed to be the one with raging hormones, but when his mouth claimed her face, neck, and lips, she guessed that made two of them now.

"I thought you'd never come back."

"I told you I'd be back." He sure knew how to make her feel appreciated.

Rohnert didn't act like he'd heard her. Instead, he held her out at arm's length and inspected every inch of her exposed skin. When he zeroed on the little bandage on the crook of her left arm, he hissed. "What is that?"

"I got this for you." She lifted the bag of blood.

Rohnert glanced at her offering, and his nostrils flared. He picked her up, snarling, his eyes wild with hunger, and his fangs elongated.

When he placed her on the bed and corralled her body with his legs, Shelly felt no fear.

"You're offering me something I don't deserve." His voice was low, but each word was clear.

"I'm giving you a little piece of myself." Her body arched upward, wanting to feel him against her.

"You've given me enough already." He hissed and tore the clothes from their bodies in swift movements.

She held the bag up. "Are you going to drink first?"

Rohnert was already seeking entry, but he took the bag from her and punctured the edge with his sharp teeth.

Shelly moaned, unable to keep her eyes off his mouth while he drank. He consumed every bit of her offering while he glided inside her, drilling harder and harder.

Her ecstatic cries mounted as the intensity built until it burst into rapture. Her vampire followed with a grunt of satisfied pleasure and collapsed next to her.

She snuggled up to him. "Hold me."

Rohnert adjusted his powerful body and gathered her in his arms. He twined his legs with hers, and they remained silent. When a soft snore drifted in the stillness around them, Shelly realized he had fallen asleep.

Undecided whether she should be offended, Shelly slipped into her own dreamland, feeling safe and loved.

Rohnert roused from the most satisfying sleep he'd had in a very long time. His arms were around Shelly's body, and it felt like the most natural thing in the world. He thought about the gesture she'd made. Although human blood could never be substituted for that of pureblood vampires, drinking hers had brought him more than nourishment.

He needed pure blood to survive, and he wondered whether Shelly would understand this. While it was true that he could go on for some time with only her blood, another source would need to be found.

"If you're worried that I won't want you to feed from someone else, don't." Shelly turned to face him. "You will need to use a vampire for blood, and that's fine."

Dumbfounded, Rohnert could only nod. She wasn't a vampire, but Shelly seemed to have picked up his mind-reading ability without even trying. How could the woman know what he was thinking?

"I've done my research, and thanks to your invaluable input, I already have a clear idea of what life will be like with a vampire." She smiled, the corner of her eyes crinkling.

"Does your research tell you what's next for us?" he asked.

"You said something about a ceremony." She placed a hand on his cheek.

He nodded. This was going to be tough. Such ceremonies were meant for parties who shared pure lineage, not inferior species. The Council rules were clear on this. A pureblood hadn't been joined to a human before as far as he knew, but then he wasn't going to let that stop him.

He'd already fallen from grace. If the binding rite wasn't possible, the next option was to follow the human tradition. "After I take you to work tonight, I will get the ball rolling."

This meant employing the help of the vampires' great Shaman. It had been years since he'd invoked Lukan's aid. The circumstances back then had been dire, but the priestess had been a great help to him. Perhaps she would help him with this, as well.

"I'm sure I can find a nondenominational minister, but I've never seen a wedding performed late at night."

Rohnert chuckled. "There's always a first time. I'm sure a healthy donation to the congregation would be persuasive."

They talked until it was time for Shelly to go to work. She had agreed to stay with him during her last two weeks at the hospital and had promised to tender her resignation that evening. Two weeks wasn't too long. They could do it.

After a brief consultation with Harrow, Rohnert had commandeered one of their fortified armored vehicles to get her to the hospital. They set out with Angus in tow—the human had been given strict orders to go wherever Shelly went.

Relieved to know that Shelly would be under Angus' watchful eye, Rohnert left the car outside her apartment and set out on foot to return to their headquarters. He had every intention of summoning the great Shaman. Once inside his room, he took the box that contained the few items he'd brought from his apartment, including the tools he needed to complete the summoning process.

Rohnert donned the black velvet robe before taking out gingko beads and a set of purple candles. Sitting on his haunches in the middle of the room, he closed his eyes and chanted the sacred words in the old language. With his arms spread apart, he ran his forefinger and thumb along the sacred beads and continued his plea for an audience.

He was almost certain the priestess would not forsake him. It took hours before a gust of wind began to circulate through the room. It was a sign that his summons had been accepted. He kept his eyes closed until he heard her speak.

"It has been a long time, oh great Rohnert. I thought you had forgotten about me."

Rohnert opened his eyes, settling on a woman with hair the color of honey and eyes like the nighttime sky. "Indeed, Lukan. I hope I found you at an opportune time."

Her smile was dazzling. Lukan walked forward and stopped before him, offering her hand. He took it and brushed his lips on the flat ring with reverence.

"It's rare for you to ask anything of me. There is no way I'm going to keep you waiting." She looked around the room, one eyebrow lifted in a questioning arch. "Is this the place you now call home?"

Rohnert nodded. "It is, oh dear one."

"What can I do for you?" She placed her hand on his bowed head to sift through his thoughts. He had been warned in the past not to challenge the woman's capacity to filter information by trying to read her mind or block her from his.

Rohnert waited until Lukan offered her hand and helped him onto his feet.

"She's the one for me," he said, leading her to the seating area. The Shaman sat down then smoothed out the material of her while silk gown. Her expression remained neutral, showing no reaction to his statement.

"So it's true that the great warrior has fallen for a lesser species."

The reference to Shelly's species left a bad taste in his mouth, but he dared not question her position.

"Go ahead Rohnert, state your idea. You have been a steadfast creature, and I value your opinion. Humor me."

Rohnert took a deep breath and chose his words carefully, not wanting to offend her in any way. "Our species is old. We've seen many things in our existence, but I don't think it's fair for us to judge a young race. Humans are capable of compassion, and they possess knowledge beyond their years."

Intent eyes watched him grapple with words before she gave him a smile. "You might be right, but old habits are hard to break." The words were almost apologetic, a concession from a superior creature.

"Understandable," Rohnert said. He tried to block Lukan's thoughts, preferring to hear her recommendation firsthand.

"You're a breath of fresh air, Rohnert. Alas, this goes beyond my authority to decide. I shall request an audience with Gastarius. If our great diviner grants a meeting, I will tell him of your present woes."

"I believe in freedom within every aspect of our existence. I don't submit to coercion, nor would I betray the race's written laws, but I feel strongly about this woman, who also happens to be carrying my child."

To Rohnert's amazement, Lukan turned pale. Her hand gripped the arm of the sofa, not releasing her hold until she had collected herself. At that moment, he was tempted to peek at her thoughts.

"I would make sure our beloved Gastarius is made aware of this development. Is there anything else that you require of me, Rohnert?"

He shook his head. Maybe it would be a good idea to request an audience with the oldest living vampire. "Would you secure a meeting with Gastarius for me?"

Lukan stood up and smiled in understanding. "I shall make sure he knows of your request. Be well, oh great one." With a flourish, she curtsied and disappeared.

Rohnert sat in the dim candlelight for several minutes, trying to gather his thoughts. Then he walked to the bureau and retrieved the black book. He went to the bed he shared with Shelly and stared at the cover. A small part of him was ready to read the written accounts of their race's history, but he still wasn't prepared to face the weight that knowledge carried. Despite Isigani's advice, prudence told him to wait until he felt the time was right.

He set the black book on the nightstand and left to seek Harrow for a sparring match. A good fight would be guaranteed to free his mind from the fucked-up fears that had taken residence inside his already crowded head.

Harrow was waiting for Rohnert in the training room, giving him a long look to size up his emotional well-being.

"Rough night?" Harrow asked.

Rohnert removed his shirt, throwing it to the side of the mat.

"Care to talk about it?"

"Do I look like I want to talk?" he bit out, crouching low.

"I think so. Why else would you call on me?" Harrow laughed and matched his stance.

"Remove your sunglasses. You don't want that expensive shit to go to waste."

"Talk then." Harrow took off his Oakleys and set them on the desk at the corner of the room. He ran back and fell into a fighting position, hands defensively poised in front of him.

Rohnert gritted his teeth. He hated when Harrow was in this talking mood. Men loved to fight, and that was what he was jonesing to do. He took a few steps forward, gauging Harrow's next move. When he jumped sideways, Rohnert spun around and landed a reverse spinning kick straight into Harrow's chest.

"I'm not sure if Gastarius will grant my request to join with Shelly in a formal ceremony."

Harrow stumbled backward but regained his footing immediately. He took advantage of Rohnert's distraction and zoomed forward with a front snap kick, clipping him on the shoulder.

"I never thought you needed someone's permission to do what needs to be done." Harrow bounced backward, waiting for Rohnert's next move.

"I happen to believe in the old ways, and I want Shelly to be recognized as my mate, not just some whore I bed."

For the next minute, they circled each other, assessing their next moves. Since Harrow seemed content to stay on the defensive, Rohnert initiated a series of jump kicks, which Harrow blocked. Rohnert tried to block Harrow's axe kick, but he was unable to get his left arm into position in time. He winced and took a step back while bouncing off the mat and rotated the arm in its socket. Catching his friend off-guard, Rohnert then employed the roundhouse technique to the temple, rendering the other vampire immobile for a few seconds.

"I don't follow the law blindly, but this is important to me. I'm an old-fashioned guy," he said, backing away and assuming a defensive stance.

Harrow shook his head and grinned. "You must do right by Shelly. I trust you to do the honorable thing. Did you ever find out when the baby is due?"

Good question. A Q&A session with Jones was in order. Harrow again used Rohnert's distraction against him and launched a side kick that struck him on the throat.

Air stopped short of reaching his lungs, and he staggered backward, coughing.

"Damn you, Gates." Rohnert raised his hand in defeat.

"You've taught me well, Sensei." Harrow bowed.

For the next half an hour, Rohnert focus on beating the crap out of Harrow. It had been a long time since he'd been able to channel his aggression onto an opponent, and it felt good to kick butt once more.

Harrow was rearranging his jaw when Rohnert decided to ease up on him.

"What the hell are you doing? Are you planning to send me to vampire heaven soon?" Harrow rolled his neck.

"So sorry, my man. Just making sure I haven't lost my touch."

"You need to come with a warning label—DEADLY IF AGGRAVATED."

Rohnert sat down in the middle of the mat and did some stretches, feeling a little tightness on his left shoulder. The damn thing had been giving him trouble lately. The rotation was off, and blocking was tricky and cumbersome.

Harrow eyed him with interest. "You should get that looked at. Shelly told me about that ossification crap."

He grunted when he moved the stiff arm around. "Yeah, maybe I should."

After their sparring session, Rohnert checked the training schedule and found that he was cleared for the night. He could hear Tor barking orders next door and decided to peek in, while Harrow excused himself to attend to business.

"With the axe, remember these key words—fling, swing, and release. The movements should be fast, and keep your eye on the target. Make sure your shoulder is straight on the take-away and your wrist squared. Gather enough momentum so your weapon sticks to your target."

Tor glanced at Rohnert, who stood by the doorway, and nodded. "It's easy once you've got the mechanics working for you."

Several students grunted in agreement. When they broke off in little groups, Tor approached Rohnert with his signature grin, flashing the tips of his fangs. "What brought you in here, my man?"

They slapped palms. "Nothing. I was sparring with Harrow and thought I'd pay you girls a visit."

Tor snorted. "Like what you see? Think you can do it?"

"Do I?" Rohnert rolled his eyes. "Fling, swing, and release. Piece of cake."

"Let's see you do it." Tor preceded him to the target area.

Taking the challenge, Rohnert followed, the students parting in deference. Tor handed him a combat axe, which was lighter and had a short handle with a single blade.

Taking his position about ten feet away from the target, Rohnert focused and kept the three pointers in mind. He raised his arm and flicked the weapon but the rotation on the socket kept him from flinging with enough force and he missed the target by a few inches.

Tor snickered. "Try using your other arm. Though it's not dominant, you might fare better."

Rohnert blew a lungful of air and concentrated on the target. He used the same tactic with his right arm. The swing went better. The lunge gathered enough speed, and his axe clipped the right side of the round target.

Everyone in the room clapped. Rohnert should have felt better, but the limited range of motion in his left arm could cause him trouble. He rotated the aggrieved arm again and tested for another run.

It was several hours later when he finished exploring this tangent and found the room empty except for Tor, who was sitting behind the desk.

"Are you good to go, Paul Bunyan?" he asked, snickering.

Rohnert grinned and took the seat opposite. He glanced over the target that had borne his punishment. His performance hadn't been bad by any means, but it still wasn't up to his personal standard.

"I guess that's good for now," he said.

Tor studied him for a moment. "Look, we all have our areas of expertise. You have the Kalimetal, daggers, and throwing stars, but I like short bursts of action."

"I get ya. I just can't imagine not being able to do something well enough."

"Hmm . . . somehow this feels like an outlet to you. Care to talk about it?"

"Why are you ladies dead set on talking? What happened to the good old 'keep-your-nose-out-of-my-business' deal?"

"I see our peerless leader had started on you, so I'm just gonna sit back and enjoy the peace and quiet." Tor leaned against his chair, watching him with his purplish red eyes.

"Why don't we take this to the bar and get some juice in our system?"

For the rest of the night, Rohnert spent time with Tor, drinking in silence. The trouble with Shelly's schedule at the hospital was the twelve-hour shift. By the time she was ready to go, the sun would already be up, and that was a no-go for him.

So for the waning hours of the morning, he drank and waited to hear from her.

Shelly found a little downtime and tracked down Rick in his office. Her boss looked up from the mounds of paperwork on his desk.

"Yes, Shelly?"

"You have a moment?" she asked, advancing into the room.

The chief-of-staff was a busy man, but Rick set aside the chart he'd been working on and gave her his undivided attention. She took a seat and got down to business. "I'm giving you my two-week notice."

Rick closed his eyes for a brief moment before opening them and focusing on her. "I see."

"I wish I could stay, but I'm needed elsewhere." She offered no further explanation.

There was no immediate response except breathing. Finally, he took a pen and scribbled something on a notepad. "I understand. I wish you all the best with your pregnancy, Dr. Anderson. You know how to get in touch with me. Call when it's time."

Rick stood up and reached out his hand. She shook it, wishing she could've given him more time, but she wanted to start her new life with Rohnert. "Thank you. I will call on you."

Two weeks was going to go fast, considering their department's workload. It seemed like every soul in the city found a way to end up in the emergency room. The time passed in a blur, and by the end of her shift, she was tired and ready to snooze.

Angus looked up from the paper he'd been reading when she appeared. "Ready?" he asked, matching her short strides.

She nodded, and they walked out of the hospital together into the early morning rush. The sun was on a slow ascent, and she shed her jacket in favor of enjoying the morning chill. Being cooped up in the ER all night made her cherish whatever passed for fresh air in the city.

While they walked in silence, she replayed the hours she'd spent in Rohnert's arms. A small smile tugged at the corner of her lips. She could get used to the idea of waking up with him, and the sex part . . . even more so. The smile stayed with her until they got to her apartment. Once she'd placed most of her things inside her luggage, Angus took the heavy load from her, and they headed to the car parked outside.

He helped her in before stowing her things in the trunk. The city traffic was living up to its reputation, and they navigated the streets at a snail's pace. Shelly had so much to do once she got to the facility, such as checking on amputees and beginning the process of fitting prosthetic limbs.

The moment the car was in park, Shelly's door was yanked open, and she was cradled in Rohnert's strong arms.

"Damn it. I thought I wouldn't survive the night without you." He took a quick glance in Angus's direction and gave him a nod. The human saluted before heading into the facility.

Tucked in his arms, Shelly felt like nothing could harm her. "Same here. All that kept me sane was remembering last night." She offered a knowing smile and then rested her head on his shoulder.

Rohnert grinned, and his eyes twinkled. "That, my dear woman, is the only thing I could think of."

Instead of taking her to the bedroom as she'd expected, he brought her straight to the empty mess hall. The scent of bacon and eggs made her mouth water. "Is that for me?"

"All for you." He deposited her on a red plastic chair.

While she ate, Rohnert filled her in on his sparring match with Harrow and his attempt to use the axe. It wasn't a surprise when he complained about the limited movement in his arm.

"Starting today, I will work on your shoulder. We'll see if we can restore some of its previous range of motion," she said between bites.

"I think I have a better idea of how to kick off our alone time." Rohnert winked.

Shelly was taken aback. Did the vampire who couldn't crack a smile, even if his life depended on it, just *wink* at her? Their time apart must've done a number on him, but she wasn't complaining—this new and improved Rohnert suited her just fine. She felt herself blushing.

"I think we're on the same page."

Shelly was desperate for sleep. Although she'd been in bed for quite a while, she and Rohnert had been going at it for the last three hours.

Crazy! Three solid hours of pleasure, screams of bliss, and nonstop trips to heaven.

This had to stop if she wanted to be able to function at work tomorrow. In all honesty, did she want to end the fun? No, sir. Until her belly prevented them doing what they loved most, she'd just have to be sleep deprived.

"Do you want me to get warm milk for you?" Rohnert asked, grinning. Contentment shined in his face, and the harsh lines around his eyes had vanished.

"That's a good idea," she said and sat up. But a strawberry milkshake would be much, much better.

He was already at the door before she realized what she had done. "One large?"

She managed a feeble nod before he disappeared from sight. Rohnert's mind-reading was something she would need to remember when her silly cravings popped up.

Left to her own devices, Shelly looked around for something to do. She had forgotten her nighttime reading material at her apartment, but she spotted a black book sitting on Rohnert's side of the bed. It made her laugh to realize they already had their own sides. That was fast!

Shelly reached for the book. It had no title, but judging from the battered cover, it had passed through many hands. Her curiosity grew, and she fingered the tattered edges before opening it to the marked page.

> On the first sign of the moon's illumination, a vampire will rise into power, his heart filled with avarice. Among his peers, he will raise havoc, and death will augment the despair within. Mortals and vampires alike shall have no power to prevent the destruction he will leave in his wake. A disinclined soul shall be called, and a child borne to the rightful guide shall come to fulfill this divination.

Shelly read the paragraph until her mind spun. When she snapped the book closed, she felt like a small-time thief who'd robbed a big jewelry store. Heart pounding hard against her chest, she tried to make heads or tails of what she'd read.

Could the book be talking about Rohnert? Was he the one who would raise havoc? Either way, the message she had read was meant for someone else.

Good thing her nerves had settled by the time Rohnert came back with her strawberry milkshake.

"Here you go—large with real strawberries." He handed her the tall glass.

"How'd you manage that?" She took the milkshake and bowl of berries from him.

"I figured it's healthy, so I dropped by the kitchen and picked up some for you."

Shelly sucked on the straw and didn't stop until she got brain freeze.

"You humans are quite fascinating," Rohnert said, removing his holster filled with weapons and placing them on top of the bureau.

He went into the bathroom, and when he came back out in nothing but basketball shorts, Shelly's eyes almost popped out of their sockets. No matter how much time she spent with the man, she'd never be able to think of him as an average guy.

"That *is* a compliment." He flopped on the bed next to her. "It's nice to know that we're on the same page."

It took a few seconds to realize her mouth was hanging open. To be fair, his massive pectorals were an impressive sight. She gave him an innocent smile and began slurping up her drink. After one long tug, she noticed that she was channeling her desire, sucking hard on the straw whenever Rohnert heaved a breath.

"You're quite distracted tonight." He lifted her to sit on his lap as though she weighed no more than five pounds.

Shelly placed the cup on the nightstand and faced him, linking her hands at the back of his neck. One look in his midnight eyes invited her to get lost in them, but she wasn't about to let it deter her from telling him the truth.

"I may have dipped my foot where it wasn't welcomed today."

Rohnert turned his full attention on her. "What do you mean? Why are you blocking your thoughts from me?" he asked.

"I wanted to keep you out until I was ready to talk." She pulled his face closer to hers and planted a kiss on his lips.

"And here I was thinking you were just interested in my good looks." He chuckled.

She shrugged and laughed. "I still want a piece of that, but not until after I've talked to you."

"Go on then." Rohnert could come across as a mean bastard, but in reality he was a good man, although he could be intense like a heart attack. Everything the vampire said or did came from deep within himself.

She pointed at the black book. "I thought that was a novel. I had no idea it was personal."

"Which part did you read?" Rohnert reached for the tome, giving no sign of irritation whatsoever.

Shelly sighed. "It had something to do with a vampire rising to power and a babe born to challenge him."

Rohnert nodded. "How did you interpret what you read?"

She couldn't answer right away. "It scared me."

Rohnert hugged her tighter, as if shielding her from an unseen enemy. "Why?"

"I'm not sure if you are the evil who raises hell or the one whose child will challenge him."

"What makes you so sure it was me that particular passage was talking about?"

"Gut feeling, I guess. It had to be you." She gripped him tighter and rested her head on his bare skin. The rapid beating of his heart excited and frightened her. "I don't want anything to happen to you."

There was a smile in his voice when he responded. "Don't worry about me. I'm always watching my back, and we have a great group here who watches out for me, too."

"I'll forever worry about you. You're out every night, and with the war out there, there's no telling."

"Rest easy, my dear woman. We're going to be together for a long, long time. Or until you decide to kick me to the curb."

She laughed and let the soft cadence of his breathing lull her to sleep. It had been a long day, and wrapped in the cocoon of his arms, she had nowhere to go but dreamland.

Sleep eluded Rohnert, although Shelly had been sound asleep for hours. He was wide awake, and there was nothing he could do about it.

Sliding away from the bed, he made sure Shelly didn't stir and then got dressed. He went up one flight of stairs and through a series of double doors into a short hallway that led to the laboratory.

There he found Jones buried in work. Though this was a much smaller version of the lab they'd had at the old headquarters, it still was complete with all the impressive gadgets and toys money could buy.

Jones looked up from the microscope and broke into a big smile. "Rohnert, what brings you here?" he asked, setting his work aside.

"I haven't gotten the chance to thank you for keeping an eye on Shelly." He advanced into the room and sat on the chair.

The scientist laughed. "On the contrary, Dr. Anderson kept all of us together. If it weren't for her quick thinking, Cyrus and Rayce might not be with us today."

That didn't come as a surprise. Shelly had been a level-headed female since day one. "Just the same, if you weren't there to help out, she wouldn't have been able to do it on her own."

"I doubt it, but if you say so." Jones accepted his thanks without any further argument. "So what can I do for you?"

"Is there any more information you can give me regarding a human mother giving birth to a Halfling?"

Jones face registered understanding, and Rohnert was glad that he didn't have to explain. The human pulled out the keyboard from his desk and began punching the keys.

"Just a few new leads, but nothing I could put my money on. Most Halflings I've contacted refused to grant me an interview. The few who have answered my questions say that their sire eventually turned their mothers, although not necessarily after childbirth. That leads me to believe that the pregnancy and the birth went fine."

Rohnert digested the information. If he were to take Jones' findings as fact, then he had nothing to worry about.

"Again, don't count on it as a sure thing. God, Rohnert, I mean I want to believe everything will be all right."

He wasn't sure whether to clap the man on the back for his honesty or shred him for not having enough faith. Shelly would get through this pregnancy. He could feel it in his bones.

"Are you able to handle labor and delivery?"

Although he'd heard Shelly asking her boss if he could help her, Rohnert didn't think it was wise to let a civilian in on their little secret, and he wouldn't want her going anywhere to deliver but there in the secure facility.

"Well, I have had a few hours of lecture in school, but it's not my forte."

From the sound of it, it would be better to have Jones assist, as Shelly had said. Then another idea hit him. Lukan had experience in birthing vampires, and it might be best to have the priestess handle the delivery in case something went wrong.

"What is the expected delivery date?"

Jones's eyes gleamed with excitement. "Most of my research came back with an average of twenty-five weeks. It could be a week earlier or later, depending on the mother's endurance. Since Shelly is more active, I think she'd be right on schedule."

Rohnert did a mental calculation before he spoke. "She's about six weeks away, if we go by your estimate."

"Sounds about right."

"Is there anything we need for the delivery? Has Shelly been informed?"

"As far as instruments, we're good. We have Cheryl on hand, too—she will be a big help to us. Shelly knows everything I told you." Jones removed his eyeglasses and ran his fingers along the bridge of his nose. "Is there anything else you need?"

Rohnert shook his head and rose to his feet. "Thank you, Jones." He offered his hand, which the other man shook with vigor.

"Don't worry, Rohnert."

Easy for him to say. He wasn't the one lying next to Shelly and watching her breathe, wondering if she was eating enough or if she was experiencing any pain.

Rohnert left the laboratory feeling somewhat relieved, yet his unanswered questions continued to haunt him.

"Mind explaining to me why we're hovering up here like damn gargoyles?" Tor adjusted his position on the ledge of the high-rise building.

"This is a perfect spot for me to catch everything in the general area." It had been Rohnert's habit as of late to scale one of the higher structures surrounding the Rockefeller Center to get a good look at every activity in the vicinity.

"Good for you, since you have that power. What are we looking for anyway?"

Rohnert's body hummed, an indication that a fight was about to happen. He strained to see more and zeroed in on a group of suspicious-looking characters walking by the rink. Their demeanor was guarded, and their attention was focused on two people seated on the bench. Rohnert smiled.

"Get ready to rock," he said and then jumped off the ledge in a free fall.

"Fuck it, Rohnert. Why must you make things difficult?" The sound of Tor's exasperated breath sounded not too far away.

The cold wind hit his face. "You wanted to partner up."

Rohnert looked over his shoulder to see Tor barreling down behind him. He tucked his legs against his stomach and did a series of flips midair to get his feet pointed at the ground, and Tor followed suit.

They hit the pavement of the dark alley with a soft thud, straightening right away. Palming his Glock, Rohnert ran at a breakneck speed, not wanting to miss the fun that had already started. Tor stayed close on his heels while they weaved through the knots of revelers at the outdoor dining area.

Rohnert skidded into a halt and turned around.

"What now?" Tor narrowed his eyes and hissed.

"I recognize some of the men." He walked farther away, but not out of earshot. The crowd swallowed them so they shouldn't be detected right away.

"And I thought we'd be going for the kill already." Tor sounded irritated by the delay.

"Hold your horses, man. I don't want to take unnecessary lives just because you're jumpy and in need of blast therapy."

Tor backed off a little. They hung around, pretending to enjoy the atmosphere, while Rohnert stayed tuned in to the conversation in process. It would be impossible to be inconspicuous, considering they towered among the others, and Tor's dreadlocks were always an attention getter.

"If I were you, I'd march into the street and get lost. Now." The firm voice ordered. Such authority came from vampires who knew their worth.

"There's no trouble from us. We're just hanging out and having a good time," a petrified voice answered.

"The disease that you carry is not welcome here."

Rohnert heard a scuffle, and from what he could make out from the noises, a fight was about to break out.

"Let's go." Unbuttoning his trench coat, he zigzagged through the thick horde of humans milling around.

"What's going on?" Tor trailed him.

"You want some action, right? I'm giving you some action."

Rohnert could hear the argument escalate, and he ran faster.

"We're crashing the party?" Tor sneered, unleashing an axe and dagger.

Oblivious folks glanced their way but must have assumed they were dressed early for a costume party.

"We're getting rusty, and it's about time we got some practice."

Rohnert pulled up the collar of his coat to conceal his face before they rounded the corner of the dark alley, just in time to witness one of the Council guards—wait.

Who in the hell sent the Elite Guards out?

One of the guards, his face obscured, tugged on the collar of one of the diseased vampires and lifted him off his feet. "I'm a reasonable man. Even if the order is to annihilate every single disease-carrying parasite, I was willing to make an exception. But you don't follow directions. Now, I'm done being merciful."

"Please . . ."

Rohnert stepped into sight, Tor flanking him on the left. "Mercy is afforded to those who ask for it."

All heads whipped in their direction. Weapons of every make and size were aimed at them, big guns were cocked, and breaths were held.

"Your opinion is not important. If you and your friend have sense, you'll turn around and leave." The head of the ten-man crew turned to face them, his eyes narrowing, still gripping the neck of the spluttering vampire.

Instead of heeding the threat, Rohnert took several steps forward and stopped just enough to get a close read on the situation. The guards on the left were trigger-happy. The ones in the back were more subdued, willing to let the team leader fry his ass first. The others were more interested in bludgeoning the diseased vampire and his super friends.

"You were given orders to kill, and yet you give ultimatums first. That is a sign of weakness."

Rohnert released the strap of his Kalimetal. The little sound tested the restraint of the jumpy guards and two inched forward. The leader released their captive, dropping him to the ground gasping for air.

Rohnert turned to Tor. "He seems anxious."

"He is a rather edgy lad, don't you think?" Tor grinned, exposing his fangs.

"As you can see, we're busy, and your intrusion is not welcome." The leader unsheathed a long-ass sword and nodded, and bullets, daggers, and throwing stars came raining down.

Rohnert kicked his heels and sprang to his left while Tor took to the right, jouncing on the walls, and they landed behind the soldiers. Their movements were precise, and they turned their weapons on the surprised group.

Four dropped like flies, and the remaining ones fired at will. The sick vampire and his cohorts started crawling away, but the leader pointed his sword at them, ready to cut them down.

There was no time to think. Rohnert diverted to fend off the attacker, springing forward and thrusting his Kalimetal within a hairsbreadth of the vampire's head.

"Try it and you'll end up like your friends," he said.

The leader hesitated and then looked around for reinforcement. One glance at Tor told Rohnert that his friend was unstoppable. Not even his prosthetic arm would slow him down. Fizzles and zaps sounded around them like goddamn Fourth of July.

"Rohnert?" the leader asked.

That glance earned him a kick in the gut. He stumbled backward as pain radiated all the way to his toes. Rohnert bared his fangs.

"Yes, and you should know better than to attack a helpless vampire. I thought I made myself clear back when I trained you."

With a lunge, he slashed his Kalimetal across the vampire's neck in a clean sweep. The severed head landed a few feet away, while the decapitated body swayed before falling to the ground. Fireworks erupted from the disintegrating remains then turned to ashes.

The three victims scooted back on the cold asphalt, too terrified to scream. Rohnert hated to see the fear in their eyes.

"Get up on your feet. You're safe and free."

The frightened beings scrambled to stand, clumsy and tripping over their own feet.

"You're not going to kill us?" one asked.

Rohnert shook his head.

"All clear. Can we go now?" Tor said from behind. His face was going to pop if his grin got any wider. That was the thing with fighters. If they were inactive for some time, they would get excited at every kill. He took a look at the men. "What about them?"

"What about them?" Rohnert returned the question.

"If one is diseased, we should take them with us."

"Then go babysit. I have somewhere to be." Rohnert turned around and headed to the corner. He heard Tor quelling the fears of the civilians.

In hindsight, he shouldn't have left Tor, but he felt like a strung cable ready to recoil. He needed to run off the aggression. That had been the first time he hadn't hesitated before taking the life of someone he knew. The change in him was rather unnerving, yet the thrill of the kill in his veins couldn't be denied.

With one kick of his boot against the pavement, Rohnert took off at a run, covering several blocks in less than five minutes, even with the thick throng of bodies zooming from every direction. He found his way into back to Rockefeller Center and tried to blend in with the crowd.

A soft knock came from the door, and Goran straightened from his desk. He'd been poring over the notes in the black book, trying to decipher the scrawled gibberish for the last two hours. He cracked his neck before calling out, "Come in."

Devereux entered with his usual swagger, wearing a confident grin. The tail of his long coat brushed the floor, swaying with his carefree strides.

"I have something that might interest you." The vampire pulled out a little square case from his pocket.

"Really? Why don't you make yourself comfortable?" Goran gestured to the seating area, flipped the case open and took the CD out. Deep down, he'd already gathered the information from the guard's mind, but a firsthand visual would be even better. He slid the disc into the player and leaned back.

Devereux did as he'd been told, relaxing on the sofa the moment his ass hit the cushion. Goran flicked on the play button and smiled. The amateur video showed Rohnert in perfect form, killing off the Council's soldiers. The homemade footage gave away the location.

What was Rohnert doing in the vicinity of the hospital? The best way to learn was to investigate.

"Well done, Devereux." Goran stood up and walked over to the adjoining room that housed his weapons. He fastened the holster across his chest and packed every weapon available. When he returned to the main room, Devereux was still lounging on the sofa. "You're excused."

The man shot to his feet. "Don't you need me with you?" Devereux asked.

"One piece of advice. Don't assume anything. Ask first." Goran marched to the door and held it open.

"My apologies, sire. I only meant to help." The vampire bowed before scampering off like a scared rabbit.

Goran smirked. Much better. Nip that shit in the bud. He watched the shadow of Devereux's retreating figure disappear before willing the invisible gateway to open and stepping outside the Council walls.

He took in a breath of the warm air and zeroed in on the hospital, not too far from where he stood. Feeling a massive dose of adrenaline course through him, he skirted around the horde of humans before setting off at a dead run.

The well-lit area surrounding the hospital made surveillance problematic. Two security guards stopped in front of the double doors, glancing around before striding away. Goran stayed hidden in the shadows across the street and waited. The sun's orange glow was peeking out over the skyline, making its slow but steady ascent, but he lingered until the last possible moment.

His patience was soon rewarded when a human walked past the dark patch where he hid. The male's thoughts broadcasted the information Goran sought, giving him much more than he'd bargained for.

Goran took it all in and smiled to himself. "It's beginning to look a lot like Christmas," he sang under his breath before leaving the premises.

He had some homework to do.

Rohnert reached the hospital a few minutes before the sun dragged its deadly claws across the horizon. The minute he arrived, a prickle of discomfort shot through his system. In the past, all hell broke loose when he ignored such a premonition.

The trouble with this strange stabbing in his chest was that there was no way of knowing to when, who, or where the warning applied.

Distracted, Rohnert flashed to where Angus had been waiting, leaning on a blue truck.

"How is Shelly?" he asked, unable to control the hiss that slipped between his lips.

Angus whipped around, startled. "Damn, you scared me."

"When was the last time you checked on her?" Rohnert asked while scanning the perimeter.

"About thirty minutes ago. She's in the middle of surgery, appendectomy. Female, Asian descent, thirty-four years old—"

"Enough. I get it." Rohnert leaned on the hood of the vehicle, suddenly feeling tired. "Noticed anything unusual?"

Angus shook his head. "Aside from the cross-dresser who was wheeled in an hour ago with a gunshot wound, it's been pretty damn quiet."

So he was a tad bit paranoid. He couldn't help it. His woman was inside those walls, and sunrise was beating him back into the darkness. Rohnert stretched his arms behind his neck and tried to quell the uneasy feeling he had.

He glanced at the pinking sky, hating the burning sensation in his skin. "I have to go. Call me as soon as you leave. It only takes twenty minutes to get back to the warehouse."

"Yes, boss. I know the drill." Angus grinned.

Rohnert nodded and flashed from sight. This 'creature of the darkness' crap was getting old. He tore through the parking lot and wove through the back alley to return to the warehouse, running against time to beat the inevitable sunrise.

It was difficult not to the trust Angus, even if his instincts were screaming to add reinforcements. The human was tight, sharp as a tack, and fast to respond. Besides, his enemies were creatures of the night, so Shelly's safety during the daytime was not a big concern. Even so, Rohnert couldn't tamp down his protective nature when his mate and child were involved.

Speaking of which, he hadn't heard from the great Shaman yet. Perhaps another summon was in order. If Gastarius didn't see fit to permit him to bond with Shelly, then her idea of a nondenominational minister would have to suffice.

He reached their new facility just as the burning of his skin became unbearable. Rohnert gunned for the kitchen, not bothering to turn on the light. He opened the refrigerator and grabbed a handful of ice cubes, letting out a loud sigh the moment the cold met his skin.

"Looks like you almost got toasted out there." Harrow chuckled from his seat at the corner table and set down his glass.

Rohnert answered with a grunt. He rolled the ice cubes along the expanse of his neck, letting the coolness soothe the blistering pain. The inflamed skin soon settled, and he felt relief.

"We all feel overprotective when it comes to our women, but you have to watch it, my man. It's not a joke. Third degree burns are not easy to deal with. Imagine Shelly breathing down your neck." Harrow shuddered and then laughed.

"Shut it, Gates."

Harrow shook his head. "I'm sorry, Rohn. If you want added security, I can give it to you. Don't fight the daylight."

Rohnert took the chair opposite his friend. It would be insane to demand additional manpower when their crew was already stretched thin, and assigning newbies was out of the question. He'd have to deal with his paranoia on his own.

"Easy for you to say. You can go out in the daytime."

"And I still won't compromise myself until we know for sure. The theory had been tested only during dusk, when the rays aren't as fierce."

True. Harrow had been quite cautious. Prudence should be the goddamn vampire's middle name. "Whatever."

"You know I have your back. Just be realistic. I can watch her for you, if it eases your mind."

Rohnert blinked. They were tight as brothers could ever be, but this kindness stumped him. He shook his head. "Nah, it's all good."

Harrow downed the rest of the animal blood in his glass and smacked his lips in contentment. Then he leaned forward with an earnest expression on his face. "You helped Jordan, and we can't thank you enough. You have given us more than friendship. It would be the least I could do."

Okay, this was making him uncomfortable. "You're going to do what you want anyway. I doubt I can stop you."

The other vampire chuckled and shook his head. "Didn't your parents teach you that kindness begets kindness?"

Rohnert raised an eyebrow. "You're not going to lecture me right this minute, are you?"

His phone rang.

"Angus." The human gave their exact location, although it was unnecessary. Rohnert's phone GPS pegged their whereabouts. "See you in ten." He placed the phone back in his pocket and looked up at his friend.

Harrow stood up and deposited the glass inside the dishwasher. "I don't have time to give you a lecture. I have a phone conference in an hour. A new client with a huge order." He walked to the doorway then turned around. "You need a haircut, my man."

"Christ sakes, will you shut up?"

The swinging door flapped like a fan behind Harrow.

Getting up on his feet, Rohnert wiped his wet hands on his jeans and took off to the bedroom. He put on his dark velvet robe and got the materials for the ritual in place. This time, the wait was shorter. Lukan's trademark wisp of smoke appeared before he had to repeat the chants.

"You rang?" she said, smiling.

Rohnert heard his knees crack when he stood and bowed his head low. "I appreciate you coming right away."

"What can I do for you?"

He dipped his head lower, knowing that the Shaman knew what he wanted, yet still gave him the courtesy. Her hands rested upon his neck, and the discomfort from the blisters disappeared in an instant.

Rohnert lifted his eyes to meet hers. "Thank you, Lukan. I meant to ask if you have had the honor of speaking with Gastarius."

Lukan's eyes rolled up, her body shook for a brief moment, and her hands fell limp on her side. He took a step forward, but she shook her head. "I made my request but was denied."

Rohnert's lips thinned and the muscles on his face twitched but he held his tongue. *So it had to be this way.* He didn't dare speak his thoughts aloud.

"We are sitting on the precipice of change. I think our aging diviner is quite occupied at the moment."

Seething inside, he took a moment to calm his nerves before speaking. He led Lukan to the sofa to distract himself. She took the ottoman, and Rohnert began to pace in front of her.

"Pardon me if words won't come easy." He stopped and looked at her.

"I understand," Lukan said and diverted her attention toward the door.

Shelly let herself in, Angus waiting outside until she shut the door behind her. She stopped in her tracks the moment she spotted Lukan. "Oh. I'm sorry, did I interrupt something?" she asked, shooting Rohnert a questioning glare.

"I was leaving." Lukan got up, her dark gown swayed with her graceful movements.

"Wait, dear Shaman. I want you to meet my wo . . . my mate. Shelly, this is Lukan, our race's healer and priestess."

Shelly's exasperation disappeared, replaced by an expression between relief and embarrassment.

"I'm pleased to meet you," she said and held out her hand.

Lukan grasped her hand with both of hers and closed her eyes. Rohnert watched her face twist into a grimace, too quick for an average human to catch, before she smiled. When she opened her eyes, they were glazed.

"You're a beautiful being, inside and out," Lukan whispered after a long moment of silence.

"Thank you."

"As I said, I have to go. It was nice meeting you, Shelly. Rohnert." She inclined her head. "I will try to return for the birth of your child," she said before disappearing in a cloud of smoke.

It took a moment for Rohnert to compose himself. It wasn't every day that the priestess could be rendered speechless.

"She's going to help with the delivery?" Shelly asked while removing her Crocs.

"You heard what she said." Rohnert drifted behind her, wrapping his arms around her waist. He sniffed her hair and basked in her scent. "How was your night?"

Shelly turned around and wound her arms around his hips, hugging him tight. "I can get used to this type of welcome."

"Soon there will be no need for welcome. You have seven more days to fulfill your duty to the hospital. After that, we'll be together for god knows how long."

He felt her smile against his chest. "True, but this is how it should be. Right?"

"You know it. How was work?"

"I'm sure you already know the answer. I was up on my feet all night.

There was no chance to breathe or even sit down. Although most cases were minor, it was busier than usual."

Rohnert ran his hand up and down her spine, rubbing the tired muscles of her back. "Why don't you change and I'll get you something to eat? Then I'll massage your tired feet."

"I'll change, but I can do without the food. I have been eating every moment I can. Jordan gave me a bag full of cookies and granola bars. I'm stuffed. But I won't say no to the massage." She broke away from his embrace and went into the bathroom. Afterward, he heard the shower turn on.

When Shelly emerged from the shower smelling like an exquisite flower with nothing but a towel looped like a turban on her head, Rohnert knew the massage would have to wait. It took two big strides to reach her. His arms went around her and lifted her, and he placed her on the bed. The towel came undone, and Rohnert held up a few strands of her hair to his nose.

"Jesus, woman, I won't ever get tired of smelling you." He pinned her down with his body.

"Aren't you giving me a massage first?"

How astute of her. "I think your body needs this more." He pressed his erection against her belly.

"I think the massage can wait," she said, pulling him down for a kiss.

Rohnert shivered at the demanding sweetness of her mouth on his. If this was a preview of their day, he was ready for it.

The thought made him smile.

"What are you grinning about?" Shelly's eyes narrowed but were full of mischief.

"I don't know about you, but I'm ready to eat."

Shelly bit her lips at the slight innuendo. "I think I'd like to get a taste, too."

Waiting was out of the question. Rohnert slid lower. The scent of her arousal made his blood run hot, and a growl sounded from deep in his throat.

It was another hour before they both had their backs on the mattress.

They stared up at the dark ceiling, spent but utterly content. The sound of Shelly's heavy breathing was music to Rohnert's ears, and he turned onto his side to face her.

"Have you thought of a name for the child?"

Her lips turned upward. "You're not willing to go with *It*?"

Instantly, his mood darkened. "You've got to be kidding me. I don't ever want you to think that."

Shelly sat up and tilted his chin until he was looking into her eyes. "I was just kidding. Forgive me?"

Rohnert sighed. "There's nothing to forgive."

"Would you prefer a name from your race, or do you want a generic human name?"

"Would you mind if we give him a name that came to me in my dreams when I growing up?"

"As long as it's not Archibald, Dick, or Gaylord, I think I'm okay with whatever you choose." Shelly laughed.

Rohnert chuckled. "How does Malin sounds to you?"

"Malin . . ." she repeated. "Does it mean anything?"

"It means strong little warrior."

She nodded. "I like it. It has character, just like his father." Then she frowned.

"Shelly, what's wrong?"

"Better make sure we have a boy. I don't want to end up with Torina or Helga if we have a girl."

"I can feel my son." He pulled her close to kiss her cheek. "But just the same, try to think of a fine name for a girl, just in case."

"I'll try."

It had been more than three weeks since Zane had walked away from the motel he shared with Cheryl. It hadn't been an easy thing to do. He'd wanted to stay with her, which was crazy.

Where was all this bullshit coming from? Never in his life had he considered anyone important until that moment. Since he'd left, he had been pining for a simple female with accusing green eyes who had defied an order from her superiors in order to protect him.

When before had he spent time mulling over what other people thought about him? Yet he cared about what she thought. The deep-seated desire to do right by her made it difficult to think rationally.

He straightened up from his bed, flinching with each movement. His muscles ached like a mother. Although he had managed to remove most of the Dangeran particles embedded in his skin, there were still some leftover granules rooted in hard to reach places.

Getting back into his townhouse had been laborious and painful, to say the least, and the place reminded him of the gruesome acts he had committed. The last time he'd been here, he had subjected Cyrus to horrific torture before changing him, all in the name of revenge.

With no one he could trust, he returned to this secure location under a veil of secrecy. Goran had no knowledge of his whereabouts, and he preferred it that way. Zane had contacted Celia, his housekeeper, who came to his aid without asking questions. The poor old lady had almost passed out when she saw his condition. At his insistence, she had agreed to keep his presence on the down low.

The old woman had taken pains to remove more of the Dangeran poison lodged in his skin. Some damage had been caused by prolonged exposure to the lethal substance. He'd live, but there was no promise he'd ever be in tip-top shape ever again.

Eighteen days, thirteen hours, seventeen minutes, and counting—how much longer until he could see her again? If Cheryl had managed to reunite with the mismatched group she called her family, she'd be safe. Until Goran . . .

No. Zane wasn't going to think about his grandfather. There were too many painful memories and too many lives sacrificed in one man's quest for power. They were all nothing but puppets, executing his orders and paying with their lives. Their crime was idiocy, believing the tangled web of lies he'd spun.

Not wishing to get more worked up than he already was, Zane pushed his body out of bed and screamed. The largest chunk of the damn Dangeran was still in his left leg, but they'd have to perform basic surgery to remove it.

The damn leg felt like lead. Zane stood up and tried to walk. He got one foot in front of the other until he reached the bathroom, but it was not without difficulty. Each stride brought gut-wrenching pain. He bit his lips to keep from crying out.

This is your penance, asshole.

He glared at himself in the mirror and wasn't the least bit surprised by his gaunt appearance. Unable to bear looking at the changes without being reminded of his past mistakes, Zane went to the shower and turned the knob on full blast. He walked in the icy water and stayed there until his frayed nerves began to stabilize.

Goran was thrilled with the information that had landed in his lap, but first things first. He needed a gopher.

There were a few people that came to mind. Devereux was smart and straight. The few times he'd forayed into the vampire's mind had proved the male was solid and loyal. However, assignments of a more personal nature should be assigned to a family member. His children were quite young, and most were female—not a whole lot of prospects there.

Then there was Zane. This reminded him that the bastard hadn't reported back for some time. His phone calls had been unreturned, and Goran wondered whether his grandson was still breathing or if he was decaying in a ditch somewhere.

He picked up the cell phone and auto-dialed. While he was waiting, he thumbed through the worn-out pages of the black book. There were many passages that remained unclear, although most of the pages were filled with a bunch of rubbish such as births and insignificant dates.

Zane picked up after four rings, just as Goran was about to hang up.

"Hello?"

"I specifically instructed you to call me as soon as you were done with the mission."

Silence.

Too bad there was no way to find out what the bastard was thinking. Phone conversations couldn't make him privy to anyone's thoughts.

"Apologies, Gor . . . Grandfather. Our mission was successful up to certain point."

"Tell me."

"We killed quite a few, but I think they're smart enough to change hideouts now. The key people we wanted to take down escaped. Their leader, the diseased one, captured and tortured me."

The story was a bit unbelievable. If Zane were indeed captured, how could he have gotten away?

"How did you escape?"

There was a stretch of silence, and then he heard a soft curse. "I conned the person assigned to watch me into letting me go."

"What did they do to you?" It was a detail he could do without, but he needed to appear interested, if not concerned.

"The son of a bitch planted Dangeran bits throughout my body."

"Where are you holing up?"

"In the penthouse. What's going on?" Zane's labored breathing revealed that the bastard wouldn't be much help to Goran.

"I want you on a stake out since you're good to go during the daytime."

"Sure. Give me a few days to recuperate," Zane said, and then the phone line went dead.

It was a good thing Goran was feeling merciful, or his dear grandson wouldn't see the light of another day after hanging up on him. One of these days, he'd have to teach the boy some manners.

Returning his attention to the black book, he went back to Gastarius' prophecy. What did it mean?

Goran stood up, his thumb wedged in-between the pages, and paced inside his chamber. To whom did the passage refer? He had so many questions, but the more persistent issue continued to be maintaining the security of his throne and his reign.

Iden's daughter had either gotten away or had perished during the raid. Who knew? Damn. Regardless, he would need to find a replacement bride right away—whomever he could stomach.

The list was rather short, since he needed a pureblooded vampire. He ticked off the names of the available candidates. Some he wouldn't ever dream of bedding.

Then there was Bretania. The woman had grace and the right disposition. She was a charmer, and people tended to gravitate to her, which would be beneficial to his cause. The iron fist with which he ruled seemed to be losing its grip, and this was not a good thing. For his reign to flourish, he needed all the support he could get.

Goran placed the book back inside the drawer and proceeded to his walk-in closet. He chose a dark tailored suit and got dressed while concocting a plan in his head.

There were no threats he could think of, and he expected nothing but a yes to his proposition. Nevertheless, Goran pocketed a dagger and several throwing stars before leaving his chambers.

He glided along the darkened hallway and slipped out of the Council walls in silence. Bretania would be in her residence since training was done for the day. Most of the elders retreated to their personal abode once Council business had concluded.

When he emerged from the hazy exit, his eyes darted everywhere, checking his surroundings. The cold wind slapped his face while he made his way toward the main thoroughfare. The shivering crowd walked with purpose, trying to hide from the lashing wind.

Something caught his attention. His eyes flickered to a bunch of men standing outside a busy bar, who were sporting concealed weapons under their heavy coats.

For kicks, Goran drifted close enough to sense their mood and to listen to their inner ramblings. The renegade trio of vampires were armed, dangerous, and on patrol.

One of the males turned, and they locked eyes. It took one look to determine that this was a carrier of the disease. In hindsight, he should've packed enough ammo for a fight. Instinct told him to walk away. This was not the right time or place.

He covered a block then turned in to a dark alley. The diseased vampire had decided to follow him and have a go-see. Goran smirked.

Just as he pivoted, a dagger swooshed by, almost catching him. Without hesitation, he unbuttoned his suit jacket, grabbed three throwing stars from the inner pocket, and shot them in his attacker's direction. One struck the male on the left arm. His presence of mind astounded Goran. Despite the dire situation, the male pulled out a dagger to sever the injured limb with an eerie calmness.

Goran dug his heels into the pavement and rushed the man. "Today's your lucky day. I'm here to issue your one-way pass to hell," he said and flicked a dagger into his victim's chest.

"We know who you are." The man spat and fell to the ground. "You're not as impervious as you think you are."

Goran kneeled down next to the fallen man. "You have no idea what I'm capable of. Sweet dreams, asshole." He yanked the dagger out.

A cry tore from the dying vampire, but Goran didn't stick around for the grand finale. He had better things to do. When he spotted the grime on the dagger's blade, he blew an exasperated breath. Although he enjoyed the thrill of kill, it was a menial job he'd much rather relegate to the guards. There were more important issues for him to pursue with his precious time.

He emerged from the alley and stayed on course. Within minutes, he reached the row of expensive penthouses. Ignoring the urge to scale the walls, he took the front entrance under the watchful eyes of the human doorman.

"How are you this evening, sir?" the piece of trash asked, giving him a suspicious once-over. Under normal circumstances, Goran wouldn't expose himself to humans, but propriety was a necessary evil in this case. It was important to appear like he gave a damn about Bretania.

"Fine," he answered, not bothering to hide his disdain for such an inferior creature.

"Which of our residents are you visiting tonight?" The question was asked without malice—just a man doing his job

However, small talk bored him, and he wasn't in the mood to waste any more time. "I'm visiting ten-thirty-two."

The doorman nodded and inclined his head. "Have a pleasant evening, sir," he said and turned to attend to another new arrival.

Goran proceeded to the waiting elevator. Once the doors closed, he glanced at his appearance in the floor-to-ceiling mirror that surrounded him. His hair was tied in a neat ponytail in his back, and his dark suit was impeccable as always. If it weren't for the harsh lines around his mouth and his black eyes, he could pass as an average human.

The ding of the elevator brought him back to the present. He located Bretania's unit and rapped on the door. The shuffling of feet sounded and fabric brushed the door before it opened.

"Sire, this is a surprise." Bretania opened the door wider. Garbed in faded jeans and a white tunic, she appeared too normal—domestic even. Not how he expected an Elder to look, even in downtime.

"I have a proposition for you," he said, glancing around the compact living room, which was filled with precious art. A notable painting caught his eye, distracting him. "Botticelli?"

Bretania's lips curled into a sly smile. "The perk of having the right connections."

Goran nodded appreciatively at *The Birth of Venus* and then returned his focus to the female before him. "As I said, I have a proposition for you."

The smile that appeared on her face could have lit up a football stadium.

Shelly woke to kicking inside her stomach, but she still felt like a million dollars. It was her last day at work, and her pregnancy had been uncomplicated thus far. Her hand moved to the space next to her and landed on Rohnert's back. This was her heaven.

She stretched and rubbed her belly. The wee one had been more active, an indication that he was growing faster and stronger. The due date had been estimated within a six-week window, but all they could do was guess.

Still, she was comforted by being surrounded with people who cared about her. "You're going to be fine, Malin,"

"He will be great." Rohnert peeked out of one eye and smiled.

"Oh, I didn't mean to wake you." Shelly sat up and leaned against the headboard.

"I'm always half-awake. It's a habit." Rohnert rubbed his eyes then focused on her face.

"You have to fully rest your mind. Studies show lack of sleep can cause fatigue, irritability, inability to concentrate, and decreased productivity."

"I feel fine. Besides, studies show that as we grow older, we sleep less. I'm almost four hundred years old. I can sleep with my eyes open."

The vampire remained an enigma. Most days, she could feel she was getting through to him, but some days she felt like he was a stranger, still holding back.

"Are you trying to read me again?" Rohnert took the hand that rested on her stomach and brought it to his lips.

"You're like a crumpled old newspaper. Unreadable. Some words are clear, but most are blurry and indistinct."

"Why don't you just ask me? No need to stress yourself out."

"What are your plans for the future? Why are you so quiet all the time? What do you think about most of the time? I feel like I know you, and yet I don't." She turned toward him, tucking her legs underneath her body. "I don't know your history. Do you have a family?"

Rohnert inhaled before releasing an embattled sigh. "You do have a lot of questions." He rubbed his head and closed his eyes.

"If you're not ready to talk about it, it's okay." Part of her wanted to leave him alone, but there was so much to learn about the father of her child.

His eyes glazed over while he pondered. "It's complicated and confusing, but if you'll bear with me, I can give you the watered-down version."

"I'm always here to listen. Bring it."

Rohnert sat up, snaked his arm around her back, and leaned her against his chest. She closed her eyes and waited.

"My childhood memories are sketchy. My parents were attentive and loving. I felt secure growing up, but I think there was more to my background and heritage. I was brought up like the rest of the vampire children who belonged to pure bloodlines. We were taught the ways of our race, how to be better fighters. We studied our history, but when it came to mine, it felt like a big chunk was missing."

Shelly tried to picture Rohnert as a young man, vibrant and full of questions, strong and exciting. However, the vision that came to mind was a quiet and intense vampire.

"When I was younger, my parents were killed while out of town on vacation. There wasn't much explanation given to me. I wanted to mourn for them, to see their remains, but they disappeared. That was when I decided that there was more going on in our lives than what I had been led to believe."

His arm tightened around her waist until it was impossible to draw her any closer. The emotions pouring out of Rohnert was more than she'd expected.

"Did you try to find out?"

She felt him nod. "Many times. Marania could tell me nothing. I left for a brief period to mourn in private, and this was when Goran rose to power amid the growing unrest within our race."

"Wait . . . your bloodline, where exactly are you in the hierarchy?"

"Our line was next."

"You were supposed to lead?" The revelation shocked her. She pushed back an inch to look into his eyes. His black irises were dilated.

"I was in no position to lead a race. I was too young and furious, hardly leader material."

"So the maniac leads your people now." Thinking of the monster that had killed countless people made her shudder.

"That decision became my burden." He let her go and covered his face with his hands.

That explained his behavior and his silence. "Then what happened?"

"When I returned from my short hiatus, I supported Goran because he was my friend. We had grown up together. I served as a tactician and trainer because that's what I was—a fighter. When he began to lead us on a path that was grossly unconventional and concentrated on his personal gain, I had to leave. The last straw was when he ordered the slaughter of diseased vampires. Death isn't a solution, and I believed we were destined for something greater. We needed peace, and the decrees he was passing left and right deviated from our goal."

"Goran is the one who killed off most of our family." Her statement came out in a rush. She had heard so much about the leader of the Council.

Rohnert's jaw clenched. "Yes."

"What are you going to do about it?"

"There's nothing I can do."

Shelly remembered the battered book. "Haven't you read that book at all?"

Rohnert raised his eyes to meet hers. "I'm not sure I have the right to read it."

"I read the first page. It was given to you, and it just might hold the key to our questions. Why are you so hesitant to use it?"

"What if it opens a can of worms?"

"You never struck me as a coward."

His brows furrowed. "Maybe I am. When I left the facility, I went to see my teacher, and he said the same thing."

"I don't think running away is the solution. Death isn't either, although it's a part of living. I think you would be doing yourself a great favor if you found your answers so you could move on."

Rohnert didn't respond. The muscles on his shoulders tightened, and he got up to his feet and began pacing the room.

"I'm afraid to find out that I'm not who I think I am." He finally stopped to face her.

"You're the father of my child and the man I love. Is there anything that can top that?" She kneeled on the mattress, beckoning him to move closer.

Rohnert came forward and took her hand. He drew it to his mouth and grazed his lips along her knuckles. "Nothing makes me happier than your forgiveness. I'm proud to have you and our son in my life."

She cupped his cheeks. "Find the answers that have evaded you all these years. Find the peace you need. I'm here to love and support you."

His expression warmed. "I don't know what I did to deserve you. I can't thank you enough for giving me a chance."

"I can think of one way you could thank me right now," she said and winked.

A slow, wicked smiled lifted the corners of his lips. "I think we're on the same page, my dear."

He seized her mouth, demanding entry. Her body flushed with heat and her heart rate spiked once she gave in to the warmth he offered. Rohnert climbed onto the bed and pushed her down on the mattress, his body growing hard against hers.

Why do we always end up like this? She grinned against his mouth.

Rohnert pulled away. "Because we're greedy bastards who can't get enough of each other?"

"You got that right." She pulled him down by the neck, clamped on to his inviting mouth, and took control.

Hours later, Shelly got up, feeling terrific. She took a shower and got dressed. Rohnert had left to go on patrol with a newbie.

Angus was already waiting for her in the break room, as well as Harrow. She might've missed the memo, but Harrow appeared to have assigned himself to be her personal bodyguard.

She didn't bother asking, since Rohnert had become obsessed with her safety and that of their child. "Ready?"

Harrow stood up with his Kalimetal strapped prominently on his back, and Angus walked ahead of them, sporting a bulky coat she wouldn't doubt was packed with weapons. One would think they were off to a war zone instead of going to a hospital.

The drive was uneventful. Her evening started with two gunshot wounds. When she was afforded a short reprieve after the first five hours, she found Rick in the nurse's lounge, sipping on his coffee.

He looked up and offered her a slight smile, patting the chair next to him. "Today's your last day. Excited?"

Shelly flopped onto the chair. "A little." She grinned.

"And you will call me when the time comes." It wasn't a question but a statement. She and Rick both served those in need without question, even if it meant crossing the lines.

Shelly still felt guilty for asking Rick to compromise his ethics, but the world in which she had been living was meant to be kept a secret. Given her situation, she had to throw the rules out the window.

"Yes. Look, I feel awful having to ask you, but there's no one else I can trust."

Rick smiled. "We've been through this before. I agreed to help a friend. That's all there is to it."

"Thank you." She placed her hand on top of his.

"Don't mention it. I'm sure you would do the same if the situation were reversed."

"You can count on it."

Rick picked up his cup and took a quick sip while Shelly leaned against the chair and spread her tired legs under the table. Then out of nowhere, gunshots were fired, and a commotion came from the hallway.

They both scrambled to their feet, and Shelly thought about Harrow and Angus, high-tailing it to the lobby where they should have been waiting for her. The seating area was empty, and patients and nurses were running to reach the exit.

Rick started barking orders, leaving Shelly to wonder where Harrow and Angus could be. Five security guards headed for the stairwell, and sirens sounded from a distance. Without giving it a second thought, she raced to the elevator where she found another security guard waiting for the car.

"Dr. Anderson. You should leave the premises," the grim-eyed man said.

"Sure, sure." Shelly pretended to turn around until the elevator doors closed behind him, then pivoted to watch the floor indicator. The elevator stopped on the rooftop. Although she knew she was being stupid, she got on the next available car. It took a little time to reach the top. Once the door opened, the shots became louder and more real. Shelly peered through the glass window but couldn't see much. She worked her way toward the rooftop door. With caution, she slipped out and slinked toward the planters, which offered her a perfect place to hide.

Shelly gasped when she spied Harrow, Angus, and Rohnert in the middle of a fight. *What the hell?* Witnessing an actual battle made her skin crawl with fear.

There was no way to tell who was fighting whom. Shouts were slinging back and forth. The guard she'd spoken to a few minutes ago fell on the ground, and the exit door burst open. Five more guards rushed out as the deafening sound of a helicopter approached.

A dark figure emerged from the shadows with guns in both hands and a sinister smirk on his face. He spoke in a foreign tongue, something she couldn't understand, then he fired. Rohnert and Harrow somersaulted away from the bullets, but Angus was struck. He fell down with a horrendous thud. Without thinking, Shelly rushed to him, just as the helicopter came in sight.

"Put your guns down. You are now surrounded." The order came from the chopper, and its bright lights illuminated the rooftop. Shelly remained where she was but took Angus's hand to check his wrist for a pulse.

The exit door burst open, and cops emerged with guns drawn. For a brief moment, the dark figure's eyes fixated on her before glancing down at her stomach. He grinned, flashed his fangs at her, and then plunged straight down the side of the ten-story building.

"Damn it."

Rohnert lingered in the shadows, away from the glaring light of the helicopter that hovered above the roof. He measured the space between him and Shelly. About thirty feet. He could sprint over, swoop her up, and make a run for it, but with all the witnesses, the plan went against their race's prime rule—keep their existence a secret. Also, knowing Shelly's dedication to her profession, there was no telling how she'd react if he tried to take her away from her patient.

"Rohn, I think it's best for us to get lost now." Harrow's bad eyesight was trained on the drama before them.

His muscles twitched with helplessness and rage while he watched his female bark orders at the officers. Gripping his Kalimetal, Rohnert cursed once more when then the chopper changed its course, moving the lights in their direction.

"I'm serious. We need to scram *now*." Harrow tugged on his arm.

Rohnert glanced at Shelly once more before he and Harrow scaled down the wall. Squad cars were parked all around the hospital, and the entire vicinity was crawling with cops, leaving them no choice but to remove themselves from the general area.

"Let's park on that building," Rohnert said, pointing to another structure not far from the hospital.

Harrow nodded. They sprinted across the street and ascended using their bare hands. Rohnert zeroed in on the hospital once they were atop the tall building, which provided them a good vantage point. Aside from the investigators and policemen still lingering on the rooftop, the place had cleared out. If he had to hazard a guess, Shelly was already hard at work on one of the injured.

"How about Angus?"

Harrow shook his head. "I can't fuckin' believe this."

"What happened?" Rohnert kept his eyes glued on the rooftop, checking the comings and goings. The helicopter moved to scour the perimeter, its megawatt light illuminating the area.

"We were in the lobby when I caught the sound of several vampires moving up the building. Then I called you."

Rohnert felt his whole body shake with rage. A male vampire unable to get to his mate when she was in danger was the worst thing that could happen.

"How in the hell does Goran know about my connection to Shelly?" he said out loud.

"That fucker was Goran?" Harrow's tone turned harsh, and Rohnert could sense the buildup of fury in his friend.

"Yes."

"He said something in your language."

"He said that since I was his enemy, all those belonging to me are his enemies, too."

"We better get ready, then."

"This is my battle. I don't want you guys involved."

"The hell it is. We're one unit. You're with us, and we go as a team. Don't forget, Jordan still has a score to settle with him, too."

Spoken like a true warrior. "If that's how you want it, but I promise you, this is not going to end soon."

"I've got your back, my brother." Harrow clapped him on the shoulder.

They stood there for a couple more hours before the threat of the rising sun forced them to retreat. They headed back to the warehouse, where Tor, Cyrus, and Zo were waiting for them in the I-room. Harrow updated the men and phoned Jordan right after.

Rohnert zoned out, his head swimming with worry. With mounting exasperation, he searched for ways to reach Shelly. He tried to get through to her cell phone, but there was no answer. That could mean that she was still hard at work, but the uncertainty was torture.

"Let's send Cheryl to collect her. I'll have Barth drive her. At least, they're both human and could pose as her family," Harrow said.

Tor nodded. "Sounds like a good idea."

"Wait—we can find out right now if I'm good to go during the daylight," Cyrus suggested.

"Don't even think about it." Harrow shook his head.

"My skin, my call." Cyrus glared at him in a rare display of stubbornness before getting up and heading for the door.

Tor followed. "Let's have Rayce escort you. If you burn, just remember, there is no doctor in the house."

Rohnert listened but offered no comment. As much as he was touched by the show of support, his mind couldn't handle Shelly being exposed to this ugliness. The whole scenario had turned into a nightmare. All he wanted was for her to be safe and back in his arms.

Harrow launched into full-scale planning with Zo while Rohnert paced the room. He hated having his hands tied, unable to do anything. After several minutes, Tor returned with Cyrus, and both were grinning from ear to ear.

"I love being a freak," Cyrus said, his eyes sparkling with enthusiasm.

"I think the idiot is ready to go." Tor parked himself in one of the chairs.

Harrow looked up. "What the hell? Really? This is good. Really good."

"Jones said that there's no rhyme or reason to the anomaly. Check out that freak, Zane," Tor said.

At the mention of Zane's name, Cyrus' face darkened and a growl tore from deep in his throat.

"Easy there, brother." Zo stood up and patted Cyrus on the shoulder.

"I'm good to go. Do you want me to take Cheryl?" Cyrus asked Harrow.

"Yeah, take her with you. Go easy on the weapons, though. That place is crawling with cops. Bring your cell phone, and call if you need anything. I'll have some guys ready for backup," Harrow said.

Cyrus turned to Rohnert. "Anything you want me to do?"

"Bring her back, unscathed." Rohnert pinned him with an earnest stare. "Please take care of her."

"I will." Cyrus dipped his head and took off.

Alonzo walked up to Rohnert and shoved a full glass of scotch in his hand. "You're a walking livewire. Drink up."

He grunted but downed the thing as if it were his salvation. "Give me another one," he said.

His faithful student went back to the bar and refilled the glass. This was going to be a long day.

Zane felt a bit better after a week of rest, but his nerves remained frayed. His mind was filled with thoughts of the woman who had touched him with a kindness he'd never known before. Sleep was impossible, filled with nightmares that echoed his waking fears for Cheryl's safety.

The phone call from Goran had offered a welcome change and got him out of his hideout. However, it also made him realize how fucked up he was. He was forced to limp, and his range of motion was limited. The Dangeran had screwed him up.

Staying in the shadows, he watched while cops breezed in and out of the hospital. The chopper was no longer in sight, but the place had been turned into a fortress, with security checking IDs, doing a thorough pat down before allowing anyone into the building. Zane remained glued to his spot.

Grandpapa wanted him to watch a certain pregnant doctor and report back. The order was by far his easiest assignment. What he wanted to know was the reason behind Goran's interest in the human. If he remembered from Demetrius's stories, the older vampire had a sick fascination with redheaded females. Perhaps that was this woman's appeal.

Zane continued to pace until a scent he'd come to know well wafted in the air. One glance was all it took before his heart slammed into his chest. Across the street, he saw Cheryl walking toward the hospital with Cyrus.

For a fleeting moment, his eyes met Cyrus'. The vampire bared his fangs and mouthed words Zane understood despite the distance between them.

I will kill you.

Zane narrowed his eyes in return, but his focus remained on Cheryl. The woman appeared subdued. Her eyes were trained on the ground, as if she were oblivious to her environment. An unfamiliar pain pierced his heart.

If it weren't for his injury, he would have rushed over and damn the consequences. But this thing with his grandpapa was far from over. He needed stay on Goran's good side for as long as it took to set his plans in motion. Cheryl would have her revenge against the man responsible for her heartache, even if she never knew that Zane had brought it about.

Cyrus held Cheryl's elbow and escorted her inside once they finished the whole security check. A thought struck Zane. The new vampire was moving outdoors during daylight. How could that be? Was that ability a gift he had transferred to his creation? The idea had him wondering.

For self-preservation, he moved toward the parking lot, which gave him a closer look at the hospital entrance but kept him better concealed. He moved between cars until he spotted an unlocked one and slid right in. The wait had begun.

Three hours later, Cheryl and Cyrus emerged with another woman. Zane recognized the doctor from the belly that protruded from her ill-fitting scrubs. He slid lower in the driver's seat to keep from being spotted when Cyrus glanced around with suspicious eyes.

"What the fuck?" he muttered. His mind rebelled against the idea of reporting back to Goran. In haste, he decided to hotwire the car he'd holed up in. His leg wasn't up to the task of following them on foot.

The trio got into a car that was parked not too far from him. When it left with its tires screeching, Zane stepped on the gas and trailed them.

Taking extra precautions to avoid being noticed, he made sure there were several cars between them. It didn't take long before they hit a block of abandoned buildings and warehouses. He stopped, turned off the engine, and parked the car.

On foot, he dragged his left leg behind him until he found a suitable place to hide. The other car stopped in front of a rundown warehouse. How odd. Despite its dilapidated appearance, the double doors opened without a sound. The dark car disappeared from view, and the door closed.

This left him thinking. Without a doubt, this was the group's new hideout, and Cheryl lived inside the premises. The newfound knowledge floored him. Zane had no idea what to do about it.

"You must be very tired," Cheryl said when they got out of the car.

"I'm beyond fatigued." Shelly straightened her stiff back, and then a set of powerful arms encircled her waist.

"Jesus Christ. I'm so glad you're all right." Rohnert tilted her chin, raining kisses over her face. His expression was intense, and Shelly could guess what had been running through his head. He looked at her face with such intensity, then his gaze slid down to the rest of her body, lingering longer at her belly. After his own version of a visual examination, Rohnert sighed and turned to Cyrus and Cheryl. "Thank you for getting her home."

Cheryl smiled, seeming pleased at Rohnert's words.

"It pays to have a pseudo-vamp in the group, doesn't it?" Cyrus chuckled and clapped Rohnert on the back.

"Indeed." Rohnert bowed his head.

He took Shelly under his arm, and they all proceeded to the I-room. "You better not pull that stunt on me ever again," he whispered, just for her to hear.

Shelly feigned innocence. She knew what she had done was dangerous, but she would do it all over again if the situation called for it.

"Oh no, you won't." Rohnert shook his head. "We're going to have a long talk."

"Whatever." She was too tired to argue. In actuality, she was beyond scared—scared for Angus and all the others. Death wasn't something she could ever get used to, no matter how many times she'd dealt with it.

"Hey, Cy, tell Harrow I'm going to take Shelly straight to bed. She's beat. If he wants to talk, it'll have to wait."

"Right on. Rest easy, Doctor," Cyrus said with a wave.

"Thanks, guys." Shelly rested her head against Rohnert's shoulder.

Rohnert led her down the stairs to their bedroom and laid her on the bed. He didn't say a word while he lifted her feet and propped them on top of pillows. When he looked up, his eyes were glistening.

"I've never been so scared in my life." Rohnert planted a kiss on her lips.

Shelly felt wretched for subjecting him to so much worry.

"Have I told you how much I love you?"

Goran slipped into his formal robe of smooth and expensive velvet in blood red. He normally wore the garment on special occasions. This was one of those days. He had extended an invitation to the Council Elders for an emergency meeting, and each had sent word back that they would be in attendance.

He checked himself in the mirror and decided to leave his hair untied, letting it flow down his back. The excitement was making him twitch.

After giving his appearance another look over, he picked up the necklace and put it over his head. He left his chamber and walked down corridors at an unhurried pace. The thoughts coming from Council room were humming with speculation by the time he arrived. Devereux stood outside and bowed his head.

"Stay put," Goran said when he passed the row of guards standing outside.

The heavy doors were opened for him, and he flitted across the room with light footsteps until he reached the front. The Elders were up on their feet, watching him with open curiosity, which gave him the opportunity to soak in their unspoken questions. Goran smirked when he caught Bretania's smile. She was garbed in a regal robe that was a match for his.

He turned around and made eye contact with the few Elders left in the Council, then moved on to those who had been inducted to fill the vacant seats. August's wafer-thin skin stretched when he smiled at him, while the rest inclined their heads in respect.

Goran gestured for everyone to sit down and took his seat. He bided his time, letting their restless thoughts swirl around the room. Once he'd gotten his fill of their collective emotions, he began speaking.

"I'm pleased to announce that I'm to be betrothed at the next full moon."

Ripples of disbelief swelled around him while Bretania beamed from her seat. The noise rose, and Goran had to shout above the din to quiet the room down.

"The female I have chosen is Bretania, esteemed daughter of Sigdor and Clementine." Goran stood up and bowed to his future mate.

"This is a pleasant surprise," August said, his frail face breaking into a grin. "I'm quite pleased with your decision."

"Aye," Wendell seconded, clapping his hands.

"About time, Goran," Icarus said.

"So this will be in a month. Have you given out invitations to the other covens? Or are you looking at a quiet ceremony?" Regrita, one of the newer members of the Council, asked.

"I'd like this to be a big celebration since it's long overdue. Bretania, dear, would you mind standing up?"

Bretania stood, looking shyer than he could remember her ever acting before. Maybe this was a good thing. She dipped her head when the room erupted in warm applause. Her smile dazzled everyone, including him.

Not bad, Goran—not bad at all.

After the announcement, they discussed a few more business items, which included the sighting on the hospital rooftop. Goran handled the questions well, avoiding any mention of Rohnert, but he sensed a slight dissention among the Elders present.

August stood up. "With all due respect, you as our leader should know better than to give humans something to think about. The last thing we need is for them to start digging. Remember, ignorance is bliss."

Goran grounded his molars to keep from lashing out. August had to know by now that he would not appreciate being reprimanded in front of the group, much less being reminded him of his job as the race's leader. He gave a quick, forced smile.

"Rest assured. I have made sure that damage control is in place. I apologize to you for my indiscretion."

He plastered a smile for the remainder of the meeting. At the conclusion of the assembly, Goran waited for the room to empty before summoning Devereux.

"Be sure August makes it home safe." He smiled and lifted an eyebrow.

Devereux stared at him in surprise before he answered. "As you wish, sire." He bowed low and left.

All that was left to do was to send word to the nearby covens about his upcoming betrothal. If everything proceeded according to plan, Bretania would be pregnant in a few months, securing his reign for a long, long time.

The prospect made him smile.

Rohnert hadn't slept a wink. After Shelly had fallen asleep, he spent the time watching her, memorizing each line on her face, every curve, and the little smile that tugged her corner of her lips.

This woman was all he ever asked for in his existence, and now that she was back safe in his arms, hell would freeze over before he would let her out of his sight. He stroked her hair and kept his vigil with an obsession borne from the fear he'd felt seeing her vulnerable, in front of the man he'd once called friend.

His eyesight blurred for a second, and he felt the weight of his terror in every inch of his body. This wasn't good. Rohnert slid off the bed, careful not wake Shelly, and took his phone with him to the bathroom.

He autodialed Harrow's number. The vampire answered right away. "Dude, what happened to quiet hours?"

"I need to get rid of some steam."

"Meet you in the training room in five." Harrow sounded much more awake, and it made him grin a little.

He got dressed in the dark without making any noise, and he was in the training room a minute before Harrow walked in. The usual Oakleys were absent, and Harrow's eyes fixed on him.

"Tell me what's bothering you."

Rohnert didn't answer but started stretching. He spread his legs on the mat until he formed a wide V and bent his head down.

"Fine, be that way. Use me as your punching bag," Harrow said, taking the opposite spot and starting with his own pre-sparring warm up. The silence stretched for five minutes before Rohnert jumped to his feet.

"I'm ready." He proceeded to the cabinet and pulled out four Arnis sticks. He tossed two to Harrow, who caught them with one hand.

"Bring it." Harrow brandished the weapons.

Rohnert thrust the sticks forward, almost taking Harrow on the shoulder. "Close your eyes, my man. You're overthinking."

Harrow sidestepped and pivoted, then clipped him on the waist. "I don't think I'm the only one here."

The smug expression was all he needed to see, and Rohnert let his instinct guide him. Harrow was operating on cruise control with his eyes closed. Rohnert was aware of the echolocation technique the vampire had begun using to compensate for his bad eyesight. From the moment they began their sparring, Harrow kept up with him, blocking and dishing out hard strikes. It took some painful hits before Rohnert found his rhythm. Expending all his pent-up rage, he pounded, slashed, swatted, thrust, and beat the hell out of Harrow. Thirty minutes passed before Harrow raised his hands in defeat.

"You're a fuckin' animal, Rohnert. Remind me not to get on your bad side." Harrow bowed before him, student to sensei.

Rohnert touched his friend on the shoulder. "Gates, I want you to be our main witness for our . . . oh damn. Vampires don't get married, but since our diviner won't see me, I'm taking Shelly whichever way I can get her. We're calling a minister to make it official. I want to know if we could have the ceremony here."

Harrow's face softened, and he nodded. "Of course you can. It'll be an honor to see you and Shelly become man and wife." Then his expression turned nostalgic. "Shit, like a best man?"

"Whatever humans call it. Yeah." Rohnert grinned, feeling some of the weight he'd been carrying dissipate.

"When is the big day?" Harrow gathered the practice weapons and strode to the cabinet.

"As soon as I get Shelly's okay."

Harrow's eyebrows shot up. "Are you telling me that you haven't asked?"

"We talked about it, but it kinda got lost in the mix. I'll mention it to her today."

"That sounds like a plan." Harrow left then returned with two towels and handed one to him.

Rohnert wiped the sweat off his face and then continued rubbing the rest of his body. Funny, he felt much better, even without sleep.

"Buzz me when Shelly is up and ready for a short meeting. I want to get more information about Angus and the situation at the hospital."

He nodded and jogged back to their room. Shelly was in the shower when he came through the door. "Shels, I'm back." He stuck his head inside the steam-filled room.

"Be right out."

Rohnert went to the closet and took a pair of shorts and a white T-shirt. Shelly was already drying her hair when he joined her in the bathroom. "Are you hungry? Do you want me to send for some food? Are you feeling better now that you've gotten some sleep?"

Shelly held a hand up. "Slow down. I had a cereal as soon as I woke up. I'm fine, please don't worry about me."

His eyes traveled down the expanse of her body and stopped at her tummy. "You're looking incredibly sexy."

Shelly smiled and opened her arms, and he walked into her embrace. "I feel sexy when you look at me the way you do."

"How is that?" He kissed her on the forehead.

"Like I'm something to eat." Her eyes went wide. "Rohnert, when was the last time you fed?"

He looked at her in confusion before it dawned on him that the last time he had taken the vein of a purebred vampire was with Marania. It had been a while. No wonder he'd been feeling a bit weak. "Maybe around eight months ago."

"For Christ's sake, would you feed now?" Shelly pleaded, tugging at his arm in desperation.

"It's not that easy. I don't know anyone."

"Isidora. She might be able to help you. She's of pure blood. You can help each other."

Since he and Shelly had gotten together, the idea of latching on to another female's vein was just wrong.

"It won't feel right."

Looking at Shelly's face and listening to her mind, he spotted the determination and refusal to accept any excuse. "This is purely clinical. Make it all about the need to stay alive."

"I don't know." This conversation was so not happening right now.

"Rohnert, please do it for your child, if you can't do it for me."

Shelly had to pull the guilt card on him. He sighed, still not convinced. "Let me think about it."

Her face lit up, and Rohnert knew that he was screwed. "Don't even think I'm going to forget about it. Well, where were we?"

"I wanted to taste every part of you, but let me take a quick shower."

Shelly smiled. "I'll be waiting."

It had to be the quickest shower he had ever taken. Within two minutes, Rohnert walked out of the bathroom and found the bedroom bathed in darkness and Shelly sprawled in the middle of the bed. He felt his insides melt at the sight of his beautiful woman and realized this was as good a time as any. Instead of jumping on the bed right away, he detoured to the closet and pulled out the trunk.

"Rohnert, is everything all right?" Shelly's voice sounded worried.

"I'll be right there. I'm just getting something." His fingers closed on the on heavy object and he slid the box into place.

He switched on the lamp before he climbed onto the bed and kneeled before her. Shelly sat up, worry lines creasing her forehead.

"What is it?"

Rohnert cleared his throat, feeling a bit choked up. This had to be done for Shelly. He took her chin with his fingers and kissed her mouth. Her response was sensual, making him harden right away.

"Shelly, I want you to share your life with me. Would you be my mate, my wife? I promise to be whatever you need me to be."

Her answer first came in the form of a gasp. "Oh, yes," she said, her voice quivering.

Rohnert leaned closer and draped the necklace from his forefathers around her neck. "I don't have a ring. This is all I have, and a pledge to love and serve you all my life." He kissed her again.

"Your unconventional ways suit me just fine. Thank you so much for everything."

And that was his cue to pull her closer and make love to his beloved.

Cyrus looked up from the desk when the door of the training room opened. The classes were done for the day, and the new recruits had left to rest before patrolling for the night. He saw a diminutive figure hesitate in the doorway. Although he tried to keep tabs on Isidora's activities, the first few weeks had been rather quiet. She spent more time in her room, which technically was Gail's bedroom. Since Harrow and Jordan's adopted daughter was staying with the general, the room had been offered to Isidora for the time being.

This was the first time Cyrus had seen her venture farther into the facility. He stood up, smiled, and tried to coax her inside.

"C'mon in. Is there anything I can do for you?" he asked and walked toward her. He saw her take a step back, confusion written on her face.

Isidora's expressive eyes locked onto his before she diverted her gaze. "Jordan told me that I could come here and learn something if I was interested."

"This is the place to be." He stayed glued to his spot, not wanting to scare her away. As it was, she looked like she'd bolt at any moment.

"Aren't you busy?" She made no attempt to advance farther into the room.

Even if I was, I would make time for you. "Class is over. I have time."

"Are you sure?"

Cyrus smiled to reassure the timid female. "Of course I am." He gestured to the chair by the desk. "Why don't we chat for a bit? I need to know your strengths and weaknesses."

"I—what?" Her confusion was evident.

"What I mean is that I want to have an idea what you have learned in the past, if anything."

Isidora finally smiled. "Oh, okay."

She walked toward the desk, and Cyrus returned to his seat, trying not to make any sudden movements that might scare her away. He didn't miss the little signs of nervousness—the way she wrung her palms together, her dark eyes darting left to right, and the way she licked her lips before she spoke.

"I'm sure I introduced myself to you before—" He cut himself off, remembering the ill-fated night when her friend perished. "I'm Cyrus, just in case you have forgotten." He reached out his hand.

She's going to leave me hanging.

Just when he thought she wouldn't shake his hand, her tiny fingers grasped his in a shy handshake. Her hand was soft, like a child's. In fact, she looked very young, like she was still in high school. It made him wonder how old she was in vampire age. Her small nose was upturned, making him think of a fairy.

"Isidora," she said. Even her voice sounded young.

He must've held her hand longer than he'd intended because she squirmed under his touch. Cyrus released her right away and cleared his throat. "What have you learned in the past? Any weapons you practice with? Do you have any preferences?"

Isidora's eyes grew big. "Oh, no. I haven't touched a weapon. My father believed that females shouldn't have to fight. That's why we have males."

What an archaic belief! Cyrus kept his opinion to himself. "So it looks like we're going to start from scratch."

"Do you think it's too late for me to learn?"

Cyrus laughed, and his fangs elongated. "You know our Harrow, right?"

She nodded.

"Well, he had been a vampire for many years when we found him. The man didn't possess an athletic bone in his body, and he moved rather awkwardly. It was his desire to learn that got him where he is now. The vampire is amazing in battle. Someone I wouldn't mind watching my back."

Isidora's mouth formed an O, making it difficult for Cyrus to look anywhere else but her lips—those sensual, red lips.

"Did you teach him?"

Cyrus blinked, too mesmerized.

"Well?"

"Oh . . . I like to think that I was his first teacher, but the Kalimetal is all Rohnert."

She smiled with fascination. "I've heard stories about him. My father, Gentry, Alonzo, and another Council Elder, Randolph, all spoke highly of him."

The woman sounded a little too enamored with the pureblooded vampire.

"So would you like to learn?" Cyrus asked, steering away from that subject.

"If you have enough patience, I will try to be a good student."

"Atta girl."

"Cyrus, are you gentle?"

He swallowed, not sure how to respond. "I always try to be."

"I'm new at this."

He smiled. "I'll take good care of you."

It was close to dusk by the time Rohnert and Shelly stepped out of their bedroom to meet with Harrow and give him an update on Angus's condition. They held hands while they navigated the stairs to get to the I-room. When the doors opened, Harrow, Jordan, Tor, Allison, Cyrus, Alonzo, and Gentry were already seated and waiting for them.

Rohnert gave each one a quick nod before pulling out a chair for Shelly and taking a seat opposite Harrow at the long table. He knew what to expect, but he would defer to Harrow's decision. Harrow removed his sunglasses and placed them on the table. He gave Shelly an encouraging smile. "I'm glad to see you well, Shelly."

"Thank you."

Rohnert grinned, a rarity for him.

Harrow didn't miss the smile and narrowed his eyes. He looked from Rohnert to Shelly and back, then his eyes zeroed on the pendant resting on Shelly's chest.

"Ah. Can I have the honor of announcing the good news?"

Rohnert rolled his eyes, and the hard-nosed doctor managed to blush.

"Our friend, Rohnert, had asked Shelly to be his mate . . . wife . . . whatever."

The room erupted in applause.

"Welcome to the club." Tor shook his hand vigorously.

Rohnert smirked. "Should I be scared?"

"Be very scared."

Cyrus clapped him on the back. "About damn time."

"This is going to be epic," Alonzo sang. Everyone laughed.

"Sire, you chose the perfect woman." Gentry bowed his head.

"Gentry, no bowing, please. And yes, she is perfect." *In every way.*

Allison hugged Shelly. "I'm going to throw you a kick-ass party!"

"I'm so happy for the two of you. This is long time coming." Jordan kissed Rohnert on the cheek and gave Shelly a hug.

"Okay, kids. Let's move on to business." Harrow sat down and waited for everyone to do the same.

"Shelly, what have you heard? How is our friend, Angus?"

"He is going to be okay. The Dangeran bullet struck him in the abdomen, but it missed his vital organs. My concern is the charges that have been filed against him."

The intercom beeped, and Harrow pressed the button to answer. "Rayce, what's up?"

"Boss, you might want to tune in to the nightly news," their tech guy said through the speaker.

Cyrus grabbed the remote and flicked on the television. He pressed the buttons until he found the right channel.

"Here's an update on the shooting at Lenox Hospital last night. Four people were injured. Three were members of hospital security. The fourth victim is being questioned about his role in the shootout. A fifth man fled the scene. Here is footage taken from the chopper."

Rohnert muscles tightened when the short video showed Goran standing before Shelly, *his Shelly*, staring her down before running off the ledge and disappearing.

Tor cursed, and Gentry pounded a fist onto the table. Harrow raised his hand, demanding silence.

"If you have any information regarding this individual, please call—"

Harrow pressed the off button and looked straight into Rohnert's eyes. "I'm open to suggestions, my man."

Rohnert took Shelly's hand and lifted it to his mouth for a kiss. Then he turned his attention to the men in the room. "Patrols continue. Our main focus is getting help for the diseased ones, but we have to step up the training. We have a good mix of humans and vampires on our team, but most are neophytes. They need to be trained well. Anyone want to help Cyrus and Tor?"

Alonzo raised his hand.

"Okay, Zo, you're up."

"We need to get Angus some legal help. I don't know how you humans do it, but if that is not possible, we can move in and take him."

"Like kidnap our own man?" Tor grinned from ear to ear. "I'm all for that."

"Harrow?"

"If that is the easiest path, I'm good with that."

"Let's do it tomorrow night. I assume that the place is still full of cops."

Harrow nodded. "Sounds like a plan."

"If you don't mind, I'd like to head the team. Gentry, Tor, and Cyrus can come with me," Rohnert said.

"I have no problem with that."

"What about Goran?" Jordan's voice was hard, and her face rigid.

It was a known fact that she had a score to settle after Goran had killed her parents and turned her. Her new family did nothing to erase her determination to avenge those wrongs.

Harrow patted her arm. "Honey, let's be patient. We're going to get there."

He wanted to get the bastard and place his head at Jordan's feet as an offering, more now than ever. Goran's tyranny needed to end, but Harrow had no idea if leading their group into a potential massacre was the right thing to do.

Rohnert took a deep breath. "Harrow is right. We must take this slow. Goran isn't your average vampire. He would stop at nothing to get what he wanted."

Gentry nodded in agreement. "I think I may have an idea of what we can do to get more information about the Council."

"It will be tough. Once we walk away, the entrance isn't available to us anymore," Zo said.

"I received word from Randolph that Goran made an announcement. Also, August wants to meet with him. I'm planning on escorting Randolph tonight, if that's all right." Gentry looked from Harrow to Rohnert.

"I'm going with you," Rohnert said.

Shelly, who had been very quiet throughout the discussion, raised her hand. Rohnert closed his eyes and gritted his teeth the moment he understood why she wanted to speak.

"Yes, Shelly." Harrow focused on her.

"Rohnert needs to feed. He hasn't taken a vein in a long time."

"Damn you, Rohnert. I thought we'd been through this before." Harrow slammed his palm on the table.

Jordan was quick to calm him while Rohnert stared at Harrow, his expression cold and detached.

"There is no one to feed from." His voice was barely audible.

"Isidora is pureblood." Shelly placed her hand on top of his clenched fist.

He was quick to notice Cyrus' reaction. The revelation didn't make him happy, and the harsh lines around his mouth deepened.

"I cannot decide for Isidora. Why don't we get her in here and find out how she feels about it?" Harrow nodded at Gentry, who left right away.

Cyrus cleared his throat. "Wouldn't this be something you'd want to ask in private?"

"I don't see any reason why it can't be discussed among us. We're all adults here, and besides, it's not like it's romantic. This is a necessity," Tor said.

The vampire seemed to be full of insight tonight. Rohnert pinned him a glare. Tor shrugged.

Gentry came back with Isidora, who looked like she had just woken up. Her short red hair was sticking out in every direction, and the sweater and jeans she'd borrowed from Allison added to her youthful appearance. Rohnert recognized the fear and loss in her eyes. He knew how it felt to lose both parents.

"Please seat down, Issy." Harrow gestured to a chair. "Dr. Anderson wants to discuss something with you."

Once Isidora sat, Shelly spoke. "Rohnert needs a vein, and you're the only one I can think of."

Isidora remained silent, which gave Rohnert the chance to scan her general emotions. Shock, awe, fear, uncertainty, and sense of betrayal swirled in her mind while she looked at Rohnert, her dark eyes dilating.

"When did you last feed?" Shelly wasn't giving up.

"It . . . has been a while."

"Would it bother you if he took your vein?" Shelly asked. "And he can serve you in return."

"Wait. Does it have to be taken from the vein?" Cyrus threw out the question Rohnert had already heard in the thoughts of Jordan and Allison. Both were squirmy about the idea of their man drinking from another.

"It has been done that way for centuries," Rohnert said in a low voice.

"Then it's about damn time you make a change," Cyrus answered.

Everyone began voicing their opinions at the same time, making it impossible for anyone to be heard. Even so, Isidora's resolute voice rose above the noise.

"I will do it."

The silence in the room was so thick that Rohnert shivered. It had been different with him and Marania. They had been friends since childhood, and it was like second nature for them. This time, things were different. He was taking a mate, and the whole thing didn't feel right.

Despite this, he couldn't deny the hunger for nourishment. If only human blood would suffice, he'd take it and be done. The thirst made it difficult for him to focus, and his body was showing wear. If he waited any longer, no one's safety could be guaranteed around him.

Shelly understood the need, and yet it felt wrong.

"Then I suggest you feed before you leave. For Christ's sake, we've gone through this shit before." Harrow didn't mince his words. The harshness in his tone showed he meant business.

Rohnert took Shelly's hands, conceding.

"Where shall we do it?" Isidora asked, looking straight at him.

"Let's do it in the clinic." Shelly tapped the table. *Under my watchful eye.*

Rohnert smiled. He loved territorial females, and Shelly sounded like a lioness.

The three of them got up and headed to the door. "Be ready to roll in thirty minutes," he told Gentry.

They walked in silence—none of them had anything to say. Still, Rohnert could hear what was on their minds. Shelly wanted this for him because she loved him, but she worried about the intimacy of such an act. Isidora, on the other hand, needed to feed, too. Her reluctance stemmed from guilt. She felt she was betraying the memory of a man she called Finn.

This was too much to have riding on his conscience, but the call of hunger overrode his better sense. He had pushed the thoughts away until Shelly mentioned it. Now, he was a mess.

The clinic was deserted. There hadn't been much action for several days. Shelly flipped on the industrial strength lighting, and it illuminated the room. She patted the first one of the three examination tables.

"How do you guys do it?"

Rohnert eyes flickered to Isidora, hoping she'd answer. When her eyes remained glued to the table, he had to say something. "We take the jugular."

His mate responded with a sharp intake of breath. "I'll be right here." Shelly stepped back and *Stairway to Heaven* began to blast from the speaker.

Her movements timid, Isidora climbed onto the exam table and sat, crossing her legs at the ankles. She pulled the edge of her collar down to expose her neck and turned her face toward the wall.

Rohnert reached for Shelly's hand. "I want you close to me." She gave no resistance. He squeezed her hand before moving forward, closer to Isidora. The positioning was awkward, but he wasn't about to make this about comfort.

This was a necessity, according to Tor. There was no need to make a mountain out of a molehill. He turned and lifted Shelly onto the table next to Isidora and wedged himself between them while leaning on the table.

Rohnert swiped an errant strand of hair from Isidora's neck and took a deep breath. He opened his mouth, allowing his fangs to elongate, and latched on to the stout vein protruding from Isidora's creamy skin. Then he closed his eyes.

The woman stayed still, holding her breath while his teeth sank into her skin, puncturing her. The first tug made them both jerk, and Isidora's hand grabbed onto his hair, guiding him. He pulled, harder, quicker, wanting this to end as soon as possible.

He reached again for Shelly's hand and held it. They twined their fingers —the real connection he wanted. Rohnert stroked her palm, grateful for her courage. The purity of Isidora's blood was undeniably delicious, and he drank with greed.

He stopped before he drained her. Rohnert pulled away, licked the puncture site, and wiped his mouth. He turned to Shelly to pull her closer. "It is over," he whispered. The nourishment had invigorated him, and all cylinders were flashing the green light again.

"I'm glad you fed. I've been worried about you," Shelly murmured in his ear.

Isidora was about to climb down when Shelly pulled away and took the woman's hand. "Thank you very much. You have no idea what your kindness means to us."

"I'm at your service."

"Don't go. You must feed, too." Shelly didn't let go of her hand.

"We can do it tomorrow. He needs to regain his strength to be able to sustain another."

Rohnert nodded and helped her down the table. "Thank you. We'll meet you here tomorrow at the same time."

The woman slid out the door like a silent wisp of air, leaving Rohnert and Shelly together.

"Go back to the room and rest. I will see you in the morning." Rohnert leaned forward and kissed her soft lips.

"I'm planning on soaking in the tub with a book," Shelly answered, draping her arms around his neck. She traced her forefinger along his mouth with a smile.

"You're beautiful and so giving. Thank you for understanding this aspect of my existence."

"You're who you are, and I've accepted everything about you. I wouldn't take you any other way," she murmured against his lips.

"You're amazing." He rested his head in the crook of her neck, gathering his wits.

After a few minutes of silence, Shelly patted him on the back. "Now do what you do best, and make me proud."

Gentry was waiting for him in the foyer. The loyal soldier's pacing stopped at Rohnert's arrival. "Are you ready, sire?"

"Rule number one, call me Rohnert. Now say it."

"Rohnert," Gentry repeated.

"See, it wasn't that hard. Besides, I don't deserve the title, so ditch it."

"As you wish." The soldier dipped his head.

"And no bowing. You're making me a target when you do that." He chuckled and patted the guy on the shoulder.

"Mode of transportation?"

"We run."

Once they reached the outside, they found the night balmy with a threat of rain. Rohnert looked up at the sky and inhaled deep. They set out at a jog toward August's residence.

August was the oldest member of the Council and revered by all. His reputation for kindness preceded him, and anyone who'd had the chance to listen to the old vampire could attest to his wisdom and his dedication to their race.

When they neared an unremarkable apartment in Upper West Side, Rohnert's ears prickled. He tapped Gentry's shoulder. "Something's not right. Let me buzz Randolph."

They jogged to a dark corner across from the apartment. While Rohnert dialed the ex-Elder's number, Gentry remained alert, scouting the entrance of the building.

"Are you in the area already?"

"About to get out of the car."

"We're across the street. Don't go in yet. I feel something." Rohnert hung up as a limousine halted in front of them.

Randolph emerged from the vehicle, wearing a dark suit. They bowed before each other and then faced the apartment building.

"What are you thinking?" Randolph asked.

"We're still going in, but I just want you to be prepared."

He opened his suit to reveal a holster filled with daggers. "I think I am."

With a nod to Gentry, they crossed to the back of the building. They climbed through the protruding bricks of the old structure until they reached the fifth floor. The windows were opened, as though someone had gone in by the same route. Once inside, the scent of one vampire permeated his nose, and Rohnert reached for his Kalimetal.

Signaling, he pointed to his eyes, then to the hallway, and took the lead. The house was quiet. There were no signs of struggle. Then he heard a little noise from another room. They made a run for it.

In the middle of the bed, August lay as if he were sleeping, except he wasn't. His eyes were open and pleading. A regular dagger was lodged in his chest, and blood continued to flow from the wound. Randolph reached forward to remove the dagger, but Rohnert stopped him.

"Don't. It'll be more painful."

"Who did this to you?" Randolph asked and took the old man's hand.

His mouth formed the name. Rohnert knew it, and Randolph understood it.

"This is the way I found Marania."

The flood of memories hit Rohnert hard. The female vampire's throat had been slit, but not enough to prevent her talking. She had slowly bled to death. Had he not come in time, she wouldn't have died as she deserved—with dignity.

"Rest easy, my friend." Rohnert patted the old man before bringing his palm over his heart. "You shall be avenged."

August's mouth quivered when Randolph began incanting the ancient rites in their native tongue. It was a farewell to a friend and the proper death he should have had.

Rohnert leaned forward and kissed the vampire on his wrinkled forehead before straightening and thrusting a dagger into August's belly. A searing sound filled the small room, deafening them as smoke rose and the body disappeared.

Randolph cursed. "What in God's name would Goran want from the old man?"

"Respect," Rohnert said.

Gentry was too stunned to speak. It was the first time he'd ever witnessed such departure. "Are you okay?" Rohnert nudged the faithful soldier.

"Yes, si . . . Rohnert," he said, blinking.

"Let's get out of here and find somewhere to talk." Randolph headed back to the room where they had come in.

Rohnert and Gentry followed Randolph, who called for his car. Safely tucked inside the vehicle, the driver had been instructed to circle the city.

Randolph was deep in thought when Rohnert turned to him. "What are you thinking, my friend?" It was common courtesy between vampires with the same talent to avoid listening in to each other.

"This has to stop. I've sat by long enough, doing nothing and seeing everyone I know and respect come up missing. I know Goran is behind it all."

"It's not that easy. He's already deployed the elite guards. We're looking at David and Goliath here." Rohnert shared Randolph's sentiments, but caution was still in order.

"I'm done being quiet. I will send word out to all the remaining Elders to watch their backs."

"That's a death sentence." Rohnert shook his head.

One look at Randolph's face told him the vampire had made up his mind. His eyes were narrowed into slits, and his jaw was clenched. Goran had pushed them into a corner, and there was nothing to do but start fighting back.

Still, Rohnert couldn't bear the thought of subjecting more people to death. It wasn't the answer, yet Goran's words echoed in his head. They were enemies, and all Rohnert's kin were targets. Where did that leave him?

Silence engulfed the car, leaving each to their own miserable thoughts. Randolph was good as gone if he decided to pursue his plan, and that left Rohnert with few options. His main concern was the elite guards and the Council soldiers. They were his friends, vampires he had trained. To go against them might be an unnecessary evil.

Of course, he wouldn't put it past Goran to breed new vampires, turning humans to fulfill his devious plans. What had changed the male he'd once called friend so much that he was willing to forsake his own people? Power? Money? Greed? Goran had been sitting at the pinnacle of success. What more did he want?

"I'm afraid the answer to your question is the threat to his throne. If I'm not mistaken, the next bloodline to ascend is your house. That, my friend, is enough to scare the hell out of Goran," Randolph said, responding to his silent musings.

Rohnert took a deep breath. He wasn't interested. Goran could stay in power for all he cared. He had everything his heart desired, except peace. That particular item was as elusive as the cure for the disease that continued to ravage their world.

"What about the rest of your people?"

He had no answer to give. When had life gotten so complicated?

"Rohnert, the time to fight is now. Bring justice to the people who died to keep the peace, and then you shall find yours."

"You make it sound like I'm the answer."

Randolph stared him straight in the eyes. "You're the only one who would know that."

Shelly awoke to discomfort radiating through her lower back. Moving gingerly to the edge of the bed, she tossed back the blanket, startling Rohnert in the process.

"What's going on?" Rohnert jumped up from the bed, grabbing the dagger he kept close by.

Shelly switched on the lamp. She squinted, adjusting her eyes to the glare, and couldn't keep herself from smiling at Rohnert's disheveled appearance.

"I just wanted to stretch a bit." Shelly rubbed her tummy, cooing to appease the hyperactive child inside her.

"Are you okay?" Rohnert replaced the weapon on the nightstand.

"He's been kicking up a storm, but this is by far is his best ninja performance." Chuckling, she continued stroke her belly in soothing circles.

Rohnert climbed back into bed, his eyes alert. "What can I do?"

Shelly took his hand and placed it on her stomach. "Rub him. I'm sure he'll like that. Talk to him, too."

He hesitated before he began to move his fingers over her. "I don't want to hurt you or the baby." His touch was tentative, slow and cautious.

"Honey, come closer. Put your mouth close to my stomach. You won't hurt me."

Rohnert moved nearer with a hint of reluctance. Just as his palm made a circling movement along her skin, her stomach shifted, following his touch.

"Did you see that?" His eyes widened with surprise. "The baby likes me."

"Of course he likes his father. Now talk to him."

"Are you serious?" He kept on rubbing, and subsequent responses to his effort made his grin bigger.

Shelly rolled her eyes. "Studies show that a baby absorbs language while in the womb around the last ten weeks of pregnancy. We are in that window already. Go on—don't be shy."

"What do I say?"

"Anything. You can even sing if you want."

She watched Rohnert. who was deliberate, his thick eyebrows lowering into a solid line. After a moment, he took a deep breath and started singing. It was a song she hadn't heard before. The words were foreign to her ears. The language sounded European, but she couldn't place it. The melody was soothing, and his deep baritone was beautiful.

When he finished, the movement in her stomach stilled.

"I had no idea you could sing. Do you have any other talents I don't know about?" Shelly grinned.

"I learned that from my mother." His expression turned wistful. "She used to tell me to keep the song close to my heart. I don't understand it still."

"Would you translate the lyrics for me?"

"I can try. Some words don't have an exact translation." He closed his eyes and paused before continuing.

Now, now that you're gone
Every minute, eternity passes away
I'm so lost without you

I'm no good without your love

Shelly grinned, not sure what to say. How could he have kept his talent a secret?

"I've only sung for you and Malin, and I want to keep it that way."

We'll see about that.

"I hear your mind churning, Dr. Anderson."

"Okay fine. Let's change the topic. When do you want to schedule the ceremony?"

"We can have it this weekend. Do you think you can find a minister on such a short notice?"

"I can try. I'll go to my office and check for listings. What other preparations do we need to make?"

"Allison has already contacted Darryl to cater the occasion. Do you have any requests?"

She shook her head. Pritchard's personal chef would know what she wanted. The guy had nothing in his arsenal that wasn't mouthwatering, and he'd created some amazing meals for the crew in the past. Too bad Harrow had to let him go for his own safety.

"Then Allison made a wise choice. Is there anything you want? A special dress? Flowers?" Rohnert watched her closely.

"I'm fine." Her mind started swirling with ideas. Although she was simple in nature, she still wanted her wedding day to be perfect.

Rohnert didn't speak but kept his eyes on her. She knew him well enough to guess that his attention had shifted elsewhere when his expression tightened.

"Well, let me get started with the phone calls. Why don't you get more sleep since you're going on 'Operation Rescue Angus' tonight." She winked at him, trying to shake him out of the gloom that seemed to have descended on him.

"I'll be here when you get back."

Shelly left the bed and got dressed. Although she had grown accustomed to his quiet nature, when he fell silent, there was no telling what he was thinking.

Rohnert jumped out of bed and grabbed the phone the moment Shelly left their bedroom. "Allison, I need your help."

She sounded sleepy, but her voice perked up when she recognized his voice. "Rohnert, this is a big surprise. What can I do for you?"

"You have connections. I need you and the ladies to take Shelly shopping for wedding attire."

"Goodness, of course! Do you think Harrow would let us go?"

"I would personally escort you, but isn't there a human tradition that the male cannot see the female's outfit before the mating ritual?" This went beyond his comprehension, but he wanted to do right by his woman.

"I'm going to call Eli now and have him close off the store tonight."

"Let me see if Harrow will agree," he said before they hung up.

His next call was to their vampire leader. "Harrow, I need a favor."

"Dude, you beat me up the last time we sparred. Can you at least let me lick my wounds for a week?"

Rohnert chuckled. "Nah, I don't think I can mop the floor with your face twice in a row. I'll enjoy the victory for now. I actually, need . . . ah, well . . ."

"Spit it out, man."

"I want Shelly to have an ideal mating ceremony. She needs a dress—"

"Shoot. Did you talk to Allison? She's the expert on shopping." Harrow laughed.

"I called her, but I don't want to overstep my boundaries. I want to make sure you're all right with them going out." Although he had reservations about them leaving the safety of the compound, his better sense told him to waylay his concerns.

"I doubt anyone is plotting to take us down in a department store. If it eases your mind, we will bring Zo and some other guys with us."

Rohnert felt better already. "That's what I was hoping you would say."

"I will coordinate with Ally, and we'll most likely head out at sundown.

You're going out with the guys, so stay on course. I'll take care of Shelly."

That was all he needed to hear. "Thank you."

"Stay focused, and be careful out there," Harrow said before he hung up.

With nothing else to do, Rohnert went to find Shelly in the clinic. She was hanging up the phone just as he entered her office. "Okay, I got a minister who said he'd make it if we pay his nighttime fee." Shelly rolled her eyes. "I told him it's at a secret location to surprise the guests. It didn't seem like he had a problem with the secrecy, so I told him someone would pick him up and that he'd be blindfolded the whole time."

"And?" Rohnert sat on the chair opposite her desk.

"The price went higher." Shelly laughed.

"I have no problem with that." He'd do anything to make the day memorable for her. "I made plans for you tonight."

Her eyebrows shot up. "Really?"

"I thought you would want an opportunity to buy your wedding attire and whatever else you'll need for the occasion." This was totally out of his league.

Shelly's mouth trembled, but she regrouped right away. "Oh, yeah?"

"Yeah."

She took his hand that rested on the desk. "Aren't you the sweetest man there is?"

"I want it to be perfect. Just the way you pictured your mating day would be."

"I . . . thank you. You have no idea how much this means to me."

Zane elected to take his roadster on tonight's stakeout. He decided against going on foot since his legs were now more of a liability. The Ducati was out of the picture since the damn thing was heavy and difficult to support with his legs once he hit traffic lights.

So here he was on the third night of his stakeout outside the hospital with nothing to show for it. He had been hoping to see the doctor again and maybe fish for some information from her, any detail to connect the elusive dots. Yeah, sure. He'd just walk in the hospital, introduce himself and demand answers. That would fly.

He was certain of one thing. She was connected with the underground vampires. Even so, it didn't make a whole lot of sense for his dear grandpapa to risk his neck over a human. There had to be reason beyond a simple wish to get all the intel on the doctor.

His legs were getting cramped in the small cab. Zane had his hand on the handle to open the car door when a black Humvee with dark tinted windows circled the parking lot.

He slid down into the driver's seat until the vehicle passed by and stopped in the darkened patch of the lot. The doors opened, and four men stepped out. Judging from the bulges in their long coats, they were armed. When the light from the lamppost hit their faces, he recognized three of the vampires he'd tangled with more than once.

The bald one, he remembered, was Rohnert. He was with the one he'd changed—Cyrus. Zane flinched at the memory. Tor was the hulking vampire with short, stubby dreadlocks. Watching their lithe, calculated movements, he knew they were up to something. The group ran across the parking lot, scaled the back walls, and entered through a dark window.

Zane fought the urge to report this to Goran. He had to find out more. What were the vampires up to? If he were in prime form, he would have followed to find out the easy way. As it was, he wouldn't amount to much in a fight at the moment, so he stayed tight.

He expected gunfire to break out at any time, but minutes passed without a noise. There were no squad cars rushing to the scene. More time ticked by before he noticed the same group emerging from the window.

Over his shoulder, Rohnert carried a man wearing a hospital gown, and the rest covered him. They made their descent with care, as if their cargo was precious. Zane watched the scene with trepidation, unsure of what to do.

He remained seated, gripping the steering wheel until his knuckles turned white. Cyrus opened the passenger door while combing the parking lot with his eyes. The others hurried to get the unknown man situated in the car. Cyrus checked the surroundings once more before climbing into the driver's seat and driving away.

Instead of following the departing car, Zane decided to wait it out. He knew where the group was headed anyway. What he needed to discover was the identity of the fifth person, and that answer would come soon on its own.

"Rise and shine, sleepyhead." Allison's voice sounded chipper.

Shelly couldn't help but smile at her friend's cheerful greeting. She opened her eyes and stretched.

Allison turned on the light, bathing the room in a buttery glow. "Today's your big day, sweetie."

"Good morning to you, too." Shelly reached into the space next to her and groaned when her hand hit nothing but pillows. She'd had a vivid and delicious dream about making love with Rohnert, as they did every chance they got. Pink crept up her face when she noticed Allison staring at her, hands on her hips.

Allison giggled. "Don't worry. I still feel the same way about Tor, and we've been together for ages." She glanced around the room. "I shooed Rohnert away, so don't bother looking for him. You won't be seeing him 'til later." She had taken it upon herself to make sure that Shelly and Rohnert wouldn't see each other before the ceremony—a foolish human tradition.

"Where is he?"

"He's bunking with Zo right now." Allison marched to the walk-in closet and took out the pale lavender chiffon gown Shelly had chosen.

"You have exquisite taste. I can't wait to see you in it with your hair and makeup done." Allison laid the floor-length dress on Rohnert's side of the bed and smoothed the fabric with her hand.

Shelly had tried on several gowns in the store with the help Allison, Jordan, Cheryl, and even the timid Isidora. This particular number had caught her eye.

The clever draping of the material highlighted her figure as a whole, taking the emphasis away from her rounded stomach. The V-neckline was studded with crystals all the way down the sleeves. The gown, with its simple detail, was elegant and Shelly couldn't be happier about finding the right one that suited her taste and mood.

She had eagerly tried it on, and judging from the reactions of everyone in the room, she knew she had made the right choice. It had been a fun night for all of them. With Harrow and Alonzo watching them like hawks, they'd breezed through the humongous department store. She had found a pair of classic ballet flats in white that would complement her outfit.

"Earth to Shelly. Hello, is anyone home?" Allison nudged her, bringing her back to the present.

"I bet Rohnert wasn't too happy about getting kicked out of our room."

"He's going to be fine. That man of yours can handle a little time away from you." Allison winked. "Darryl made a special breakfast just for you. Why don't you get up and find him in the kitchen?"

Shelly grinned. This already had the makings of a perfect day. Her mouth watered just imagining what the celebrated chef had cooked up for her. Shelly scooted to the edge of the bed and swung her legs onto the floor. After she got her morning ritual out of the way, she and Allison wandered down to the small kitchen.

"*Ma belle dame.*" Darryl beamed the moment she walked in. He opened his arms, and Shelly walked into his embrace. "*Vous êtes aussi exquis comme une fleur-de-lis.*" He kissed her on each cheek.

Shelly looked at Allison for translation.

Allison giggled at her confusion. "He said you're as exquisite as a fleur-de-lis."

"Thank you, Darryl. It's nice to see you again."

"*Madame*, I made your favorite, flambéed crepes Suzette." Darryl pulled out a chair for her. "Would Ms. Allison join us, too?"

"I may not allow you to leave," Shelly said, eyeing the plate. The pungent aroma permeated her nose, and her stomach growled.

"I will have a little. I've missed your cooking, Darryl." Allison took the chair next to her.

"Don't worry, *madame*. I went easy on the Grand Marnier." Darryl's rich French accent made Shelly smile.

They ate while Darryl regaled them with stories about his new restaurant—a gift from Pritchard in exchange for his services as their personal chef. At one point, Allison excused herself while Shelly and Darryl caught up. Shelly hadn't noticed the time and was on her second serving of crepes when Allison returned.

She grimaced when Allison picked up her plate from the table. "Hey, I'm not done yet."

"Yes, you are, missy. You have one little vampire in there, not ten, so don't eat like there's no tomorrow." Allison smirked, making Darryl laugh so hard, he was close to tears.

"It's nice to know that you guys are having so much fun at my expense." Shelly crossed her arms.

"Chop-chop, we have so much to do." Allison pulled her up to her feet. "So here's the deal. I want you to soak in the tub for thirty minutes. I have to do my last minute walk-through of the ceremony and reception. Isidora volunteered to do your hair, and I will take care of your makeup. Then we'll get to the gown and all that good stuff." Allison's rapid-fire delivery was endearing and annoying at the same time.

"Good thing you are a vampire, Ally, because at the rate you are going, you'd die of a heart attack otherwise."

"Did you hear what I just said?"

"Yes, ma'am." Shelly saluted.

"March in the bathroom like a good girl, and I'll be back for you in an hour. Don't worry about anything. Tonight will be magical," Allison said before she darted out of the room.

Rohnert stood next to Reverend Tillman, growing more and more anxious while he waited for Shelly's arrival. Allison had sent word that they were almost ready. He swore under his breath, catching the attention of Harrow, who was standing next to him.

"Are you solid, my man?" Harrow asked, patting his shoulder.

"Tight as a strung cable." Rohnert glanced at the rest of his friends.

He wore the ceremonial black robe with golden specks he had used in the past as a member of the Council. It seemed appropriate to wear it on this special day to represent his lineage and his race. He caught the minister looking at him several times, and he had to make a conscious effort to conceal his fangs.

Rohnert looked around the training room, which Allison had magically transformed into a ceremonial area. She even managed to arrange a few chairs on each side, and a carpet runner in deep red lined the path from the door to the front of the room. Flowers were in abundance, too, as well as petals littering the floor.

Foregoing the traditional wedding march humans often used, Rohnert had decided at the last minute to give Rayce an instrumental CD often used during mating rituals. When the music filled the room, he felt a nervous tug in the pit of his stomach. He watched the door with excitement, knowing that his future and the mother of his child would be walking in any time.

The doors opened, and Shelly appeared, making her way to him. Rohnert had always thought she was beautiful, but tonight, she was in a class of her own. He marveled at how her glowing face radiated warmth when she smiled at the people in the room. Rohnert watched her, mesmerized, until their eyes locked and his body came alive. Shelly was the epitome of everything that was beautiful and graceful.

He could hear the beating of her heart when she walked closer. Her eyes never left his, and just like a magnet, they were drawn to each other. Shelly had been worth waiting for.

He reached out for her hand and kissed it. Someone in the back of the room coughed, and the lights of the room were dimmed. The warm glow of the circle of candles illuminated the room. Rohnert led her into the circle, and Reverend Tillman followed. This was the vampire tradition, to start their life as mates in radiance.

Reverend Tillman cleared his throat. "Friends, we have been invited here today to share with Rohnert and Shelly a very important moment in their lives. In the few months they have been together, their love and understanding of each other has grown, and now they have decided to live their lives together as . . ." the minister paused, "as mates."

Somebody snickered.

Rohnert couldn't take his eyes off Shelly's face. Time stood still while he stared into her expressive eyes.

"They have prepared their vows for this unique occasion," Reverend Tillman announced.

Rohnert had nothing prepared. Digging deep into his soul, closed his eyes for a brief moment. When he opened them, he spoke.

"Shelly, I look at you, and my heart is overflowing with love. I am certain that I will feel the same way for all eternity. I pledge, with all of what I am, to cherish and nurture you as we build our lives together. I will always strive to be the man you came to love."

Shelly's eyes began to fill with tears, but her smile exuded happiness. She unfolded a piece of paper, sniffled once, and took his hand.

"I've always wanted to share my life with a man who was gentle, kind, and courageous. I dreamed of someone who would love everything about me. I never thought I would get everything I wished for. When you came into my life, I knew my wish had been granted. You offer yourself and your love fully and unselfishly. I give myself to you as your mate. I promise to treasure the love we celebrate today for all my days."

As instructed, Harrow produced a red cord and bound their hands together. They both recited the vows together, then Reverend Tillman concluded the ceremony with the declaration of their unity.

"Rohnert and Shelly have exchanged these vows of love in our presence. We now recognize them as . . . mates. Congratulations, you may now seal your bond with a kiss."

Rohnert looked at Shelly with the eagerness of a hopeless lover. When their lips touched, he felt the tingle throughout his body, sending his whole being into a pulsating frenzy.

"Ladies and gentlemen, I now present to you . . ." Reverend Tillman turned to him. "What's your last name?" he whispered.

Rohnert grinned against Shelly's mouth and broke their kiss. "Just Rohnert and Shelly."

"I now present to you Rohnert and Shelly."

The room erupted in a deafening applause and the stomping of feet on the floor. Rohnert lost his grasp of time while he held Shelly in his arms, exploring the sweetness her mouth had to offer.

"Are we there yet?" Shelly straightened in the seat of the Humvee and strained to see past the jet black tint of the windows.

She had been on constant alert, making sure he was entertained and asking questions that made him laugh while they drove through the dead of the night to their destination.

"Thirty more minutes," Rohnert said, glancing sideways at her.

"You said *that* thirty minutes ago." Shelly laughed.

"Are you really this impatient, or do you just enjoy being a pain?" He took her hand, which was resting on her thigh, and twined their fingers.

"I enjoy hassling you." Shelly leaned against the door and watched him. There wasn't much to see, with the darkness looming ahead and around them.

Rohnert knew this was the best time to give Shelly a glimpse of his past. His childhood vacation home might not be the perfect location for a honeymoon, but since Shelly was on the last leg of her pregnancy, he thought it was best to take it easy and stay close to the city.

Rohnert rubbed her palm with his fingers, while halfway concentrating on the road. The drive was tame considering the distance. They'd left the city hours earlier, heading to a quiet hamlet in East Hampton. Shelly had been excited about the prospect of getting away, and he knew it was in part because she wanted to know more about his background. His decision to bring her reeked of sentimentality—he wanted to share a piece of himself with her.

He remembered her face perking up when he proposed the getaway. Although he hadn't visited his childhood home in years, he knew that it had been kept in good repair. After phoning the caretaker, he was assured the secluded cottage was tidy and safe.

The modest home had been a retreat for his family back before the town became a summer getaway for New York City's affluent residents. It was also the place where his parents had disappeared.

Rohnert took Route 27 and slowed down when they passed through villages. The towns were much different from what he remembered. More retail stores, art shops, and restaurants lined the highway, giving it a more modernized feel.

With their fingers laced, he navigated through the deserted highway until they reached the hamlet known as Wainscott. Rohnert drove further down the street until the road was no longer paved, and the ride became somewhat bumpy.

"Hang on." He let go of Shelly's hand and held on to the steering wheel.

Within minutes, they reached the end of the road and turned onto a winding driveway. They took the path amid long and unruly bushes and vegetation that lined each side. The cottage was perched on the edge of the lot, overlooking the ocean.

Shelly peered from her dark window, in an obvious state of excitement. Rohnert parked the car in front and hurried out to open the passenger door and hold his hand out to assist her.

"Ready?"

"Since thirty minutes ago." Shelly, with an eagerness he hadn't seen before, placed her hand in his and allowed him to lead her out of the car and toward the house.

Rohnert grinned and squeeze her hand. "You're too much for me. You know that?"

"I'd like to think of your comment as positive." Shelly smiled.

"I have nothing negative to say about you, my female." Knowing the ins and outs of the property like the back of his hand, he opened the front door with keys he'd rarely used.

He turned on the light, and the house came into clear focus under the ambient glow. Shelly let go of his hand and advanced into the room. "Rohnert, this place is precious." She rushed to the wall lined with glass display cabinets and gushed.

The curios housed memorabilia belonging to his family. Sensing her eagerness to connect with the little mementos, Rohnert opened the glass doors. He took out one of the two muskets inside the case.

A barrage of unfamiliar images flashed before his eyes upon contact, making him stagger backward.

"What is it?" Shelly was quick to sense his distress.

He tried to brush away the unknown memories he couldn't understand. "Oh, nothing."

Shelly knew better than to buy his half-assed excuse.

"Rohnert, spill." She held his chin bring them face-to-face.

Rohnert closed his eyes and honed in on the visions. "This particular weapon was used in a sinister plot. I see a man, no face. No one has a face, but the background is vivid as hell." A jolt ran through his body, leaving his body humming. He scrambled to replace the musket in its spot.

"Rohnert, what is it?" Shelly's voice rose, tinged with worry. She searched his face.

"The weapon was used here. The massacre. The cries and accusations." He pressed his palms on his temple, trying to stop the flood of information. "They were killed here."

Shelly took his hand and led him to the Victorian couch. "Sit and try to calm down. You're scaring me."

Rohnert settled on the sofa, rested his elbows on his thighs, and covered his face. *Perfect! What a way to start their honeymoon.*

Her hand rubbed his head, making him look up. "Shells, I apologize for scaring you. I have no idea where that came from."

Her face softened, and she shook her hand. "No apologies necessary. Take all the time you need." She wrapped her arms around him, barely covering the breadth of his shoulders.

"I still can't understand why you're in love with me."

"Because"—she grazed her fingers on his temple—"you're strong in mind"—then glided down his chest—"heart"—and pulled him closer —"and body."

Rohnert couldn't speak. All he could do was bask in the grace of her affection.

"We can go to bed, if you want," Shelly said after a few minutes, rubbing his back.

Rohnert shook his head. "Let me show you the rest of the house, unless you're tired."

Her eyes twinkled with mischief. "Well . . . why don't you show me around and we'll see what happens next?" She winked at him.

There was a stirring deep within him, but he tamped it down. He pulled her to her feet and gave her a quick hug. "I love you so much, just in case I haven't said it lately."

Her body molded to his, fitting just right. "You did, an hour ago." She kissed his lips. His reaction was instantaneous. He caressed her face with his hands and deepened the kiss until they both gasped for air.

"Where were we?" Rohnert looked around, composing himself. He led her closer to the same display cabinet. "Ah, that was where my father kept all of the weapons used by our family." He pointed to a black, rusty metal dagger with five blades. "My father's favorite."

Shelly pressed her nose on the glass to get a closer look. "Did you come from a long line of warriors?"

"Yes. Apart from being in the Council for centuries, my father was also the weapons expert for Goran's father." The image of the two older vampires brought back warm memories. As a child, he had often wandered inside the Council walls and would witness them sparring or practicing with the samurai swords.

"What happened to Goran? Why did he turn the way he did?"

Rohnert had asked himself the same question one too many times. He shook his head. "There were stories swirling around the deaths of his parents. Many think that he lost his mind when they passed away. Perhaps he wasn't ready to take responsibility. I wish I knew."

"You were friends?" Shelly turned to him as if gauging the shift in his mood.

"That's what I used to think. We were like brothers. We fought many battles together. I don't understand." He swiped his large hand over his head, wiping off the sweat.

"I wonder what drove him that way."

"Me, too." He opened the next display case, which contained more weapons. He glanced at Shelly, hoping he wasn't boring her to tears, but her face shined with excitement.

"I wished I could've met your parents."

Fresh pain tugged his heart. "I wish for it with all my heart."

Then he remembered the pictures on the mantle. He tugged at her hand, and they crossed the tiny room to the hearth. Rohnert picked up a frame with a fading picture of a family in sepia tones. The contact brought another jolting revelation. His hand released the frame, but Shelly caught it.

"Tell me what you see." She cupped his face and urged him to focus on her face. "What did it remind you of?"

Rohnert fought the nonstop flashback and the subtle hints that were making his head spin. The memories were of an event he couldn't recall witnessing himself. He closed his eyes. "There's a baby . . . a boy being handed to another."

"And?" Shelly tightened her hand on his face, willing him to open his eyes.

"All I see is the baby—crying—and the hands taking him. There were no other details. None that I recognize."

Shelly turned silent for a moment, and when she opened her mouth, her voice was clinical. "I think you're getting overly anxious. It's obvious that being around this place triggers memories you've worked hard to suppress."

"What are you saying?"

"Read the book once we get back to the city. I believe it holds the key to your questions," she said. "Let's finish the rest of the tour."

Rohnert took the cue and shook the miserable flashbacks away. Whatever it was, he wasn't going to let it ruin their short vacation. "How about I show you the bedroom?" He held her by the waist and cradled her in his arms.

Shelly's answering giggles were electric, and the scent of her lust rose to the surface, filling his nostrils. "I thought you wanted to save the best for last?"

"Fine, I'll show you the stunning vista first." Instead of letting her back onto her feet, he carried Shelly outside, where the sound of the crashing waves greeted them. The scent of the salty air penetrated their noses.

The third quarter moon hung low as though it was close enough to touch. Its glow made it possible for Shelly to appreciate their immediate surroundings, the lush landscape that bordered the property and the scent of the flower blooms. He deposited her in one of the aging Adirondack chairs and sat down next to her. The stillness of their environment added the allure to the ocean's ongoing symphony.

"Thank you for sharing this place with me. I couldn't be any happier." Shelly closed her eyes.

He took her hand. "There is no one I would rather share this place with. I'm glad you like it."

"This is heaven, if there's one at all." Shelly took a deep breath, and the ensuing sigh was like music to his ears.

He traced rhythmic patterns on her palm. "I'm touching heaven right now."

"Would you sing for me again?"

She didn't have to ask twice. Rohnert leaned back, looking upward and keeping their fingers twined. He began singing softly, music he had known by heart since childhood. As words and music began filling the air, his voice soared, setting his anxiety free. Shelly's hand squeezed his, removing all doubts of his past and present worry. The future was theirs to hold on to.

When he finished, Shelly was quiet, but he knew the questions of her heart.

"The main idea of the song is my wish to see the sun in your eyes."

Rohnert couldn't wipe the stupid smile off his face, but that was understandable. He'd had the most amazing five days of his life. It hadn't been limited to sex. He and Shelly had walked on the beach, shared childhood stories, and showered together.

"Where do you want the bags?" he asked, slinging the backpacks and suitcases into his arms. It remained a mystery why women needed to pack so many clothes for a few nights away.

"Just leave them by the door, and I'll unpack later. I'm going to the clinic first. I'll see you in a bit." Shelly kissed him on the cheek before she left.

He smiled and caught Harrow smirking from the door of the garage.

"You're whipped, my man."

"It takes one to know one," Rohnert shot back. "What's up? Don't tell me this is the welcome wagon. I'm hurt."

Harrow snickered. "I want to run some info by you. Swing by the I-room when you get a chance. Oh, and by the way, wipe that smile off your face. You look like an idiot." Harrow disappeared from the doorway.

Rohnert unloaded the bags in the bedroom, leaving them by the door as Shelly had requested, and his eyes settled on the black book. Isigani and Shelly were right. It was time he read the contents and got the answers he needed. He grabbed the book, tucked it into his waistband, and proceeded to his meeting with Harrow.

He found Harrow in the I-room on the phone, deep in a strained conversation with Leo. The bits and pieces of the one-sided conversation he overheard told Rohnert that the general was concerned about the recent spate of vampire sightings and had been drilling Harrow for information.

"Leo, be reasonable. My men are good. We stay away from humans. We go about our business quietly."

For once, Leo sounded pissed, which was a reasonable reaction, considering the potential repercussions of such sightings.

Rohnert hung around, helping himself to a scotch from the bar while Harrow continued the heated conversation with the general. In the end, Harrow seemed to get through to their military friend, and he promised to be more vigilant for the sake of everyone's safety.

Harrow blew a relieved breath when he punched the speaker button. "Tough guy he is."

Rohnert nodded. He'd met Leo several times and liked the man. He was the father figure they'd missed since Pritchard's demise. Leo was a level-headed person—fierce and loyal in the way he upheld his dead friend's wishes.

"So what's up?"

Harrow didn't answer right away. He got up and poured himself a stiff drink. "I have some information you might be interested in," he said after downing half the glass.

"Tell me." Rohnert sat down and leaned on the table.

"I heard from one of our boys that there are rumors Goran is getting married."

Rohnert blinked, unable to comprehend the news. He'd heard about the pressure the Council had been putting on Goran to find a bride. Since Isidora had gone missing and was now in their protective custody, he hoped that would cause a delay and prevent Goran from further solidifying his power.

"Is that so?"

"They overheard a vampire who claimed to be an elite guard say that the female was their weapons expert and tactician. Do you know her?"

"Bretania." Not good—not good at all.

"Well, what do you know about her?"

He rubbed his forehead and thought about the Council Elder. "She's smart and excellent with sword and dagger. She's also shrewd and quick to retaliate." No wonder Goran went for her. Teamed up with such a crafty vampire, the sky would be the limit.

"I'd better get hold of her," Rohnert said out loud. Maybe she would listen to him.

Harrow eyes rose from the rim of his Oakleys, and he shook his head. "Preposterous. Dangerous."

"Do you have a better alternative?" Rohnert challenged.

"I—I," he stuttered. And Harrow never did that. "Well, you're courting danger."

Rohnert chuckled. "I think we're in a dangerous situation already, being hunted as we are. I've sat on my ass long enough doing nothing. If things are left as they are, it's not going to get any better. If I get through to her, there might be hope for our race. That includes you, my friend."

The vampire seemed unconvinced. Harrow took off his glasses and rubbed his eyes. He glared at Rohnert. "This has trouble written all over it."

"It's the first step to getting things done. Besides, I have a score to settle. Goran killed another Elder, and who knows how many more."

"Then I'm coming with you." Harrow's eyes flashed with determination.

"You'll just get yourself killed, too."

"Don't be so morbid. It ain't over until I say it's over." Harrow chuckled, but his eyes were far from amused.

"You're an arrogant SOB, aren't you?" Rohnert replied with resignation.

"I'm surrounded by the best."

"So be it."

"When do we leave?"

"Tomorrow. I'm off tonight, and after Shelly is done at the clinic, we're going to see Jones for a check-up."

Harrow's face perked up. "Great. When is she due?"

"In a week or so. According to Jones, she's going to have a C-section. It's best for the baby and her. So I'm bringing another doctor in here." Then he remembered he had forgotten to ask. "My apologies. I assumed it would be okay. He's a friend of Shelly's, and she trusts him."

"You know the drill. We'll do anything for the doctor."

After their short meeting, he proceeded to the control room, and found Rayce watching the exterior cameras.

"Hey, boss, how's it going? How was the honeymoon?" Rayce glanced at him and quickly returned his focus to his camera vigil.

"It was great. Thanks for asking. Everything okay with you?"

"I feel like a brand new man, thanks to Dr. Anderson. She's given me a new lease on life." Rayce flashed a thumbs-up, his eyes never leaving the monitor.

"That's good. I'm glad you're feeling much better." Rohnert smiled. "Hey, I just wanted to let you know that I'm going to hang outside, maybe on top of the roof. I need fresh air and some time alone to read."

Rayce nodded. "No problem. I'll open the exit door for you. Once you're out there, I'll drop a ladder. Watch your head."

He saluted Rayce and walked to the end of the hallway to the foyer, where the first door awaited him. Properly warned, he watched a ladder materialize on the wall. Very clever. Rohnert took it and climbed until he reached the top. The wind gust was mild, and the night chill wasn't too bad. He found a good spot overlooking the tall buildings and its glittering lights. Perching on the ledge, he pulled out the tome and started with the same worn out page Shelly had read.

> On the first sign of the moon's illumination, a vampire will rise into power, his heart filled with avarice. Among his peers, he will raise havoc, and death will augment the despair within. Mortals and vampires alike shall have no

power to prevent the destruction he will leave in his wake. A disinclined soul shall be called, and a child borne to the rightful guide shall come to fulfill this divination.

If he was going to make an assumption, he suspected that this referred to several people—him, Goran, and his child. Damn, his child. Back when he'd first come across the passage, it didn't make sense, but he hadn't suspected that he was going to be a father. The words held a new meaning now, and he shuddered at the weight of their significance.

He decided to start from the beginning. This time, he'd be diligent. Rohnert flipped the pages until he reached the dedication. He read Marania's heartfelt inscription, and his chest tightened. Not a lot of things frightened him enough to give him pause, but Marania's exposition made him question the future.

Rohnert flipped through the next pages, the same ones he'd seen before. Births, deaths, missing vampire children . . . then the flashback from that first night in the Hamptons came rushing back to him. The crying baby in his vision—who was it?

He closed his eyes, trying to trigger something, anything. Still, he came up empty, so he read on.

The next page gave him more information—more than he'd ever bargained for.

> Cantor, head of the Council circa 1732–1799, sire to two boys, Ronestus and Goran, mate to Divina, had given his firstborn up for adoption upon the urging of the diviner, Gastarius.

Rohnert tried to slow his racing mind. Goran has an older brother? Man, isn't this the breaking news of the century?

He continued reading.

> Arron, Council member of Anatol's bloodline, and mate Hedy had graciously accepted the duty of watching over Ronestus until he came of age, where all would be revealed to him. The child's name was changed for his protection.

Selected members of the Council had the full knowledge of this delicate matter. Among them were August, Randolph, and Marania, being the current keeper of records.

Rohnert stopped breathing, feeling the invisible walls closing in on him. He rose to his feet and walked off the increasing discomfort inside him. For fuck's sake, this explained everything. The pieces were falling into place.

His inexplicable feeling of alienation had a name. No matter what he had done, his parents had always been restrained though affectionate with him. Was it because they feared losing him? The constant instructions they had given him to remember, and the song passages they'd urged him to understand and keep in mind were now making better sense.

Christened as Ronestus by his real parents, he had been given a new name to secure his safety. The image of the crying child flashed before his eyes.

He was that child.

And he was Goran's older brother.

He was the rightful heir to the throne.

Rohnert tried to stifle the emotions hitting him from every direction with this revelation.

A faint noise sounded from behind him. He tucked the book in his waistband and readied the dagger. Poised to strike, he relaxed once the thoughts of the party crasher alerted him.

"Jordan, this is not a good time." He returned the dagger to its holster.

Jordan came into view, her face illuminated by the faint glow of the moon. "I knew I made the right call coming here." She came closer, watching him. "Seems to me that someone needs a friend."

"I need answers. Would you be a good girl and tell Shelly that I'm going to pay Randolph a visit?"

"Don't you want company? Last time we had an outing, we kicked some serious butt."

"The only butt I'm dying to kick is Goran's," he said, feeling his jaw clenching.

Jordan's face hardened at the mention of the vampire's name. "Then you need me to be there."

"This is not the time. When it finally comes around, my promise to you still stands. For now, deliver the message for me. I will be back in time to be with her to meet with Jones."

She seemed to weigh his words. "I would much rather you go well armed. Your dagger is not going to cut it out there."

"I'm just going to visit an old friend." The last remaining person who can confirm what I suspect.

"Then be careful out there," Jordan said and left.

Rohnert looked up at the sky and cursed. This sick twist of fate had left him reeling. Everything he'd known about himself was a lie, and he felt more alone than ever.

Jumping off the ledge, he tried to break some cross-country speed records in his haste to get to Randolph.

The last conversation he'd had with the vampire echoed in his head.

"You make it sound like I'm the answer."

"You're the only one who would know."

The goddamn puzzle pieced itself together for him, but the nagging question continued to haunt him.

Why me?

Shelly sank wearily into the office chair and hoisted her swelling legs onto the foot stool. She had just dropped by the clinic to check on things after being away, not expecting she'd end up treating two die-hard wannabes. The night had been pretty busy after the two humans checked in with deep lacerations and contusions from trying to keep up with their vampire comrades. In all likelihood, these newbies had missed the memo that explained there was no keeping up with vampires.

Cheryl peeked through her office door. "Doc, is everything all right?"

"Hey, c'mon in."

The only nurse to survive the last raid seemed too withdrawn after her ordeal. Shelly didn't expect her to be happy and untraumatized, but there was something off about her.

Cheryl hesitated before taking the seat opposite hers. Her hands shook when she rested them on the table, prompting her to remove them. Shelly didn't miss this.

"I just wanted to check on you, make sure you're okay. I could've done it if I wasn't too shaky," Cheryl said, sounding too apologetic.

This made Shelly upset. She hated seeing her friends in distress, and she knew better than to bother them with personal questions. Then again, Cheryl had been unable to perform the simple task of dressing and cleaning the lacerations. The sight of them seemed to scare the hell out of her. Worse, she even looked repulsed by them.

Shelly gave a smile of concession. "I'm fine. Just a bit tired. My feet look like they're going to burst soon." She glanced at her swollen lower extremities with disdain. "But let's not talk about my pregnancy. What I want to know is what happened back there."

Cheryl started fidgeting, avoided looking at her. "I get a little jumpy around wounds lately."

"That's what I thought. I don't mind stepping in for you from time to time—that's what we do. But I need to know that you can still do your job, because you're all I have here."

"Doctor Anderson, please, I promise to stay focused. I—I'm just distracted, I guess."

"I don't want to pry into your personal business, but as your boss, I need to know I can depend on you while I'm on maternity leave."

It was a nice angle, framed that way. Shelly didn't care about the details. She wanted Cheryl to be happy, or at least back to how she was before. She'd had a tough life. The few times they'd hang out, Cheryl had given her a glimpse of her rough childhood. This was the reason behind her decision to abandon the outside world in exchange for living in the facility.

Cheryl had been repeatedly molested by her step-father, and her mother had refused to believe her. Once she turned eighteen, she left their house. She lived on her own, put herself through nursing school, and ended up working for Pritchard. Shelly wouldn't have found out about if it hadn't been for Cheryl's request for an unscheduled day off, when she told Shelly she'd be attending her mother's funeral.

The brown eyes that gazed up at her were brimming with tears. "Remember the night of the raid?"

It still gave her nightmares. "Yes."

Shelly planted her feet on the floor, leaned forward, and took hold of Cheryl's hand.

"I watched over the one they captured. He was tortured, and I can't bear the thought of the abuse." Her lips quivered as tears began to fall.

Shelly took a deep breath, got on her feet, and walked around the desk. She put her arms around the shaking body and chose her words carefully. "I don't condone any form of torture, but we are in the midst of an unusual world, where ethics and morals are blurred. Harrow is a good man, and I trust his judgment. I wish you weren't subjected to that. I'm sorry."

Cheryl's sobbing intensified, and Shelly rubbed her back in soothing strokes. The nurse was a tough cookie. If she'd lasted this long being around here, there was no doubt Cheryl would be all right.

When the worst of the tears were over, Cheryl looked up at her. "I removed the Dangeran from his body," she whispered.

Shelly swallowed. So that was how the vampire had gotten away. The Dangeran was not a substance vampires would mess with, although it was harmless to humans.

"Zane is dangerous. You have to make every effort to avoid him." She left it at that. Cheryl was a grown woman and capable of discerning right from wrong. The nurse nodded, but made no attempt to speak. The silence hung thick until Shelly continued. "You're a valuable employee. If you need some time off, I can give you a few days."

"I'm going to be okay. It was just a case of nerves." Her expression turned to pleading. "Can you keep everything I said between us?"

Shelly nodded. Call it feminine intuition, but she sensed Cheryl felt something for the man she'd allowed to get away.

Rohnert reached Randolph's hideout and was surprised when no one came to the door. Randolph had several servants who answered each caller promptly. Maybe they'd let the wrong person in.

He unzipped his leather jacket, palmed his dagger, and then kicked open the door. There was a bit of resistance when he tried to push it, and he discovered the dead weight that was preventing him from opening it. The only sound he could hear inside the house was his own movement. A body lay at the foot of the door, dead and cold.

Rohnert realized he was too late. Pulling out the dagger, he ran on stealthy feet to the sitting room and found another servant lying on a pool of blood. Judging from the position of the body, he had likely been struck from the back. Rohnert began to feel desperate. He continued combing the rooms, opening each doors, still fisting the dagger, ready to fight.

As I go unto the afterlife, cleanse my soul and grant me everlasting peace.

His shoulders sagged upon hearing the last invocation. He turned the knob and found Randolph in the same state in which he'd discovered Marania and August.

"Randolph." He rushed over.

The Elder was sitting in a chair, hunched over his desk, pen in hand. Rohnert looked around, and the traces of blood from a few feet away marked the place of the attack. Randolph had dragged himself to the desk to write something.

Rohnert lifted Randolph's shoulders to turn him over, but the elder began convulsing. He sat on his heels so Randolph could see him. A long slit on the vampire's neck prevented any verbal communication, and blood continued to gush from the wound.

Randolph let go of the pen and struggled to hand the paper to Rohnert. Read it later. I have no more time. I did what I was supposed to do. The rest is up to you. Keep our memories alive by upholding the beliefs our forefathers set for us.

He held Randolph's trembling hand and bowed. "I will do whatever I can, my brother."

Promise me.

"I promise."

Randolph's breath hitched, and Rohnert launched into chanting the rites in their old language. The hand that gripped his slowly slackened until it lay limp. Cursing under his breath, Rohnert slid the paper into his pocket and lifted his hands to his eyes, trying to block out the gruesome picture.

Another person had fallen victim to Goran's evil plot. This had to stop. The death, the lies, and the manipulation had gone long enough. No more blood must be shed if he could help it.

Hysteria began to claw its way into his psyche, and the stench of blood became too much to bear. He carried Randolph's body to the bed, then plunged the dagger into his chest. Rohnert didn't bother to look back when he departed the bedroom.

Vengeance wasn't his to seek, but justice was his to uphold. He would do anything within his power to carry out the wishes of the friends he held dear in his heart.

Shelly was getting worried. Dawn was close to breaking, and Rohnert had yet to make an appearance. Sure, he'd sent word through Jordan about visiting one of the Elders, but she couldn't help the frightening images that kept creeping inside her mind.

What if something had happened to him?

Jordan had no answers to her repeated inquiries. Her subdued behavior raised some warning bells, and Shelly couldn't wait until Rohnert was back in the warehouse, safe and sound, where he belonged.

She turned to check on the luminous clock on her nightstand, as she had done many times throughout the morning. It didn't help that Malin was kicking harder than ever, keeping her awake and uncomfortable. She had gone to the bathroom to relieve herself too many times, since the baby seemed to enjoy pressing on her bladder.

The doorknob jiggled, and she sat up, turning on the bedside lamp. Shelly held her breath until Rohnert walked in. His face had the look of death, and his clothes were bloodied.

"Rohnert, oh my god. Are you okay? Are you hurt?"

She jumped out of bed, despite her swollen feet and aching back, and rushed to him. Panic gripped her heart when she opened his jacket, searched his body for the source of the blood. A quick check told her he wasn't injured. The blood belonged to someone else.

"Shelly, I'm fine. Just hold me." Rohnert's voice sounded hoarse, as if he'd been crying.

She looked up at him but saw no trace of tears. Her arms went around his waist and held him. "I was so worried about you." She stifled a sob.

"I should've called, but things got rough, and I forgot."

"It's okay. Jordan told me. Will you tell me what happened?"

Rohnert's chest heaved, as though breathing had become difficult. "I will, but let's go see Jones first."

"I told him we might be late."

"We're going now. I could use some good news." He looked down at her feet, and his jaw clenched. "You need to be off your feet."

"I feel fine," she said. It was a lie, of course, and Rohnert would know.

Without saying anything, Rohnert lifted her off the floor and brought her to bed.

"What clothes do you want to wear? I'll get them for you." He looked around and saw the bags still sitting by the door.

"Everything that fits me is inside those bags. I can get them."

"Please let me do it." Rohnert's tone sounded like a plea, like he needed to keep his mind off whatever had happened earlier.

Shelly stayed put and nodded. "You can grab the beige sweat pants and matching top." Rohnert rummaged for a moment before finding the clothes she'd asked for.

"Rest for a bit while I take a quick shower," he said and disappeared in the bathroom.

Shelly heard the shower running and closed her eyes. She dared not think of anything else but her love for the man. Fatigue had set in, and she didn't realize she'd fallen asleep until she woke, hours later.

When she stirred, Rohnert turned to her. His eyes were bloodshot, and his muscles looked like coiled cables, straining underneath his cotton shirt.

"Why didn't you wake me up?"

"I couldn't bear the thought of disturbing your sleep."

At least he looked better than when he'd come home. "Shall we go?"

"If you're ready."

She pushed her body up and turned to him. "We'll talk later, okay?"

Rohnert nodded.

Jones met them at the clinic and waved when they walked in. Instead of the music she usually had blaring while she worked, the morning news was on. Cheryl lowered the volume once she spotted them.

"You look ripe and ready," Jones said, then laughed. "Hello Rohnert."

Rohnert inclined his head in greeting while Shelly snorted. "Aren't you perky this morning? On your tenth cup already?"

"I've given that up. I've been too shaky lately." Jones snapped on the latex gloves. "Shall we?"

Shelly knew the drill and climbed up the examination table. Cheryl pushed a brand new ultrasound machine closer to her. Bless Harrow's heart for anticipating her needs and ordering the medical instruments to accommodate the impending birth of her child. She rolled up her shirt to expose her belly.

Jones applied the gel on her abdomen, the cold making Shelly squirm. Then he pulled out the wand and placed it on her belly.

He moved the transducer around her stomach, glancing at the monitor that showed a black and white visual of the baby. Jones adjusted the controls until the sound of the baby's heartbeat filled the room. Shelly glanced at Rohnert and caught him with a little smile on his face. He stepped closer and took her hand.

Jones continued to move the wand along her belly, taking pictures, before gliding it to another spot.

"Do you know what you're doing?" Shelly asked, smiling.

The scientist raised an eyebrow. "I've been deep in study since you asked for my help. I find the sound of the heartbeat calming." He turned to Rohnert. "Don't you think so?"

Rohnert could only nod, but he squeezed Shelly's hand, a gesture demonstrating his happiness and nervousness.

"Okay, here we are. The baby is growing beautifully, and the position is good. Since we're still unsure how this type of pregnancy goes, I still believe C-section is the best way to deliver."

"Then we should decide when," Shelly said. She looked to Rohnert for guidance.

Judging from his expression, she could see that such decision was something he hadn't been prepared for. His Adam's apple bobbed when he swallowed. "Tomorrow's the beginning of a full moon."

"What does that mean?" Jones stopped moving the wand to look at Rohnert.

"We see it as a new beginning, with power and clarity coming into full focus. It also symbolizes an ending of a phase in someone's life and the cycling to begin a new chapter."

Rohnert's words sold Shelly on the idea. There had to be another reason behind his suggestion, but she'd ask later.

"I'll call Rick to see if he is available in the next few days."

"I wouldn't wait any longer. We're already sitting on the period we've pegged from our research." Jones' warning rang in her ears.

She didn't plan on waiting. There was nothing she wanted more in this world than to meet their son.

"Fuck you!" he cried, trying everything he could to clamp his muscles together, to keep the throbbing pain from pushing him into insanity.

"I think you're the fucked one here," the bastard said, sounding very sure of himself.

Then there was another turn of the screw. He bit his lips hard, tasting blood. Sweat broke out on his body at the effort to keep from crying out. With each slight movement, he inched closer to hell. The device opened farther apart. The sound of metal grunted against him, followed by the unbelievable pain of his skin tearing apart.

"Look at that! You're bleeding like a bitch."

His screaming woke him up. Drenched in sweat, Cyrus scrambled out of bed in the darkness. Another fuckin' nightmare. When would it ever end?

A loud banging came from the door, just like the ones before. He was getting tired of this.

He walked to the door but paused to check that he was decent. He had on shorts and no shirt, and his skin glistened with perspiration.

Cyrus yanked open the door. "I'm fine."

Tor stood outside, his dreads in disarray, looking as though he'd scrambled out of bed in a hurry. However, his eyes were alert, searching Cyrus' face just like he did almost every night. "You're having another wet dream?"

"Ha-ha." He didn't open the door wider.

"Dude, I think it's time to talk about it."

"Do I look like I want to talk?" This was getting old. If he wanted to talk, he'd find a shrink.

"You're about to crack."

"I'm good." Yeah, shit. He was strung way too tight. "Go back to sleep, Tor."

"I'm going to leave you alone for now, but you better keep your head straight. You're scaring me." Tor continued to watch him. It was disconcerting.

Cyrus bared his fangs. "Go back to Allison and leave me the hell alone." He slammed the door, not wanting to hear it.

So he was messed up. Tell him something he didn't know. He'd been running on auto-pilot ever since his captivity. When the memories rushed in, Cyrus gritted his teeth and clamped his mind shut.

He'd have to figure out a way to stop these nightmares. Maybe forgo sleeping. Did vampires fare well with little to no sleep? He bet they could. Seeing a therapist was a no-go. That would mean confiding in someone from the outside world and airing his dirty laundry. The thought made his stomach churn.

Seeing Shelly was another option, but what good would that do? Although he'd forged a close relationship with the doctor, he still felt all alone in this and terribly ashamed. Did he want to relive the past? Hell no!

Since sleeping was out of the question, he walked to the closet and pulled out a cotton T-shirt. He might as well burn his excess energy on the treadmill. At this time of day, he'd be alone to sort out his thoughts.

After the excitement of the ultrasound and getting their arrangements in place, Rohnert studied the paper Randolph had given him. With Tor, Zo, and Gentry flanking him, he unfolded the bloodied parchment and began reading.

He sagged at what it disclosed. Randolph's testimony confirmed that Goran was his kin. He was the older brother who had been given up to fulfill Gastarius' prophecy.

It was the same information he had gathered from the black book earlier. What Randolph didn't explain was the silence from the Elders regarding the Goran's rise to power. Was fulfilling his destiny more important than bringing a wrongdoer to justice? They must have known that they would eventually pay with their lives for this decision.

Rohnert crushed the paper with his hand and growled. "If I find an opening tonight, I'm moving in to kill that fuckin' shit Goran."

"Hey, hey, bud. What the hell is going on?" Tor moved closer, placing a massive hand on his shoulder.

Rohnert threw the paper, which Tor caught with his prosthetic hand. Seconds later, Tor also cursed. "What the fuck is that about? The son of a bitch is your brother?"

The air around them chilled while fury rolled off in them in thick waves.

Gentry hissed. "I have no idea if I should weep for you, sire."

Rohnert ground his molars, trying to hang on to his last thread of sanity.

Alonzo jumped up and hollered. "What's next? Superman is Batman's bitch?"

Rohnert kept his eyes glued to the vicinity of the plaza. There was a subtle glow he could see from where they were perched, high up on the roof. This was the entrance to the Council walls. Humans, oblivious to the beings in their midst, and the vampires mixed together. He could surge through the opening, but he wouldn't dare gamble with the others' lives. Without a plan, penetrating the Council would be like walking through darkness without a flashlight. Besides, knowing that Goran was utilizing the elite guards, he knew he would be walking into an ambush.

Rohnert sat tight, then he pointed out an oddly costumed civilian below. "Darth Vader is a cross-dresser. Check out the skirt."

Tor laughed without mirth.

It was obvious they were just as shaken as he had been when he first discovered the secret behind his identity. Stupid lottery. He had to be big brother to Satan himself.

All their eyes were trained on their surroundings, paying close attention to the behavior of the vampires. Most of the Council guard appeared subdued. For Christ's sake, Satan was getting betrothed. Why the long faces?

His phone rang. "Rayce, what's up?"

"Shelly and Harrow are on the line. Putting them through now." There was a click, then he heard Shelly's breathing. His heart hammered in his chest.

Once he'd listened and then barked some orders at Harrow, he tried to calm his voice. "Shelly, you'll be fine. I'll get Rick now. Take care of yourself."

Rohnert hung up, and the others surrounded him. "Plan's changed. Looks like she's going to have the baby tonight."

He didn't wait for them to say anything, jumping off the building in a free fall and sprinting. Seconds later, he heard their footfalls behind him.

Once he reached the hospital, he tracked Rick to where he sat in his office, alone.

What a great way to reintroduce himself. He climbed through the window of the lounge once the last of the employees had left. His mental clock was ticking, reminding him not to waste time.

Rohnert rapped on the door marked Hospital Chief and didn't wait to be invited in. Rick looked up from his desk. "Who the hell are you barging in my office without—"

"Shelly's water broke. Excuse me if I forgot my manners." He eyed the human and began reading his thoughts.

Taken aback, Rick stared at him, trying to decide if he was a vampire or human. Rohnert pulled back his upper lip to expose the tip of his fangs. It took a few moments for the surgeon to collect his wits.

"You're her—"

Rohnert nodded, hating the slow reactions of humans in general. "We have to go now."

"How?" Do vampires fly?

He snorted, impatient. "We run, but since you can't, do you have a ride?"

"Yes, yes." Rick eyes snapped into alertness. The early surprise was gone. Rohnert watched him gather his keys, pull his backpack from a closet, and buzz someone. "I'm leaving. Emergency. Call if you need me. Tell Murray he's in charge tonight."

"Where's your car?" Rohnert followed the doctor out of the room.

"In the parking structure." They got into the elevator in silence. Rick had many questions and had been constantly sneaking glances at him. Once out of the elevator, they took an exit marked for employee use and headed to the reserved area. Rick's gleaming Benz responded to the click of a button. "Show me the way," he said, getting in the driver seat.

"Drive out and head west." Rohnert took out his cell phone. "Tor, we're in the car. We'll meet you there."

Shelly adjusted herself in the tub and luxuriated in the lilac scent of the bubble bath. Rohnert was out for the night doing his good deed, as she called it. She still worried about him. After the ultrasound, they'd begun planning, and she'd called Rick to check on his availability. It was agreed that the best time would be tomorrow.

Her baby's impending arrival sent shivers down her spine. The idea of motherhood hadn't even been a remote possibility a year ago. Not in her wildest dreams would she have predicted this could happen, and certainly not with a vampire. Shelly wasn't complaining. The complexity of their situation was nothing compared to the happiness she felt being with Rohnert, even with all the baggage he carried.

After several more minutes of relaxing, Shelly drained the tub then grabbed on to the handle bar to hoist her body up, but her foot slipped, and she landed on her butt. Hard.

Shelly cried out when her body reacted to the painful landing, and she felt her stomach muscles tighten. She remained seated for a few minutes until the discomfort ebbed, rubbing her stomach in soothing motion. Then she attempted to get up again.

Water gushed from between her legs, and she froze.

Oh shit!

She stepped out of the tub and pulled the robe from the counter. This wasn't good. Rohnert wasn't slated to be back until much later. Shelly moved toward the phone and pressed Rayce's extension.

"Get Harrow and Rohnert on the line for me."

"Is everything okay, Dr. Anderson?" Rayce's voice was filled with worry.

"It will be once I've talked to them. Hurry." Within seconds, Rohnert and Harrow went live.

Rohnert jumped in right away. "Shells, what's going on?"

"I'm here, talk to us," Harrow said.

"My water broke. I don't think I can wait until tomorrow."

She heard Rohnert curse. "Okay, hang tight. I'm going to get Rick right now. Harrow, you take her to the clinic, call Jones, and get Cheryl on it, too." Rohnert was speaking a mile a minute, and Harrow grunted in agreement. "Don't worry. We'll be there in no time."

"I'll see you in a bit," she said before the line was disconnected.

All it took was a couple of minutes before Harrow came to the door with Jordan and Allison. "Let's go, my dear." He lifted her from the bed.

"Are you all right?" Jordan fixed her robe.

"I can walk," Shelly said.

"I'm not letting you. You heard Rohnert. He'll have my head on a plate if something happens to you." Harrow marched to the door, which Allison held open.

They proceeded to the clinic in an awkward silence while Shelly's head swam with worry. If Rick couldn't make it, who would take his place? She'd seen Jones under pressure. The human would crack, and his limited knowledge was another cause for concern.

She regulated her breathing, and focused on Harrow's calm. Underneath his dark lenses, she could see him looking at her, and his mouth quirked into a smile. Jordan and Allison sandwiched them, banging on the doors of the suites when they passed them.

There was no labor pain yet. Thank goodness. Shelly wasn't looking forward to it after the horror stories she'd heard.

Jones was already waiting for them with Cheryl. One long look around the room told her that all instruments were ready. Jones was acting nervous, despite his smile, but Cheryl seemed more like herself. Shelly took comfort from the nurse's composure.

Harrow laid her on the table while Jordan and Allison hung in the background. "Are you okay?" he asked.

Shelly smiled. "I want DM."

Cheryl scuttled over and switched on the MP3 player. The intro to "Gravedigger" burst from the speakers, and the nurse's face turned beet red.

"Sorry." She pressed a button, then "The Space Between" played.

Shelly began to relax and closed her eyes while Jones connected her to a monitor, starting with her belly. A blanket was placed over her legs, and she sang in her head, willing good vibes in. She thought about Rohnert and Malin.

And the wait began.

Goran waited in his chamber for a cue from Devereux. He still hadn't gotten over the excitement of extracting information from Randolph. The thrill burned in his system like fuel, making the impending union with Bretania bearable.

In truth, he didn't care about the female. The driving force behind the decision to take her as his lifelong mate was practicality.

Randolph was the last living Council member who had opposed his rule. With a slash of a dagger, he'd solved that little problem. Now, he could breathe easy. With the elite guards and soldiers behind him, his continued reign was guaranteed. No one, not even Rohnert, could derail his plans.

Once he set his last maneuver in motion, the rest would be on cruise control.

A quiet knock sounded. "Come in," he said.

Devereux entered, wearing his elite guard uniform. It was a loose, black garment with the Council's gold emblem set on the left breast. The tunic was tapered at the waist, with dark trousers underneath. His sword hung at his side next to a holster of daggers.

The clock in the corner of the room chimed eight o'clock. "It's time, my lord." The guard's head bent low, his thoughts muddled with excitement.

"I'm ready." Goran took one last look in the mirror. His red caftan was immaculate, held together by a single black cord. The golden pendant that had been passed down for generations hung proudly around his neck and nestled on his chest. His sleek black hair was pulled away from his face with a leather band.

They walked the bright hallway together in silence, his companion on his left. The sound of voices came from the farthest wing of their headquarters. The rarely used shrine had been readied for this special occasion and was brimming with guests.

Goran straightened his back when they neared the sanctum of his forefathers. The heavy wooden doors carved with images of their beloved oak bush opened upon his arrival. Devereux stopped short and bowed before he proceeded inside.

A hush fell over the room, and familiar faces turned to the middle aisle while he progressed to the altar, which was filled with relics that had been collected throughout the years. The jewels, artifacts, and precious pieces of art were a magnificent backdrop for this occasion. Traditional music provided by a string ensemble wafted around the room, lending an elegant but somber air. Goran reached the steps and ascended. He turned around, smiling at the sea of faces that watched him with awe, admiration, and envy. This was the response he'd been looking for—not the contempt, suspicions, or distrust he often received from the members of his Council who were no longer around.

He glanced and inclined his head toward the remaining Elders. They raised their clasped hands to him in a sign of honor.

When the music became more joyous, all eyes turned to the far end of the room where Bretania stood. Everyone's breath held for a second before they broke into applause.

Bretania beamed from beneath the light veil that covered her face. Her red velvet gown was exquisite, bejeweled and sewn to her body like second skin. She was radiant, and Goran almost felt his shaft tingle. Almost.

The female vampire walked down the aisle, her eyes trained on him. Her smile gave away her excitement while the steady thrumming of her heart rose above the whispers of admiration. Goran extended his hand as she ascended the steps. When their hands met, the room exploded in another round of applause.

Lukan stepped forward and raised her hand. Looking lovely and vibrant in her black robe, she opened her arms and beckoned them. Goran smiled at the priestess, whose mind shut down, preventing him from reaching into her deepest thoughts.

They placed their right hands in hers, and Lukan shut her eyes. She didn't smile or frown—she showed no reaction at all. With her eyes and mind closed off, Goran had nothing to go on while he waited for her proclamation.

Once she opened her eyes, she looked down at her feet and took a deep breath.

"Dear members of the Council, esteemed guests, and loyal friends of Goran and Bretania, I am pleased to announce a good match. With the power bestowed upon me by our fathers and our ancestors before them, I proclaim our leader, Goran, and our lovely Bretania mated."

The room erupted in frenzied clapping while Lukan gestured for them to lean forward. She placed her palms on their bowed heads and chanted the mating rites. When her quiet incantation ended, she pulled him into an embrace and then turned to hug Bretania as well.

"Let everyone realize your greatness, my beloved Goran. Show them a dutiful companion, Bretania," she whispered.

The guests continued clapping until Goran raised his hand and the room quieted down. "From this day forward, may our reign go down in history as being devoted to ensuring that our race continues to flourish and to ensuring a peaceful existence for ourselves and our children."

Afterward, they sat on the seats while each guest offered their gifts, talents, or vows and embraced them. A lively beat began coming from the great room where the celebratory meal was to be served. Goran held Bretania's hand when they entered the dining area, his grin stretched from ear to ear.

Three long tables were arranged parallel to each other. A white topiary graced the middle of each table, and crystal doves perched on branches and strings of pearls hung from the gigantic chandeliers. The silver tablecloths made the crystal stemware gleam. It was a feast fit for the leader he was.

"This is breathtaking." Bretania squeezed his hand. "Thank you, my lord, for making this day memorable for me."

Her jet-black eyes sparkled with sincerity, and Goran was moved to plant a kiss on her forehead. He led Bretania to the center table and seated her next to her mother. Goran took his seat beside her and combed the guests for Lukan. The female was nowhere to be found. At another table, he spotted his children, all from different women, from the oldest boy, Nathaniel, who was fifteen, to the youngest girl, Esmeralda.

Each of the children gazed at him with admiration, making his chest puff with pride. As the night progressed, wine glasses continued to clink in celebratory toasts. The music played nonstop, and they danced the night away.

At last, his plans were falling into place, and this made him a happy man.

Once they reached the warehouse, Rohnert all but dragged Rick out of the car in his haste to get to Shelly. It had been more than an hour since she called, and his mind was ready to combust. Add the damnable New York City traffic, and he was ready to put the doctor on his back and make a run for it. The doors leading to the interior opened when he steered Rick in the direction of the clinic. He could hear DM blasting on the speakers when they neared the room.

Cyrus burst out of the clinic and took Rick's backpack to get the human moving faster.

"Hurry up. That woman is going to eat us alive in there." Cyrus flashed his fangs, and Rick stumbled.

"I'm trying." His voice came out in a croak, making Cyrus laugh.

When they entered the room, they found Shelly on the bed, her face dripping with sweat, and her mouth expelling ragged breaths.

Rohnert forgot everything and everyone when his eyes focused on his mate. He rushed to her side and began kissing her face, cheeks, and mouth. She looked tired, but when she smiled, he relaxed a little.

"How are you?" He watched her chest heave up and down.

"I'm fine." She offered an unconvincing smile then turned to Rick. "Doctor, will you hurry up and get this over with?"

"Dr. Anderson, what happened to patience?" Rick's voice sounded normal, now that his initial shock had worn off. Rohnert listened to his internal musings and learned the man was comforted by having several humans in his midst, in addition to Shelly.

"It's at zero percent." Shelly closed her eyes, riding an invisible wave of pain.

Rick finished scrubbing his hands, and Cheryl helped him into a sterile gown, mask, and gloves. After a quick introduction to Jones, who was suited up and ready to assist, they launched into checking the monitor readouts.

"Let's do this," Rick said and looked at the rest of the people around them. The room emptied out once Cheryl began shooing them away. It was Shelly's turn to be prepped for the procedure.

"Doctor, I already inserted the catheter. We're just waiting for you to administer the anesthesia." Cheryl was back in tip-top shape.

Thank heavens. Shelly sighed in relief.

Rohnert heard her thoughts. "Do you want me here?" he asked Rick.

"Oh, what the hell. Let's make this a party," Rick said, his voice muffled by the cloth covering his mouth.

"Where should I park?" Rohnert's insides churned with nausea from the sterile aroma of the enclosed space.

"If you're the jumpy sort, stay away from me. I don't enjoy distractions." Rick sounded like a man who was used to being in charge, and Rohnert began to relax a little. Besides, the human had come with a glowing endorsement from none other than his mate, so he wasn't going to sweat it.

"Come here, sweetie, hold my hand." Shelly reached out for him.

Rohnert caught Rick's thoughts and knew the doctor wanted to say something. "Say it Rick, if it would ease your mind."

Rick stared at him. "You have to keep in mind I'm not an obstetrician or an anesthesiologist. I'm crossing ethical boundaries here . . ."

"We've gone through this before. This is in the baby's best interest. You're the only one who can help us." Shelly's tone held the desperation Rohnert felt inside. They had no one else to turn to in this delicate situation.

Rick was all they had.

The doctor sighed. "Ready?"

Shelly shifted into a fetal position, and they exposed her back, ready to jam the needle into her beautiful body. Rohnert caught sight of the long-assed thing and focused on Shelly's face instead, determined to distract her. "I forgot to tell you what I found out last night."

She flinched, and he rubbed her forehead. He felt dread it in its purest form. What if something—no he wasn't going there.

"What?"

"I know why I've always felt out of place with my family." He glanced at Rick, checking to see whether the injection was done.

"Twenty minutes," Rick said.

"Tell me?" Shelly took a deep breath, her eyes becoming glassy.

Rohnert squeezed her hand. "Because they're not my real family."

Shelly's eyes got bigger. "What do you mean?"

"I was given to them in order to protect me."

"So the memories back in the cottage were real?"

He nodded. "And I found out who my younger brother is."

"Who?"

"Goran." He said the word through gritted teeth.

Shelly stared at him as if he suddenly sprouted horns. "Are you kidding me?"

Rohnert sighed. "I wish."

"What are you planning to do?"

"I think it's a good time to have a little restructuring in the Council."

They continued to talk about his discovery, Rohnert holding Shelly's hand while Rick and Cheryl began prepping her for the procedure.

"It's almost time." Rick cut through their conversation.

"You'll be fine, Shells."

For the next few minutes, the music of Dave Matthews blared in the background while they worked on Shelly. From Rohnert's viewpoint, he couldn't see what was going on. He heard the hushed orders, and Rick's mental rambling gave him a front seat, as if he were witnessing the procedure with his own eyes.

The scent of blood drifted inside the room, and Rohnert braced himself, concentrating instead on Shelly's breathing.

"Look at me," Shelly whispered, as though she understood his predicament. "I love you, and I don't care if your brother is the devil incarnate."

"You say the funniest things."

She smiled, leaving him to concentrate on her mouth while they waited. They listened to the sound of suctioning.

"We got him," Rick said after ten minutes. His words were followed by a robust cry. He lifted the baby for them to see.

Shelly's hand tightened around Rohnert's as tears began the trek down her face.

"Congratulations, Shelly and . . ."

Damn. Had he forgotten to introduce himself?

"Rohnert." He offered his hand, which the human grasped into a firm handshake.

"You have a healthy baby boy."

"Our Malin," Shelly murmured.

The baby began crying when Shelly uttered his name. Malin's tiny voice intensified, and Rohnert's heart swelled with pride. His eyes misted, then blurred, and he realized he was crying.

"He's beautiful." And so tiny.

"He's an angel." Shelly brought a hand to her mouth, stifling a sob.

Rohnert watched while Rick handed the baby to Jones, who in turn brought Malin to a table to perform an initial evaluation.

He felt Shelly's grasp tighten, and his attention whipped back to her face. "What's wrong?"

"It's just pressure. Rick is putting everything back in place."

It felt like forever before Rick announced that the procedure was over and successful. Cheryl removed a bag filled with . . . ugh . . . Rohnert didn't even want to ask. He'd been watching everything in a dazed stupor.

"Can you move her to that clean bed?" Cheryl nudged him.

He lifted Shelly to the waiting mattress while the nurse shuffled the IV tubes around to accommodate the transfer. Rohnert had just straightened his back when Jones walked over with the baby in his arms.

The little angel was swaddled in a light blue blanket, looking like a badly rolled burrito.

Jones smiled apologetically. "Sorry, Rohn. This is the product of a crash course in wrapping babies. Congratulations," Jones said and placed Malin in his arms.

Rohnert felt a shock hit his system while his body cradled the little one. Everything seemed to move in slow motion. Nothing else existed, just him and his son, and all else faded to the background. All it took was one touch to feel their connection. Son to father, father to son. A primal desire awoke deep within him. The intense urge to possess, to mark, had been so great that Rohnert staggered at the savage instinct he couldn't contain. It crept up like a blazing inferno until he could no longer deny his nature anymore.

Malin let out a lungful of air in a wail while Rohnert chanted his name over and over. The urge to taste him was so great that Rohnert's tongue darted out of its own volition. He licked his son's face, marking him as his own. The baby quieted down before Rohnert had finished this ritual introduction to life.

The room had fallen silent, and Rohnert got the distinct impression that all eyes were on him. He was still suspended in a vacuum of joy and paid no mind to the stares. This was his time with his son, the one destined to bring comfort and hope to their race.

The tiny guy began to move. His arms wanted out of the blanket, and his little lips started moving, then he expelled a cry.

A loud cry.

This was real. They had a son. Malin wasn't an intangible concept anymore, but a living, breathing bundle. Rohnert's heart swelled with happiness, and his eyes blurred yet again with tears.

His existence couldn't get any better than this. "Malin," he whispered the name with reverence amid the robust crying of his son.

"Does the baby have fangs?" Tor entered the room, grinning like an idiot.

"What happened to knocking?" Rohnert rushed to quiet down the arriving group while the baby stirred inside his crib, making those little sounds that he was getting accustomed to hearing.

"We're celebrating." Tor took out several cigars and waggled his brows. "Cuban."

Harrow walked in after him, shaking his head. "I tried to duct tape his mouth, but he's too damn strong for me."

Allison, Jordan, and Cyrus followed, bearing flowers, balloons, and gifts. Rohnert eyed them with wariness. Human tendencies were hard to shake off. It was a touching scene, nonetheless.

"Whatever you do, keep it down. The boy is jumpy. He wakes up at every sound, and Mommy needs a little rest."

Shelly was in a deep sleep, thanks to the sleeping pills Rick had prescribed before he left. The male doctor had been a real trooper. Although he had reservations about being in a building full of vampires, he had done what he came there to do and more. He had promised to come back later on in the evening once the hospital could do without him.

Harrow and the rest went to the adjoining room and hovered around the crib. Rohnert fought the urge to kick them out once Tor began cooing like an idiot.

"Why don't we step outside?" Harrow gestured to the door.

"We'll watch Shelly and Malin," Allison offered. Jordan nodded with the same excitement.

With two of their finest female fighters guarding his precious family, Rohnert couldn't deny the invitation to be with his friends.

He took quick glance at Shelly then at the sleeping angel and walked to the door. The men followed him out into the hallway. "I don't think it's a good idea to smoke that thing here, so close to the baby."

"Let's go to the I-room," Harrow said.

Tor was already halfway down the hallway by the time they caught up with him. "Why are you so excited?" Cyrus asked.

"Hello?" Tor glared at Cyrus. "Haven't you guys realized that this might be the last time we'll have a little child in our midst?"

"What do you mean?" Cyrus pressed.

Tor tossed the rest of the cigars to them and bit off the end of his own. "Allison and I can never have one." Then he pointed at Harrow. "Lucky bastard here has Gail. Unless you snag a human, you'll be like a cactus, too."

Rohnert jumped in to change the topic. "I thought we were celebrating." He placed the end of the cigar in his mouth. He had no taste for these types of vices, but hey, if it was a tradition, he'd go with the flow.

Tor rushed over and flicked a golden lighter to light Rohnert's first. A cloud of thick, chocolate aroma wafted in the air.

"That is what I'm talking about," Tor said, sitting down and getting comfortable.

"Drink orders, anyone?" Cyrus strode to the mini bar.

"Patron, make it double." Tor raised his prosthetic hand.

"Make that two," Harrow said.

"Lag for me." Rohnert took another hard puff and coughed. "This is considered a delicacy? This thing is awful."

Cyrus came back, balancing four glasses in his hands. After handing the drinks around, he raised his glass. "Let's toast to new beginnings, long life, and messy diapers."

Rohnert snorted, while Tor wrinkled his nose, then they clinked their glasses and downed their poison.

Harrow took a drag of his Cuban. "Rohnert, pay attention. Don't inhale the smoke. Puff like this." He placed the cigar in his mouth, sucked slow and easy, and then released the smoke. "See?"

Tor and Cyrus laughed at Rohnert's next attempt, which was another fail.

He shook his head and let the cancer stick burn itself out on the ashtray, preferring the easy glide of alcohol.

"What's next?" Cyrus settled on the chair next to him.

"I have a personal score I need to settle once Shelly is up and about," Rohnert said.

"Vendetta. Ah, I love the sound of the word, my man. It's about time." Tor leaned forward, his prosthetic hand making a slight noise when it settled on the wooden table.

"What are you talking about?" Harrow asked.

Rohnert had expected that Tor would have mentioned something to the others by now. Weird. In normal circumstances, the guy was prone to gossip. "There are things in our lives that we're embarrassed to put out there, but since you are part of the aggrieved party, I'm letting you in on my little secret."

Harrow removed his Oakleys and blinked. "What secret?"

"I found out that our notorious enemy is also my brother." Extreme disbelief showed in the men's faces while they stared at him. This prompted Rohnert to explain further. "It seems like a sick prophecy. From what I read in a sacred book, one will rise into power with pure, dark deeds until someone steps up to challenge him. And guess who the designated idiot is?"

Tor snickered.

"Wait . . . what the fuck! Why you?" Cyrus took one hard puff from his cigar.

"Because I'm the older brother."

"What? How in the hell did that happen? You belong to a different bloodline. Different parents," Cyrus said.

"It seems like I was given to a childless couple in the next line for safekeeping until they could figure out what to do." Even to Rohnert, the concept was unbelievable.

"Who are they? What made them so afraid?" Harrow asked.

"This is all I could gather from the book. It was prophesied that Goran would commit these atrocities until the time came to stop him—"

"Oh, no. Hell, no. That sounds so wrong. You guys sound like puppets."

That was Rohnert's exact sentiment. If higher beings were privy to future calamities, why couldn't they dip their powerful hands in the small pool and change the outcome?

"And you're going to do it? Why can't your parents stop him?" Cyrus said.

Rohnert had forgotten no one except Shelly knew a thing about him. He'd given bits and pieces of his life, but he'd offered nothing concrete. He was still as mysterious as the day he had first come into their lives.

"Because our parents were killed."

This bit of information plunged the room into silence. Everyone seemed to hold their breath. The only sound came from the burning cigar on the ashtray and the tick, tick, tick of the wall clock.

After a few minutes, Tor recovered. "I bet that fucker killed them."

Rohnert's head whipped in Tor's direction. "What the hell!"

"Think about it. Goran is capable of the unthinkable. He sent his Harem to their deaths and killed half the members of the Council. Do you doubt for one minute that he's incapable of this crime?"

Rohnert's skin crawled as anger surged to the surface. Why hadn't he connected the dots before? He pounded his fist on the table.

"If you're blaming yourself for not knowing, stop right there." Harrow seemed to have read his mind. "We can't always know the depths of a man's wickedness."

"You have much to do, my friend. Tonight, let's celebrate your son's birth." Cyrus had refilled their glasses.

Rohnert rose, holding his glass in a tight grip. "To my son—may he grow up bearing his mother's gentleness."

"And his father's courage," Harrow added.

Shelly emerged from a deep sleep, feeling refreshed. When was the last time she'd felt this way? Her hands went to her still-swollen belly, but the tightness and the weight was gone.

She opened her eyes, and the sweet scent of baby powder struck her. Shelly tried to wrack her brain to remember anything past Rick's announcement that she had given birth to a healthy baby boy.

"You have a heartbreaker here," Jordan said, cooing to the bundle cradled in her arms.

"Oh, Shelly. He is the most adorable thing I've ever seen." Allison was rearranging the flowers from across the room.

"How long have I been out?" She opened her arms, wanting to hold her child for the first time.

Jordan walked to her bedside and handed her the swaddled baby. "You've been out for about six hours."

"Why can't I remember?"

"Rick gave you something strong. He said you needed the sleep first."

So this was how everyone felt when she'd knocked them out like animals. *Payback's a bitch for sure.*

Cradling her precious baby in one arm, she loosened the blanket to reveal his entire face, his mouth moving in a sucking motion. Shelly stared at her baby boy, memorizing his little features, taking note of the mass of black hair and the prominent nose before she started counting fingers and toes. She kissed the newborn's head, loving the way he felt so right in her arms.

Shelly lost track of time. She didn't even notice that Jordan and Allison had excused themselves to give her some private time with her baby. It wasn't until Malin cried that she snapped out of her happy daze. His mouth quivered, and when she touched his lips, he wanted to suckle her finger.

She lowered him down to her chest and offered a breast.

The first tentative suck made her squirm. He pulled harder and then began to cry. His face moved from side to side, and his cries intensified while her frustration mounted.

The door burst open, and Rohnert ran inside.

"I heard him crying." He rushed to her, his eyes trained on their child. "What's going on?"

Her frustration manifested itself in tears. "He can't get any milk from me, and he's getting upset."

Rohnert's worried expression softened. "Oh, baby, just keep offering it to him. You said so yourself—it takes some babies more time than others."

His calm reminder gave her enough courage to try again. She angled Malin's chin to her breast, teasing his mouth with the tip of her nipple. He took it again after several tries and latched on again. Then off again, and more tears. Rohnert rubbed her back while they kept at it. With a few tentative pulls, Malin became impatient, flailing his arms as he sucked harder and with urgency. After a moment of coming up empty, she felt him relax when she started producing what he wanted. He fell into a comfortable rhythm and dozed on and off. They stay cuddled together while Rohnert looked on.

Satisfaction radiated within her when Malin settled into a comfortable pace. The first feeding took about thirty minutes, and the baby fell asleep with his mouth still clamped on her breast.

"Good god, I didn't think feeding would be this difficult," Rohnert said, looking as spent as she felt.

"I've heard the horror stories, but I didn't believe it." She laughed, watching the peaceful infant sleeping in her arms.

Rohnert sat on the mattress next to her, wrapping his arm around her back. She rested her head against his chest, and they gazed at their child's face.

"What are you thinking?" she asked after a long, drawn-out silence.

"I'm thinking of the future." His voice sounded distant.

She turned her head to look at him. "What about the future?"

He kissed her hair and sighed. "I don't want Malin to grow up in hiding.

I want him to feel free. No one is going to harm him. Not humans and especially not his own people."

Shelly looked up, but no words were necessary. This was the moment they'd been waiting for. Tears pooled in her eyes when she thought about how fate had brought them together to create this adorable new being.

"I still can't believe it."

"He has your eyes."

"And that head of hair has to be from your side of the family." She snuggled closer to his body and closed her eyes.

The last thing she remembered before drifting back to sleep was Rohnert's voice singing a song, lulling her to dreamland.

Rohnert's phone beeped, and he rushed to answer. In the weeks following the birth of his son, he'd learned two important things. First, keep the phone on vibrate so as not to startle the little one, and second, follow the strict feeding schedule.

"What?"

"We have some new leads. We're tracking down a number of elite guards." Alonzo sounded breathless.

"Where are you?" He glanced at the clock. Two in the morning.

"Fifth and eighty-second."

"Give me fifteen. Sit tight, and don't dance until I get there."

"Hurry," Alonzo said before the click.

Damn. He was on child watch since Shelly had been called to attend to several injuries stemming from a club brawl. Rohnert dialed the extension. "Cheryl, can you put Shelly on the phone?"

He heard the loud music in the background and rolled his eyes. Shelly preferred ear-splitting rock music while she tended to her patients.

"Hey, what's up?" Her voice sounded strained. Although she was still technically on maternity leave, any medical emergency was enough reason to bring her back to work.

"I got some leads I need to work on. Are you almost done?" he asked, feeling like an asshole for bailing.

"Our little human here is a bleeder. I'm still giving him a blood transfusion. Might take a while. Can you call Allison and ask if she can watch the baby?"

As much as Rohnert hated being away from his family, he still had an obligation to fulfill. "I'll call her now."

"Hey, you—take care of yourself." He heard Shelly blow him a kiss before she hung up.

After speaking with Allison, who was more than happy to help, he walked to the closet and armed himself. He threw on a dark trench coat before strapping on his Kalimetal.

He gave Allison a quick rundown of Malin's schedule, where to find Shelly's breast milk, and all the other goodies. After the instruction was over, he left on foot. He pointed his head at the sky and breathed deep. This evening had the makings of a disaster, but he was done staying in the shadows. Ready or not, he'd tango with the best of them.

He dug his boots into the gravel and broke into a steady jog, taking in all the thoughts around him, picking, choosing, and discarding unimportant ramblings. When he neared The Met, he caught up with the group.

"What's going on?"

Alonzo's group of misfits were perched on the rooftop of an art gallery, monitoring the elite guards converged on the stairs of the famous museum below. Judging from the guards' body language, they were aware they were being watched and were waiting to react to any provocation.

"They have been talking like women since we tracked them down." Alonzo glanced over his shoulder at him.

Rohnert wracked his brain. The group was itching for a confrontation. Though the match would be dead even, their side was almost all newbies, not counting Alonzo, Firman, and Gentry. Robin, Markus, and Jared were still in training. They had grasped the fighting guidelines fast, but they were far from being battle ready.

Then there was Zo, Gentry, and Firman—three solid fighters. The odds didn't seem insurmountable. They looked to him for guidance, fidgeting in their fighting gear like little children ready to pounce on the playground. Rohnert had to think fast. If they didn't make a move, the opposite group would. Their leader was already forming a plan to surround them.

One thing the head vampire had forgotten was that they were on low ground and at a disadvantage.

"Firman, stay here with the boys. I'm going down there with Zo and Gentry. If the situation gets dirty, rain bullets on the bastards. No hesitation," Rohnert whispered.

Firman saluted and pulled a Sig from his holster. The neophytes followed without hesitation. "Throw me a signal." His eyes were fixed on the other group.

"Ready?" Rohnert straightened his back, marking the points around the group in his head, their possible exits, backup plan, and best course of action. Alonzo and Gentry fell in line, their heads free of doubt, almost to the point of recklessness. "Stay tight," he said through gritted teeth.

They jumped off the building and landed on their feet. The targets were across the street about thirty feet away, and their heads whipped in the trio's direction. The fighters spread like a goddamn disease to surround them. Three against eight—not at all friendly.

Rohnert maintained his stride, and his buddies didn't falter either. Assessing each opponent's mental state, he reached into their minds. *If you don't want to look like a fool, don't follow the orders of one.*

Then he recited an important quote in his head. The supreme art of war is to subdue the enemy without fighting.

It was one of Sun Tzu's proverbial reminders. He wasn't going to waste lives if he could help it.

A few staggered back in confusion, causing the leader to panic and react. Wrong move. The head of the group leveled his daggers at them and swung. Alonzo shouted, identifying himself as an ex-elite soldier, reminding them of the strictest code.

"The shame you bear is yours to resolve with the tip of a dagger."

This had been Rohnert's stringent policy before he left, upheld by every member of the elite group. Gentry plowed straight ahead, deflecting the dagger meant for Rohnert. Feet shuffled, and the bolder vampires surged forward. The ones he'd had an effect on stayed rooted, but the other five refused to accept his directives.

"Whatever you're doing, I'm all for it." Alonzo yelled, tackling one vampire to the ground. Rohnert crisscrossed, avoiding anything that flew in his direction, while Gentry engaged in a fiery battle.

Rohnert reached the leader, tossing daggers to repel the onslaught of blades blazing toward him. "You're wasting your time following the wrong leader."

"I was told you would try to manipulate us."

As bullets and weapons buzzed by them, Rohnert stop and circled, watching his assailant. "If you're quoting my brother, then you've been manipulated."

The opponent faltered, confusion lacing his feral expression. Rohnert took this opening, flipped over, and landed a kick straight to the chest. The force shoved the other man several feet away, where he landed on the steps and jumped to his feet.

"I sense your confusion. When in doubt, you either fall back or dance. Which will it be?"

The vampire's eyes flickered but refused to consider, and he went for Rohnert. Rohnert met him and when their bodies collided, they fell to the ground. They struggled against each other, Rohnert lashing out mentally at the man with possible scenarios of his death, but the guard refused to accept his final offer.

No weapons were involved, which made it even better. Rohnert twisted and turned, freeing his arms from the other's hold and managing to get a grip on the other's neck.

"Last chance." He pressed at the jugular.

"I shall die with honor," the man said through a burst of breath.

Rohnert increased his chokehold, straddling his opponent on the ground. "You will die in vain." He closed his eyes, refusing to see the look in the soldier's eyes. He clamped hard until he heard sputtering, and the hands trying to pry off his fingers loosened.

There was no need to sacrifice lives. He took a dagger from his chest holster and plunged it into the soldier's unbeating heart, ending what could've been a more fruitful existence.

Choices had been made, and he couldn't change them for anyone. But he could still give them the opportunity to change on their own. The fighting around him reached a standstill, which was good.

Alonzo had killed one and subdued another, while Gentry had two kills to his credit. He waved at Firman to stand down before addressing the other three who hadn't taken part in the party. Rohnert expected their reactions. Each one pulled out a small weapon and dropped to their knees.

"You don't have to do this. Atonement is offered to discredit your grief-stricken mind."

Hesitation marked their puzzled faces. "But this was your legacy," one said.

"And I take them back under these circumstances. I free you from the ties that bound you to the greed that exploited your services."

"We know nothing else but to fight," another said, his features besieged with guilt.

"Then you shall fight freely for what you believe in. Go, and never return to the insatiable power that dominated your lives."

The last vampire shook his head. His miserable thoughts couldn't afford him reprieve. In a rushed decision, he plunged his Dangeran weapon through his heart and fell to the ground.

The vampire fizzled in an instant—a life that could've been spared. Rohnert shook off the feeling of culpability that gripped him and turned to the remaining two, as well as the subdued man still pinned underneath Alonzo's weight.

"It didn't have to come to this. Go on, and live your lives as you see fit."

He turned to leave, his feet heavy underneath him. Killing and death were an acquired taste, and something he should've gotten used to by now. However, the sting remained, and he knew that it would linger.

Alonzo spoke to the remaining vampires and offered the same suggestion before Rohnert heard them following behind him and Gentry.

"If we choose to serve you, would you accept our regrets and take us in?" one of the remaining vampires asked.

Rohnert pivoted and cursed. This was unexpected, but if fate dictated more vampires would leave Goran's army, he wouldn't stand in the way.

Alonzo jumped in. "If you would indulge me, I'd like to take responsibility over them."

He nodded. "Let's go home." Rohnert took one final look at the ashes on the ground being blown away by the wind and chanted a quick entreaty.

Not a day went by when Cyrus forgot the torture he'd suffered under the enemy. His heart burned for revenge. The more he pushed back the vengeful thoughts he harbored, the more he ached for retribution.

He had to stay focused now that Rohnert had everyone on alert. After the last face-off against the Council elite guards, they'd stepped up their training. All his waking hours, when he wasn't patrolling, were spent at the training room, teaching and supervising most of the classes.

Their collection of fighters came from different backgrounds. There were elite members of Goran's army, Council guards, stray humans who had been victimized by diseased vampires, and other vampires in search of a goal. The term *misfits* came to mind, and this made Cyrus chuckle.

"You look like you're in a good mood," Tor observed during a break. The vampire had been on his case.

They taught back-to-back classes since their areas of expertise were related—weapons, planning, evading, and when to engage. Although both had been hotheads in the past, they'd learned to curb their explosive natures.

"I'm always in a good mood," he said, then turned to the class. "I'll meet you in the shooting area in three."

"Sure. I noticed that when a certain female is around." Tor snorted, taking a big chug from his water bottle.

Cyrus ran his palm over his short crew cut. There was no point in pretending he had no idea who Tor was referring to. "You're full of crap. I'm old enough to be her father."

"That is true," Tor said. "Well, since you are now a bona fide vampire, it doesn't matter." His eyes glistened with his trademark mischief.

"And I'm not going after her. You know I've always been helpful to the women." He might as well pretend to keep Tor from teasing him.

No break there. "Pfft. You can say whatever you want, and I'm not buying it. You haven't seen yourself around her. Your eyes get this dreamy look, and your voice changes, like you're going to sing." Tor had the nerve to laugh, getting everyone's attention inside the small room.

The doors opened, and the subject of their conversation walked in. Cyrus felt his body slacken. It was a weird phenomenon that happened every time the woman was in close proximity.

"Cyrus?" Isidora walked over to the desk.

"Hey, Issy. What's up?"

"Yep. There you go," Tor said and got up, giving them some privacy.

"I wondered if you'd have time to go over dagger throws with me later."

"Sure, I'll be done in an hour."

"Great. Can I watch?"

"Sit here." He stood up and offered his seat.

Tor caught Cyrus' eye from the corner of the room and mouthed, "Goddamn whipped." And then laughed.

Zane's phone went off, and he stared at the familiar number long enough to let it go to voicemail. This might just piss off dear old gramps, but he had no new information to give. He's given him enough to go on but had withheld a bit for personal reasons.

Whatever Goran thought, he'd worked for the damn vampire long enough to repay him for the monetary gifts he'd received. Yeah, he was a goddamn parasite who'd never done a day's work in his life. Shameful? Yeah. Even worse, he had taken from those who'd loved him in the past. All were now dead.

Guilt was alien to him, but it had taken up residence in his psyche, often pushing him into a spiral of guilt-ridden angst for taking advantage of Demetrius' and Melissa's kindness. However, he felt no remorse for taking everything he could from Goran. The bastard had holdings everywhere. The small change given to Zane in exchange for the 411 was nothing. He'd watched the hospital like a hawk. Even after the doctor had gone, he still came to investigate from the shadows. He'd seen Rohnert leave with another doctor and disappear inside the walls of the warehouse. He'd seen the medical chief, Rick Whitaker, visit there once more. He didn't have to be a brainiac to guess that Shelly had given birth, and he could assume who the baby's sperm donor was.

Zane was bone tired and sleep deprived. When he got a short reprieve, he'd awake drenched in sweat, haunted by faces. There were many faces, but Cheryl's remained the most prominent of them all.

Zane walked with difficulty over to the window of his townhouse. The wounds on his left leg and other parts of his body had healed, but the limp remained. It was proof that all evil deeds were punished. The wounds might have closed, but the imbedded bits of metal would forever be his burden to bear.

He looked outside the window of his secret hideout and watched the early evening traffic. He'd holed up in here rather than the penthouse he'd placed on the market in order to get away from dear Grandpapa. Once it was sold, the proceeds of the sale would be wired to an overseas account to sustain him until he got his shit together.

His mind raced back to Cheryl. Her kind eyes still haunted him, bothered him. All her words had been spoken from the heart.

His phone rang again, and once more, he let the call dump into his voicemail. This time, the caller left a message. Zane dragged his leg behind him to the desk and checked the call log. An unknown number registered, so he pressed the button to listen.

A swoosh of air in the background was all he got before the caller hung up. The number was untraceable, and every code he punched failed to reveal a call-back number. Zane remained unmoving and listened to the message once again. There was breathing once he amplified the call—a female. His muscles twitched at the random thought. Could it be?

This was too much wishful thinking on his part. Why would a woman, and a human at that, who had plenty of reasons to hate his existence, spend a minute to call him? His mind suggested several scenarios, but most of them were unthinkable.

The air around him felt suddenly stifling, and he was sweating underneath his shirt. He'd learned in the past never to ignore his basic instincts, the gut feeling. Good or bad, he had to continue watching, even if it was from afar.

He rushed to his closet, which was small compared to the space he had back at the penthouse. He'd deliberately left most of his things and had come with just a few basic items. For some reason, those things didn't matter anymore. All he needed were weapons, most of which were leftovers from the last raid on the Tack Enterprises facility.

Zane grabbed a Smith and Wesson and checked the barrel. He armed himself with the gun and a few throwing stars. Since he was just an onlooker, there was no need to arm himself to the teeth.

He carried his leather jacket until he reached the garage. His leg wouldn't carry him to his destination fast enough, but the bike would. He hopped on the Ducati and raced out of the secured parking structure. Navigating the street at this time of day was hellish, since the commuters battled for every available lane, honking and screaming obscenities. He was cursing under his helmet the whole time until he reached the hospital.

The hospital was a zoo. There was no need to hide—he would be taken for a civilian needing medical help. He parked the motorcycle and hurried to the entrance as fast as his feet would take him.

Upon reaching the front desk, he asked to see Doctor Whitaker. After a short Q&A, he slapped a visitor name tag on his chest and moved along the hallway in search of the man who might be able to answer some of his questions. Zane ran those questions in his head and decided against using any scare tactics to get information.

The elevator took him to the sixth floor, and he found the office without difficulty. Employees were scarce. Patient meals were being served, and most visitors were already on their way out.

Zane was about to knock when he heard a skirmish inside. He palmed his nine millimeter and pressed his ear to the door.

"You will tell me how to find her," an unfamiliar voice said.

"I will not," a man answered.

Someone laughed, then a loud whack sounded followed by a thud.

Zane's ears pricked up. He was pulling out a gun when a nurse appeared from the end of the hallway. He was left with two options—barge inside the office, or get the hell out. He opted for the latter since he had no idea of how many people were inside the room.

He went into an empty room until the nurse passed, but more footsteps sounded in the hallway, preventing him from coming out. By the time he found an opening, the doctor's office was locked, and the room was silent.

Half-running and half-dragging his leg, he made it outside, but there were no traces of anyone suspicious.

"Damn it!" He slammed his fist on the handlebar of the motorcycle and pondered his next move. His frustration mounted while he worked on connecting the dots. Was Dr. Whitaker connected to Shelly? What did the interrogator want with the female doctor? And why?

These were questions for which he'd never find an answer, and he wasn't going to sit around and wait. Zane turned the ignition, pumped the gas, and sped out of the hospital parking lot. He drove faster, snaking in an out of little spaces between cars until he reached the vicinity of the warehouse.

Zane turned off the headlight and drove forward in the darkness, taking note of the dense plants surrounding him. If this was the end of the road, so be it. He drove close enough to trigger massive lights that bore down on him. He knew he was being watched, and he stayed on the bike to wait.

Cyrus had just stepped out of the bathroom when his cell phone and speaker phone chimed at the same time. He wrapped the towel around his waist and hurried to answer.

Rayce's voice shot through the phone line, sounding frantic. "Come right now. You need to see this."

He pulled on the first clean clothes he could find, dressing in a hurry. He was gunning down the hallway when he saw Harrow emerging from his bedroom.

"What's going on?"

Harrow grunted and shook his head. They reached the I-room and found Tor and Alonzo hovering by the monitors, surrounding Rayce like a glove.

"I think it's a fuckin' death sentence." Tor hissed and created a space for Harrow and Cyrus.

A new brand of fury shot through his system upon seeing the man who waited outside the warehouse door. Cryus pounded on the table, rattling everything. "What is that fucker doing here?"

"Did you check the entire perimeter?" Harrow's face was almost pressed against the monitor, trying to get a good look at the picture and the timestamp.

"He came alone." Rayce punched several keys, and more segments showed in the overhead monitors. "I'm sure of it."

"I'm going out." Cyrus turned for the door.

Harrow held his arm, pulling him back. "Man, you can't just walk out. It could be an ambush."

Cyrus threw the vampire a don't-fuck-with-me glare, and time stood still while he waited for Harrow to pull the leader speech on him. Seconds of tense silence ticked by before he yanked his arm back.

"Try and stop me." He threw the careless warning without thinking of the repercussions. He ignored Harrow's call to take a minute to think about the situation and left the room.

Once inside his bedroom, he threw on his jeans, boots, and black shirt and armed himself. Without looking back, he hurried to the exit, expecting to claw his way out, but every door opened just as he reached them. Before he arrived at the last door that led to the outside, he heard footsteps behind him. He looked over to see Harrow, Tor, and Alonzo catching up to him.

"This is my fight," he said.

"We're just going to watch." Tor's expression was grim.

"Don't even fuck with me. I mean it." Cyrus found the warehouse door open, and Zane was still sitting on the motorcycle.

Cyrus felt fire blaze in his gut as rage consumed him. This was his chance to get back a small amount of dignity after what the motherfucker had done to him. He took a step forward while the others stayed glued to the spot. They didn't follow, nor did they pull out their weapons.

Zane got off the bike and raised his hand. The bastard flinched, which didn't escape Cyrus' notice. He also saw the obvious limp when the vampire took a few steps. There were no weapons drawn, and his jacket was zipped up.

"Stop," he ordered. Cyrus pulled the Glock from his waistband and aimed dead center at Zane's skull. With his keen eyesight, he didn't see Zane twitch or exhibit any aggression.

"I came here to give a warning," Zane said, his hands coming up.

"It's ballsy of you to show up here. Mind if I kill you first and talk later?" Cyrus' finger was itching to pull the trigger.

Zane's eyes were trained on him alone, as if he didn't care whether the others jumped him. "I know I have no credibility whatsoever, but I—"

"Fucker, shut up. You've talked enough. Say hello to Satan—"

"Stop this! Don't do it, Cyrus."

Cyrus turned at the shrill female voice and found Cheryl rushing out of the warehouse, catching them all by surprise. Before any of them could react, she planted her small body in front of Zane, protecting him.

Tor cursed. "Cheryl, stay away from him."

"Oh, for Christ's sake, Cheryl, don't do this." Harrow stepped forward, unsheathing his Kalimetal.

"I won't let you," she said. "Please, we've done so much killing already."

"Cheryl, listen to me. You have no idea what kind of person you're defending. That vampire has killed many, including people you cared for and loved," Harrow pleaded.

His appeal had fallen on deaf ears. Cheryl had a determined look on her face, despite the tears streaming down her cheeks. Where was Rohnert when they needed someone who could suck information from the bastard's mind?

"We've seen enough bloodshed to last us a lifetime," she said through her sobs. "You will have to shoot me first before you get to him."

"Cheryl, no. Please don't do this." Zane pulled her to his side.

Cheryl wasn't listening. She struggled to shield Zane with her tiny body. "No . . . this is enough. I can't take this anymore."

Cyrus lowered his gun, not liking that his attempt to rid the earth of the motherfucker had been thwarted. "You're a lucky son of a bitch to have a woman protecting you. I will let it go this time, but mark my words, I will find you."

"What did you say?" Rohnert knew what he'd heard, but for some insane reason, he couldn't process the information.

"Cheryl rushed out and begged Cyrus not to shoot Zane."

He cursed. This cemented two facts in his mind. Cheryl was digging on the vampire, and the fucker was lucky as hell not to have gotten his head blown off. Another fun piece of trivia was that he was the fucker's great uncle. Woo-hoo!

"That's insane," he said. He kissed Shelly on the mouth, did a quick check on the baby sleeping inside the crib, and disarmed.

Though Malin was still an infant, he'd taken the precaution of locking his weapons away from curious hands. It was never too early to practice safety.

"I don't know." She sighed. "I understand where Cheryl is coming from."

"Love is a complicated thing. I won't even begin to say that I comprehend all its intricacies." He sat on the bed. When the mattress dipped under his weight, Shelly slid closer to him.

"Do you understand ours?" Her voice took on a seductive tone.

He stroked his chin, baiting her to react. "I don't think I do."

A playful slap landed on his arm. "Are you sure?"

Rohnert took a deep breath. Oh, the mysteries of such feelings, the cloud nine moments once you let someone in, and the glory of indefatigable love. Yup, he was whipped, shackled in a happy, happy, joy, joy relationship with a woman who meant everything to him.

To think that he had almost let her get away because of his stubborn resolve to protect her. Thank heavens that several people had knocked some sense into him, or it would have been too late. Well, there was no use in worrying over the past, because here he was in bed with the woman he adored, and a child, to boot. What more could a man ask for?

"I don't understand how you could've forgiven me after I pulled that stupid disappearing stunt on you. But I thank my lucky stars every day we were brought back together. I'm lucky to have a smart, beautiful, sexy, adorable woman like you. I will move heaven and earth to give you everything that your heart desires."

His words seemed to have an effect on her. She inched closer, letting her hand rest on his thigh and rubbing his bare skin, until she reached the bulge between his legs.

"This is what my heart desires." She offered her sweetest smile.

"And I don't even have to move mountains to give you what you want." He twisted their bodies until she was pinned against the firm mattress.

"Whatever you do, be quiet about it. She pointed with her chin toward their baby's room.

"Aye."

He worked on disrobing her and tossed the garment on the floor. Then he did a whole lot of drive-by on the creamy expanse of her body with his eyes. He eased back, kneeling and letting his eyes feast on the female who never failed to drive him to edge of ecstasy.

Rohnert ran his palm along her silky skin, starting at her legs and working his way to her chest. Her lactating breasts were healthy mounds he wanted to sink his face into, so he did just that.

Shelly responded with little mewling sounds that came from deep in her throat. Even in her fevered arousal, she controlled herself, avoiding loud sounds that would wake up the sleeping one. Rohnert let the tip of one fang create friction against her skin, feeling his body come alive. His teeth were like an extension of his cock—ultra sensitive and easily aroused.

With her head resting on a pile of pillows, she was glorious, waiting for him to taste her. Her blond hair lay in beautiful waves all around her. Then he was struck stupid by a thought. She'd just given birth. What, six weeks ago? And he was about to take her like a sex-starved maniac. He backed off, easing his body off hers.

She stared at him with confusion in her eyes. "What's wrong?"

"You just had a baby. Rick hasn't cleared you yet." Yep. His damned scruples always got in the way.

"I'm a doctor. I know what my body needs right now." That tone of voice never failed to burn deep in his gut.

Yet he hesitated, even though the hunger in him multiplied with every passing second.

"Rohnert, please . . . all I want is you . . . right here, now."

Shelly's whisper echoed inside his head. Rohnert continued to stare at her, a full-blown struggle raging within. He was conflicted, lustful, and wanting.

He made one last attempt to get her to hear him out. "Are you sure?" Rohnert placed his hands on her shoulder, trying to draw her away. Her proximity was intoxicating, and his body ached to take her. It didn't help when her eyes smoldered with want.

"All I want is you."

Who in their right mind could resist such inviting words from a beautiful woman? With one swift move, he pushed his concerns aside and wrapped his arms around her waist. Drawing her closer, he crushed his mouth to hers. This was no gentle kiss by any means. Instead, it was filled with hunger—over a month's worth of pent-up desire.

He should take her with gentleness, but the urge to possess was uncontrollable once the floodgates had been opened. Rohnert tried to calm himself down, to take it slow, but the more he tried, the more his irrational side got the best of him.

Without breaking their kiss, he fondled her breasts, getting lost in a sea of lust while she arched her body to meet his demand. His tongue penetrated deeper into her mouth, harder, until her warmth and eager responses pushed him closer to the edge.

She worked on yanking the shirt over his head, and when he was free of the material, her hands glided along his chest, creating a wondrous sensation that sent bolts of electricity everywhere his blood flowed.

Rohnert hissed at the surge of pleasure her touch had created, overwhelming his senses. Everything about the woman made him want to scream. Tor had been right—he was whipped beyond measure. He was her slave and worshipper, and he'd stay that way for all eternity.

Rohnert ran his hands along her neck and down to her shoulder blades, knowing each contour just by touch. His mouth traced the path of his hand, tasting her skin and smelling her delight.

He listened to her accelerated breathing and the drumming of her heartbeat. Every moan added to his desire to possess her. He continued to tamp down the primal instinct to hurry, letting her enjoy each sensation so he could hear the sound of her moans.

"You're so beautiful."

Her mouth quirked into a contented smile, and then she licked her lips. "And you, my love, taste divine."

Her words unhinged him.

"Touch me again." The woman was practically purring.

Rohnert indulged her. He cupped her breasts, feeling the softness of her flesh in his hands. She shivered and groaned with pleasure while he palmed her nipple, circling it in a way that brought a throaty moan from her. Christ, he'd give anything for a chance to lick her breast and tease her with his tongue.

Shelly brought one hand to his head, and her thighs rubbed against his stomach. He looked up momentarily and saw the fever raging her eyes.

"I want to feel you inside me."

"It won't hurt you?" It was his last effort at reason.

"Nothing will hurt more than not having you inside me."

Rohnert's felt his resolve fall apart. He tore his shorts off, reminding himself that although Shelly was all for it, he needed to be careful around her. He attempted to calm himself down. With care, he lowered his body onto hers. Shelly pulled his neck down until their faces touched and his length rubbed her belly.

"I'm not going to last long, darling." His breath came in ragged spurts. There went his last ounce of control.

"Come inside."

He accepted her invitation and slowly slid his way into her opening, feeling her tightness right away. He paused, even though her slick entrance didn't offer much resistance, while her body adjusted to his length, embracing him. Shelly bucked her hips when he filled her. They moaned in unison, hanging on to each to each other while he rotated his hips, gently gliding in and out.

"Damn it, woman. I'm very close." He thrust a few times to wring more whimpers from her. Her response was exquisite, and she dug in with her nails, scraping his skin. Rohnert kept his pace steady, not giving in to the urge to pound into her. He took her mouth when he closed in on the imminent pleasure. Hoping Shelly would come before him, he held back. She arched and took his hip, helping him thrust into her until she cried out in ecstasy—calling his name out loud.

Rohnert glanced at the sleeping babe, hoping the little one wouldn't wake up. Shelly clutched him tighter and breathed hard against his ear. His own climax hit, and he jerked, shattering with rapture. She wrapped her legs around his thighs while he released inside her, then they held on to each other, spent but cocooned in total bliss.

He collapsed next to her, and they both stared up at the ceiling in satisfaction. "I wanted this to be slow and special, instead of turning into a raging madman on you. For that, I apologize." He took her hand and kissed it.

Shelly seemed bewildered by his statement. She squeezed his hand. "It was special, Rohnert . . . it's what we both needed." She paused for confirmation. When he nodded, she continued. "We can always do it again and take it slower."

Ah, the prospect of a marathon brought a wicked smile to his face. "I can work up an appetite in a few minutes."

Shelly giggled and turned to face him. Her leg landed on top of his thighs. "I never want this to end." Her eyes were earnest, and his heart melted.

"This . . . we . . . will never end."

Rohnert drew her close, feeling every inch of her body against his. His hands, of their own accord, ran across the smooth planes of her back while he nuzzled his face in her glorious mane. He pondered the concept of time between vampires and humans. How could he explain the fragility of humans without sounding morbid? He tossed the idea aside.

"Have I told you how much I love you?" she said softly into his chest, her voice trailing off with fatigue.

"I love you more, so much that I can't breathe sometimes." He felt her smile.

She was drifting off to sleep. "Sing . . ."

Rohnert chuckled. It took him a moment to decide what song to sing for her. He started humming the melody while stroking her hair. Shelly was already sleeping when he sang the first note.

Rohnert's dreams had dried up the moment Shelly came back into his life, so this vision of Lukan ushering an old guy—damn, a really old guy—with a long beard that almost touched his belly and eyes that screamed wisdom couldn't be real.

The searing, blistering light that made him wince and cover his eyes seemed authentic. He felt across the bed, and Shelly stirred, her softness bringing him comfort. Okay, so this was just a dream. He took a quick peek at the dynamic duo invading his subconscious.

"Rohnert, oldest son of Cantor and Divina, rise so I can see you," the gravelly voice commanded.

Funny, the apparition knew his real parent's names. What's next? He'll call me by my given name?

"Ronestus, you're not stuck in a dream. You asked to see me. I'm here at your request."

He squeezed his eyelids first, then peeled them open, even though he thought they already were. "I beg your pardon?"

The light dimmed, affording him a chance to check his surroundings. Lukan smiled, hovering close to the crib. A growl tore deep in his throat, that indescribable instinct to protect his own.

Rohnert jumped and grabbed the dagger on the bedside table. He bared his fangs and lowered his stance, ready to attack.

"That, my boy, is what I've been looking for—the inherent instinct to defend your keep." The old man stroked his long beard, his smile barely discernible.

"Rohnert, your eyes are open, and yet you refuse to see. We've given you facts, visions, and eventualities to support our reality, and still you deny the truth," Lukan said.

She waved her hand, and strips of images flashed before his eyes. The same pictures he'd seen back at their summer retreat—the crying infant, the massacres past and present, and endless images of faces he recognized, most of who were deceased.

"What more do you need to see to believe?" the old man asked.

This is a damn dream.

"You are awake. Look around you, my child." And as if as an afterthought, the stranger added. "Look at yourself."

Rohnert shook his head, dispelling the wave of discomfort that filled him. "Lukan . . ." Then he glanced down, realizing for the first time that he had nothing on. Flustered, he grabbed his discarded shorts from the floor.

When he looked up, he saw Lukan smile, a playful expression on her lovely features.

"This is Gastarius."

Rohnert scrambled backward, unable to believe his eyes. In the years he'd been around, the diviner rarely made an appearance, much less made house calls.

The old man beamed, the tips of fangs punching his lower lips. "Come closer, Rohnert, and let me look at you." He opened his arms.

Rohnert hesitated. The elderly vampire seemed frail, but somehow he doubted that he was. He sensed power beneath the shriveled skin. "Gastarius?" He proceeded with caution, unsure whether to shake the vampire's hand or walk into his embrace. He reached for the man's palm instead.

The grin got wider. "You have so much strength in you, but your doubt is clouding your judgment."

Rohnert let go of his hand. It was too weird for him. "What can I do for you?"

"I think the question is what we can do for you."

Shelly stirred and opened her eyes, then she blinked before shooting up like a rocket on the bed. "Rohnert, who are these people?" Upon realizing she, too, had no clothes on, Shelly grabbed the sheet and covered her chest.

Rohnert ran to the bed and held her trembling body. He soon realized her reaction wasn't fear, but embarrassment. "Hey, it's okay."

Shelly lifted her eyes to meet his. "Who are they?"

"This is Gastarius, our race's forecaster." The old man nodded at the introduction.

"And this is Lukan, our Shaman. You've met her."

What the two did next took his breath away. Lukan curtsied, while Gastarius bowed his head, bending low at the waist. For a moment, Rohnert thought the man's body would crack, given his advanced years.

"We're here to give you the belated blessing you seek," Gastarius said when he straightened his body.

Shelly looked at Rohnert before returning her attention to the age-old vampire. "What?"

Rohnert couldn't believe his ears. "But the rules, the traditions . . ." This was downright unbelievable. For centuries, they'd frowned on mixing their race with humans. Requests for leniency had been turned down left and right, and now him.

He'd given up on the idea of Shelly being accepted into their tight little circle of aristocratic snobs. Truthfully, he didn't give a fuck anymore.

"We make amends to those we offend. We've gone long enough without affecting change, and this time, I feel the need to make alterations. Our race is evolving faster than we can process, and because of this, we must start with the rightful leader." Gastarius' voice was pure gravel, but his spoken sentiments were passionate and almost heartfelt.

"Are you saying you will grant us a mating ceremony?"

Gastarius nodded, his opaque eyes gleaming. "Although I expect you to wear something more appropriate." There was humor in the suggestion, and Rohnert carried his bride inside the walk-in closet and closed the door.

"What the hell is this about?" Shelly kept her voice down.

He silenced her with his lips, bruising her mouth with the hunger and happiness swelling in his chest. Shelly responded, her body curling against him until he let her go.

"Gastarius doesn't leave his den too often. House visits aren't his thing. We're not about to make him regret making the trip. Where is that lovely dress of yours?"

They worked fast inside the closet. Shelly put on her gown, which took a bit of time to fasten, given the gazillion buttons running from her tailbone to the nape of her neck. Rohnert donned his one and only robe, and then they walked out together hand-in-hand.

They both froze on their tracks when they glanced at the home improvement their bedroom had undergone. All furniture had been pushed to the side. Even the bed was next to the wall, leaving space in the center of the room.

Gastarius was standing in the middle of the room inside the circle of suspended candles, cradling their baby. Surprisingly, Malin was dead to the world, contented and sleeping in the old man's arms.

"Ready?" Lukan regarded them with approving eyes.

Rohnert gathered his bearing first and led Shelly, mouth still hanging open, into the luminous circle. "This rite includes your son, who as you already guessed will follow in your footstep as the rightful heir to the top Council seat."

"The prophecy! You're the caretaker. It is true," Shelly blurted out, no doubt remembering the piece of information she'd gathered from the sacred book.

Rohnert squeezed her hand and pleaded to the diviner for understanding. "She read the book without knowing. Please forgive me for being careless."

Gastarius nodded. "You have been denied your rightful place in the hierarchy, and this is a small recompense for your troubles, past and present. Come. Let me grant you your heart's desire."

Lukan began chanting in their ancient tongue, her voice as fluid as calm waters. When the rhythmic recitation was over, a blinding light appeared from nowhere, illuminating the circle in which they stood.

Shelly fidgeted, her eyes attesting to her nervousness. Rohnert was quite taken aback, too, but he had to get a grip on himself, to show that he was tight and all.

Gastarius closed his eyes while holding Malin close to his chest.

"Sacred is a mating between two entities. A life celebrated in pursuit of dutiful service, physical desires, sacrifice, and spiritual enrichment. Grant each other a hand in the darkest hours, and love one another through this life and the one after. Strengthen your bond by mutual reverence and adoration. Uphold the values of your ancestors and impart them to your offspring so they would know their purpose in life."

Rohnert glanced at Shelly. Her eyes were closed, a small smile on her lips, as if she were mesmerized by the words. She seemed at peace, and everything felt right in his world.

After Gastarius sealed the short ceremony in their old language, Rohnert felt lighter than he ever had before—like he was buoyed by serene waters and basking in light. Gastarius placed his hands on his head, then Shelly's, and finally on Malin. As blinding light illuminated the face of his son, Rohnert believed in the prophecy for the very first time.

Goran surfaced from the delirious pleasure of Bretania's body at the sound of persistent knocking. The sheets tangled around them, and he frowned. Devereux knew better. He wasn't going to be disturbed unless the world was falling apart. He glanced at the clock and hissed.

"What is it?"

"My apologies, sire, but I have news that you might need to hear." The second the command's voice was muffled by the thick mahogany door.

This had better be worth his while. "Give me a moment." He turned to face Bretania, her mouth bruised from hours of punishing foreplay, and her neck ravaged with bite marks. "This will just take a second."

"I'll be here," she said and buried herself under the glorious covers, smiling.

Goran stood and picked up the discarded robe on the floor with his toes.

He put it on and blurred to the door. Devereux better back his shit up, or he'd be toast. "What is so important that couldn't wait?"

Devereux took a step back, smelling the stench of his annoyance. "Sire, I had reports that most of your Council members are missing."

He had called for an emergency meeting to discuss the changes after the death of August, which, of course, was an act of violence as far as he was concerned. The rounding up of the Elders was necessary to get a feel of their stance in the wake of August's demise.

"Who are missing?"

"Wendell, Icarus, and Serena." Devereux refused to meet his eye.

Goran felt the rage coming. The remaining Elders were goddamned parasites—new fixtures in the seats for decorative purposes due to their bloodlines, but without influence or experience.

His cry tore through the room, shattering the crystals and shaking the foundation. Anger blasted from his chest as he reached for the first thing he could get his hands on, and flung it across the room.

Devereux stumbled back, while Bretania rushed to Goran, her face pale with confusion. He slammed the door and raised a hand, halting her steps.

"Don't come near me." His voice came out in a deep growl.

The female vampire's eyes were alert, as if taking in all that she'd missed. Without taking a step forward, she beseeched him. "Let me ease your worries, my lord."

Panting, and on the verge of losing the last thread of his sanity, Goran lunged at Bretania like a predator.

They ended in a heap of limbs on the floor, him on top, and her underneath his body. A slap of lust consumed him, fueled by fury. He forced her legs apart and thrust himself into her. He penetrated while her surprised cry ricocheted off the walls.

Goran pumped, dug even harder, and kept at it. Bretania held on, fear and pleasure mixing in her widened eyes. His animalistic grunts echoed in his ears while he pummeled harder and harder, until he reached orgasm. Goran didn't let up until he was dry and dead tired.

When he collapsed on top of her, his muscles continued to tremble underneath his skin, and his mind raced.

If these idiots thought they had gotten the best of him, they'd be surprised to learn that they were mistaken. Nobody played him for a fool and lived to talk about it.

"I want you to gather the Council guards and kill them all—spare no one. I mean it. If you return without completing this task, better to not come back at all."

Bretania's bliss was replaced by indelible fear. He sensed it. Hell, he even smelled it.

"Yes, Goran." Breathless, she scampered off the floor and into the dressing room to carry out his bidding.

And this is how it's supposed to be, my dear mate.

Goran was still seething long after Bretania had left. It seemed like all his Council brothers and sisters were ganging up on him. So be it. He wasn't the slightest bit afraid of them or concerned about what they could do to him.

Leadership came with sacrifice. For many years, he had watched his father's lax rule, which had allowed repeated rebellions to sprout like mushrooms around them. Furthermore, the bastard's plan to give up his seat to the next bloodline was just wrong, adding cowardice to the long list of his sire's blunders.

The Council needed a strong leader, someone who wouldn't balk under pressure. Someone willing to squash any wrongdoers without losing sleep over it.

Goran knew he was up for the task. He recalled the night he'd confronted his father and mother about the rumors. When the expected denial hadn't come, he had taken matters into his own hands.

Staging the murder was relatively easy. No one suspected the grieving son of the heinous crime. Everyone accepted his rise to power without question, until Rohnert's parents voiced their displeasure, then he had to eliminate them, too.

So this latest development had to be treated as a crime, and he was well within his authority to hand down swift punishment. It was a good thing that the new Council Elders were easy to intimidate. He had no doubt in his mind that this next step would be easy, and he didn't mind doing the dirty work himself.

Shelly had just finished feeding the baby when Rayce put in a stat call to Rohnert. She propped Malin on her shoulder and started patting his back, encouraging the burp to come out and trying not to listen to the one-sided conversation. Of course, Rohnert didn't say much past the occasional grunt.

"Go to this place." He recited an address. "Call the rest, and I'll meet you there. Keep this on the down-low. You know how he can turn things around."

She busied herself with patting the baby until he burped. He was already asleep by the time she laid him in his crib, and she kissed his tiny pink lips, loving his scent.

In two months, Malin had grown several inches, and he was sporting the appearance of a six-month-old child. He definitely had his father's genes, and it wouldn't be a surprise if he grew taller than Rohnert.

Rohnert hung up the phone and leaned against the sofa. His eyes were fixed on her. "That was Icarus, one of the Council Elders. It seems a few of them have abdicated their seats, and they want to talk to me."

"Oh?" She tried to sound nonchalant, although she was dying to hear the details.

Rohnert smiled. "Goran has been left with just the new members."

"What does that mean?"

When he patted his lap, she walked over and obliged. Shelly rested her head on his bare chest, loving his masculine scent. His strong arms slid around her waist, and he started skimming his mouth along the nape of her neck. She moved to give him more room to work with, and Rohnert began hardening underneath her.

Then he abruptly stopped and inhaled a sharp breath. "I have to go. This is not going to end well. I'm sure Goran is already hunting them down. I told them to hide in my old apartment until we get a solid plan underway."

She turned around to face him, locking her legs around his waist. "But you're off tonight."

"Off or not, I don't think this is something that can wait."

"But you are . . ." *Hard.*

Rohnert swore. "I know. Can I take a rain check? I promise I won't take longer than necessary."

A pout was already forming on her mouth, but she stopped. Her work took precedence over holidays and birthdays, with no regard for sleep or exhaustion. If a job needed to be done, or if someone needed her help, she must go. This applied to Rohnert, too. His responsibilities couldn't wait. There wouldn't be a time when she would ask him to choose between his duty and his family. It wouldn't be fair.

"I get hard when you get all noble on me." Rohnert continued caressing her through the V of her robe.

Shelly gave a short laugh. "Rain check, then. You need to stop by later." She waggled her eyebrows at him.

After he kissed her temple, he murmured, "You're on. Get ready for my healthy appetite."

The promise made her tingle, especially in the area where she wanted him the most. "You'd better be on time." She captured his lips for a tender kiss.

Rohnert responded with the heated passion she'd grown to appreciate. He might not be the most vocal person when expressing his sentiments, but his actions provided all the assurance she needed.

When he broke their kiss, he held her gaze a moment longer before he spoke. "I love you."

"I love you more." She planted another kiss on his lips. "Off you go." Shelly rubbed his back before unclasping her legs.

"Who's on babysitting duty tonight?" Rohnert stood up.

The massive tenting in his shorts made her smile. She watched him stride to the walk-in closet and closed her eyes, savoring the prospect of their time together once he returned.

"Jordan's watching Malin." She tracked his movements while she lounged on the sofa. In a few minutes, she'd be up on her feet.

He emerged wearing his usual jeans, black cotton T-shirt, and trench coat. Shelly could see the bulge at his back, knowing his favored weapon was strapped underneath.

"You'll be careful?"

"As always." Rohnert proceeded to the adjoining room and gave the baby a quick kiss. Then he walked over to where she was seated, his eyes focused, and his mouth set in a fierce line. "I hate rain checks, but you do understand, right?"

Shelly smiled. "You have nothing to worry about. I'll be waiting for you." She rose and pulled his neck down until their noses touched. "I love you."

"I love you more, my woman." He brushed his lips against hers.

After Rohnert left, she basked in the few minutes she had to herself before reporting for her duty at the clinic. Time had flown since their reunion. With the birth of the baby, their relationship had become stronger than ever. Words weren't necessary to convey their affection anymore. It was a good thing. They moved in synchronicity, aware of each other's needs. Even if their separate responsibilities got in the way, they managed to scrape some time to be together. She smiled at all the good things that had happened in her life.

Jordan knocked while she was putting on the finishing touches to her light makeup.

"You look different," Jordan said, watching her with those knowing amber eyes.

"Of course, I look different. I'm much smaller after the baby."

The vampire shook her head. "No, that's not it. You seem really happy. That smile of yours is wider than I remember."

Shelly rolled her eyes. "Oh, be quiet. Can't you leave a mated woman alone?"

Jordan smirked. "And risk your reputation?"

Hours into her shift, the clinic remained idle, which was a good thing. Shelly preferred to be bored to tears instead of seeing people hurt. She let Cheryl off early. It was not that she didn't appreciate the company, but the woman's constant sighs were driving her nuts. She had heard rumors that

Cheryl had protected Zane. Although Shelly had no idea why the nurse would do such a thing, she figured Cheryl would explain herself when she was good and ready.

Her phone rang, and one look at the caller ID got her smiling. "Rick, how are you?"

"Shelly, I need help here if you're not too busy." There were no pleasantries, just straight business. She respected that.

"I'm not doing anything. What's up?"

Rick recited a number of cases he had to deal with, and Shelly salivated at the idea of helping. Not to mention she owed the doctor. It made sense for Rick to call on her since she was still on the active roster at the hospital. "Hang on. Let me clear it with Harrow," she said and pressed the hold button. She punched Harrow's extension. When he came to the phone, she gave him the skinny on Rick's request.

"I have no problem with that. Make sure your husband knows. I don't want him biting my head off." Harrow chuckled.

"Thanks."

He was still chuckling when she cut the line and returned to Rick. "I'm good to go. Give me twenty minutes to get there."

Scrambling to her feet, she called Jordan to let her know that she needed to stay a few hours more and then arranged for one of the newly inducted fighters to drive her instead of taking a cab. This way, she could leave as soon as the schedule eased.

"Ready?" Markus was already behind the wheel of the Humvee by the time she reached the garage.

Shelly took the front passenger seat and strapped on the seatbelt. "Step on it," she said when the massive doors parted like the red sea.

"Yes, ma'am," Markus replied and lead-footed the accelerator.

She left a quick message to Rohnert while they sped out of the warehouse and onto the city streets.

The traffic wasn't bad, and they reached the hospital ten minutes later. Markus dropped her off at the employee entrance in the back, and she hurried down the hallway until she reached the nursing station.

"Where's Whitaker?"

One of the nurses looked up, surprised. "Doctor Anderson. I didn't expect you back so soon. Doctor Whitaker is in his office."

She raised an eyebrow. "Aren't we busy tonight?"

"Sure, but—"

"That's okay. I'll go see him." She whipped down the stairwell and marched one floor up to Rick's office. She banged her knuckles on the door before she turned the knob and breezed in. "Rick, don't we have stuff to do?"

The office was dark, and she wondered what the heck was going on. Then she froze where she stood. Behind his desk, Rick was tied to his chair, his mouth gagged with a cloth. His frantic eyes were locked on her, and standing behind him were two hulking figures. Menace rolled off them in waves. The water that had been running in the private bathroom shut off, and another man emerged. Without warning, the overhead lights switched on, and Shelly had to stifle her scream when she recognized him.

"Ah, there you are—the famous Doctor Anderson."

He glided closer until she could see the tips of his fangs when he gave her a broad smile, his eyes narrowing.

"Goran." It came out in a whisper.

He seemed pleased by her recognition. "I'm flattered. But then again, you're with Rohnert. I'm sure he's already filled you in on all the necessary details."

Fear found its way through Shelly's defenses, and she started to backpedal toward the door. Her eyes darted from Goran, then to Rick.

The next minute, Goran was standing behind her, his expression reeking of evil. "I didn't call for you just to have a short rendezvous, my dear."

If Shelly looked past the wickedness, Goran wasn't a bad looking vampire. He was smaller in build than Rohnert, but he was just as intimidating. There were no telling features that would give away their relationship except the prominent nose and dark hair.

Goran staggered back and braced one hand on the wall, catching his breath.

One of the statues behind Rick made a move to run to his side, but Goran stopped him with a wave of his hand.

"Sire, are you all right?" the man asked, throwing a suspicious glare her way.

Goran sputtered before he could reply. "I'm fine, Devereux. Sit tight."

Then he yanked Shelly's arm, drawing her close until she was face-to-face with him.

"Let me go." Shelly tried to free herself from his grasp, but Goran dug his fingers deeper into her flesh, and twisted her arm behind her back. She let out a howl.

The woman with the piercing blue eyes glared at Goran, throwing off fear, defiance, and anger while he harnessed her mind. With those thoughts, everything he had ever believed crumbled in front of his eyes. It was unbearable, weighing him down until he could not breathe.

"He's not my brother," Goran said and hissed. His body rejected the idea, and his mind couldn't process the knowledge. Had he spent his life blindfolded?

"But he is, and you took the rightful seat from him. You killed his parents, too, I suppose." Her voice got stronger with each accusation.

"Of course—just as I killed his *real* parents."

The woman knew too much. He gripped her arm tighter until she flinched. Bringing his body closer to hers, he felt burning hatred radiating from her.

"Rohnert won't let you get away with everything you have done."

"He has nothing on me. I will crush him with my bare hands."

Oh, yeah—she was beautiful. A bit crass, but she definitely had an allure. He gathered a handful of her honey locks with his other hand and brought it up to his nose and sniffed.

"You need to shrivel up and die." Shelly pivoted, pushed hard against his chest, and found the dagger tucked in his waistband. She waved the blade in his face, making it difficult for him to get closer.

If he hadn't needed to capture her alive, there was no way would he would have allowed anyone, especially a human woman, to disrespect him. Given his strength and agility, subduing her should be a piece of cake. However, he had to use caution. The dagger she had stolen was infused with Dangeran, and no vampire wanted to fuck with such a deadly weapon.

"Don't play with fire, woman," he said, watching her clumsy movements.

"Don't fuck with me, Goran."

He sifted through her mind as though he was sucking her blood dry and got more than he'd bargained for.

"You have a child with Rohnert. He plans to lead the people against me." Goran sneered. *Ain't gonna happen, sister.*

She continued to wave the weapon in front of him while she moved toward the door. Goran shook his head. "I'm not going to let you go. I always want to be a step ahead of the game."

Shelly lunged at him, but he slipped out of her way, and she hit nothing but air. This seemed to aggravate her even more, and she slashed at him again. Tears were raining down her cheeks.

Shelly almost got a clean hit at his waist. Blind rage was a tough opponent, and the doctor was going at him with utter fury. Goran tried to grab her from behind, but she twisted her body fast enough that the dagger knicked his right thigh.

He cried from the sting of the Dangeran on his skin. "Damn you."

"I'm not letting you get close to my family." Spoken like a true lioness protecting her keep.

Goran smirked. Ignoring the weakening effects of the deadly blade, he shifted in time to avoid another attack. She attempted another thrust, but he managed to catch her wrist. He spun her around, except the blade caught him in the arm. The slash went deeper this time, and it hurt like hell.

Gritting his teeth, he looked at her and hissed. "Game over."

Before he could make a move, a shot rang out.

He felt no sting and checked himself for damage. Nothing.

Then Shelly hit the floor.

The female fell to her side on the carpet. Blood pooled around her body while she gasped for air.

Goran nodded to Devereux, who executed his unspoken order with rapid movements. He released the bindings on Doctor Whitaker. Before the hysterical doctor could take off, Devereux pulled out his dagger, pinned him against the chair, and made a minor adjustment. He forced the mouth open and hauled the tongue out and cut.

One clean sweep.

A hoarse, grinding sound filled the room.

"Why did you shoot?" Goran focused on Carson, the jumpy guard.

There was no need for an answer because the trigger-happy fuck had just earned his ticket to hell. Goran moved swiftly, not giving the vampire any time to beat feet. He wrapped his arm around Carson's neck and twisted. Hard. A crack like the snapping of a twig sounded. The guard hung limp, and Goran let the body slide to the floor.

Goran did not appreciate having his plan to use Rohnert's wife as bait thwarted. Her capture would have been the perfect way to force Rohnert into submission. She was no use to him dead, and the loss of his woman might make Rohnert even more of a threat than he already was.

Doctor Whitaker's cries continued while he slumped to the ground, blood gushing out of his mouth. Goran's instincts told him to stick around and enjoy the scene, but the stench of blood overcame him. He didn't have time to suck them dry at the moment. Considering the noise the doctor was making, they had to make a quick getaway.

Before he and Devereux exited through the window, Goran glanced back at the damage. The male doctor, in spite of his wounds, was staggering toward Shelly, who was barely breathing.

"Always a step ahead," he said, and turned to freefall six stories down.

Rohnert made it to the meeting place on time. The abandoned building looked squalid, just the way it always had. In the darkness, he moved with caution, making little noise in case vagrants had taken up residence since he left.

A clap of thunder sounded, followed by lightning as the nighttime sky brought the threat of rain. Rohnert heard hurried footsteps from behind him, heavy and definitely more than he could handle by himself. He pulled out his Kalimetal and swung around, ready to draw first blood.

"Rohnert, it's us," Icarus said, his arms raised. Flanking him were guards Rohnert hadn't seen before. They wore the crest of the Elder's bloodline on their breast pockets. There had been some buzz about members of the Council building their own armies, and Rohnert couldn't blame them. Considering the rapid disappearances, and members dropping like flies, it was high time they took their safety to heart. Rohnert made a mental head count—a good thirty able-bodied guards were at hand.

"I'm glad you came to me," Rohnert said.

Icarus gave him a good-natured slap on the shoulder. "Are we the first ones here?"

He nodded. The sky was letting up, and trickles of rain prompted them to take cover inside the building. Just as the last man walked in, more footfalls sounded outside. Rohnert glanced out the grimy window just in time to catch Wendell and Serena's arrival. The rain was pelting harder now, and they were running toward the building, followed by a number of vampires. Males and females were in the group, lugging weapons on their backs, their mindsets focused and intent on protecting their masters.

Icarus opened the door wider, looking pleased with the huge turnout. As embraces were exchanged, Rohnert's chest tightened. He staggered and braced his hand on the battered wall.

"What is it?" Serena asked. Her hand shot out to steady him, her eyes searching, no doubt getting a feel for his emotions.

"I don't know." Rohnert brushed away the well-intentioned offer. The odd feeling at the pit of his stomach persisted, so he eased over to the wall and leaned against it.

Wendell came up to him, his eyes narrowed. "What's wrong?"

Rohnert had no idea. He felt in his pocket for his phone and realized he'd left it on the nightstand. "I need a cell phone."

Three phones appeared. He took Serena's and dialed the number Rayce had everyone memorize. The call was routed to the main line, and he had to leave a message since he was calling from an unrecognized number.

He rubbed his chest, trying to ease the tightness, when the phone rang. "Rayce, it's Rohnert."

"Hey, what's up big guy?" Rayce asked, sounding cheerful.

"I forgot my phone in our room, can you check to see if I have any missed calls?"

"Sure thing." He heard pounding on the keyboard while Rayce worked his tech wizardry. He came back after a few minutes. "Dr. Anderson left you a message."

Rohnert's heart hammered against his chest, making it impossible to think straight. "Put the message through."

Another clicking noise sounded, and Rohnert gripped the phone when he heard Shelly's voice.

"Hey, I got a call from Rick. He needs backup, so I'm going in. You know, it's the least I can do after what he'd done for us. Markus is driving, and we're on our way. I know you left your phone on the nightstand, so I wasn't in any hurry to call. I'll be back before sunrise and will be ready to collect that rain check. Love ya."

Rohnert almost shattered the phone in his palm. "I have to go," he said, staggering to the door. In an instant, everyone was right on his heels.

"We're going with you." Wendell's voice was firm, and Rohnert didn't bother denying him or the others.

He flew out the door, his boots sloshing on the rain-soaked earth.

She's all right. I'm being paranoid. She's going to be okay.

Rohnert repeated the mantra in his head while he made headway through the evening traffic, not caring if he garnered stares from surprised humans. He ignored all the questions coming from his companions' thoughts.

One thing kept playing in his head like a broken record: *Shelly is fine. Shelly is fine. Shelly is fine.*

Shelly tried to lift her eyelids, but they refused to open. She tried again and was rewarded with hazy vision. Not a single muscle in her body cooperated when she attempted to worm her way to the door.

Rick's agonized cry filled the room. Her instincts to help flared, but she was too weary to move. A gurgling sounded, and she realized the noise was coming from her. Her gaze slid down to her chest, and she could tell that the hit was fatal. She'd seen enough of this to know the real deal.

Fading footsteps moved away, and she heard Goran's taunting voice. "Always a step ahead," he said.

Her heart throbbed. The cavity continued to ooze warm blood. Feebly, she tried to use one hand to apply pressure. Damn it, she had no strength left. What happened to that rush of adrenaline? Fear gripped her when the pain began numbing her body.

"Rick . . ." Her voice barely rose above a whisper. She had to try again. "Rick . . ."

Shelly heard scratching noises when Rick wobbled in her direction. Unable to move her head, she struggled to breathe. She tried to conserve whatever remaining energy she had.

When Rick came to view, his mouth was bloodied, and a steady stream of blood gushed down from it. His eyes were filled with terror as he looked down at her.

He pointed to the door.

"No time." She fought to stay conscious. "Tell Roh . . . nert . . . love him . . ." She gasped for more air, begging the divine to give her more time. *Oh lord, no. Please. I don't want to leave my son, and Rohnert . . . help him.* "Kiss Malin . . . for me."

Rick's tears mixed with the blood on his face. He coughed and made a strange noise as he attempted to speak.

Shelly tried to lift her hand to touch him, to let him know she was okay with this. "Love . . . my family."

Her friend stumbled away, and she heard his labored footsteps moving to the hallway before a burst of shouts rang out and sound of rushing footsteps drew near. Then someone gasped.

"Code blue to Doctor Whitaker's office! He and Doctor Anderson are down."

Shelly closed her eyes, and prayed for strength to get through this. Her mind went into overdrive, flashing fond memories, the ones worth remembering. Her parents, her graduation from med school, her first job, then her stint at Tack Enterprises and her first glimpse of Rohnert, and then the mating ceremony, followed by Malin's birth.

Tears blurred her sight when she opened her eyes. A nurse was kneeling in front of her. Shelly's chest heaved, begging for air. She was choking. Nothing was passing through, not even a tiny amount of air.

"Stay with me, Doctor Anderson. You're going to be okay." The strangled voice of the nurse confirmed what she already knew in her heart.

Shelly could feel herself slipping away. Thudding footsteps were the last thing she heard while she fought against the tide.

She was losing . . .

Rohnert was flying on his feet. He sped through the puddles in the alley, snaking between cars, whichever way he could get ahead. Icarus, Wendell, and Serena were right behind him, keeping pace. These people were of noble blood, but they were right there with him, getting just as soaked in the rain.

They reached the hospital within minutes, but it still felt like the longest journey of his life. When they arrived, his heart plummeted to his feet. The entire place had been cordoned off. No outsiders were granted access.

Cops were in abundance, and more came with each passing minute. Patients were out in the parking lot. It seemed like they were evacuating the whole hospital.

Rohnert felt sick to his stomach, unable to make heads or tails of what was going on. He tried eavesdropping on a conversation between two rattled employees, but they were also in the dark.

With the place swimming with police, there was no way to get in undetected. They tried to blend in with the onlookers who had turned out to watch, and he strained to get something out of the stray thoughts around him.

His frustration mounted, and Wendell patted his back. "I'm sure your mate is all right."

The soothing words did very little to ease him. Rohnert wanted to see Shelly with his own eyes. When he did, he would kiss her, punish her with his mouth for gambling with her life, and then he'd make love to her. The wait was killing him.

Several vans pulled up, the name of television stations emblazoned on the sides. This was good. At least, they'd be able to get more than the gossip passing between the humans. He glanced at his faithful companions. Everyone appeared intent on getting answers for him.

Rohnert watched the camera crews set up, a reporter arranging the bud in his ear. He tapped the microphone several times, testing the volume, and then looked grimly at the camera.

The vampires heard it before anyone else did. There had been an attack inside one of the offices. No names were given, no confirmed identities yet. Rohnert had no idea whether to laugh or cry. His instinct was firing inside his body, turning him to a churning mess.

"I can't stay here and do nothing." He lost himself in the shadows, looking for a way to get in.

"There is no way to infiltrate the building looking the way we do." *Unless you wrestle your way in.* Wendell didn't have to say the last part out loud.

"If I have no other choice . . ."

Out of the corner of his eye, he saw a diminutive figure shifting in the shadows.

Blood ties bored him, especially a direct descendant of his younger brother, yet he glanced at the quiet vampire leaning by the tree. Their eyes met, and Rohnert was hit with the strangest feeling just before he caught the man's thoughts.

His phone rang, pulling him out of the confusing cesspool of information.

"Harrow . . ."

"Rohnert, where are you?"

"In front of the hospital, waiting."

He heard a sigh of relief from the other end, and wondered what it meant.

"We're a couple of blocks away. I, uh—"

Then a three-way announcement came from Harrow, the newscaster, and Zane's thoughts, hitting him from every direction.

"I'm so sorry, my man. I have no words." Harrow's.

"I tried to warn them." Zane's.

"We have the name of the lone fatality . . . Doctor Shelly Anderson." The newscaster.

Rohnert heard everything, but processing the information through his short-circuiting brain was impossible. His eyes blurred, and sounds were sucked into a vacuum, until all he heard was his heart slamming hard against his ribs.

He sucked in a breath and wished the nightmare would end, but reality stuck as he frantically rubbed his temple, hoping for a do-over of the last several hours.

Just this once, please let this be a dream.

Everything was in goddamned slow-motion. Each picture flashed in a warped tempo, drilling into his head until he numbed out, and all he could do was let out a scream.

A blast of anger splintered out of Rohnert's body, mixing with cold reality and dread. He staggered to stay upright while his vision swam and his mind fought to deny the truth. These people were mistaken. His Shelly was alive, and she would be coming out soon and walking straight into his arms.

Propelled by the rage flowing through his veins, his scream cracked into the charged night, breaking nearby car windows.

Rohnert's cry rose higher, and his chest constricted so tight he could no longer breathe.

Dead! She can't be dead.

"Rohnert, you need to calm down." He saw Wendell mouth the words, but he couldn't hear him.

All he heard was the pounding of his heart, and the nonstop words replaying in his head. *Shelly's dead. Shelly's dead. Shelly's dead.*

In the midst of his agony, Rohnert's tears streamed down his cheeks like angry torrent. He heaved and gasped, wishing the earth would swallow him and end his torture. Bile rose in his throat, until his cries turned hoarse. His heart, which was once filled with compassion, was now an empty vessel, beating with no purpose.

He pointed his head upward, beseeching a higher power to take back the cruel joke and return Shelly to his arms. Misery blanketed him, and he crumbled to the ground.

"My brother, this is a sad day for us all," Icarus said, hovering above him. His voice strangled.

Rohnert shook his head, still hoping to dispel the ugly truth. In his woe, he begged for strength he no longer felt and forgiveness for whatever havoc his misery would create.

Shelly isn't dead. Shelly isn't dead.

"Shelly isn't dead." He hadn't meant to say it out loud, because he didn't believe it. "I don't fucking believe it." He'd always suspected he was capable of great rage, but nothing could have prepared him for the tremendous fury he now felt.

No longer caring about the well-kept secret of their existence, he jumped to his feet and set out in a dead run.

"I will fuckin' kill Rick," Rohnert said in a voice he couldn't even recognize.

He covered a decent amount of mileage, determined to get inside the hospital, before steely hands grabbed him by the shoulder and his waist was yanked from behind. It was no surprise when he landed on the wet ground, taking Harrow and Tor with him.

Rohnert snarled. "Don't even think of stopping me." He got back on his feet before the others could contain him, but now there were more obstacles in his path as Serena, Icarus, and Zo moved to intercept him.

Serena's anguish was palpable, halting his momentum a bit. "I'm sorry, Rohnert, but you'll have to wait this out. I know your pain—"

"You don't know my pain. You have no idea what it is to lose the woman you love." The voice, the tone was not his anymore. It was the sound of a broken man.

"That might be the case, but going in there and throwing a fit won't bring her back." Harrow held his shoulder, stopping his movement.

"Sire, with due respect, there isn't much we can do right now but wait." Alonzo knew better than to get in Rohnert's grill.

He balked under the pressure he faced, and the little air in his lungs released in a long, pitiful sigh. Transferring his weight to Harrow, he bowed his head and sagged at the hopelessness of his situation.

"Let's hang around and let the situation calm down before we make a move." Tor squeezed his shoulder.

"Sunrise is up in an hour," Alonzo said from behind him.

Footsteps shuffled toward them, then Cyrus spoke. "I'm tested not to melt under the sun. How about I stay here and be your eyes?"

Rohnert shifted his eyes to his friend, feeling an overwhelming desire to scream again. It should be him standing out there waiting, but the damned daylight would not yield to his need. Ever.

"You need backup," Harrow said.

Tor went right to work, flicking on his phone and assembling a human team to come. Once satisfied with the arrangement, he hung up. "They'll be here in thirty."

There was nothing to do while humans swirled around them like damn moths. The wet air hung like an acrid reminder that his existence had taken a nosedive to the bowels of hell.

Another cry tore from his lips, and he surrendered to the miserable reality.

The voices of the newscasters drifted around him. They repeated the same old same news over and over, only adding that another doctor had sustained serious injuries.

When Rohnert's knees could no longer sustain his trembling weight, he stumbled, but several vampires came to his aid and steadied him.

"We have to go," Harrow finally said.

Rohnert surrendered to the urging of his friends and lifted one heavy foot after the other, taking himself away from the bitter reality.

Zane watched the men walk away. In the thick of it all, Rohnert stood, aided by several vampires, bleak and broken. Zane's once-unfeeling heart constricted with pain at the cruelty of the situation. He'd tried to warn them, but no one had listened. Could he blame them? His reputation was as murky as muddied glass.

His mind urged him to stay behind in the shadows where he belonged, but his heart prompted him to say something—to offer words of sympathy. Then what?

The internal warring over what was right continued until the group walked away and disappeared in the waning darkness. Cyrus lingered, and Zane moved away—not because he was afraid of confrontation, but to avoid further ruffling the feathers of the humans who'd already seen enough for one night.

While Cyrus paced back and forth, watching and sometimes stopping to glance around at his surroundings, Zane continued to keep vigil. Minutes later, a group of humans garbed in bulky clothes came and conferred with Cyrus. There was no doubt they were packing enough ammo to blow anyone away. Then the woman who'd been haunting his every waking hour and the object of his nightly dreams came into view. Wearing a light sweater and dark jeans, Cheryl approached the group.

Zane closed his eyes and took a deep breath, catching a whiff of her scent that the wind blew in his direction. Despite his present predicament, his insides went haywire on him.

He retreated deeper into the shadows while he deliberated his next step. Sure, he had amassed enough cash to stay afloat and get some men back on payroll. If he intended to keep on, going solo was out of the picture. He'd made a long list of enemies who would fall in line for a chance to off him.

The group hung around, moving closer to the hospital entrance, trolling and waiting. Cheryl stayed close to Cyrus, and the sight created havoc in Zane's system. Part of him wanted to clobber Cyrus, but the other half knew that he'd already overstepped the boundaries.

Where was this emotion coming from?

He cursed when Cheryl began an earnest conversation with one of the cops. His chest burned like hell, wanting to pry her away from the male—any male, in fact. Then he overheard her. "I'm a cousin of Dr. Anderson's. I'm afraid there are no other living relatives this side of the country."

Her voice sounded timid, and he realized the woman wasn't comfortable with lying but had no choice.

The cop appraised her like he would a gleaming brand new car, and this further infuriated Zane. The impulse to plow over the man and get him out of the picture was overwhelming, but he hung back. The place still had a healthy amount of police, and attacking would be stupid on his part.

After a few more words were exchanged, he was surprised to see Cheryl crossing the yellow tape, escorted by another human from the team. The desire to follow her, to ensure her safety, grated at him, but considering Cyrus was there, as well as the hordes of officers, Zane sat tight and gritted his teeth.

He waited like a sentinel until she emerged an hour later, her face tear-stained. Zane strained to listen to her report amid her endless tears. Another doctor had been injured. Although he was expected to live, his ability to talk had been taken.

Zane thought of the bastard Goran, the grandfather he wished he never had. Damn his family and the genes that came with them. After more waiting, Cheryl left with another human, and Zane was left to ponder how fucked his once-orderly existence had become.

Back at the warehouse, Rohnert leaned against the wall outside their bedroom, his chest stinging with pain and uncertainty.

"Are you okay, buddy?" Harrow asked, his hand resting on Rohnert's shoulder.

Rohnert's head throbbed like it had its own heartbeat. He nodded, not trusting himself to speak.

"We're going to be in the I-room in case you need something. I will halt all patrols for the night." That was Harrow, all proper and shit.

Rohnert listened to their retreating footsteps before he turned the doorknob. The moment the door opened, a blast of Shelly's scent assaulted his nostrils, mixed with the smell of their baby.

His heartbeat quickened as reality slapped him hard. His son was motherless. The poor thing would not know a mother's love. Rohnert's chest constricted until he could no longer breathe.

"Rohnert, is that you?" Jordan asked while she rocked Malin in her arms.

He raised his eyes to meet hers and let his gaze slide down to his child, who was tucked in Jordan's embrace.

Her face was filled with wretchedness when she looked at him, and her voice quivered. "I'm so sorry, Rohnert. I'm so sorry." It was almost a whisper.

Her steps were slow and unsure when she walked up to him. Once she got close enough, she lifted the swaddled bundle and offered his child to him. "I will leave the two of you alone. If you need anything . . ." She paused, as if at a loss for words. "Anything you or the baby need, just call on me."

Rohnert took his son. When their skin connected, he felt a surge of energy that wasn't his own. It was as though his son was lending him the strength he no longer possessed. He glanced at Malin's cherubic face, and his heart tore to pieces. "I know. I don't know . . . I can't do this . . . how can I . . . we move on?"

Jordan's arms wrapped around his back, shielding him from the unseen terror of the future. "We're going to miss her. Shit. I loved the woman, too."

"I love her still." His voice grew hoarse.

"That's never going to change." Jordan wept, her tears dripping onto his shirt and soaking the material, making this all seem so final.

Cradling his child who was sandwiched between their bodies, he lowered his head to her shoulder and let his feelings out in the open.

"Go ahead, let it out," Jordan whispered while rubbing his back.

All his life, Rohnert had never allowed himself to break down like he did at the moment. He had no idea how long they stood there, mourning their loss, until Malin started squirming. Rohnert wiped off his face and tried to find some form of composure.

"Call on me for anything. We're here for you." Jordan straightened her body and swiped her own tears away.

After she was gone, Rohnert sat on the bed, still clinging to his child as if he were a lifeline. Malin's eyes were trained on his face, and sure as hell, it felt like he understood where they both stood.

He held the baby close to his chest and marveled at the strength his son transferred to him. Bizarre didn't cover it, but he needed all the help he could get. Rohnert hung on to his son for the longest time, wishing things would go back to where they had been.

Remembering his last moments with Shelly was painful enough, but what else could he do?

What would happen to them? His son needed his mother, and Rohnert ached for the love of his life. He closed his eyes and let the anguish take over. Pinpricks of sadness taunted him until his body grew weary. With his son sleeping in his arms, he repositioned himself in bed and glanced at the empty space next to him.

Before yielding to the reprieve only sleep could offer, he decided that whoever had taken Shelly's life would pay with his. Even if it was the last thing he'd ever do.

Goran appeared in his chamber, expecting Bretania to have returned, hopefully bearing good news. The visit to the hospital hadn't gone well. The plan had been to seize the doctor and use her as bait. Who could have known the bastard soldier he had in tow would turn out to be a trigger-happy piece of shit?

Adjusting his eyesight in the darkness, he muttered a curse. Goran flicked his fingers for some lighting and marched straight to the bathroom. When he glanced at the mirror, he gasped.

On his forehead, a purplish lesion ran from his hairline down to the bridge of his nose. He moved closer to the mirror for a better inspection. The wound appeared scaly, and a pink crust surrounded the six-inch vertical gash on his forehead. He staggered backward, repulsed by his own appearance. On impulse, he removed his jacket, followed by the rest of his clothes, to check for any other affected areas.

He dared not speculate, but his heart pounded hard against his ribs while he got rid of his black sweater. Sitting low on his collarbone was a bump the size of a quarter. It had the appearance of a boil and the same pink discoloration. Goran stumbled backward, running his palms over the rest of his body.

His fingers came across another raised waxy wound behind his shoulder blade, and further exploration revealed the same type of manifested lesions elsewhere on his skin.

Terrified at this discovery, Goran scrambled to the closet and retrieved his old trunk. In his naked glory, he hauled the square chest into the middle of the room and got everything he needed to make a direct call. With the candles lit and the beads pressed between his fingers, he began the chant. He stumbled through the words, distracted by fear and the implications.

Goran tried again, beseeching the Shaman, although maybe wringing her neck would be a better idea. As far as he could remember, Lukan had pronounced him free and clear that night. These welts, lesions, or whatever they were didn't seem something he could shrug off as nothing.

He'd gone through the beckoning process twice, but after an hour, Lukan was still a no-show. Goran gritted his teeth, trying to quell his mounting frustration. Bretania still hadn't reappeared as well.

What if something had happened to her?

A hot breeze swirled through the room, which was uncharacteristic of Lukan's arrival. Goran looked around, expecting the priestess to materialize at any second, but as minutes ticked by, there was no sign of her.

Goran retrieved a dark robe with an attached hood to conceal his body. He had no idea what was going on, and he didn't want anyone to make the assumptions. The wounds started to throb on cue.

At his desk, he pressed Devereux's number and summoned his second-in-command. The elite guard arrived in a heartbeat. His face registered surprise when the question swirled in his head. *What is wrong with him?*

Goran ignored this unspoken inquiry and dove down to business. "Assemble your best men and annihilate every living Elder outside the Council walls."

"Sire?" Devereux's eyes flickered.

This was a sure sign of faltering, a no-no in Goran's book, but just this time, he was willing to let it go. "You heard me. Kill them all, and while you're at it, destroy every diseased vampire out there. Come back here with results." He didn't bother hiding his disdain for the momentary hesitation on his subordinate's face.

Devereux's voice took on an aggressive edge. "Yes, sire." He bowed his head before leaving Goran's presence.

Goran then eased his body onto the bed. He had to hang around and wait in case Lukan showed up, but he hoped the female appeared before he had to take drastic measures.

Rohnert awoke with a start in the middle of his nightmare-ridden sleep. He glanced at the blue luminous display of the clock. It was already noon. Malin was still enveloped in his arms, sleeping peacefully. It might sound crazy, but he felt like the little one understood where his mind was and had left him alone without a fuss.

He looked at his child's face and felt a tug of guilt that made it difficult to breathe. What had he done? What had he failed to do? While his mind twisted around every imaginable scenario, he continued to berate himself for his inability to save his beloved.

Listening to the sound of the baby's breathing helped a bit, giving him focus. What could he do now? Everyone in their little hideout was dead to the world, and the few humans were out with Cyrus. Feeling desperate and restless energy flowing through his veins, Rohnert placed the sleeping babe in his crib.

A soft knock came from the door. He hurried to the door as Malin stirred and made a little noise.

"I'm here for my babysitting duty." Allison smiled. Her eyes were puffy, and Rohnert knew the reason behind it. There was no arrangement for this time of the day, since he was always on babysitting duty while Shelly swung back and forth at the clinic.

But he appreciated Alison's gesture. Maybe he needed the time alone. Rohnert offered a smile that he was certain never made it to his eyes.

Allison tried to return the smile, but the anguish was too much to bear, and she broke down outside the door. "Rohnert, I'm so sorry. I miss her already."

He pulled her into his arms and rocked her. This was what he needed— to shift the pain away from himself and focus on others. Besides, he had no idea how much longer he could bear to be inside the room he'd shared with Shelly. Everywhere he looked, something reminded him of her. Her white Crocs by the door, her robe draped over the chair, the novel she'd been reading on the nightstand, and most of all, her scent all around him. They were reminders of how good he'd had it.

He held Allison for a few more minutes before letting her go.

"I appreciate your help." His voice croaked.

Rohnert thought of the black book. It might help him pass the time. With all the activities after their mating ceremony, their short honeymoon, and the birth, he'd forgotten about the tome. He opened the drawer, grabbed the book, and slipped away from the room.

Out in the hallway, he braced his hands against the wall as nausea engulfed him. He hated the thought of walking away from his son, but he needed some time to think—or maybe not to think. After the wave passed, he tucked the book in his arms and headed to the recreation room. At this time, he expected to have no company there, which suited him.

Once inside the room, he closed the door and locked it then settled on the leather sofa. He thumbed through the book, starting where he'd left off. Marania had many entries, most of them speculations, but the more he read, Rohnert realized that what had been predictions when they were first written had since come to pass.

For instance, Gastarius' prediction of a disease that would decimate the vampire community. The diviner had seen it coming long before Goran's line began their rule.

According to Marania's chronicle, Gastarius had seen the death of Rohnert's biological parents at Goran's hands.

> The greed from the younger seed shall supersede ethics or kinship. On a night when the moon fails to illuminate, the wickedness in his heart will dictate the course of the race for over three hundred years.

Rohnert did the math. It had been over three centuries since Goran had risen to power. Thirst for more information lead him to a gruesome truth he hadn't foreseen or even expected. He gripped the battered book in his palms, feeling his fangs elongating from fury. So Goran had killed his adoptive parents, too. No wonder nothing had come up from the investigation.

How could the Council allow such crimes to happen? What had become of the protection they vowed toward their race, their people? Nothing added up. Even for the sake of argument, why would the Council allow such massacre to happen?

And the answer hit him square in the face.

Because Goran is the Council.

Now, everything clicked into place. Goran had offered no resistance when Rohnert left, respecting his wishes and letting him go without repercussions. This was unheard of, unless a Council member was sick. There was no going away or severing ties.

Each Council Elder had been killed when they discovered the truth or began questioning Goran's leadership. Rohnert had wanted nothing from anyone—not the seat, not fame or responsibility. All he'd craved was peace and to be left alone.

Almost ripping the next page in his haste to get to more information, Rohnert's eyes bulged from their sockets when he read the first line.

> The firstborn, after centuries of living under a veil of mystery, would come forth to challenge the leadership, but not without sacrifice. The human mother of the son destined to rise to the highest seat of the Council would be taken.

Rohnert stared at the words, reading them over again, not realizing his tears had fallen and drenched the page of the old book.

He hurled the volume across the room and bellowed a cry from the pit of his stomach. The pain of the wretched death of the woman he loved was too great, and hatred oozed out of him in furious currents. They had known all along, and yet they'd done nothing to prevent this from happening.

They wanted the son, *his son* to lead them, but they had to answer to the father first.

The door burst open, wood splintering everywhere when Harrow and Tor rushed inside. "Rohnert, what the hell is going on?" Harrow said, running his weak eyes over him before scanning the ruined pages scattered on the floor.

"I fuckin' need to spar. You and Tor better give me your best shot." This was not a request, but an order.

Harrow nodded grimly, because he knew where this anger would lead him. Rohnert didn't care. For once in his life, he'd lost the power to care. All he had was hatred in his heart, even for the very people he'd tried to protect and the beliefs he'd upheld. Just like that, any respect he had felt went up in smoke, and the rest would have to deal with his Kalimetal.

Rohnert jogged out of the room, shedding layers of clothing and dropping them with careless abandon along the way. Tor swore behind him, and the sound of their footsteps rang in the quietness of the hallway. Once they reached the training room, Rohnert was down to his jeans. He strode straight to the metal cabinet that held the wide variety of training weapons and grabbed four Arnis sticks and a heavy wooden axe for Tor.

He tossed the sticks to Harrow and the axe to Tor and bared his fangs. "I so fuckin' need this. Be prepared to haul ass."

"You're insane, but I'm your man." Tor shed his shirt and calibrated his prosthetic arm.

"Don't forget the values you uphold." Harrow's reminder ricocheted like bad news around him.

Rohnert shook his head. "Better remove your sunglasses."

As the two vampires, his friends, readied and widened their stances, Rohnert twirled the sticks between his fingers. Aggression flowed in his veins like adrenaline while he calculated his first move.

From their defensive positions, Rohnert already knew he had to strike first. Letting his anger rule him, he lashed out, hitting Harrow's stick hard enough that it cluttered to the floor while punching Tor's arm with the tip of the stick, making him release his weapon.

"You're an animal," Tor said, shaking his head.

"It's about time I explore that part of me." Rohnert wiped the sweat off his forehead.

With Tor weaponless and Harrow left with one stick, Rohnert moved faster, using the mind tricks he'd rejected for so long. He scrambled their thoughts, creating confusion in the frontal lobe while he jumped in the air in one quick burst and landed behind them. He struck Tor behind the knees with one blow, and the big vampire landed on the mat. Then Rohnert popped the stick still in Harrow's hand at its tip hard enough to send it flying in the air.

"Not fuckin' fair." Tor got to his feet and punched his fist into the metal prosthetic. "Don't use that crap on us. Fight fair and square."

Harrow recovered, and before Rohnert could drop his weapon to the floor, the vampire had already landed a hard kick to his jaw. His neck jerked backward, and he landed on his ass.

The two circled him like animals, their fangs punching their lower lips. Tor curled his prosthetic finger, beckoning and taunting him.

Rohnert lunged at Tor while Harrow jumped him from behind, grabbing his head in a vise-grip. He staggered and tried to smack his elbows backward, but Harrow twisted his body until Rohnert could no longer breathe.

"You told me to think before I act. That is the cardinal rule."

"And you always reminded me not to let my anger get in the way," Tor said, and smacked his palm against Rohnert's forehead so hard he literally saw stars.

Fury seeped out of his pores like acid, but then reality crept in. Rohnert rejected the idea of forgiveness. "You're . . . a bunch . . . of sorry asses." He choked out the words.

Harrow relaxed his grip a fraction but didn't let go. "We're in this together, because we're your friends. We feel your pain, no matter what you think. Use your head, because your son still needs his father."

There went Harrow spouting his infinite wisdom. However, Rohnert was too far gone, and reasoning held no weight anymore. The one thing that still mattered was revenge, and he could almost taste it.

Cyrus wasn't a quitter. This was one thing he knew for certain. In all the days of his human life, he'd never surrendered to fear or pain. He wouldn't balk now that he was a vampire.

He glanced at the people around him and absorbed their emotions. This was real. Shelly was dead, and he could imagine the events that would follow. Rohnert had been the quiet one, peaceful and intuitive. Always the one who would give sound advice or just quiet camaraderie without the pressure to speak.

With this recent nightmare, he guessed the vampire would seek revenge, and he understood the need for it.

As for him, he knew Zane had been lurking in the shadows, but this wasn't the right time, even if the bastard was within reach. Cyrus was here for one mission alone—to get the necessary intel on what had happened to Shelly. Patience had never been his strongest virtue. Today, he was making an effort. He leaned against one of the news vans and waited for updates.

So far, the only fatality reported was Shelly, and Rick Whitaker, the doctor who had delivered Malin, had been injured. There had been no update on his condition except that he would live. If the doctor was in critical condition, it would further complicate the situation. Cyrus needed answers. His group had been hanging around for hours without getting any concrete details, and the wait was chipping away at his nerves.

He glanced at the farthest end of the lot and saw a group of dark cars approaching. When he recognized the license plates, he moved closer. Car doors opened, and General Leo Krever stepped out, his face grim. Had Harrow contacted him?

"Hey, General." Cyrus waved.

Every head whipped in his direction. Though he hated the attention, this would be his ticket to getting into the hospital.

Leo looked over his shoulder and narrowed his green eyes. It took him a few moments to recognize Cyrus. By this time, Cyrus was already elbowing his way through the crowd. Two cops stopped him.

"No one's allowed past this line."

"He's with me," the general said.

Cyrus crossed the demarcation line and almost flashed his fangs at the man in blue, but stopped himself in time.

Leo clapped him on the back. "This is a sad day."

He could only nod while they walked together amid the commotion around them. Surrounded by two armed men, he and the general walked past the throngs of medical personnel, cops, and plain-clothes personnel. Cyrus took note of the agency name on their badges and committed the information to memory. Leo seemed uptight, which was understandable under the present circumstances. This was a massive loss to them, considering Shelly had been with the group since day one.

"Did Harrow call you?"

"Him and a host of other people," Leo said, then abruptly pulled him aside. He nodded to his men, who turned their backs, eyes alert. "There are rumors of vampire involvement."

That explained the people who seemed out of place, running around with some GPS-like gadgets. Cyrus shook his head, wondering if he would set off their devices. It was just another thing he needed to look into after everything was said and done.

"What are you going to do?"

Leo closed his eyes and took a deep breath, then he focused once more on Cyrus. "What I've always done. Damage control. I'm afraid the doctor might have given information away."

"Rick?"

"Yeah."

"Nah. I don't think so. He's cool. He delivered Shelly's baby."

"We'll see. I'm planning to visit with him."

"Why would they think vampires were involved?"

"Camera," Leo whispered, moving closer. "The exterior camera hadn't been disabled like the one in Dr. Whitaker's office was."

Damn it. At least, this would identify whoever killed Shelly. It would offer a little consolation to counter their grief. Leo resumed walking, and Cyrus trailed behind. They reached the reception area, which had been converted into a command station.

A dignified-looking gentleman wearing large-rimmed glasses walked over when he spotted Leo. He eyed Cyrus with wary interest before extending his hand to the general. "General, I'm pleased to see you here."

Leo took the outstretched hand and shook it. "What are we looking at?"

The man glanced at Cyrus again. "Do you want to talk in private?"

"Pete, we're good here. Cyrus is one of my most trusted men."

Pete still threw a distrusting glance Cyrus' way before he ran a palm over his face. "These are the preliminary reports. I sequestered the video tapes upon your request. I'm afraid vampires were involved." At this time, Pete lowered his voice so that only they could hear. "They got in through the window in Dr. Whitaker's office. Before they disabled the camera, we got a good look at all three men."

"Are you sure about this?" Leo gnashed his teeth. "Did anyone see the tapes before you got to them?"

Pete nodded. "I'm afraid so. The technician and whoever was inside the room saw them."

Leo's expression was beyond pissed off. "What are the preliminary findings?"

"Dr. Anderson was shot in the chest, and Dr. Whitaker was maimed. It is safe to say he won't be able to talk again. God, Leo, what's up with this? I think it's about time we focus on these rats. I'm sick and tired of seeing humans suffer, and yet we're keeping quiet about it."

The hostile reference to his kind spiked the anger in Cyrus' blood. He clenched his fists, wanting to strike the man down, but Leo threw him a warning glare.

"Where is Dr. Anderson right now?"

"She's been taken to the morgue for autopsy. I believe there's a woman who claims to be a cousin waiting to take the body. I'm afraid we can't grant her request until the process has been completed."

Oh, shit. Rohnert won't be happy with this piece of news.

"And how long will that be?" Leo knew the drill, but he asked for Cyrus' sake.

A colleague called for Pete. "Be right there." He turned to Leo. "One week. Listen, the technicians already blabbed to the media. I can't stop them, so I'm going to leave it up to you to work your magic."

Leo nodded. "Can I see Dr. Whitaker?"

Pete chewed on his lower lip. "His tongue has been mutilated, and he's under sedation. I'm not sure he'll be able to answer your questions." Pete had the audacity to chuckle, which made Cyrus ache to punch him on the face.

This bastard is pushing it.

"What's the room number?"

Pete gave the info, and once the men exchanged another handshake, he left. Leo looked at Cyrus. "I'm going to check on Shelly after I see Doctor Whitaker. Are you coming with me?"

Cyrus nodded. He wanted firsthand information so he could give a full report. They took the service elevator without their escorts. The walk was long and spent in tense silence. Judging from the set of Leo's jaw, he had his work cut out for him.

They reached the ICU, and once they located the room, they headed inside despite the glance of disapproval from the nurses. Two policemen had been assigned to guard the door. Leo took a deep breath, and Cyrus tried not to mimic him. The scent of blood was too much for his neophyte taste.

Rick looked deathly pale, lying in bed with numerous tubes running from his arms and surrounded by machines. The area around his mouth appeared swollen beneath the wads of bandage covering it. The two men walked closer to his bedside.

Cyrus fought hard to keep from retching from the god-awful stench of blood and medication swirling around him. Leo gave him a sideways glance and patted him on the shoulder. "It's all right."

"I'm trying not to puke here. So much carnage around us."

"I wonder where Dr. Whitaker came in."

On cue, Rick's eyes fluttered open. They both leaned forward into the doctor's line of vision. Rick's eyes focused on Leo first before rolling over to Cyrus, and instant recognition marred his battered face. Agitated, Rick tried to speak, but nothing but muffled and hoarse sounds came out.

"Rick, don't try to speak. If you can, just nod your head for yes and shake it for no."

He nodded.

Cyrus looked at Leo for permission to start into the countless questions he'd been dying to ask.

"Did vampires do this to you and Shelly?"

Rick bobbed his head several times while tears trickled down his mottled cheeks.

"Who killed Shelly?"

Rick's eyes began blinking, and the noise he made no sense. Wrong question. Cyrus placed a palm on the doctor's arm to calm him down. He tried again. "Was Goran the one who came for her?"

The doctor closed his eyes, leaving Cyrus to think that he might have fallen asleep, but then Rick nodded.

"Are you sure about this?"

Rick continued to nod while tears fell in a relentless rush.

Leo cleared his throat before he spoke. "If it's not too much to ask, can you deny these allegations to the media? I'm afraid several employees have leaked the information already."

Another bob of the head.

"Is there anyone you would like us to call?" Cyrus asked.

Rick's head moved from side to side.

"We have to check on Shelly, but we'll be back. Hang on tight for now."

The doctor's body began to quake at the mention of Shelly's name, and the awful sound of his cries was enough to tear Cyrus's heart apart. He rubbed Rick's arm in an attempt to console him.

Outside in the hallway, it took them a while to collect themselves enough to go down to the morgue. Cyrus had never seen one, and it was enough to start the dry heaves. The mortician took one look at him and shook his head. Leo followed the man while Cyrus trailed, feeling sick to his stomach.

"Are you sure you're up for this?"

Cyrus nodded, despite feeling his knees about to buckle underneath him.

They passed rows of stainless cabinets until they reached the far end. The mortician opened a door and checked the toe tag before pulling on the handle. A whirring sounded, and then the entire body appeared before them, covered with white linen.

Cyrus held his breath once more while the man lifted the cloth to expose Shelly's face. One look at her and he had to glance away, unable to keep his emotions at bay any longer. He felt hot tears bursting in a mad rush, angry and miserable.

Shelly had been a friend. She hadn't deserved this. Nor had the family she'd left behind.

Rohnert kneeled in the middle of his room, not bothering with the ceremonial garment or etiquette, and awaited Lukan's appearance. His muscles twitched with aggression as well as the beating he'd taken from his friends. No matter how much Harrow and Tor had tried to drill their advice into his head, he was beyond listening. Reason was overrated, and it was high time he relied on his instinct instead. Every piece of him demanded vengeance.

With the cloud of smoke, Lukan appeared before him. With her face concealed by the white hooded robe, she extended her hand to Rohnert. He didn't take it and ignored the customary greeting.

"Let me in the Council walls."

"You're not thinking clearly. You'll get yourself killed." Her voice lacked the usual levity he'd grown accustomed to.

"Show me the way to get in." Forget niceties. Fuck everyone. If he was their answer to unseating his bastard brother, the damned diviner and priestess knew better than to deny his order.

"You wouldn't deprive your race their rightful destiny." Lukan's tone held a tinge of nervousness.

"Watch me." He stood up to his full height and towered over the Shaman he now loathed with a passion.

A tiny vial containing clear liquid appeared in her palm. "It's a one-way ticket. I'm afraid you'll have to find your way out on your own, if you're —"

"Go to hell," Rohnert didn't allow her to finish. He grabbed his Kalimetal and dashed out of his bedroom.

"You must feed . . ." Lukan said before the door slammed shut.

He expected resistance from his comrades as he went through the exits. For once, he felt no shame using his mental power to open every door, disengaging locks and safety devices along his way. This was his moment.

Harrow, Tor, Alonzo, and Gentry stood by the final exit, their faces marked by worry. Rohnert passed them by, not saying a word. These men knew better than to stand in his way.

Rohnert's mind ran through the brief phone call from Cyrus in which his brother had been named. That had been enough. Hell might as well hold its breath, for his fury would spare no one.

Why did it seem like they were always regrouping? Harrow tried to fathom the latest tragedy that had befallen his team. Shelly's death was another blow to their peaceful existence, and probably the worst yet. Rohnert had always maintained a neutral approach in most situations. The vampire had wanted peace above everything else and had avoided taking precious lives as far as he was able. Looking at his friend when he left the warehouse, Harrow wasn't sure Rohnert was that man anymore.

Harrow surveyed his group, uncertain what their next course of action would be. From Leo's phone call, the general expected him to lay low and keep his men away from conflict, and he didn't want them patrolling for weeks. Harrow could do the first, but the latter might be impossible.

"What's next, Gates?" Tor drummed his prosthetic finger on the table, which was annoying.

The door burst open, and Cyrus walked in, his hair still damp from the shower. "Excuse me for being late." He took the chair next to Harrow.

He nodded. "Leo doesn't want us patrolling."

There was a collective groan from everyone present. Tor grunted in frustration. "With all due respect to the general, but this sucks. I think we need to be out there more than ever."

"I agree with you, brother, but Leo is concerned about the recent leak from the hospital incident. There could be a backlash from humans. I'm sure you're aware of vampire hunters, right?"

Harrow had wanted to laugh when he first heard about these hunters, but the general had cautioned him. They were real, and that would further complicate their lives.

The intercom buzzed. Harrow punched the button, and Rayce's voice came on the speaker. "What's up?"

"There's a call for you from Icarus."

It took several seconds for the name to register. "Put him through."

As soon as the line was patched in, it was apparent that there was trouble in the background.

"Harrow, we have insider information that Goran has instructed the Elite guards to kill every single one of the Elders."

His jaw tightened. They weren't supposed to do anything but stay inside their hideout, but he wasn't going to sit around and wait for others to get slaughtered. No, sir.

"You need back up?" Stupid question.

"If you have fighters to spare. I want to turn this around on the bastard."

That's the spirit. Harrow eyed Cyrus and Tor, and he could see from their faces that they wanted this—needed it, even.

"Would thirty men make a difference?" His mouth parted into a harsh smile. Harrow was so ready to do battle. It was time they made a stand.

There was silence on the other line before Icarus replied. "My brothers and sisters would be forever indebted to you."

"No need for that. We're doing what we think is right." Revenge would never taste so good.

"Just the same. Know that we will do whatever we can for you, should the time come." The voice held a trace of sentimentality that made Tor roll his eyes, and he rolled his hand to get Harrow to move the conversation along.

"Where are you guys holed up?"

"I sent word out that we'd meet the others in the Catskills in three hours."

Harrow glanced at the clock on the wall. That meant one thing—they'd better get going. "We'll see you there in three."

There was loud clapping, hoots of approval, and fists pounding the table the minute Harrow hung up the phone. He raised his hands to quiet down the jubilation and eyeballed each of the men in the room.

"This might not turn out like you expect. There is a good possibility of death, and the guy next to you might not make it through alive. So I'm giving you the option to walk away now. I won't hold it against anyone, but I want to be clear that this may end badly."

Silence followed his announcement before everyone started talking at the same time.

"I want in." Angus raised his hand.

Harrow shook his head.

"Fuck death. I'm ready to kick some Elite ass," said Jared.

Markus waved his fist with arrogance.

"Dude, I thought I'd never see battle." Tor laughed, flexing his biceps.

"I'm ready to haul ass." Cyrus bared his fangs.

Okay, this would be interesting. They were on the verge of marching to their deaths, and the idiots were celebrating like it was the Super Bowl.

"Angus, I want you to stay and watch over the warehouse. Rayce will need backup, and I hate to leave Jordan and Allison by themselves." Harrow waited for the human to answer.

He didn't seem to mind. The assignment was meaty enough to satisfy his fighter soul.

Then Harrow turned to the rest. "See you girls in ten minutes." He was out the door before anyone else.

Jordan was suiting up when he reached their bedroom.

Damn it. "I'm afraid I need you and Allison to stay here to guard the place. It's a very tricky situation, and I'd hate to be blindsided. With Zane knowing where we are, there's a possibility of an ambush."

Jordan flashed her fangs, a rare occurrence nowadays. Her goal remained the same, even though she hadn't mentioned it much. She still wanted to kill Goran.

"I will stay because this place and you mean so much to me, but you won't be able to stop me next time."

The threat sounded real, but Harrow wasn't going to get in a tiff with her—not tonight. He nodded before striding to the walk-in closet to grab a few necessities. He slipped the sunglasses on his face, strapped on a holster filled with daggers, throwing stars, and knives, and grabbed his Kalimetal.

Harrow walked back into the room and found Jordan sitting on the edge of the bed. He lifted her chin with his hand until she was looking straight into his eyes. "I've never forgotten what is important to you," he whispered. "I love you."

He didn't wait for an answer. It pained him to know Jordan's purpose hadn't shifted, now that she had him and Gail. Deep down, he understood her determination, and he wasn't going to stop her.

"Come back to me . . . please."

He pivoted and offered a grim smile. "I will."

Rohnert's mind was in shambles while he ran across the city at breakneck speed. If he'd cared before about humans and staying out of their way, those silly concerns were nonexistent this time. He jumped over cars, raced through thick hordes of pedestrians, and plowed through some to get him where he needed to be sooner.

Thunderclaps rumbled above, while trickles of rain descended from the evening sky, causing people to run for cover. By the time he reached the famous landmark, rain was pelting his back. The area was almost deserted. Few people remained, getting soaked under the prodigious downpour.

He fished for the glass container inside his jacket pocket that held the key to his old stomping ground. Since he had no idea where and how the entrance would appear, he smashed the bottle with his palm and threw it on a random wall.

A billow of smoke rose from nowhere, accompanied by a whirring sound, like a washing machine with a full load. It was dark inside the circle of smoke as Rohnert held on to his precious weapon and dove into the abyss. Seconds into his freefall, an odd feeling crept through him, and he looked over his shoulder to see Alonzo zooming in behind him.

Goddamn it! "What's wrong with you? This is my score to settle. You have no business following me."

"I came here of my own accord. I vowed to serve you, and I'm fulfilling that promise. Besides, I owe you for making me what I am today."

This was so un-fucking-believable. Zo was making conversation while gliding into the unknown, possibly going to his death.

"You owe me nothing."

Alonzo let out a raw curse in Spanish. The demand to translate was about to leave Rohnert's mouth when they landed just outside his old bedroom. Their arrival made enough noise to wake the dead. "If I can't make you leave, just promise me you won't get killed on my watch."

Rohnert shot to his feet and looked around the familiar surroundings. The same old heavy damask curtain covered the window, the same old paintings adorned the walls, and the same old heavy wood furnishings occupied every single space available.

"I don't plan—"

"Ssshhh." He cut him off when he heard someone outside.

They waited until the sound of the footsteps faded before Rohnert opened the door. He glanced from left to right in the darkened hallway before stepping out. He knew where to go and just what he needed to do.

Rohnert broke into a run, barely registering the sound of Alonzo following close behind. He veered off to the left and stood outside Goran's door. Using all his active senses, he listened for any sound, calibrated his mind for errant thoughts, and inhaled hard to catch any identifying scent to alert him of danger.

Then he kicked the door hard.

Brandishing his Kalimetal, he entered fast. The room was dark . . . and empty. Except for the lingering scent he'd grown accustomed to smelling on the diseased comrades in their group, the room held nothing for him.

"Are you looking for me?" The voice he knew so well spoke from behind him.

Rohnert pivoted around, but he was not fast enough to stop the dagger that went straight into Alonzo's heart.

"*Madre de dios*," Alonzo said, crumbling to the ground. "Sire, I didn't plan on this."

Rohnert's quick strides brought him to Alonzo's side, where he dropped to his knees. Before the vampire fizzled, he held his hand and made another vow. "I'll kill them all for you," he whispered.

Goran clapped his hands as the disintegration process began. "How mighty arrogant of you, my brother. But I like it. You're as dimwitted as you were when we were young."

Rohnert rose and pointed his Kalimetal at Goran. "You might think that you've gotten the best of me, but hear this brother—the last thing you'll see when you leave this miserable life will be my face."

An arrow struck Rohnert in the neck from behind, and he was certain that he was being put to sleep. He collapsed on the floor, feeling the drug snaking inside his body at an alarming rate. Before he knew it, his eyesight had blurred, and Goran was standing over him.

"Plans change. I'm always one step ahead of you, big brother."

Rohnert saw the sole of Goran's shoes descending on his face before the lights were rudely turned off.

Hours later, the buzzing in his head finally stopped, and his senses began calibrating again. Rohnert had to deal with a splitting headache, and his eyes refused to open. He willed his hand to move, but rattling chains prevented any movement. Doing a quick check, he could tell he'd been beaten to a pulp. His body ached everywhere, and going by the pounding in his head, the bastards had used it as a punching bag.

Someone found his predicament funny, even without making the slightest sound. "Ah, our guest of honor has awoken," Goran said from his right.

"Sire, would you like me to put him to sleep once more?" A shrill, stupid-sounding voice came from the left.

Rohnert whipped his head at the scattered noises around him. He could tell he had an audience. The bastard was a coward.

"Eh, be careful what you think."

Then there was the scent of blood. His. "Goran, you know damn well that the only way you can stop me is to kill me."

"I'm working on it, but first, let's talk."

Rohnert yanked on the chain, but it got him nowhere. "There's nothing to talk about. But I can tell you this—I would love to see you dead."

Goran's laugh echoed across the room. Judging from the way the sound bounced, he was in a big room. There was a burning sensation on his skin. He tried to force his eyes open, but the lids were too swollen.

"Can you feel that burn, my brother?"

Rohnert turned his face to the heat source and recoiled. The bastard was going to kill him in the worst possible way. His self-preservation instincts flared up. If he was going to die now . . .

He stopped thinking.

"Yes. You're as vulnerable as that son of yours at the moment." Goran was so close Rohnert could smell his breath—and the lesions, and the disease.

"The breath of a dying man."

It was obvious he'd struck a chord when Goran growled. "Go to hell."

Another blow landed on the side of Rohnert's face, hard enough to turn his lights off for a second time.

With Rayce guiding them through his satellite navigation system, Harrow and his group arrived at the clearing, finding the Council Elders without a hitch. Harrow scanned the environment and felt his muscles twitch in anticipation.

There was no room for fear, and even if there was a sliver of doubt that they'd come out alive, he pushed it to the back of his mind. Tonight, they would fight against the tyrannical ruler who should have been protecting their race instead of destroying them for standing up for their beliefs.

He spotted the company awaiting their arrival. By the scent in the air, he grasped the general emotions of those around him—excitement and hope mixed with implicit fear. All together, their group was big enough to cause damage. The rest was up to fate.

"Just in time." Wendell offered a tight smile. He was garbed in dark, loose pants and a black turtleneck, and the Elder's group was dressed in similar fashion. Harrow wondered if it was to be able to identify each other in a battle.

He inclined his head to get a better look at the faces of the people he'd be fighting alongside, while Tor positioned himself next to him, bodyguard style. Cyrus took the other side, and he could feel the man's aggression rolling off him in thick waves.

"Are we expecting anyone else?" Serena asked. In her red robe, the female appeared lethal, despite her subdued persona. Holstered around her waist were guns of different types and models, and Harrow couldn't help but smile.

"Rohnert won't be here, if that's what you're asking," Tor answered. If he suspected the female's motives, he showed no indication.

Serena looked away, arching her neck at a proud angle.

A gust of wind alerted them to an incoming group. Everyone readied themselves, Wendell taking the front, which was stupid but very noble. His obvious second-in-command took his flank, and the rest assumed an upside-down V formation.

"If I die tonight, look after Allison."

"Rotten weeds don't die. They linger to annoy the rest of us." Harrow patted Tor's back in understanding.

"Are you ready?" Wendell shouted above the din of rumbling footfalls that spilled like a goddamned disease over the field, surrounding them.

"Here's what we're going to do. Let's wait for them to come to us, and then we can rock and roll." Tor's eyes were trained on the soldiers headed their way.

Harrow flicked his wrist, loosening the joint, and eyed his first target.

"Hold!" Wendell raised his hand. The group drew nearer. The sounds of their boots crunching against the ground echoed all around them. "Hold," he said again when they didn't stop. When they were a hairsbreadth away, he gave the signal. "Let's do this."

Off everyone went. While Harrow concentrated on one man at a time, he tried to keep tabs on his group, making sure Tor and Cyrus were within easy reach should anyone need assistance. A soldier ran toward him at dead speed, aimed his gun, and fired nonstop. Harrow leapt out of the way, avoiding the incoming bullets and deflecting a few with his Kalimetal. He whirled just as the vampire pivoted, the muzzle of his gun trained at Harrow.

It was either him or his opponent. Harrow jacked up and punched the tip of his Kalimetal at the gun, taking the vampire by surprise, and dropped to his feet for the final blow. He sliced through the shoulder down to the torso in one quick swipe. He didn't even look back to see the result before he gunned for his next victim.

The battle swelled with the stench of blood and burning ashes, and he knew that the casualties would be massive. Harrow took the gun from his waistband and fired at will, slinging bullets anywhere he saw robed figures and taking down several vampires.

With one quick glance, he saw Serena being corralled by two opponents, and Harrow wasted no time. He sprinted toward the trio and struck the closest one to him from behind. Serena shrieked before slicing the remaining vampire with her sword.

Harrow moved around, striking and trying to keep up an inventory. Wendell was supremely skilled, while Icarus pranced around like he had built-in hooves. Their confidence radiated in the flow of their movements.

"Gates, don't just stand there. Give me some love here, will ya?" He heard Tor's voice booming from his left.

Sprinting over in his friend's direction, he stopped a few feet away and aimed his gun. He kept firing until he had to reload. Tor flashed a thumbs-up and worked on his next victim. Harrow was pushing the last bullet into the chamber when the sound of a gun firing registered, giving him little time to react. Another blast sounded just before he fell to the ground.

"This sucker came in handy," Serena said of her gun before rushing to his side. "Oh, my." Her hand went to her throat when she got a load of the damage.

"Don't worry. I'm not susceptible to Dangeran," Harrow assured her while he unsheathed the dagger from its holster and worked on a quick fix. He dug the regular blade into his thigh muscle, creating a round entrance, and pulled out part of the bullet. Until he got the other half, he'd be a sitting duck in the middle of the battle field. Out of the corner of his eye, he saw a vampire aiming at Serena, and he pulled a fast one, downing the bastard with a shot to head.

Serena breathed a sigh, and her dark eyes gleamed. "Thanks. Don't worry—I got your back from here on." She jumped up, and Harrow stayed low. Like an imitation of the famous duo, Bonnie and Clyde, they went on a murderous rampage with her covering him from behind.

Smoke from disintegrated ashes rose up into the night sky, filling the air with the scent of burning and blood. Harrow took a quick glance around him to find many of his men still standing. Six out of the thirteen humans he had in tow were still looking for their next victims. Gentry was a tiger unleashed. This was good. Cyrus' every strike was designed to kill, and Tor continued his chatter, not unusual for the character whose voice box had become a curse to them all.

"Stop! Hold your fire." Wendell's order shot across the field. "Devereux is surrendering." It took several tries before every combatant stopped.

When the uneasy announcement was clarified yet again, Harrow tried to get to his feet, but the numbing agent had moved its way down his leg, and he went down on the ground. "Fuck," he said.

"What the fuck, Gates." Tor was at his side, pulling him to his feet and propping his arms around his shoulder. "We're getting out of here."

"The hell we are. This isn't over yet." Harrow tried to push the vampire away, but Serena muscled him back into submission. Tough gal. "This is the thanks I get?"

"Consider the debt repaid." She smiled and left.

"Let's move closer." Harrow tried to move with his good leg until Tor threw him over his shoulder.

"Much better."

"I don't need a babysitter."

"Heard that before. Try using another line." Tor chuckled while they waded through bodies and pile of ashes to get a closer view of the newest development.

Weakened, Harrow caught the part where the man called Devereux announced their surrender before his lights shut off.

The end was near. Rohnert could feel it in his tired and weary bones. Sure, he was still alive and breathing, but the fire burning in his chest would not sustain him for very long. Subjected to twenty-four hours of beating with a Dangeran-tipped whip was beginning to weaken him, and he was close to being useless.

May the best man win.

At least his bastard brother had refrained from beating his face, and his vision was somewhat restored. Though the view was blurry at best, he could tell where he had been taken. The infamous room he'd heard about from wagging tongues was indeed real. The Blanch room was where countless humans were processed like animals to undergo the change. Since when did killing hapless humans become a sport?

"I'm glad you're awake now. I have a proposition to make."

Rohnert threw a disgusted look at Goran, who sat in across from him on a beaten-down chair. More than ever, he swore he wouldn't die now. Not here. Not leaving his son alone without a mother or anyone to show him what living was all about.

With great effort, he summoned what energy was left within him. Rohnert twisted his body until his skin stretched, and his bones rebelled under the shackles binding his ankles and wrists.

He looked at Goran, curling his lips to bare his fangs. "Proposition won't get you anywhere. You've burned your lifeline." His voice came out strangled.

Goran stood up, walked closer, and tilted up Rohnert's chin with the tip of his sword. The blade cut through his skin, but he swallowed back the yelp of protest.

"You and I—let's see who wins."

Fury shot through him, and he tried to break free from his bindings. The struggle was futile, yet he must persevere. Death was knocking, but he sure as hell wouldn't answer the door. Gritting his teeth until his jaw rattled, he pushed against the cold tile.

Goran had the audacity to offer a fight, knowing he had the edge. Rohnert was much too weak to put up much of a challenge.

Who *would* emerge as the victor? Memories of what he'd lost flashed across Rohnert's eyes. It was a reminder that he had failed many, but most of all, he'd failed his family . . . Shelly.

Rohnert nodded. This would be quick, but he wouldn't go down without a fight. Fuck Gastarius and his divine intervention. He would be proven wrong. He probably hadn't foreseen Rohnert's cowardice coming into play.

"Release him!" Goran ordered, circling him.

Two minions ran forward and pulled Rohnert to his feet. The room swirled around while his blurred eyesight tried to register that he was at last vertical. His knees couldn't support his weight, and he stumbled forward. If it hadn't been for the chain still connected to his wrists, he would've face-planted on the floor.

Trying hard not to think of how he'd even compete, he staggered to stand up by widening his stance. The two vampires worked on removing the shackles while Goran continued pacing before him, no doubt trying to read his mind.

Slapping his mind shut, Rohnert arched his back until he heard his bones crack. It provided small relief. He followed Goran's movements with his hazy vision and remembered Lukan's words. He must feed.

Damn her and her warning. He began to hear more voices, those of the new Council members giving Goran a warning before they were shot down with dagger glares from their leader.

"No one interfere here. This is between me and Rohnert." Goran's order reverberated in the silent room. Murmurs of approval and consent rang loud. "Give him back his weapon."

The command was heeded, and the two Kalimetal were tossed in his direction. Powered by the desire to live, or maybe his dumb notion to postpone the inevitable, Rohnert caught the weapons with one hand.

He gripped the handles and ignored the pain shooting from his back with every flex of his muscles. The whip had done its job well. The Dangeran tips had sucked the energy out of his body with every lash. He could barely move his arms, let alone raise the weapon to defend himself.

Goran shed his robe, followed by his shirt, earning a loud gasp from the spectators. Even so, no one dared to say a word.

"You're a vessel of hypocrisy," Rohnert said. He noted the welts across Goran's chest and the wound on his face, which had been concealed from everyone until now.

"Be that as it may, I'm still going to kill you."

Goran threw a death glare across the room, eyeing each one of his minions, guards, and Elders, daring them to say anything about his disease. Everyone kept their traps shut, and that was how it should be.

With a smirk, he unsheathed his sword and raised the weapon above his head. Light hit the metal, casting an ominous gleam for all to see. He looked across the room to his brother, the great Rohnert, Cantor's firstborn, and heard his mutinous growl.

Damn the black book and its missing pages. If it hadn't been for the doctor, he would still be in the dark about too many details. That Rohnert was his older brother was a well-kept family secret. The Council Elders who had protected that secret were now rotting in hell.

Everything boiled down to this moment.

Him against Rohnert.

It was funny how things had worked out. He wasn't the least bit surprised at finding the vampire inside his bedroom, because he'd dreamed about it. Goran had never understood what the dream meant until the sudden prickling of warning he felt. He could thank his dead parents for the gift of self-preservation, because he wasn't ready to go. He planned on hanging around for centuries more.

With his wife, the bitch who'd been missing for several days now, he'd take the Council by its throat and run the show for as long as he liked. Until then, their race would be ruled as he saw fit.

"So much introspection, my brother. Are you getting cold feet?" Rohnert said, his fangs bared, and the look of death swirled around him like nasty weather.

Goran's lips peeled upward to expose his fangs. "Let's see who gets the last laugh."

He watched Rohnert struggle forward, his body undulating on the uncooperative legs beneath him. The whip had been a great idea. He should thank Bretania later on for her creativity.

Gripping his sword, he waited for Rohnert to let go of his thoughts so he could seize the inner secrets his brother was keeping from him. So far, there was nothing.

Short-tempered, he eased into the center of the room, eyes alert and studying Rohnert's every movement. He watched the other vampire raise his weapon to a defensive position with difficulty. Goran noted Rohnert's gnashing teeth while rivulets of sweat mingled with the crusted and fresh blood on his temples and cheeks.

Goran beckoned the guy to move forward, assessing his uneven gait and haggard breathing. This would be too easy. Swinging his sword, he found a good rhythm and was able to gauge his opponent's response.

He tested and pointed the tip of his sword toward Rohnert's chest. Rohnert's eyes locked on his before he batted it away with the Kalimetal. He'd seen his brother at work, remembered the grace and raw power of his strokes, but none of those were present at the moment.

All he got from the man was his agony and the stench of hatred. So be it. He wouldn't let the man wait a minute longer. With a quick thrust, Goran struck hard, landing a descending diagonal blow that Rohnert managed to block with his weapon. His blade slid down the stout Kalimetal blade.

Smart. Rohnert was making up for his weakened condition. He was known for his defensive tactics, which made him lethal in Goran's book.

"Don't make it easy for me to kill you."

Rohnert laughed, but the mirth didn't reach his murderous eyes. "Don't pat yourself on the back too soon. We're not done yet."

In successive motions, Goran rained down strike after strike, hitting nothing but metal. Rohnert continued to block, but Goran could see that his opponent was tired, so he parried some more. Not once had Rohnert counter-attacked.

Goran continued parrying, moving faster to confuse the vampire. Rohnert seemed uncoordinated when he moved around, following Goran while dragging his body with difficulty. Goran attacked again, aiming to split his skull and be done with it, but the one-handed block was solid. Rohnert countered fast with his Kalimetal and struck close to the hilt, and Goran lost his grip, sending the sword flying from his hand.

"So let's see—should I still be worried?" Rohnert lifted a bloodied eyebrow to taunt him.

This time, Rohnert moved faster than Goran would have thought possible. He crisscrossed both metal weapons, despite the pained expression marring his face. Maneuvering against the incoming attack, Goran jumped away, avoiding the slow but precise strike coming his way. With Rohnert's inability to execute a quick offense, Goran managed to evade each fatal blow. With every missed strike, the growing number of spectators reacted louder and louder.

"I didn't think you had it in you to continue living after your human's death."

The room hushed at his callous taunt, everyone watching them with the utmost interest. Goran got to his sword and punched the tip with his foot, and the weapon flew into his grasp. Rohnert's cry filled the room with primal anguish that sounded like it was coming from an animal.

It seemed as though the sucker had enough energy to pose a threat. Enough dallying on his part. It was time to dive down to business. Goran took a deep breath and started on the offensive. With blurring speed, he moved with efficiency, tipping the Kalimetal, pushing Rohnert's defenses to the limit, and confusing the hell out of the weak vampire.

Surprising Rohnert with a kick to the gut, Goran took advantage of his momentary distraction to dislodge both Kalimetal from the vampire's grip when he went down to the ground. With Rohnert cornered and in the worst position possible, Goran stood above his writhing form and sneered.

"I think you're ready for that date with your puny human in hell." He raised his sword tip-down and aimed for the heart.

"Not so fast."

Rohnert looked up and saw the blade descending upon him. Goran had chosen the wrong thing to say. Shelly might not be alive, but wherever she was, she wasn't burning in hell. Unlike where the asshole staring down at him would be heading.

In a burst of energy fueled by rage and the thirst for revenge, Rohnert mustered enough strength to kick Goran in the legs, sending him crumbling to the floor like a broken piece of furniture.

The vampire howled in pain, his legs bent at an angle. Rohnert leered and leapt to his feet, kicking the sword out of the way. He took his time to retrieve his Kalimetal, glancing at the faces of those who were watching them. There was nothing but surprise etched on their expressions, as well as unspoken admiration.

He walked around Goran, checking his emotional grid and knowing full well his brother still had fight left in him.

"I will make this perfectly clear to all. I am Rohnert, son of Cantor, the firstborn denied his rightful place as leader of the Council." Gasps followed his revelation. The Elders present conferred among themselves, but it didn't concern him at all. "Gastarius saw Goran killing both our parents and those who adopted me. All his predictions have come to pass. The truth was hidden from us so that we would become the powerful race he had envisioned."

Rohnert landed a hard kick to Goran's face, sending his brother flying across the room and taking down an innocent bystander with him. His rage continued to boil, which made thinking difficult. His panting breaths were hot, while his chest tightened at the pain he would soon share with the people. His people. He let the idea sink in. These were the same people his son would rule in the future. Somehow, the future didn't seem as appealing as it once had.

"Our race is dwindling because of Goran's greed and ambition. Because of this, I will exercise my authority to execute a course of action. Goran's decree to eliminate every diseased vampire is immoral, and I will grant him the same leniency he afforded them. As a carrier of the disease, he shall be the last one to die from it."

One thought broke into his concentration and altered the course of his actions. Eyeing the dagger in an Elder's waistband, Rohnert zipped faster than the eye could follow and pulled it from the startled Council member's grasp.

Without a word, he pulled Goran up by the hair and dragged him mercilessly to the middle of the room, giving the man who had governed their race into the ground center stage. Defiant onyx eyes met his, and Rohnert ran his tongue along the sharp points of his fangs.

Goran's eyes widened after reading the thoughts Rohnert allowed him to see. Had he seen a lick of fear in the pitiless vampire's eyes? It was too late. Rohnert plunged the dagger into Goran's jugular, and his blood began squirting from the major artery like a broken hydrant. Rohnert walked away, pointing his nose upward at the tainted scent of blood. Death wouldn't come as rapidly as one would wish under the circumstances. The regular dagger would prolong his suffering—a fitting end for a poor excuse for a living being.

A commotion came from the entrance, and Rohnert let out a thundering order. "No one is allowed to kill in this room from now on without my direct order. Let them through."

Wendell, Icarus, and Serena led the group of vampires that included the familiar faces of his friends. Jordan stood proud and tall next to the Elders, and her fangs bared at the sight of Goran. She flashed to Rohnert at an unbelievable speed and got into his grill.

"You promised that I would get to kill him." Her eyes flashed with fury, and she hissed.

Rohnert closed his eyes for a moment, picturing Shelly in all her living glory. He hoped to someday forgive himself for the fate he brought her. Peace would come at a price, but for now, he'd take comfort in the impending demise of the evil in their midst.

He opened his eyes and smiled. "He's not dead *yet*. I saved him for you."

The satisfaction in Jordan's face eased the pain in his tight chest, and she pulled the Kalimetal off her back.

And then he turned away.

The last thing Rohnert heard before he left the room was the pitiful cry of a dead man.

With the Vampire Council in shambles after Rohnert left, a phone call with Wendell had to suffice for the time being. The Elder promised to hold down the fort until the Council had their first post-Goran meeting. Back at the warehouse, Rohnert went straight to the clinic to check on Harrow, who'd been in terrible shape. There had been no medical personnel available since . . .

Damn, he wasn't even going there.

Cheryl looked up from Harrow's bedside. "I did what I could. I don't have enough experience, even after watching Doctor . . ." She paused and shut her eyes, no doubt dispelling painful memories. "I think I got most of it out, but we need a doctor to do the rest."

Rohnert nodded, feeling helpless. He glanced at Harrow on the bed, pale but still obviously in command. Tor was standing in the corner, his eyebrows furrowed with worry. He uncrossed his arms and pinched the bridge of his nose.

"Cheryl, it's okay. We'll figure something out." Harrow acknowledged Rohnert's presence and gestured to the chair. "Is . . . Jordan back yet?"

"She's on her way. Don't worry. She's got Cyrus and Gentry with her." Rohnert parked himself in the chair.

Harrow closed his eyes and sighed. Words weren't necessary to understand his friend's deepest worry. Pain lanced at his heart at the thought of an existence devoid of passion, companionship, and love. He ached for Shelly.

He had to change the topic before he broke down. Rohnert blinked and focused on the IV hanging on a pole. "What's this?"

"Antibiotics. Since Cheryl isn't sure if she got all the Dangeran out, she thinks this will help if infection sets in," Tor replied. "We need to get him to a doctor."

Rohnert clenched his jaw. They had one . . . fuck this.

"It's okay. I think Cheryl did a great job." Harrow struggled to sit up.

"No, it's not, and you know it. Remember what you did to Zane? Want that for yourself?" Tor asked, indignant.

This was more than anyone had bargained for. Rohnert had no idea what to say.

"Will you lay off me? Do you think I enjoy the fucking pain?" Harrow's eyes blazed with annoyance.

The door burst open, and Jordan rushed in. It was safe to say that she had gotten the job done, judging by the blood that stained her face and clothes and the gleam in her eye. She went straight to Harrow.

"Thanks for letting me go," she said, taking his hand and kissing it.

"I can't and won't hold you back." Harrow pulled Jordan closer and pressed his mouth to hers.

Rohnert looked away. While he struggled with his emotions, he began wringing his palms together. What should he do next? Leave?

"Tell me the gruesome details." Harrow patted the mattress, and Jordan sat next to him, her eyes glittered with satisfaction.

Rohnert didn't miss it when Jordan silently asked if she could talk about Goran's demise. He nodded and leaned against the steel chair. Though he knew how things had gone down, Jordan needed this closure.

She took Harrow's hand and began rubbing it, a small smile appearing in the corner of her mouth. "Rohnert left him for me, incapacitated with a regular blade."

Harrow and Tor flinched at the image.

"Since he could no longer talk, I stood over him and waited until he recognized me." It was obvious Jordan was enjoying reliving the moment.

"Did you say anything?" Tor rubbed his palms together.

She grinned with a pure, honest-to-goodness glee that Rohnert had never seen in her. "I just said 'fuck you' before whipping my Kalimetal across his neck. Nothing to it." She smiled with smug satisfaction.

Harrow let out a long sigh while Tor clapped his hands. "Is that the end you were seeking?" Harrow asked.

"Yes." Jordan turned her gaze to Rohnert. "Thank you."

He felt just a sliver of satisfaction. "I have fulfilled my promise. Now if you'll excuse me, I have things to do." He stood up, but before he could clear the doorway, Harrow spoke.

"Listen, we want to give Shelly a proper burial. That is, if you're on board with it. After all, she's your—"

"We leave tonight at sundown. Whoever wants to come is welcome." He scrambled out of the room before he started weeping like a child.

Cyrus paced in his bedroom. This had been become a habit since his transformation. Whenever thinking became a pain in the butt, the repeated movement became an outlet. With Harrow injured and no physician to treat him, permanent damage was a possibility, and that wasn't sitting well with him.

He glanced at his watch and sighed. If he waited until nightfall, it might be too late to reverse the damage of the Dangeran on his friend. Whatever. Since he had no problem with the daylight, he could march into the hospital and figure out how to get help.

Yeah. Sure. Walk in, demand a doctor come with him at gunpoint, and voila. Cyrus shook his head. He needed finesse. Um, another problem there. With him, it was brute force, little yap and more action. That would get him thrown behind bars faster than it would charm anyone.

Nevertheless, he glanced at the mirror to check his appearance. Maybe some of the business clothes Allison made him wear before might soften the rough edges. A blazer to hide the tattoos, a little gel to lighten the severe crew cut, and a smile might do the trick. Maybe not the smile—he doubted the humans would appreciate the fangs.

In a hurry, he shed his jeans and black shirt in favor of the business duds and fixed his hair. He shuddered when he saw the finished product. Oh, well—enough of the make-over. Passing by Rayce's station, he did a quick check on all fighters who had made it back. He had his work cut out for him once he returned.

"I'm taking the Humvee. If Harrow asks, just tell him I'm attending to personal business."

Rayce raised an eyebrow. The human knew him well enough to know this was bullshit. "Need me to track you down?"

"Nah, I'll get back right away." Deep down, he knew the man followed Harrow's orders like they were his bible, and Cyrus would be tracked on his phone's GPS.

It took half an hour to reach the hospital. Damn city traffic. He parked in the marked space for registration and strode to the building. Gone were the caravans of news vans and police cars, but there were a healthy number of security personnel walking around. He kept his head down, trying to blend with the rest of the human population.

There was a somber feel to the atmosphere inside the hospital when he made his way to the elevator. Cyrus had no exact plan, but he would start with the only person who might be able to help him. He tugged at his cream blazer, feeling like a fraud in this get-up.

He stepped out of the elevator and past the nurse's station on his way to Rick's room. There were no guards assigned outside, unlike the first time he'd visited the doctor. He gave a soft knock before pushing open the door. Inside, he found Rick Whitaker sitting on the bed, propped up on several pillows.

Brooding brown eyes met his. Not the warmest welcome, but considering the man's situation, he didn't take offense.

"Hey, Rick, how are you?" Cyrus tried to sound as cheerful as possible.

The doctor gave a nod before pulling a pad and pen from the bedside table. He wrote on the tablet and turned it around for Cyrus to see. *I feel fuckin' great. Thanks for asking. What's going on?*

Cyrus smirked. He liked that—no fuss and straight to the point. "We're in a little bind. With Shelly . . ." He paused when the doctor flinched and closed his eyes.

Rick's lips quivered, no doubt trying not to wuss out in front of him. It took a few moments before his eyes snapped open, but by then he seemed more collected.

Cyrus continued. "Harrow has been injured, and he needs medical attention. I wondered if you know anyone who could help us."

Rick didn't move or make any attempt to use the pad to communicate, prompting Cyrus to think that maybe he wasn't going to help. "Well, I apologize for wasting your time. I'll leave you alone now." He blew out an impatient breath and turned for the door.

A god-awful sound came from the bed, and he whipped around to see Rick trying to speak. Damn it. He walked back to the bedside and placed a hand on the doctor's shoulder. "It's okay. No need to get excited. Write it down."

The man scribbled in a mad rush and showed him the paper. I want out. They're conducting an internal investigation, and I will be questioned. I don't think I'm up for it. Will you put me up at the warehouse?

Okay, so the doctor was basically seeking asylum. Who was Cyrus to turn him away? Their group needed a resident physician. In a normal situation, he would ask Harrow's opinion, but the vampire needed to be seen right away. Cyrus could make the decision and face whatever repercussions there were later.

"Is it going to be a problem to get you out of here?" he asked, already casing the entire room, the windows, and the door.

Rick wrote on the pad again, the tip of the pen making a furious scratching sound on the paper. We're not using the windows. We'll pretend to go out to get some air. We can use the service elevator. Get your car and meet me in the physicians' parking garage.

Cyrus was so on board with Rick's idea. After the doctor managed to climb out of bed with his assistance, they walked out of the room, past the nurse's station to the service elevator commonly used by maintenance and nursing personnel. He took a quick look to see if anyone was paying attention to them. Every employee seemed too caught up in their own tasks to even notice them. Once outside, he left Rick leaning against the wall and ran to get the car. Within minutes, Rick was loaded in and they were flying down the city streets en route to the warehouse.

Rohnert felt something tug in the pit of his stomach when he was getting out of the shower. It had been a painful morning so far, both physically and emotionally. He couldn't stop thinking of Shelly, and the more he tried, the more agitated he'd become. The one thing that helped pass the time was sparring. Tor had been gracious enough to oblige. Maybe it was his need to feed that made him almost nauseous, because Tor had easily beat him twice before he called it quits.

Dressing up in jeans and a dark long-sleeved shirt, he walked out of his room to visit with Malin. Allison had been kind to offer to watch the baby for him while he sorted out his head. In the hallway, he was alerted to a one-sided conversation between Cyrus and . . . shit. Rick.

Rohnert broke into a jog and found the two men walking into the clinic. They both looked over their shoulders at him. Their eyes met, and in an instant, Rick's mind went into overdrive. A cacophony of broken memories chronicled that fateful night, and the horror of what he'd seen and what had been done to him and Shelly came into clear focus.

Cyrus looked at him then at Rick. Rohnert couldn't take another step, and he braced his body against the wall, weak with grief at the images he'd seen. Rick appeared confused until Cyrus ushered him into the room. He came back to Rohnert, who was still leaning on the wall and heaving.

"I know from experience that is a sign you need to feed."

"I can't. There's no one . . ."

"Shelly told me that you fed from Isidora once."

Rohnert couldn't take it. It felt like he was violating his vow to his mate. Not now, not when she'd just died.

"I can't." Before Cyrus could do anything, he made a run for it back to the silence and comfort of his room.

Once alone, he went to the walk-in closet and pulled out a regular dagger. He shed his shirt on his way to the bathroom and stood in front of the sink. Turning on the spigot, he twisted his left arm around and began slashing through his healthy skin. This would mark the beginning of the daily purging he would observe for the rest of his existence. He would bear the burden of his wife's death.

Tears trickled down his face when the first drop of blood slid down his arm. He cried while chanting the silent prayers for the soul of his beloved.

It might have been due to exhaustion or lack of proper nourishment that Rohnert had passed out on the bathroom floor. Next thing he knew, Tor was nudging him awake.

"Hey, my man, what's going on here?"

Rohnert squint his eyes, trying to get a grip on himself. He looked around in daze and discovered his body sitting in a pool of blood.

"Nothing." He ignored the outstretch hand and got up. His eyesight spun, and he braced himself on the bathroom sink. "What time is it?"

"Seven. I'm going with you." Tor didn't wait for a response. Instead, the vampire walked out of the bathroom and hovered by the sitting area.

Rohnert appreciated the time alone. The last thing he needed was someone fussing over him. He washed up and retrieved the discarded shirt from the floor.

"I'm ready." He didn't bother securing his weapon. He didn't expect any more threats in their lives now that the bastard had bitten the dust. His only concern was to get Shelly back and properly mourn her.

Tor pulled up in the bulletproof sedan, and Rohnert slid into the passenger seat. They drove through the city in total silence. Nothing needed to be said. Tor understood this, and Rohnert was grateful for the moment of peace. He leaned against the headrest and tried to calm his shot nerves. Once they got to the hospital, Rohnert took advantage of his mind-scrambling ability on each human who laid eyes on them, putting them on momentary pause. Tor hurried to the hospital control room and did a loop-de-loop on the cameras and met Rohnert on his way to the morgue.

Rohnert continued to mess with the brain circuitry of anyone they encountered. Tor did a quick scan on the computer to locate Shelly's body while Rohnert waited with mounting impatience.

"Fuck!" Tor muttered.

Rohnert didn't bother asking but shoved his friend aside. The mortician's remark stated that Shelly's body had gone missing. No clearance had been given, and no trace had been left behind.

The room grew quiet except for the hum of the air conditioner. Tor looked at Rohnert, mouthing words he couldn't understand. Total stillness. Eerie silence. He couldn't move for a moment . . . or two.

Rohnert blanked out for several seconds before the neurons began firing and this new discovery seeped in. Little by little, the fact slithered into his brain while rage worked its way into his heart. He screamed until the whole room quaked under the intense weight of his raw fury. Air sucked in, vibrated and splintered everywhere as if oxygen had its own solid form.

Flat on his back again. *This shit is getting old fast*, Harrow thought as he made himself comfortable in the narrow bed in the clinic. Just like Shelly had liked it, the machine with its cord attached to his body made a loud beeping sound, alerting everyone within a one mile radius.

"For crying out loud." He began peeling off the wiring connected to his arm

"Doctor's orders," Isidora said when she entered the room, followed by Rick. She reconnected the wires while Rick issued silent orders. As it turned out, the female had the same talent as Rohnert, in part thanks to Iden, her murdered father. This gift came in handy, considering Rick's inability to communicate. It made the process easier and gave Isidora something to do. Plus, the doctor obtained a translator.

"Why am I not surprised to see you trying to be a he-man?" Rick said via Isidora.

"Oh, shut it. I just wanted a drink of water." He eyed the doctor with calculating eyes. Rick was Shelly's friend, and as such had been a part of the collateral damage.

There was a soft knock on the door, and then Cyrus slipped inside. "I heard the beep." He nodded at Rick before his gaze lingered on Isidora, who returned a shy smile.

Harrow grinned. This felt like déjà vu. He'd seen it between Rohnert and Shelly when Cyrus was flat on his back. Jesus, give him an arrow and dress him as cupid.

"That sucker isn't a beep. It's a freakin' siren."

"Shelly told me a lot about you people. Stubborn asses . . ." Isidora stopped, turning red. "Um, I'm not sure I can do the, um, *blunt* kinds of comments you guys are used to."

Rick placed a hand on her shoulder and tipped her chin so she could watch his face. During their silent conversation, Harrow watched Cyrus's body turn taut while he ground his molars together.

Bingo! And he'd thought the man was a monk. Harrow almost chuckled but stopped himself in time.

"Ah, okay . . . what's next for me?" he asked, breaking the silence for the sake of his friend's sanity.

"You're going to be on bed rest for two more days, then no patrolling until I clear you."

Harrow narrowed his eyes. He'd heard this before. "Are all doctors out to punish their patients?"

"Only . . ." Isidora's eyes widened, and she continued. "Only when you're acting like a child. I changed that. I'm afraid Rick will need a few lessons in the use of vulgar words." She laughed and threw a quick glance at Cyrus.

The vampire squirmed in the corner, making Harrow shake his head.

Another knock came from the door.

"We know, you heard the beeping," they said in unison, then laughed when Jones peeked in.

"Wow, looks like there's a party here." Jones let himself into the already crowded room. "Am I interrupting?"

"Hey, my man. No, you're not. What's up?" Harrow watched the scientist fiddle with a piece of paper, a nervous expression lacing his face. In the year or so he'd known Jones, he hadn't seen him nervous. The guy was a walking mass of self-confidence.

"I think I may have found the cure for our little disease." He held the paper up, waving it in the air with a triumphant grin.

There was another knock on the door. Jordan, Tor, and Allison squeezed into the tight space.

"Hey, honey. Jones said to meet him here." Jordan walked toward Harrow's bedside and pressed a kiss to his mouth.

"This is cozy. I'm so touched, you guys." They laughed. "Where's Rohnert?"

"He passed on coming," Tor said in a solemn voice. "I already discussed this with him and Jones this morning."

"What's going on?" Harrow held Tor's gaze.

"When Rohnert threw that black book in the lounge, I picked up the papers and read a few. I came across some scribble about a disease and the cure. It said something about a baby, so I ran it by Jones. Turns out, Shelly also instructed him to cross-check Malin's blood. Why don't I let Jones explain the rest of the mumbo jumbo?"

Harrow took a deep breath and readied himself for the news. "Bring it, Jones."

Jones adjusted his glasses and waggled his eyebrows. One would have thought the scientist had finally lost it. "I have here Leroy's theory about the disease and how animal blood might be the solution. In his notes, he claimed that when a diseased vampire consumes human blood, which is what its body is used to, it feeds and keeps the virus active and running. Human blood triggers action in the virus, keeping it alive.

"Then with an animal blood's X-protein, you get the opposite effect upon ingestion. The virus, like the animal blood, is foreign matter. They are both threats to your system, but combined together, they don't impede on each other. The X-protein neutralizes the virus on contact, so it halts the virus in its dormancy. Your immune system sees the animal blood as food and does not push it into any adverse reaction."

Everyone stared at Jones, and he chuckled. "Sorry. I had to give you the preliminary findings that worked to put the disease in an inactive state. When Tor mentioned Malin, it reminded me of one conversation I had with Shelly. She instructed me to draw a small amount of Malin's blood and cross reference it with your blood, Harrow, since you're our guinea pig."

Harrow drew an impatient breath. "I know, I know. Then what?" he prodded.

"I drew a small amount after Rohnert gave his consent and placed a drop of the baby's blood inside a vial that contained yours." Jones paused, waving his hand with dramatic flair.

"What?" everyone asked at the same time.

"Well, it seems like Malin's blood acts like a repairing agent."

When everyone shot him a blank stare, Jones took the piece of paper and started a haphazard illustration. When he finished, Rick took the piece of paper, studied it for a moment, and nodded.

"Rick is saying that he's following your train of thought now." Isidora smiled.

"Which is still Greek to all of us," Tor interjected, making everyone in the room laugh.

Jones rolled his eyes and shook his head. "Okay, see these little dots with the tiny follicles?" When they nodded, he continued. "That is Harrow's blood."

"You need a shave, man," Cyrus, who had been quiet up till now, quipped.

"Will you guys cut out the jokes? I'm dying here," Allison said.

"Okay, Malin's blood contained a healthy dose of plasma. A normal human's blood is a little over fifty percent plasma. Because of the disease, Harrow's blood doesn't have enough. Ingestion of blood, human or animal, gives him strength and energy, but it fails to get rid of the infection. However, mixed with Malin's blood, Harrow's is less sedentary."

No one seemed to follow him. Rick was the lone person nodding. "Look at it as the enabler, transportation, or anticoagulant. There is more flow or action in the system."

"Okay, I think I'm grasping the concept. But if Malin's blood is the answer, how come Goran was susceptible to the disease? And Shelly was human." Jordan's eyebrows creased.

All heads whipped in Jones' direction for the answer. "I have two theories on that. One, the mix of Rohnert's and Shelly's blood mutated, creating a little miracle worker. Number two—divine intervention. Shit. I don't know. This is something I haven't seen before. I can't explain it yet."

"Let's say I'm buying your bullshit—what happens to them now?" Tor challenged.

"Since our source is a child, and an infant at that, I suggest we go slow and draw a small amount. One small vial would be enough to cure two infected vampires a week." Jones shrugged.

"And do we take human or animal blood after that?" Harrow asked, still unable to wrap his mind around the new discovery. After all these years, they might be staring at the answer he'd been waiting for.

"Here's what I suggest. Keep with the animal blood diet for the first week, since we already know that the strain responds well to it. Then we can have you try human/vampire blood after, and see how your system reacts. You would do the same activity as before, and if the results are positive for noninfection, then you can make your choice," Jones concluded.

"And how about the *you know*," Tor asked, looking hopeful.

"We'll be doing active tests after that. I can't promise it'll be safe to do *you know*, but further testing will give us more answers."

After a few more questions and answers, everyone dispersed, chatting about the possibilities that were lining up on the horizon. Each of them felt hopeful, which left Harrow reeling.

"What if it goes flat?" He took Jordan's hand and kissed it.

"Then you are no worse off than you are now," she said, smiling at him.

He thought about her response and sighed. "I'm going to cross my fingers."

"Hey, I loved you then, and I love you more now. Infected, diseased, or not, nothing is going to change."

Harrow pulled her into an embrace. "I love you more than ever, you know that?"

Jordan nodded and then looked up, her amber eyes sparkling. "I worry about Rohnert."

"I feel the same way, but he's tough. He'll get over it."

"I don't know. I have a bad feeling about this."

He traced his fingers along her face. "I feel his pain, and I can see him holding back. My concern is for when he blows up."

"Then we'll be there for him."

He closed his eyes, holding Jordan close. "That's all we can do."

Rohnert heard a soft knock outside his chamber. "Enter."

Massey, Wendell's trusted guard, entered and bowed low. "Sire, the Council is waiting."

The first Council meeting under his rule had been postponed several times in the months following Goran's death. Rohnert's inability to function, to even think, had led to the suspension of the assembly until further notice. However, he could no longer delay the reunion, even if his heart wasn't in it.

"I'll be there in a few minutes." He waited until the guard left before he collapsed into a chair. Before him were journals, petitions, and proposals awaiting his stamp of approval. Although he felt he wasn't ready for life-altering decisions that could change the race's course, there wasn't a good reason to wait any longer. He had to do this for his son and the thousands of souls who deserved a fair ruler.

He took a bracing breath. The sting lingered, and he doubted that it would ever go away. There was no forgetting the woman who had made him a better man, and yet her death shook the very foundation of his being, leaving him bereft. Sure he woke up, fed, and attended to everyone's needs, but just to keep himself occupied. His responsibilities to his son and the

Council kept him from dwelling on the pain of Shelly's absence.

Hatred was a punishing companion. It was eating up his soul little by little until soon there would be nothing left but an empty shell.

Rohnert shoved himself to his feet, putting one foot before the other until he stopped in the doorway. He needed another minute. One question kept jabbing at him. How could he lead if his heart, mind, and soul had been taken from him?

Frustration hummed in his skull, yet he walked down the hallway and into the limelight to face the firing squad. The medal hung heavy around his neck, a grim reminder of the task before him. Garbed in the finest robe, as befitted the leader in the highest seat, he tugged at his black and golden garments and gestured to the guards at the door.

The two guards bowed and opened the door to reveal the surviving Elders who had not been caught in the killing spree. Once the door closed behind him, Rohnert walked the length of the red carpet, which bore the seal of the Council. He took note of the general emotions of those around him. Wendell, Icarus, and Serena, the loyal Elders who had stood by him and his group, dipped their heads in veneration, and he acknowledged their respect and loyalty with a handshake.

Rohnert took his time with introductions to the newer members, intent on solidifying their commitment and trust. After all, it was imperative that all members be on the same page. With the new proposal he was about to present, there was much to be done toward rebuilding their beleaguered group.

He reached the bottom of the five steps that would take him to his seat, thought better of it, and spun around.

"I'd rather sit next to you, my brothers and sisters. We all share the same importance, and I would rather see each one of you on equal footing."

A general roar of approval greeted his declaration. Rohnert pulled up a chair next to a newly inducted Elder, prompting everyone to form a circle, which gave each one a better view of the others.

Rohnert proceeded. "Our pride and belief in a common goal had been tainted, and I expect every single one of us to restore that and embrace our given responsibilities. I have made an informed decision about what each of your primary tasks will be going forward."

He looked over at the vampire on his right. "Icarus, you will be the designated keeper of records."

"It would be an honor to serve in this capacity." He inclined his head toward Rohnert and then to the rest.

"Serena, I entrust the Council's finances to you. I expect a written report on a monthly basis."

"As you wish." Serena smiled.

"Wendell, your courage and leadership were proven in the last conflict. I believe you would better serve this Council by taking charge as a tactician and weapons expert. Will you take on that responsibility?"

The vampire gave a tentative nod.

"Excellent. I have good people who would be happy to serve under your command."

This brought a grin to his face. "I have seen them firsthand, and it would be an honor to have them in the group and to serve under your rule, sire."

Rohnert paused. Titles didn't interest him at all, but this could be addressed later. "Bardos, you will be the Council liaison," he said to a young vampire sitting next to Icarus.

Bardos bowed his head. While Rohnert called out the roles of the other two members, he finally began to see a ray of hope. Maybe it wasn't too bad after all.

When the group settled, he went for the meatier subject.

"There will be no hunting of diseased vampires from now on. We have a cure in our hands. The process will be slow, but I expect we will able to reach out to most of our population over the next two years."

The announcement sent everyone's spirits soaring. Rohnert couldn't help but smile at their enthusiasm. "I forbid the mass initiation of humans. They are to be left alone. If feeding is required, it is to be done with the utmost secrecy." This would be tricky, but their genetic make-up gave them no other choice.

"Bretania is still unaccounted for. We're not sure if Goran's mate has been killed, but we will continue to search for her."

Icarus raised his hand. "I will make it my personal mission to find her, or information concerning her fate, as soon as possible."

Rohnert bowed his head in appreciation of the vampire's initiative.

"I will personally look at our by-laws and make changes as I see fit. Those changes will be subject to the Council's approval. There are many outdated rules I feel are no longer necessary. We need to usher in change, good change that will benefit our people."

"I agree," Regrita, a female vampire with an intense expression, chimed in.

"We will hold a monthly meeting, and I expect each of you to attend. Remember, we are building from the ground up, so I need everyone's cooperation. I don't plan on residing here full time since I have a child who needs my attention, but I will be at your disposal any time of the day or night."

At the conclusion of the meeting, Rohnert felt lighter, as if a burden had been lifted from his shoulders. If he could just get rid of the weight of guilt in his heart.

"Hey." Serena approached him, looking quite regal in her ceremonial robe. Her easy smile made Rohnert relax a bit.

"Hello, Serena."

"You did well today."

"Thank you. It's a relief to get over the initial hurdle." Rohnert began walking toward the exit. He didn't want to cut the conversation short, but there was a part of him that couldn't reconcile being in the company of another woman.

"I meant to tell you because I am aware of the complications on your part—"

"Yeah?"

"If you need to feed, I would be happy—"

"Thank you for your kind offer, but I have to go." Rohnert fled the assembly room as if his ass was on fire. That was so not happening.

An hour later, he was back at the warehouse, ready to tackle another meeting with his family and friends. But first, he had to take some time away from it all. He took the stairs until he reached the deck.

Aside from the muted sound of the city traffic, there was a serene quality to the environment. The night air was clear and crisp. Bright stars were evenly spaced in the nighttime sky, lending a soft illumination to the otherwise dark surroundings. Rohnert sat on the ledge and let his legs dangle idly.

The deaths of so many friends had been a substantial setback for them all. Now that each deceased member had been memorialized, they were yet again in the rebuilding stage. Having Rick at the helm in the clinic had been both a blessing and a curse, since the physician would always be a grim reminder of what he'd lost. With Isidora as his willing source of nourishment, Rohnert himself should be on the path toward healing. Each feeding brought physical gratification, but it was also killing him inside. Shelly's memory continued to haunt his every waking hour, and the fact that her body had disappeared left unfinished business that continued to claw at his sanity.

They still had so much to do, but they were a resilient group, and each adversity made them stronger. Rohnert wished he could make himself believe the same was true for him. Perhaps only time would tell.

A familiar thought pattern flitted from behind him.

"Jordan, I don't mind company." Rohnert looked over his shoulder at the woman he considered both a sister and a friend. He patted the space next to him. "Come enjoy the quiet with me."

Jordan walked with grace and leapt to the spot with confidence. He watched her close her eyes and take a deep breath, contentment radiating from her.

"I want to thank you again for giving me the closure I needed." She opened her eyes and let her gaze linger on his face.

He turned away, refusing to let her see his true emotions. "I try to make good on my promises."

"Hey, look at me," she said, taking his hand in hers.

Rohnert moved his head until he was looking into her eyes. It was difficult not to yearn for Shelly while in the presence of one of her dearest friends.

"It's going to be tough, I know. I won't even begin to tell you how bad it might get. But I want you to know that I'm always here for you, even if it's just to listen or be silent company."

"Thank you."

"I can't promise a happy ending, but with the same strength you provided me in my darkest hours, I won't stop looking for Shelly, to get you the closure you seek."

Rohnert smiled, remembering the time when he'd convinced Jordan to find her way back into Harrow's arms. He could only wish a higher being would afford him the same reward. Perhaps the key to happiness was letting go of the guilt and accepting what fate had handed him. It would be a long path to healing and acceptance. With the aid of his friends, the family he held dear to his heart, it wasn't impossible.

He looked up at the stars and located the brightest one. This made him think of Shelly with all her spunk, spirit, and zest for life. His chest constricted once more, an all-too-familiar ache that would undoubtedly be his constant companion.

"Shelly's up there." Rohnert pointed at the brightest star of all. "She's looking down at us, telling me to stop sulking, get my head out of my ass, and fight on."

"Indeed, she is," Jordan agreed.

Sneak Peek from
Reckoning,
the fourth book in
The Gates Legacy series
by Lorenz Font

"Please don't hurt him," the woman pleaded.

Cyrus stepped out of the darkened patch in which he'd been hiding and broke into a sprint. The air was stifling, and even at midnight the summer heat was on full blast. He moved quickly, passing parked cars and rundown establishments, while his boots slammed on the pavement with dull thuds. From the corner of his eye, he saw Gentry streak across the street in pursuit of their newest project.

The female's plea echoed in his head.

The male vampire Cyrus was pursuing was fast, considering his ailment. It made Cyrus wonder what in the hell he was worried about. In the six months since Jones had introduced the idea of a cure, a flood of diseased vampires had lined up on their doorstep. Well, that wasn't exactly accurate. They had been given an address where they could sign up. After attending a few counseling sessions, they were deemed worthy of little Malin's gift.

It had now been six months since they'd discovered the gift Malin's birth had brought them. The son of the Vampire Council's new leader, Rohnert, the half-vampire, half-human child, had no idea how precious his blood was to their race. From the time he was two months old, he had been contributing small amounts of blood, which was used to cure those infected with *Incomis Sippanus*.

Tack Enterprises certainly had come a long way. What had begun with one man's search to cure his infected daughter was now an organization dedicated to protecting and treating the diseased vampires who had, until recently, been hunted down and reviled. No matter how slow the production of the antidote, the positive results spoke for themselves. Harrow Gates, the unwitting source of the contagion, had taken over Tack Enterprises upon the death of its founder. He led the Tack team in its efforts to respond to the countless requests for help from the vampires who suffered from his legacy.

"He's going to jump." Gentry's warning broke into Cyrus' rumination, and he refocused. The male they'd been pursuing had reached the harbor. He stopped, looked over his shoulder with a laugh, and plunged into the water.

That was where Cyrus drew the line. He wasn't going swimming. Skidding into a halt by the edge of the waterfront, he traced the man's trajectory.

There was no sense in wasting precious time and resources on someone who didn't want their help. It was time to move on.

"Have fun swimming," Cyrus muttered under his breath.

"Where to now?" Gentry asked from behind him.

The soldier had been an excellent addition to their group. A vampire loyal to Rohnert and the Council, he had been relegated to serving as the royal babe's bodyguard since the child's human mother had been killed. When he found some downtime away from his prime responsibility, he served as the point of contact for those who sought the cure.

"Back to the facility."

They turned to the deserted street and found the woman waiting for them. Her face fell when she realized her runaway son was not with them.

Cyrus offered an apologetic smile. "If he doesn't want our help, we can't force him. I'm sorry."

"He doesn't know what's good for him," she said, her voice breaking.

"That is why we prefer they come to us on their own."

"Will you give him another chance?"

How touching. If all mothers were like this female, then there might be some hope left after all. At least Rohnert's reign had stopped the shunning and slaughtering of the infected ones that had been carried out under Goran's orders.

"Of course. Gentry here will take care of him." Cyrus turned to leave.

The woman caught his arm, and when their eyes locked, she offered a feeble smile. "Thank you. You're heaven sent."

Cyrus didn't bother telling her that he and heaven were poles apart. The truth was he was living on borrowed time, and his sworn vendetta against Zane, the man who had robbed him of his humanity, cast a shadow over whatever was left of his soul. Once Tack Enterprise's new venture was up and running, he planned to heed the dictates of his heart and follow a different path. He wanted revenge.

It was easier said than done, of course. There were a million things that needed his attention before he could pursue Zane.

Rayce paged him with a summons to the control room the moment they reached the underground facility. Then his phone beeped with a message from Harrow to meet him in the I-room. Yeah, he was everyone's go-to guy.

"Go ahead. I'll catch up with you later." He slapped Gentry on the shoulder and made a beeline for the control room.

Before Goran had been defeated, he had ordered his grandson, Zane, to take them out. The damage had been substantial, and Cyrus' blood boiled whenever he thought of the asshole who had changed him. His *daddy*, as Tor never failed to remind him. With Goran's downfall, they had returned to the Tack Enterprises' original underground facility. The place had been retrofitted and given an extensive make-over after a security breach and infiltration.

During that dark time, they'd had to abandon the facility and set up shop in a refurbished warehouse. However, the Vampire Council had begun to move in a positive direction under Rohnert's guidance. Since their lives weren't threatened anymore, returning to their first home had been an easy decision to make.

"You need me?" Cyrus asked when he entered the control room.

Rayce spared him a quick glance before returning his attention to the bank of ten monitors. His mop of brown hair was sticking out in all directions, which made Cyrus wonder if the man had trouble sleeping—or just grooming. If it was the former, that would make two of them.

The tech guy punched the keyboard, and several monitors flickered then zoomed. "Look at this," Rayce said.

Cyrus directed his attention to one, and his heart skipped. Isidora was inside the shooting range, firing a Sig. Her form was perfect. Her stance wide enough to withstand the recoil, and her focus was intent on the target.

She had been a diligent student—always on time, never missing a session—but she preferred one-on-one instruction, which still baffled him. Not that he was complaining.

"Um . . . what made you think I needed to see this?" he asked, eyeing the younger man with annoyance.

Rayce gave him a sheepish grin. "Well, she's your student. I thought you might be interested in keeping tabs on her progress."

And there you are, folks. The teasing has already started. Cyrus regulated his breathing before flashing his fangs at the human. "Stop hanging out with Tor. He's turning you to the dark side."

Cyrus took one last look at the monitor before exiting the room. Rayce's laughter followed him on his way to the I-room. Blast the damn human. He was lucky his control room was such a godsend.

Harrow and Tor had complained about the lack of privacy before, but Cyrus had thought it was silly. After all, it was for their own protection. But now that he, too, was under the microscope, he realized he wasn't too crazy about the cameras pointing in every direction. Their fallen leader, Pritchard Tack, had been too engrossed with his people's affairs.

Cyrus opened the door of the I-room and found Harrow watching the same segment. "You guys are not funny," he said, marching straight to the libation station. He picked his favorite bottle and poured.

Harrow turned and snickered. "You're like a brother to me, and you know I only want what's best for you. Right—"

"Cut the crap, Gates. What do you want from me?"

Harrow turned somber, which made Cyrus roll his eyes. *Here we go.*

"I want you to be happy . . ."

"Oh, please. Not that speech again. Can we just skip the sentimental bullshit and tell me what you want to do with the Naples account." That should shut the boss up. Slap Harrow with business decisions to take the focus away from Cyrus. It always worked.

Harrow gave him a knowing look—no doubt the man had caught on to his evasion tactic. "You have a meeting with the CEO tonight?"

Cyrus nodded and pulled the glass to his lips, downing the first of many drinks of the night. At the rate he was going, he might as well buy stock in Caol Ila. He'd been drinking the single malt whiskey like it was water.

"I'm meeting him at his home. I told him I have an early flight, and that was the only open time in my schedule." That was bullshit, of course, and Harrow knew it. He had reserved his daytime hours for scouring the city for traces of Zane, who had vanished without a trace.

Harrow gave him a dubious glare but said nothing. Cyrus waited while he pulled a sheet of paper from a folder, signed it, and handed it to Cyrus.

"That should seal the deal. Tell Jack that his order is guaranteed to ship in four weeks."

Cyrus scanned the contract, and after a thorough check, got to his feet. "I'll pass it on." He turned to the door.

"Hey, man, are you sure you're all right?" Harrow asked, removing his sunglasses to look him in the eye.

Despite the cure, the damage to Harrow's eyes had been too extensive to reverse. Looking into his whitish eyes was a bit creepy, but this was getting old.

"I'm great. Couldn't be better."

Cyrus left him shaking his head and marched straight to his bedroom. Any more questions about his state of mind and he was going to scream. He slammed the door and collapsed on the sofa. If everyone kept treating him like a live grenade, he really would explode. He glanced at the digital clock on the wall and gritted his teeth. His appointment with the guy from Naples was in an hour. If he wanted to make it on time, he'd better get in the shower quick.

Isidora worked the mouse and moved her target closer. On inspection, it was riddled with bullets, which were concentrated around the chest area. This made her smile. She moved the target back then reloaded.

This had been her nightly ritual since she began training with Cyrus eight months ago. Once her teacher left for the night, she would engage in nonstop practice, further developing the skills she wouldn't have in her wildest dreams imagined she possessed. Under Cyrus's tutelage, she had tried several different weapons, and the guns seemed to be the ones that worked for her. They also spent countless hours sparring, which had produced dismal results, in her opinion. Though Cyrus continued to encourage her, she wished he would give up on ever teaching her hand-to-hand combat.

She had been cooped up inside ever since she arrived—first in the warehouse, and then in the underground facility. It wasn't much different from the conditions she'd left behind except that instead of being hidden away in a mansion, she was thirty feet underground, in the company of both humans and vampires.

However, this time it was no one's doing but her own. She hadn't expressed a desire to go out to anyone at the facility. The first and the last time she had ventured outside her sanctuary, her world had been turned upside down. Her beloved Finn had been killed trying to defend her, and the little hope she had of a normal life had blown away with his ashes.

Pushing aside her gloomy thoughts, she focused on the target once more. Isidora cleared her mind of all the clutter, zooming in on the limbless, headless torso and firing. The sound exhilarated her, and the force of the recoil pulled at her strengthening muscles. She was getting better.

The door suddenly opened, and Jordan, Harrow's mate, walked in. Her red hair was pulled into a severe ponytail, but her eyes were much kinder than they'd been the first time they met. After Goran's defeat, Jordan's personality had undergone a drastic change. The female had been one of Goran's many creations, and her life's purpose had been to eradicate the vampire. Her mission had since been accomplished, and the facility inhabitants reaped the benefits of her new positive outlook.

"Issy, you've already proven yourself with the guns. I think you're ready for the Kalimetal," Jordan said. Her eyes had same the familiar twinkle they held whenever she suggested the idea to Issy.

Isidora put down the gun and removed her protective goggles and ear plugs. "I'm not as graceful as you want me to be. We both know it." She smoothed her long floral skirt and headed to Cyrus' desk. Without him around, she took comfort in spending her quiet hours using his desk to read.

"Well, let's see. Recalling my first time, I wasn't exactly well coordinated. Ask Rohnert—he'll tell you how many times he wound up smacking my hands with the Arnis." Jordan shed her jacket to reveal a well-formed upper body that hadn't lost its feminine curves. "And you have to lose the skirt. I believe in freedom of movement, and dresses and skirts would be a liability during a fight."

"I'm open to suggestions," Issy said.

Allison, the coheir of the Tack fortune and Pritchard's daughter, had asked her several times what she needed. Too timid to impose on her benefactors, Issy had asked for the type of clothes she had been used to wearing at home.

"If you're serious about this, I'm going to get you the proper clothes, although I think it'll be better if you choose what you prefer." Jordan sat on the chair, grabbed a pen and paper, and scribbled down something. "Here— it's the link to a site that carries every style you can think of. We have an account with them, so all you have to worry about is finding what you want."

Issy glanced at the paper and grimaced. She hadn't been taught how to use the computer, let alone go shopping on the Internet. Her father hadn't believed in modern technology, preferring to raise his daughter according to the old traditions.

"Hey, what's with the long face?" Jordan was too perceptive.

Isidora shook her head. "Nothing."

Jordan studied her for a moment and then sighed. "Tell me if I'm overstepping my boundaries here. I'm going to make a wild guess and say that you're not quite sure how to use a computer."

Issy looked down, feeling suddenly small. For Christ's sake, they were in the twenty-first century, but she'd been left behind after being sequestered all her life. She slowly nodded. There was no use hiding it. When she looked up again, Jordan was watching her with those kind, amber eyes.

"You have nothing to worry about. I'm going to teach you everything you need to know."

Grateful, Isidora could only smile.

Rohnert collapsed on the chaise after concluding his fourth official Council meeting. He had retreated to his personal chamber in the hopes of getting a short reprieve from the never-ending demands of his position. Being the head of the illustrious group was just as tough as he'd imagined it would be.

The Council had been through rapid and extensive changes. This growth pleased him, but at the same time, his energy was at an all-time low. Even so, the repeated pleas for him to take a break had fallen on deaf ears.

As long as he was working, he couldn't think, so he spent all his time with his child, running the Vampire Council, and training. He didn't want to remember why he was taking care of a growing child single-handedly— didn't want to think of the hole in his heart his mate had left behind when she died. Teaching and training gave him the chance to impart his knowledge of martial arts, but they also gave him an outlet for his pent-up rage. He was hurting more than he let on.

Parenthood had its rewarding and frustrating moments. Jordan and Allison had both been a great help to him, as well. When the two female vampires had offered their babysitting services, Rohnert took them up on their offer, knowing his little boy would be in good hands. They would give their lives for Malin and protected him as if he were their own.

A loud knock sounded at his chamber door. There was no need to look to know who was waiting outside. Such a loud inner voice could only belong to someone with an equally big mouth.

"Come in, Tor," he called out and leaned against the chair to wait.

Tor opened the door with his usual flourish, chuckling. "You're one piece of work, you know that?"

No matter how long they'd been friends, Tor still couldn't come to terms with his mind-reading skills. Rohnert gave a hearty laugh.

It went without saying how grateful he was for Tor and Cyrus' help with the new soldiers' training. Tor had been a mean machine, working the troops to the ground under the watchful eye of Wendell, the newly appointed tactician and weapons expert. Cyrus also had been pitching in whenever his schedule permitted.

Tor sat on the ornate chair opposite him and glanced around. "You know, I still can't believe that you're actually here. This place is creepy. All those wood carvings, heavy curtains, and artsy-fartsy paintings don't suit your style."

"What is my style, if you would be so kind as to enlighten me?" Rohnert lifted his legs and rested them on the table.

"Well, first of all, the robe makes you look fat," Tor said and then laughed.

Rohnert shook his head. Some people would never change. "And what kind of clothes should I be wearing?"

Tor pretended to think. "Jeans, black shirt, and your Kalimetal."

The vampire might have been an ass, but he was also an integral part of the group, especially when things got rough, so Rohnert was willing to tolerate his endless witticisms.

"And what about the decor?" he asked, looking forward to a good laugh.

"It's grandpa-ish—makes you look old."

"What should we do about it?"

"Um, I have the newest issues of *SI* and *Playboy*. The centerfolds could breathe life into this lonely place." The moment he said the words, Tor drew back. "Man, I'm sorry. Foot-in-mouth disease is next in line for a cure."

Rohnert faked a laugh. Indeed, he was lonely, and he feared he'd never find a reason to *really* smile again. It might have been six months since the dreadful day of his mate's murder, but not a minute had gone by that Shelly didn't make an appearance in his mind.

Every memory he had of her only strengthened the pain of knowing he'd never get over her. Time didn't heal some wounds. He couldn't stop the longing in his gut, erase the memories from his mind, or fill the void in his heart.

He learned the art of faking it, just to appease those around him. It was easy to pretend that he was all right instead of answering questions about his mental well-being. In truth, he was sick of it—sick of his whole goddamned life without Shelly.

"It's okay, my man," he finally said.

Tor watched him with those concerned purplish-red eyes, staring long enough to make Rohnert uncomfortable.

"Rohn, you'll have to talk about it at some point, you know."

Talk? Talking would make it more real, and he still couldn't wrap his mind around the idea that Shelly was gone. His very soul refused to accept the finality of it.

"Excuse me, but I have some important Council matters to attend to," Rohnert said by way of dismissal. He didn't look Tor in the eye, afraid the vampire would see right through him.

Well, he did, but thankfully he didn't prod further. "I'll be in the training room if you need me." Tor left in total silence.

Rohnert bolted to his feet and walked off the anxiety. He didn't want to go there—not to the place where darkness, sadness, and isolation shackled him. His muscles were coiled tight while he paced the room like a caged lion.

Bretania stirred from a short, nightmare-ridden sleep. Her lids fluttered open, and the piercing glow of the light, no matter how insignificant, stung her eyes. For some time now, darkness had been her constant companion. It didn't take a genius to discern the problem. She had been hoping the great Shaman could aid her, but alas, Lukan had failed to respond to her summons. With difficulty, Bretania pushed her body out of bed, feeling her energy seep out her with the slightest movement. She braced her hand on the nightstand.

"Greta." Her voice came out strangled.

Her loyal housekeeper answered her call but then stopped dead in her tracks. Judging from her expression, the sight before her was gruesome. The scent of the lesions was far from her preferred Chanel No. 5, and the thoughts swirling in her servant's mind confirmed what Bretania already knew. She was a card-carrying member of the diseased.

Despite Greta's qualms, she rushed forward to steady her mistress. Fire raged down Bretania's throat when her faithful servant's scent grew stronger as she moved closer. The hunger didn't listen to reason nor adhere to proprieties or scruples. If she denied its call, she would go mad.

"Madame, you must not exert yourself." Greta hefted her onto the bed.

Blocking out the guilt and pushing pride aside, Bretania eyed her servant's jugular hungrily. This was her life now, and there was no denying what she had become. With the element surprise on her side, she was able to grab the woman by the shoulders and pin her against the mattress. Bretania mustered enough energy to overpower her victim, despite the fight the woman tried to put up.

"Ssh, this is going to be fast," she whispered in a voice that sounded foreign to her ears.

In quick movements ignited by the hunger she had denied for months, she punctured the skin, probing deeper until she caught the sweet taste of blood.

Her salvation.

Bretania sucked at the vein with greedy pulls, taking what she needed to build her strength. Then she did the unthinkable. She utilized her talent for manipulating weak minds to insert thoughts into Greta's cerebrum. The one person who had been aware that she possessed this gift had taken his knowledge to grave with him.

The suicide mission on which Goran had sent her and the group of new vampires had spelled trouble from the get-go. Their little rebellion was no match for the Elders' army of disciplined fighters. Had she not used her gift, she would have perished in the battle.

Seizing Greta's mind, she planted vicious images, ruthless ideas, and added a fondness for butchery into the mix. Life had handed Bretania lemons, so she would squeeze everything to a pulp and leave a trail of bitterness and carnage in her wake.

With one last look, she got up from the bed, marveling at her renewed strength. The night was far from over. While her servant went through the writhing and pain of the transition, she had better things to do and questions that required answers.

Energy coursed through her veins. Gone were the dreary nights spent cooped up in her apartment. This was her time to shine and deliver a blow to the belly of the beast. She would take down those who had thwarted and denied the legacy of her beloved. Hatred burned inside her while she wrapped her body in a black-hooded robe. She holstered her weapons around her waist and took one last glance in the mirror, pleased to have the chance to regroup and build her army.

Centuries of solitude, following the rules governing their race, had been her life. Motivated by her infatuation with the leader who had finally noticed her adoration, she finally came to a conclusion. Rules bored her, allies often led to betrayal, and survival meant looking at the big picture.

Bretania smiled at the mirror, studying her disease-ravaged features. Her once-onyx eyes held a tint of whitish discoloration, and her formerly smooth, silky skin had taken a light pallor, with painful lesions running across her limbs, torso, and face. Her pale, full lips still held a drop of blood from the feeding, and she greedily licked it off, savoring the taste of the temporary reprieve.

She would go to whatever lengths were necessary. After all, she was married to the ruling blood line, and by the grace of that union, she would take what was rightfully hers. The tip of her sword would ensure this path, and damn anyone who dared step between her and her goal.

Acknowledgements

First of all, I want to thank my Sensei, Mavvy Vasquez, who made it her personal goal to monitor my progress as a writer. I couldn't have been any luckier when you took me under your wing. I'm forever grateful.

To my friends and beta readers—Kristen Giles, Wendy Depperschmidt, Trenda Lundin, Lucia Morales, Judith Somera, Claudia Trapp, Eric Banaag, and Ching Yu. It takes a special kind of person to endure my never-ending prattle about my stories. I couldn't have done it without your help.

To Sidney Lorenzana— 'Tol, your song lyrics are amazing. Thanks for letting me use them.

To my family, friends, and readers—thanks for your continued support.

About the Author

A professional daydreamer, Lorenz Font discovered her love of writing after reading a celebrated novel that inspired one idea after another. Since being published in 2013, she has been conspiring, butting heads, and enjoying her spare time with vampires, angels, samurais, and other creatures she has created in her head.

Her perfect day consists of writing and lounging on her garage couch (a.k.a. the office) with a glass of her favorite cabernet while listening to her ever-growing music collection. She finds writing urban fantasy exhilarating and places an intense focus on angst and the redemption of flawed characters. Her fascination with romantic twists is a mainstay in all her stories.

Lorenz lives in Southern California with her supportive family and three demanding dogs.